SUMMER ROSE

CAROLINE HARTMAN

Red Dobie
PRESS

EXTON, PENNSYLVANIA

Summer Rose

First Edition
Library of Congress Control Number: 2013937690
ISBN 0981595499
ISBN 13 9780981595498

Published by:
Red Dobie Press *an imprint of Alexemi Publishing*
P.O. Box 1266
Exton, PA 19341

www.AlexemiPublishing.com

Cover Design by Bradley Wind, www.bradleywind.com
Please visit the author's website: www.carolinehartman.com

Printed in the United States of America

SUMMER ROSE IS DEDICATED TO THE MEMORY
OF MY MOTHER, HELEN FURST GILLESPIE.

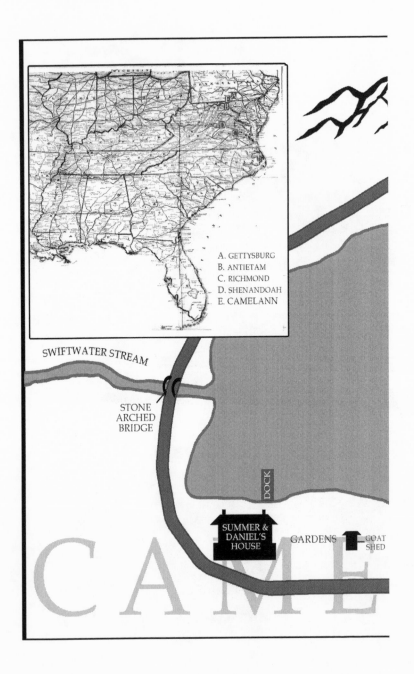

A. GETTYSBURG
B. ANTIETAM
C. RICHMOND
D. SHENANDOAH
E. CAMELANN

SWIFTWATER STREAM

STONE
ARCHED
BRIDGE

DOCK

SUMMER &
DANIEL'S
HOUSE

GARDENS

GOAT
SHED

CAME

PART ONE

LOVE AT FIRST SIGHT

CHAPTER 1

A LITTLE PIECE OF PARADISE

June 30, 1863
Maryland Pennsylvania Border

T wo Union officers halted their horses at the edge of the forest and peered through the feathered branches of pine, considering the lake beyond. Daniel removed his hat, squinting against the sun then wiped his forehead with his sleeve. He used the brim to fan his face, ignoring his sun-streaked hair as it flopped back over his eyes. Though the air, heavy with the scent of pine tar and heat took his breath away, the soldier in him noted the undisturbed sand, the circling hawks, the echo of a distant woodpecker's rat-a-tat-tat, the sound of the water. Nothing hinted of human.

Chester blew and snorted. "Good boy," Daniel murmured, running his hand down the stallion's sweaty neck. He urged the animal into the sunlight, but neither the horse nor his friend and fellow officer, Hal, needed any prodding. As they eased nearer the water, Daniel blew out his breath, ruffling his thick blond moustache and making a sound much like what the horse had just done.

Two days before Custer's spies had reported Lee, deep in Pennsylvania. Word from York County had come of Confederate cavalry helping themselves to barrels of whiskey and brandy, bacon and hams, and horses. One Pennsylvania housewife told of being forced to use all her reserve flour to bake bread for the rebels. Rumors said the *secesh* were ready to pounce on Harrisburg. Where in the devil are they? Daniel and Hal hadn't seen one enemy soldier. *Stay smart, stay alive,* whispered a voice in Daniel's head.

Free of the smoldering humidity of the forest and roused by the breezes off the water, Daniel's face cooled a little, but sweat still soaked all the way through his wool uniform. Hal pulled up beside him and Daniel couldn't help flinching. His friend smelled rank. No surprise. Daniel supposed he did, too. They edged forward another step and the entire lake and valley came into view. In the distance, two waterfalls cascaded from the sheer granite walls of the hills. Nearer, an island strewn with boulders and ancient pines, beckoned.

In a voice fit for church, Hal said, "Good Lord. Is that beautiful?"

Daniel nudged Chester toward a patch of grass and dismounted. He removed the tack and gear, and both he and Hal let the horses amble across the sand into the lake. Just like the men, the animals needed water and rest.

Daniel glanced at Hal, who nodded. Without a word, they stripped to the skin. They'd been friends since before they could walk. Most times Hal didn't even need to open his mouth. Daniel blinked away a bead of sweat and wiped his arm across his brow. *Hell*, he thought, *he knows as well as I do that taking a dip in this lake is stupid, irresponsible, and dangerous. But I'm so hot I can't think.*

As they stepped into the water, Daniel spotted the familiar birthmark on Hal's left hip, a port wine stain in the shape of a flying wild goose. Daniel had teased him about it ever since they could first talk. "You better be careful. Some sharpshooter will line up that goose on your ass and put you out of commission."

Hal chuckled, settling low in the cooling water. "You're just jealous. Every girl at Mary Hall's loves my wild goose. In fact, they fight for a wild goose ride."

Daniel snorted. He and Hal had a running argument about Washington's whorehouses. Hal spent many spare hours there, Daniel didn't.

Daniel pointed toward the island. "How far do you think that is?"

"A hundred, maybe a hundred and twenty yards."

Hal stood and dove. Daniel followed. The cool water cleared his head as the long muscles of his arms and legs stretched into a rhythm. He heard Hal splashing beside him, and they tagged the island beach at almost the same instant. Daniel stretched out in the shallows, feeling the pebbly bottom tickle the tight line of his back. His lungs strained and burned, but the cleansing swim had been worth it.

"God, this feels good."

Hal was sitting, skipping flat stones over the water. "Wonder what this—"

Gunshots: one, two then a quiet pause. A third shot rattled up in the hills. Daniel reacted out of instinct, shoving at Hal's shoulder and pushing him deep into the water, then sinking beside him. After a few seconds, Daniel raised his head, cleared the hair from his eyes, and checked the far shore. The shots had been far enough away, maybe a mile. Their horses still stood in the water, apparently undisturbed.

Hal whispered, "Sounded like a shotgun to me."

Daniel nodded. They both knew a sharpshooter with a good rifle and a scope would have picked them off by now. He turned, shading his eyes, and quickly surveyed the hills. "Some farmer's hunting."

Daniel's attention dropped to the rocks and trees on the island, and he smiled. The place was perfect. He settled back down on his elbows and let the water cool his body.

Hal sighed. "Imagine coming out here on a moonlit night with a girl. Just listen to those falls."

Daniel's lack of interest in Washington's brothels didn't mean he didn't like women. Not at all. He adored the fairer sex. Philly and Washington considered him a most eligible bachelor, and he was all but engaged. Being with a girl was about the only thing that kept the war at bay. Even then, thoughts of what he'd seen and done never entirely left him.

He slapped Hal's back. "Maybe we can do that in another lifetime. Better swim back." His eyes lifted to the hills and he frowned. "Somebody's around. Keep your ass down," he said with a grin. "I swear that damn goose will get us both killed."

He swam back slowly, searching the breeze for any sound out of the ordinary. Once on shore, he dug soap out of his saddlebag, returned to the water, and gave himself a good scrub and rinse. He tossed the soap to Hal, dried himself, tugged on his pants, then rolled up the legs. Hal did the same.

When they finished with themselves, they retrieved the horses, knowing well that a cavalryman was only as good as his horse. Brushed and buffed, the animals seemed in much better spirits. Daniel cleaned and checked Chester's shoes, then hobbled both animals before repacking his saddlebags.

Now that all the important jobs were out of the way, he sat in the shade and cleaned his boots while Hal studied their maps. When the sun lowered and the air began to hum with the war cry of mosquitoes, they shrugged into clean shirts and socks, pulled on their boots, and rolled down the legs of their pants. Daniel surveyed their surroundings, on alert as he always was. Some part of him never relaxed.

Daniel lit a small fire and set some coffee beans Hal's mother had sent them to roast in a pan. Hal pulled out a fishing line and dropped it into the lake while Daniel swirled the fragrant beans around on the hot metal.

After many attempts but no nibbles, Hal returned to the fire and watched Daniel pour the roasted beans onto a piece of cheesecloth, which he'd smoothed out on a flat rock. He smashed the beans with the butt of his revolver, tied up the ends of the cloth then tossed the bundle into a pot of boiling water. The aroma bloomed. Even the horses looked over. Hal took a deep, appreciative sniff, then stood and checked his rifle. When he sat back down he leaned it against his leg. Real coffee, a rare treat, as opposed to the Union Army's dehydrated stuff, which tasted like boiled paper, could alert rebels for miles. But they'd decided earlier that the risk was worth it. They might only be living off jerky and hardtack, but they had coffee.

CHAPTER 2

KIP

Daniel heard a cheerful whistling melody and tensed at the obvious movement of someone coming down the slope. He pulled his revolver close then relaxed a little at the appearance of a thin boy, maybe eleven or twelve, approaching from across the meadow. The boy touched the brim of his shabby straw hat in a mock salute.

Two healthy, foxy-looking dogs brushed against the boy's knees. A shotgun hung broken over his arm, and against his shoulder, rested a thick stick with three pheasants, all cleaned, plucked, skewered, and ready for the fire. Glistening with lard and sprinkled with herbs, the hens, even uncooked, looked mouthwatering. Daniel's stomach growled. He took in the boy's ragged, dark cotton pants, his long-sleeved, tan shirt, and his loose, many-pocketed canvas vest. When the boy knelt and laid down his shotgun, Daniel noticed his tanned skin, dark hair, and the brilliant whites of his eyes. Daniel's attention went to the hens again, and he swallowed hard as saliva pooled in his mouth.

Hal, too, eyed the hens. He leaned forward. "I'm Hal. That's Daniel."

They nodded to each other, and Daniel grinned, leaning around the fire to shake the boy's hand. Military protocol wasn't Hal's strong suit. "The skinny, dark haired guy is Captain Hal St. Clair. I'm Captain Daniel Charteris. We're cavalry scouts. Help yourself to the coffee, Son."

The boy's voice came out raspy. "Folks call me Kip. I shot these birds, thought you might want to trade coffee for a couple." He expertly placed two prepared, Y-shaped branches to hold the skewer, started the hens to cooking, then raised his hands. "I have potatoes, onions, and some squash." He pointed to his knapsack, assuring the men he meant no harm. "I'm just getting them out."

He set the vegetables in the coals, then poked at them with his stick. After a moment, he nodded toward his dogs. "Meet Nip and Tuck." Then he added, as if to apologize for their names, "My mom named them. She sewed a lot."

He snapped his fingers, and the dogs, red-gold with yellow eyes rimmed in black, hunkered down with their muzzles on their paws, their eyes unblinking. He pointed up into the hills. "We live around here. Every once in a while I get hungry for talk with someone other than the dogs. I heard your horses and smelled the coffee." His eyes drifted to the pot. "I love coffee."

"That's the real kind. Help yourself."

As the boy withdrew a cup from his knapsack and filled it, he nodded toward their Yankee blouses still drying on the rocks. "We don't see too many officers out this way. I saw a couple rebs last week. Scouts. Couldn't make out their rank.

They didn't act like officers. I stayed my distance. Looked like they were headed toward Chambersburg. You see any?"

"Not one."

"Did you hear that Meade is now head of the Army of the Potomac?" Hal asked.

The boy shook his head. "Last I heard, Lee'd crossed the Potomac. Rumor is he might try to take Harrisburg, even Philadelphia." He smiled when Daniel lifted his brow. "Not just coffee. I'm hungry for news, too."

"We don't know much more than you, but I do have a newspaper." Hal reached in his saddlebag and pulled out two tattered sheets of newsprint. "Most of it, anyway. Want it?"

Kip nodded and Hal handed him what pages he had of the *Washington Chronicle*. Daniel was a little surprised when the boy settled, his back against a rock, and took his time studying the thin paper, reading from beginning to end. When he'd finished, he laid the paper beside his pack.

Later, while they ate supper, Hal asked. "How did you fix these birds? I haven't eaten this well in months. I love the squash, too. Thank you."

"Nothing too hard. I larded them, rubbed them inside and out with salt, pepper, and herbs. I like to cook. My mom taught me."

"She must be a great cook," Daniel said.

Kip shook his head. "She was. She died last year, right after my father and two brothers were killed at Antietam. My da was a colonel, Colonel Micah McAllister. My brothers, William and Colin, were captains. I live pretty much by myself now, though there are neighbors. I have a brother in

Washington. He comes by as often as he can. Were you there? At Antietam?"

Both soldiers nodded. "You seem young to live alone," Hal said. He threw a bone to the dogs, but neither moved a muscle.

One side of Kip's mouth curled up at Hal's lifted brow. "Trained 'em not to take food from anyone but me. Keeps 'em lean and a little mean."

Across the fire, Daniel stretched, then leaned his elbow against a low rock while he studied the boy from head to toe. Kip's odd, blue-green eyes came around and locked onto Daniel's, and Daniel couldn't look away. Something about the boy bothered him. He sensed something. Not dangerous, but odd.

Daniel had learned to trust his hunches. Even before the war, he'd been a good judge of character. His first assessment of his classmates had always been on target, and he'd further honed the skill as an officer. This boy possessed an attitude, an air about him, as if he knew some secret. His looks and actions didn't tally somehow. Then again, he figured, losing your parents so young might make a kid savvy. War certainly had smartened Daniel up. He shook his head. No. There was something else about this boy that just didn't ring true.

A skein of ducks wheeled through the darkening sky, squawking and quacking, and everyone's attention shifted overhead. The sun settled below the horizon, and the sky took on a soft purple hue. The ducks swarmed to the far end of the lake, and the other water birds, soft as the night, headed for their roosts. Bullfrogs bellowed from a patch of reeds, a strangely comforting sound.

"Is there somewhere you could go? Grandparents? Relatives?" asked Daniel.

All hell was about to break loose near here. He didn't like the idea of this kid being alone. The boy lifted the paper and used it to sweep the horizon. He snapped his finger against it, making a loud smack on the paper.

"Why? You think I should leave here and head into the cesspool of Washington or Philadelphia?"

Daniel stiffened, taken aback at the boy's flare of anger. "I'm concerned for your safety, that's all."

Kip flicked his finger against the newspaper again. "All I read tells of riots, robbery, and murder. A girl found with her throat cut, a child gone missing right out of his home. I sell eggs and vegetables at the markets in Gettysburg, and my skins in Westminster. I hear what it's like in the capital. Mud to your knees, charlatans gypping country men, boys my age conscripted."

He motioned again with the paper, then his posture softened and his voice became as velvety as the lake and the night air. "Tell me something. If you lived here, Sir, would you leave?"

Bats flitted like shadows above the silver-tipped water, and an owl hooted from the hidden depths of the pines. Daniel let out a slow breath and one corner of his mouth curled. He nodded, just a slight bob of his head. He knew, in that instant, if he made it through the war, he'd come back and find this place. It was that special.

"Does this valley have a name?"

"My da called it Camelann, from the myths. The legends, you know? Of King Arthur. The place where he died."

"Camelann? As in Camelot? Magic? Druids? Arthur?"

The boy shrugged and rolled his eyes. "It's just a name, a story. My father came from Scotland. He told us all the old tales. Don't think it's on a map." He sat abruptly and glared at Daniel. "And don't you go putting the name on your maps, either. I don't want anybody finding it."

He leaned against a rock and drank his coffee, watching Hal add wood to the fire. Sparks puffed and flew into the darkening sky. "Not too many folks find this valley. Seems you stumbled onto the only easy way into here." He lifted his cup, indicating the silhouette of the mountains, now black against the lavender sky. "You'd need to use ropes to get in any other way. The few people who did happen upon the lake didn't stay long."

The fire flickered orange and red on Kip's face, making his eyes flash and dance over the rim of the tin cup. "It's a lonely place."

An owl hooted somewhere behind them and the wind lifted the branches of the pines, whispering secrets through the needles. Kip picked up a handful of sand and let it trickle through his fingers. "Most of the time I like lonely. I think this valley is the most beautiful place on earth." He sniffed. "I haven't been to a lot of places, but it sure seems better than Philadelphia or New York."

The boy suddenly rose without a word, moving with the smooth grace of a deer. From behind Daniel's left ear came a dry rattle, and every inch of his skin prickled. The hair on his forearms stood straight up and he fought the urge to bolt. He didn't breathe as Kip eased his cup to the ground, and, with great economy of movement, slipped a Bowie knife from beneath his pant leg. In a single, fluid motion, as slick and athletic as any master knifeman, the boy threw the knife. It swooshed by Daniel's ear, slicing the air and ripping into the snake. Daniel leapt into a crouch when the rattler whipped around, smashing and beating the dirt in a futile attempt to free itself from the blade. After an eternity, the snake and the knife stilled. Daniel's heart slammed into the bones of his chest and his blood raced. He hated snakes.

Hal stood, chuckling, and headed toward the reptile. "Danny finds these beasties more offensive than rebels." He grinned from ear to ear as he freed Kip's knife with the point of his sword, then speared the snake and lifted it. "Damn, look at those rattles. He's a beauty. Must be close to eight feet."

The dogs sat up, alert and waiting for a signal from their master. Even as far away as the meadow, the horses snorted as they caught the scent. Hal slung the carcass into the night and they heard it splash. When Hal turned back and saw Daniel's face, he chuckled again. "Easy Danny, it's dead."

Daniel got to his feet, shaking his head, then bent and picked up Kip's knife. Kneeling at the edge of the water, he cleaned the blade then wiped it dry with his handkerchief. He weighted it in his hand, ran his thumb over the razor sharp blade. Not a cheap knife; the balance was excellent. He stood and headed back to the fire, handing the hilt of the knife out for the boy. He stuck out his other hand for a grateful shake.

"Your throw was slick. Best I've ever seen. Fast, too. Thank you."

Kip took the knife and accepted Daniel's offered hand. "My da taught me, taught all of us."

Something about how Kip lowered his eyes caught Daniel's attention. He shook the boy's hand and held it for a moment, noticing how his large hand swallowed Kip's. The delicate fingers and knuckles, with bones like those of a bird, were small and featherweight beneath Daniel's rough and calloused skin. His thumb slid over and found Kip's pulse: strong, fast, sure as a drum. Their eyes locked again.

"Thank you. I suspect I owe you my life."

Kip shrugged, pulling his hand free. "Weren't nothing. Thanks, though, for the coffee and the news." He replaced his knife then shouldered his pack and shotgun and patted his thigh for the dogs; they bounded to his side. Just before he walked into the night, he glanced over his shoulder, his big eyes riveted on Daniel.

After he'd disappeared, Daniel led the horses back to the campfire. He and Hal shuffled around, preparing to ride and rendezvous with Buford at Gettysburg.

"Is Kip a boy's name or a girl's?" Daniel asked.

Hal's head jerked up, and he snorted. "No girl could throw a knife like that kid did."

CHAPTER 3

GETTYSBURG

July 3, 1863

Daniel leaned against an ammunition crate, thick smoke blinded him, blotting out the carnage. But the smoke couldn't take away either the stench or the cries. Nausea weakened him, tilted the earth, and he leaned to one side and retched. Through his misery flashed an unbidden image of the lake, and he marveled. Hard to believe he'd been there, how many days ago? Now he was dirtier than he'd ever been in his life, and his body longed for the blue-green water.

A shudder jolted through him, knocking the breath out of him, making his blood race in a throbbing path throughout his body. Cries and moans pressed in on him, suffocating him. He'd wondered if anything could be as bad as Antietam. Today, this third day of hell, was worse. A picture played repeatedly through his head, and he attempted to wrap his arms around himself for comfort, but the effort hurt too much.

The air, the goddamn air had turned pink with blood. He still saw it, smelled it. Pictures barged through his mind, showing him the poor trooper's head as it ripped from his body and catapulted toward him like a wild billiard ball. He'd stared in horror as the ball exploded, disintegrated into gray pink slush, then slid in a warm mess of gore down the inside of his blouse. He dared not close his eyes, for fear of seeing it again. Would the image ever go away?

In shock, he'd fallen from Chester, and a *minié* ball, like an exclamation point to a cruel declaration, had whistled then thudded into the meat of his thigh. He noticed not the pain but the jarring. He remembered, too, Sergeant Munro, one of Hancock's sergeants, ripping off the slime-soaked jacket, which clung to his skin, and attempted to wipe up the mess. He remembered, too, as clear as when it had happened, the tooth and part of the trooper's ear where it had stuck in his suspenders. All the while, the bugles blew, the cannon boomed as Pickett's division marched toward him. Rebel officers, their horses, chest-deep in the tall grass yelled, "Forward!"

And the drums. If he lived to be a hundred he'd still hear those goddamn drums rolling through his blood. He cried out when someone dragged him behind a fence row, then propped him by a tree, and threw him his Spencer rifle and ammunition. He watched Pickett and Pettigrew's divisions, shoulder to shoulder, the flags flapping as they marched, then ran toward Hancock's guns. The booming and the smoke consumed the air, and when the big guns stopped, Daniel fired the Spencer until his ammunition ran out.

Beside him, the young corporal stirred again. He couldn't have been more than fifteen. Daniel lifted the canteen to the young man's lips, remembering how he'd helped him earlier, but the boy made no sign of seeing him then or now. Shot had blown off most of the kid's hands, but he didn't cry or moan. His big brown eyes just stared at a spot somewhere in front of him. A half hour earlier, the stretcher bearers had passed him, carrying another body to the surgeon's table. Daniel knew the bearers took the worst first, but only those with a chance of living. The boy knew, too.

Darkness, like a stage curtain, descended, leaving only fires and torches to provide light. Daniel dragged himself into the shadows. Shivers he couldn't control jerked through his body. *Christ*, he thought, *I'm not ready for the orderlies.* He was a captain. He knew they'd take him soon. *Where in God's name is Hal?* It seemed like hours since he'd left Daniel, heading out to find his horse. Chester couldn't be that far away. His eyes drifted back to the boy without hands. *I have to get out of here.*

Someone, maybe Sergeant Munro, had wrapped a bandage over his ripped trouser leg and around his thigh, trying to keep the raw flesh from oozing down Daniel's leg. A sane part of his mind acknowledged he might lose the leg, while another part screamed, *Not so fast!* He knew it was bad, but not deep. He didn't think the bone was broken. Hal and he had vowed to protect each other, not allow the surgeons to simply hack off a limb. Where the hell was Hal? He took a deep breath, but the acrid air only brought him images of thousands falling like pigeons at a pigeon shoot. Just before his mind shut down, Daniel dragged himself further away from the firelight. Each movement jolted hot rivets of pain down his leg while a cold sweat ran over every inch of skin.

The pain like blades, fingers of knives thrusting, travelling down through his body, filled his throat, and he threw up bile then blacked out.

He awoke to Chester's snort, coming from the blackness beyond the fence. That horse had a snort like no other. Somehow Daniel managed to lift his fingers to his lips and whistled a signal, one he and Hal had used since they were boys. Moments later, Hal knelt beside him, slipping an arm under Daniel's shoulder.

"Here. Drink this."

Daniel smelled the bourbon and couldn't help himself. He grabbed Hal's hand, choked and laughed out loud. Hot tears streamed down his cheeks and every syllable he uttered cut straight through him.

"Where did you get this?" he wheezed then took a big swallow. Warmth spread like a wildfire through him.

Hal levered him to his feet, grunting with the effort. "Okay, big fellow, help me out here. How in hell I let you talk me into this, I do not know."

"What's happening?"

"Your Chester was right where he was supposed to be. Our troops are scattered from here to the Monocacy, guarding supply lines. That's a thirty mile ride. I spoke with Captain Keogh. He gave me the bourbon. He said to either shoot you or take care of you. He'll see to our men and let General Buford know our whereabouts."

With his foot, Hal nudged the wooden crate end over end until it stood beside Chester. He helped Daniel step onto it then groaned as he heaved his friend onto the saddle. "Christ. You weigh a ton."

Daniel fell across the horse and slowly swung himself around so he had a leg on each side of the saddle. For a moment, he pressed his cheek against Chester's mane, wondering if he'd ever sit up again. Pain and nausea came in waves and he retched, leaving a little whiskey and bile on the side of his mouth. He lay with his hand on Chester's chestnut neck, petting the horse, thinking, *Good old Chester.* With a monumental effort, he pulled himself upright, wiping the vomit off his cheek and lips with his sleeve. He managed to get his left foot in the stirrup as Hal gently nudged the right, the wounded leg, into the other stirrup. The searing pain brought tears to Daniel's eyes.

"Head toward the lake," he said with a grunt. "And keep those bloody surgeons away from me. They'll take my leg."

Hal didn't have to ask which lake, and Daniel's stomach threatened to heave again, though this time it was because of the sight spread before him. Dante's descriptions of Hell had nothing on this scene. He passed stretcher-bearers as they sorted through the slain by torchlight, seeking the living. Following them came crews, usually punishment details, who lined up the dead, who would be buried little deeper than potatoes. He saw pallbearers checking for the bodies of officers. They would be crated into coffins and shipped home. Huge teams of draft horses dragged dead beasts, shot in their traces, clear of the artillery. The screams, the heart wrenching cries of men, cut through the night as Confederate and Union passed each other in the dark.

The town itself, every street corner, private home, and church, had become a hospital. They passed through a maze of wounded, and Hal pointed to a church where limbs lay stacked like firewood outside a gaping doorway. As they rode closer they could see the wooden doors had been taken down and placed over the pews. The surgeons wearing filthy aprons and doing their bloody work stood over the makeshift operating tables. Small fires burned at every street corner.

They crossed the railroad tracks, and once they were safely out of town they headed west toward the lake. Daniel gave Chester's reins to Hal then slumped forward, his forehead heavy on the horse's neck. *If I have to die, let it be at Camelann.* Hal left the crowded road and Daniel squinted beyond. Through the firelight danced shadows of Lee's army, forming their wagon train of wounded. Again Hal changed direction, and Daniel said nothing. Hal was good at maps and had an iron trap memory. He knew the way.

Two or three agonizing hours later—Daniel lost track of time—he rolled out of the saddle and landed in Hal's arms. His leg was on fire, and his back had seized, having been tensed for so long. Hal lowered Daniel to the ground and dragged him under a tree, where he leaned his weary friend against a rock. The moon was bright, maybe full, and it spilled silver across the calm surface of the water. A family of ducks complained at the intrusion, and Hal broke out the bottle again.

"Drink more."

Daniel took a long drink of the whiskey, then handed the bottle back. Hal took a big swig and blew out a long breath. "God, that's good stuff."

He passed it back to Daniel, who took another drink. Hal unsaddled the horses and led them to the meadow, where he hobbled them. When he returned he dropped cross-legged onto the sand beside Daniel, and they passed the bottle back and forth between them. Neither had eaten for what seemed like days. Daniel tasted both bile and bourbon, but with the whiskey's heady power, the pain took its teeth out of him. The horrors dimmed and blurred, swirled around him as they drank, until he blotted out the moon and the lake and the pain. And the fear.

From deep in his stupor, Daniel heard something grate against the sand. He squinted in the dim light, watching a slim figure load their gear into a canoe and float away. He wanted to protest, knew he should, but couldn't find the energy to lift his arm. Later the canoe thudded on the sand again and, in a boozy fog, Daniel managed to rise, then fall into the canoe, nearly capsizing it. He was aware of it floating across the water, of strong arms helping him out of it.

A figure—maybe an angel—built a fire, removed Daniel's bandage, enlarged the tear in his pant leg, and inspected his wound, cleaning it several times with water warmed in a kettle sitting on the coals. As the sky grayed with first light, Daniel leaned forward and squinted through the dregs of his drunken stupor, watching as the angel strode down to the water's edge. The blurry figure stripped off pants and a shirt, peeling down to just frilly white bloomers and a lacy camisole. The water barely rippled when she dove deep into the lake and disappeared.

CHAPTER 4

DREAM GIRL

Midmorning, someone unbuttoned the sky. Torrents of rain plastered Daniel's clothes to his skin, freezing him to his core. His teeth chattered, and he curled into a ball to stop the shaking. Hal rigged the canoe across some rocks then draped the tent over the boat.

"Crawl under there, Danny. Here's your poncho. Slip it on."

He did as he was told, and Hal followed him. "Good Lord, it's like the inside of a drum in here." He held up the bourbon, dark brow raised in question.

Daniel shook his head. The shivers wouldn't quit, so he rolled into a ball on the damp sand. Hal spread his poncho over the two of them and the beginnings of warmth took root.

Above the thunder and drum of the rain, the lightning ripped about them like artillery at close range. Hal took a swig and offered him another drink, but Daniel shook his head again. Hal draped himself over Daniel, but Daniel still shivered.

About noon they crawled out of the makeshift cave. The sky was still dark and bursts of rain were now sporadic, and thunder still rolled over the mountains. That was when the angel walked out of the lake and lit a miraculous fire. Through the haze of Daniel's pain and fever, the roaring inferno warmed him. The blur of white threw more pine boughs on the fire, causing the flames to leap and throw sparks into the sky. She led Daniel to a table-sized rock, fed more pine into the fire, and helped Hal stumble to a nearby tree. Great billowing clouds of white smoke covered the island, lifting high under the grey sky.

Daniel jerked and protested as she pulled off his boots, unsnapped his suspenders, and eased off his trousers.

"Hush," she said as she hauled out her big knife and cut off the leg of his underwear. As she had before, she cleaned his wound with water warmed at the fire, then pulled a glass bottle of greenish-yellow, honey-like liquid from her basket and poured the concoction into the wound, smearing it around the opening.

At one point the pain ripped clear through him and he screamed. Her strong hands pressed against him and held him down, and she murmured, "Easy, Daniel, easy."

Taken aback that she knew his name, he let the idea calm him, and his fear dissolved into the smoke. Sure fingers probed deep into the wound, and he thought later he must have passed out, because the pain seemed a dream, and time didn't matter.

Later, through his lingering haze of delirium, he became aware of the girl in white throwing more pine on the fire. The needles crackled and swooshed as they caught, and the billowing smoke blotted out the bluing sky. When she was satisfied, she sat beside him and used her Bowie knife to cut long strips from the cotton ruffles of her pantaloons, then tied the cloth around his leg.

"I'm tying these firmly, but not too tight, Daniel. It's to speed the healing. I want a little air to get under the bandages and help that salve reach deep into the flesh of your leg. I pulled out the *minié* ball. Now we have to get your fever down."

She left him for a minute then held a scalding cup of tea to his mouth and urged him to drink. He gagged. She chortled lightly and kept pressing the cup to his lips, insisting he drink."I know it's bitter, but it helps." When he'd managed half of it, she eased him to a blanket by the fire and held cool rags to his forehead, then swabbed his neck, back, and chest. In a moment of clarity, he heard Hal snoring a few feet away, and felt a rush of panic when he noticed the crackle and roar of the fire, the smoke rolling over all of them. *God. They'll see that smoke in Harrisburg, maybe Philadelphia.* He tried to sit up, but the angel leaned against him, forcing him down, then curled up beside him. She held him close, and when he threw up, she cleaned his face, gave him water. At last the shivering stopped, and he fell asleep.

He didn't know how long he slept, but his dreams were strange. At one point he was almost sure the dream was real. From the depths of the white smoke, an old man spoke, hugged him like a son. *"I'm Colonel Micah McAllister. These two are my sons, William and Colin, both captains with the regiment."* He nodded toward the angel. *"My daughter thinks you're worth saving, Danny. Make sure you deserve her trust."*

When Daniel awoke, the smoke was gone. Stretched beside him, asleep, wasn't an angel, but a beautiful girl, blanketed in dappled sunshine. Silky, sable-colored hair sprawled halfway down her chest, the ends curling over her breasts. He moved his eyes to her face, where thick dark lashes brushed against honey-hued skin. His attention, like a magnet, drifted back down to the silky skin stretching over the most beautiful arms and shoulders he'd ever seen. His gaze drifted lower, taking in the cream-colored flesh at her waist as it peeked from below the hem of her little camisole. Above the ruffled bodice, her breasts swelled, gently rising and falling with every breath. *Right now,* he thought, *I want to lay my cheek there.* The urge was so strong he could practically feel the soft skin against his face.

As he considered doing just that, the girl opened her eyes and caught him ogling her breasts. They were Kip's eyes. She sat with a jerk and her hair tumbled down her front.

He glanced quickly up and caught her surprise, then tried to blink away the heat in his cheeks. He hoped he hadn't insulted her. The last thing he wanted to do was offend her. It's just that breasts and the unexpected abundance of hair on Kip's head confused him. He hadn't been prepared for either, and he definitely hadn't expected Kip to be beautiful. He wanted to tell her as much, but his tongue had wrapped around itself. Feeling as daft as an eight-year-old, he stared up at her, suddenly awkward under her great, ocean-blue eyes.

She didn't seem to notice. Instead, she turned to his leg and pulled the bandages back with a feather-soft touch. She leaned in and lowered her head, then sniffed the wound and smiled.

"Look," she whispered, happiness dancing in her voice. "No redness, no putrid smell. Oh, Daniel, you'll be fine.

We'll watch it, but I know you won't lose your leg now." She giggled and winked, as if sharing a secret. "My da made good medicines. Before the war, we stashed a keg of it in a cave under the lake."

A long breath shuddered through him as his fear slipped away again. He'd not known, until this moment, how terrified he'd been of losing his leg. She refitted the bandages and another beautiful smile crossed her face. Like the sun bursting from behind clouds.

"I put your horses in my lean-to and plucked out some nice long hair from your horse's tail to use as thread for your stitches. Only took nineteen. I boiled the hair to soften it – a trick my da taught me. Horsehair works better than thread."

When they'd first come to Washington, that summer before Bull Run, Hal had visited the whorehouses. The tales he'd told hadn't impressed Daniel. Neither man needed such establishments; impending war somehow changed the rules. A lot of women, respectable women, went wild, finding creative ways and places to seduce these handsome heroes to be. Neither he, nor Hal, nor their following of classmates who had hoped to pick up their leftovers, gave a damn. They were a herd of young bucks, loose and kicking up their heels for the first time in their lives. While McClellan dallied, they gathered the spring bouquets of wartime Washington: in cabs, in empty bedrooms and horse stalls, in rowboats, haylofts, and even once in a darkened coat closet in the Executive Mansion.

On the surface, they were just being young, enjoying their lives to the fullest. In the depths of their souls, they'd known exactly what they were doing: crowding a lifetime into a few weeks, making a mad attempt to become immortal. Hal and Daniel had relished the hunt, the pursuit, and the conquest. To the two friends, love, lust, and war had all been part of the same game. *Veni, vidi, vici.* 'I came, I saw, I conquered' applied to women as well as battle. They moved from one part of the game to the other as easily as a sleek horse moves from a walk to a canter to a gallop.

Now his breath hovered at the top of his chest, and he felt dizzy with need of it. He grabbed her hand, suddenly filled by a horrible, irrational fear of losing her. Never had he wanted a girl like he wanted this one. 'Want' wasn't even the right word. He knew right then that he wanted her more than just how a man wants a woman.

Across the fire, Hal stirred, then awoke with a start. He stood and shook himself like a dog, then walked to the water's edge, where he splashed water over his face and head. He nodded to Daniel and the girl, then knelt and inspected his friend's leg as she rose to feed the fire.

"It looks good." He angled his head toward the girl, and whispered to Daniel. "I was out-of-my-mind drunk. She's gorgeous. I thought she was an angel."

"I did, too," Daniel admitted. "She might just be."

The afternoon sun beat down so hot the wet sand steamed. Daniel sat back, leaning against a rock and aching all over, his leg throbbing. The girl, now with her tan shirt over her cotton camisole and bloomers, moved about the campsite, picking up and cleaning up. She enlisted Hal's help and they flipped the canoe then twisted water out of the blankets and bedrolls. They rigged a clothesline and slung the damp blankets over it. Hal said something; she laughed. An enormous pang of jealousy grabbed Daniel's chest.

She turned back toward Daniel. "You two get some rest now. I'll be back in an hour or so with dinner. I put your horses in the lean-to before the storm. No doubt they're ready to graze."

She stooped, fiddling with something at the fire then walked toward Daniel, smiling as sweetly as a cherub. She knelt beside him, handed him another scalding cup of the foul-smelling tea, and brushed his blond hair out of his eyes.

"It's made from willow bark and herbs. I know you don't like it, but it helps with the fever and pain. Drink it." She glanced over her shoulder. "Hal, make sure he does."

She turned back toward him, and a lazy, sweet smile twinkled in her eyes. She swept her hand across his forehead again, gentle as a feather. "Sleep is the best thing for you right now, Daniel."

His name came out as a caress. Her fingertips may as well have been her lips. A sweet shudder ran through him and the jealousy that had practically ripped a hole in him a minute before flew away.

His voice came out full of wonder, just a touch above a whisper. "What should I call you? Kip?"

He knew the poets raved about the beauty of porcelain white flesh, and Philadelphia debutants bathed in milk to whiten theirs. But from the moment he'd first seen her, even when she'd been Kip, he'd noticed her golden color, and he loved her creamy honey hue. His mind spun, looking at her. He'd never seen skin so perfect.

She shrugged and imitated a Scottish brogue. Her strange eyes danced as her r's rolled off her tongue. "Well, ye saw through me Kip disguise, did ye? Fiddlesticks! I'll need to think of another." She arched her eyebrows. "An old man, perhaps?" She stood, shouldered her shotgun and knapsack, and placed them in the canoe.

"I've always been called Summer Rose," she said shyly, then put one foot in the canoe and pushed off from the beach. "Drink that tea."

As the canoe pulled away from the shore, Hal spoke. "Should I go with her? I mean, should she be walking around in her undergarments like that? Do you think she's safe?"

Under his breath, Daniel said, "You stay right here."

Hal's thick dark eyebrows jerked up. "Daniel, I'd never hurt a girl."

A smile softened Daniel's voice, but it had an edge to it. "I know, Hal. Neither of us would. We're honorable men. I just don't want you to fall in love with that particular girl. If you want this one, we'll have a problem. I want her," he said as he let out a deep, low breath, then his eyes flashed to Hal. "Not only like you think. I want to keep her."

Hal clucked his tongue, looking scandalized. "You're all but engaged to Miss Mary McGill, aren't you?"

Daniel let loose another ripping breath. "Good Lord, I missed that one, didn't I? I almost asked her on my last leave." He shook his head. "My mother, you know her. She was dropping hints, pushing me." He tossed a twig into the fire. "All hell will no doubt break loose, but no. I want this girl."

"You sure?"

He took a long swallow of the tea, watching the canoe grow smaller, its tiny wake smoothed by the lake. He nodded then rolled onto his side. "I'm sure," he said, then slept.

CHAPTER 5

LOVE AT A FULL CAVALRY CHARGE

When she returned with her tawny dogs, the sun had inched toward the treetops. Daniel awoke with a jolt as the dogs jumped from the canoe, greeting them with sniffing and yipping, kicking up clouds of sand. Hal shot to his feet, petting the dogs and reaching to help her with the canoe. Daniel rose slowly, testing his injured leg. Its solid strength surprised him.

Hal knelt by the wriggling dogs, who leapt around him. "How do you tell Nip from Tuck?"

She shrugged. "Don't try. Nip has one white toe, but usually it's dirty and you can't tell them apart. They both answer to either name, and they're always together. My oldest brother, William, helped me train them." She snapped her fingers, and they settled down on the grass.

Now she was dressed, and Daniel noticed Hal surveying her. He did, too. Couldn't help himself. She was fresh as sunshine in a simple navy skirt with a half-inch of white eyelet ruffle showing at the hem. A white blouse, also of eyelet, covered most of her arms and shoulders. Dressed, she seemed younger, and to Daniel she still appeared more beautiful than any woman he'd ever seen. Her skin, her hair, even her teeth radiated health and beauty. The thought made him chuckle to himself. *When have I ever used the word 'healthy' to describe a girl?* Her long, dark braid had been tied with a red grosgrain ribbon, and she wore no shoes. He dragged his eyes from her toes. Even her toes were perfect.

She noticed his attention and pointed out the red ribbon. "Today is the 4th of July, but I don't have a flag," she said, carrying cotton sacks and baskets to the table-sized rock by the fire. "My red, white, and blue will have to do."

She gestured for Daniel to sit on the big rock, then lifted the edge of his bandage and sniffed the wound again. She indicated the large wicker hamper, still in the canoe. "Gentlemen, fresh clothes and everything you need to clean yourselves is in the basket. Take it out of my sight and bathe." From her pocket she pulled the bottle of thick yellow liquid and handed it to Daniel. "When you're clean and dry, rub the salve around the wound again. I put some clean bandages in the hamper. Tie them loosely."

She stood and pointed toward the shorter waterfall. "If you're up to moving a little, there's a wonderful pool at the bottom of Forty Foot Falls." She pinched her nose dramatically and puffed out her breath. "You both are filthy, and you smell even worse. Wash out your clothes. I'll mend your trousers before you leave. Those," she said, glancing back at the hamper, "are my brothers' things. They should fit. While you bathe, I'll fix supper."

Suddenly all of her face smiled, transforming itself with dimples, crinkles, and dancing eyes. "I believe the three of us deserve a feast. After all, it's the 4th of July. May I dip into your supply of coffee?"

Close to an hour later, the men returned to the fireside, where Summer Rose knelt by the pots and pans. She almost didn't recognize them. "Good grief! All that grime hid two decent-looking men. I must tell you, gentlemen, you looked a little frightening before."

She sniffed deeply and giggled. They smelled much better, too. They must have been liberal in their use of the Bay Rum bottle she tucked in the hamper.

The week before she'd noticed their looks, but hadn't been able to quite get past her wariness. Now she looked them over more carefully, studying their faces while keeping hers as smooth as a pan of cream. They were both tall, over six feet. Lean, maybe a little too thin. Hal had dark hair, sparkling blue eyes, and sported long, dark sideburns that matched his thick eyebrows. Daniel was blond and wore a thick and trimmed, sun-bleached moustache. His eyebrows were almost white. Both men had rock hard bodies, easy smiles, and good teeth.

But Daniel, well, even the hint of Daniel's smile took her breath away. When his eyes, clear and green as river ice, locked on hers, her heart raced so hard it hurt. She remembered the moment when his big hand had swallowed hers, and she could almost feel the calloused warmth of his palm again.

The men shrugged. They'd been in military school since the age of twelve. Now they were in the Grand Army of the Potomac, they knew how to kit themselves out. They had scrubbed and shaved, clipped each other's hair, and trimmed the back of the other's neck. To be out of their heavy wool uniforms and dressed in rolled up, blue work pants and rough shirts, they knew they smelled and looked better than they had last week, when they had first encountered the lake.

Despite their outward appearance, they were army officers to the bone. Even in their bare feet, they stood and moved like soldiers. They hung their wet things over low bushes and leaned their boots against the back of a big pine. Daniel noticed her holding a cup of coffee, so he poured Hal and himself some then sat on a boulder as she balanced a large skillet over the fire.

"Thank you. You gave us everything we needed. And whatever is in your salve worked magic. My leg feels strong. How long should I leave in the stitches?"

"A week? Ten days? You'll be able to tell. Just snip them. Keep putting salve on it. I'd like to check it again tomorrow. It's not deep, but we'll be careful."

He nodded toward the fire. He hadn't eaten for at least a day and a half, and the aromas rising from the skillet twisted cramps in his growling stomach. "Can I help you?"

Smiling, she shook her head and expertly turned the sizzling slices of ham, adding cut up potatoes, green beans, and onions to the mixture. His mouth ached as he watched her cover the pan with a lid. He gestured with his chin toward another deep, covered skillet sitting on a tripod of stones.

"Biscuits?" he asked.

"Yes." She pointed to a basket sitting further back on the rocks. "Would one of you get the bowl of salad greens out of the basket for me? The lettuce is from my garden, I found the watercress by the stream, and there's a jar of dressing in there. Jars of honey and butter, too."

Hal handed her the entire basket. "A salad? I haven't eaten salad in months."

She set the bowl and jars on a low, flat rock which she'd covered with a faded blue and white checkered tablecloth. Tin plates and bowls, glasses, silverware, and napkins also sat on the makeshift table, along with an open bottle of red wine. She'd even added a little bouquet of white snapdragons and red zinnias, arranged in a blue and white cup beside two fat candles.

"I haven't cooked for anyone except the dogs and me for a lot longer."

She must have sensed Daniel watching her, for she turned and lit his heart with her smile. "My garden's my pride and joy. The tomatoes have started …" She removed the skillet from the heat, raised the lid, and threw in a jarful of chopped herbs and spices. With a sure hand, she jiggled the skillet and replaced the lid, then set it on a nearby rock. As she tossed the biscuits into the cloth-lined basket, she asked, "Would one of you light the candles? Oh, Hal, would you please add the dressing to the salad? And pour the wine?" She frowned. "You like wine, don't you?"

Daniel set about taking care of her requests, though questions bounced about in his head. This girl was an enigma. How old was she? With her clothes on she might be fourteen, maybe seventeen in her camisole and bloomers. And now she's offering wine? Where did her poise come from? Why had she corralled them on this island? To keep them safe from marauding rebels? To keep her safe from the two of them?

He set the salad on the table, still surprised by such sophistication. To find a girl anywhere who was equally at ease in either her underwear or a proper dress …

Before serving the plates, she reached to her ankle and hauled out her Bowie knife to slice the ham steak. He'd almost forgotten about the knife, her speed and expertise with it. He watched her spoon sauce onto the ham, then place the knife next to her plate.

"Delicious!" Hal exclaimed. "What spices did you use on the ham?"

"I use a mixture of rosemary, thyme, chives, garlic, and some hot paprika my grandmother sent me. She has a Hungarian housekeeper who gets it from her sister in Budapest. They live in Philadelphia."

"What are your grandparents' names?" asked Daniel, cutting a piece of ham.

"Martha and Ralph Fitzmartin."

Daniel sat a little straighter. "You've heard of the Fitzmartins, Hal. Fitzmartin Hall, north of the city. It's out near Chestnut Hill and Fort Washington."

Hal nodded absently and spooned more sauce on his ham. "I love this sauce. It tastes sweet, tart, and spicy."

She wiggled her eyebrows. "Brown sugar, vinegar, and paprika."

Daniel clung to little tidbits of information. "He's into lumber, coal, and something with canals and the railroads, right?"

Summer Rose shrugged and sipped the wine. She'd finished one glass and was starting her second. "Lumber, yes. I don't know about the other things. I remember hearing about a canal and a toll road. Do you want more potatoes? I grew those, you know. I think I overcooked the beans. Are they still good?"

Hal bit into a bean. "You didn't overcook them. They're perfect. My body's starved for decent food." He chuckled. "The army doesn't feed us real vegetables. Once in a while the troops will raid someone's garden and steal or trade some carrots or onions, but the army packages dried vegetables. They call them dehydrated vegetables, but the troops call them desecrated or dissipated vegetables. The cooks add water, boil them, and they end up tasting like paste." He popped another bean in his mouth and grunted with appreciation.

Daniel sat back, watching and listening. He could tell she was hungry to talk, as if she'd bottled up words all year, and now all her thoughts came uncorked in a champagne gush. He guessed, too, she made a good front about living alone, and he admired her mettle. Her scrubbed face glowed in the firelight, her sable hair glistened. In fact, he was impressed. He wasn't sure he could have lived alone for so long. He checked her over again, letting his eyes graze from her toes to her nose, making sure he didn't spend too much time eyeing her breasts. Had he ever met a girl so lovely in so many ways? His eyes dropped to the big knife and he shook his head.

He knew what was happening to him. Soldiers, even officers, talked of falling in love. Several of the officers wrote daily to their wives, arranged for them to live nearby. It was something Daniel had always had trouble fathoming. Men in the Charteris family, if they went to war, more than likely did so to *escape* their wives. Daniel's parents barely spoke to each other. Two uncles kept mistresses, one of which had two illegitimate children, another never married. In his family, marriage was serious business, intended to keep the wealth among a chosen few. God forbid if you fell in love with the wrong woman, wrong meaning one without money.

She laughed, presenting him with an image of loveliness. He chuckled silently at his naïveté, and a warm softness thrilled through him. *I haven't fallen in love,* he realized. *I've crashed, smacked, a full cavalry charge into love.* He thanked God or the heavenly powers or whatever, so relieved he hadn't proposed to Mary. The thought of being married to that sweet, pale girl sent his stomach into somersaults. The only reason he'd ever considered marrying her was because of his mother's urging.

Summer Rose sipped the wine and regarded them both through eyes flashing in the firelight. Her lips glistened red from the wine. "What do you think of President Lincoln? Do you think he did the right thing with removing *habeas corpus*? When Da and my brothers first went to Washington, they had great difficulty getting there. The southern sympathizers in Maryland burned the bridges in Baltimore. My father commandeered boats, found railroad men among the troops, rebuilt track, then took his boys across the river and into the capital." She took another sip. "I believe President Lincoln had every right to lock up the Maryland legislature."

She expelled a loud breath and blew a fringe of hair from her forehead, then lowered her voice. "You know, it's all about slavery, though they try to whitewash it with talk about states' rights. Ever since Clay and Calhoun dominated the Senate, they proposed state's rights—of course they did—the right to buy and sell slaves in the new territories."

Her lips tightened and her eyes, if it were possible, burned brighter. "We went to Washington when I was nine. I saw them chained together, tied up like I tie my goats. Negro women came around begging for money so they could buy their children. It makes me sick even now. Have you read *Uncle Tom's Cabin*?"

She didn't give them a chance to answer. "And did you ever meet Generals McClellan or Alexander Webb?" Large pink circles bloomed on her cheeks. "I'd spit on them if I ever met them. You know, at Antietam they held back a division and my father and brothers died …"

Daniel and Hal had dined at the Executive Mansion with President Lincoln, and to Daniel, this conversation wasn't far removed from what he'd experienced there. While most people didn't say so out loud, he was well aware a number of them wanted to spit on several generals, including those she'd mentioned.

As darkness settled over the lake, Hal cleaned up the dishes and pots while Daniel observed. Hal fixed more coffee, and the three of them sat, drinking it, around the fire. The dogs had settled beside her as they always did, their golden eyes never seeming to blink, though every once in a while a pointed ear would come to attention.

She held up her coffee cup. "You'll have to forgive all my talking. The wine went straight to my head." She nodded sweetly to Hal. "Thank you for the coffee and for cleaning the dishes."

Hal returned her smile, nodding amiably, then sat back down.

She took a deep sip of coffee. "Tell me what you can of the battle yesterday. I could hear the cannon. It had to be the loudest thing I'd ever heard. My house shook." She petted the dogs, smiling fondly at them as she did so. "My brave beasts hid under the porch."

Daniel reached for a handful of small sticks to the side of the fire and started snapping them into smaller pieces. "On Wednesday," he said, laying out the twigs in a pattern of some kind, "we were some of the first troops on the field. We carried messages from our headquarters to the other generals, so we saw a lot."

Hal went to the water's edge and brought back a handful of pebbles, dropping them by Daniel's twigs. Together they drew maps in the sand showing the locations of regiments, the formations of each day of the battle.

"What you heard was just about every cannon in North America firing at the very same time. I never saw anything like it before," said Daniel. "We were supposed to go back to Maryland to protect supply lines, but our colonel lent us to General Hancock's division to protect the flanks of a battalion of light horse artillery. I ended up having a front row seat."

He shook his head and told her how the *minié* ball had hummed before it drilled into him. "I heard the damn thing coming at me. Sounded like a killer hummingbird." He winced at the memory. "After I was hit, one of Hancock's sergeants pulled me out of the way and wrapped a bandage around my leg."

Hal let out a nervous chuckle. "That's not the worst thing, either." He related the story about the artillerist's head. "I saw it happen, Summer Rose. It happened during the cannonade, before Danny was hit by the ball. The poor fellow's head flew like a missile and exploded a few inches from Danny's chin. Blood and gore and his teeth like dice ... all over Danny. I almost got sick."

Even Daniel grinned when she cringed, then he picked up the telling. "Then Lee sent about fifteen thousand men marching, flags and guidons flapping, drums pounding, straight at us. I swear I heard a piper." He shook his head. "They knew we were there, but they still marched uphill toward us. Our cannon cut 'em down with canister and shot." He hesitated for a breath. "Mowed them like grass. I never saw such a slaughter, such bravery." His voice cracked as he recalled the collapsing wall of men, then he took a deep breath and swallowed down the memories. "Our forces held and wiped out Pickett and Pettigrew's divisions. Wally Stackhouse, from our class, was one of Pickett's captains. He grew up in Philly, but his father's family came from Virginia." His eyes burned with unshed tears. "What unit is your brother with?"

"Last I heard he was on General Heintzelman's staff in Washington." She made a dismissive motion with her hand, stood, and poked at the fire. "Jack wasn't wounded physically at Antietam, but he's not well. They created a staff job in Washington for him."

She took her knife to the water's edge, washed it, and dried it on her skirt. Glancing down, she slid the knife back into its sheath then sat beside the dogs, petting them. "We should sleep out here tonight. The heat will be unbearable away from the water. In the hot weather, we often sleep on the island." She leaned back, taking in the sky full of stars. "I feel close to my family here, and it's safe. The dogs will let us know if anyone even comes near the shore." She laughed. "Oh, and you'll meet the geese tomorrow. They'll let us know if anyone comes over the bridge."

Daniel didn't want to talk about war anymore. But he didn't want to go to sleep yet. He wanted to know more about her. He leaned forward and spoke gently. "Would you tell us what happened earlier? We saw you dive into the lake. Where did you go? How did you come to live here?" His voice softened even more. "And another thing. I dreamed of three men last night. I think they may have been your father and brothers. The dream was so real I could have sworn they were ghosts, actually. Their names were Micah, William, and Colin."

Her eyes went dark, staring past him toward the night horizon.

"Would you tell us about … you?"

CHAPTER 6

STORIES

Her legs were tucked beneath her, the head of one of the dogs resting in her lap. She settled back, not seeming the least bit cowed by his questions.

"I dove into the lake to fetch the medicine. I swam to an underwater cave, one an old Indian showed my father when he first moved here. The entrance is down about five feet on the side of the island. You swim through a wide tunnel, then up, then left, then down again," she said. Daniel was fascinated by the way she moved her hands, showing the path. "It's frightening down there. The first time you do it, you need someone to show you exactly where to turn and where to push up or down. My father said the cave sprawls under the entire valley."

She chuckled. "It's very damp, but there's a little light from fissures. I was afraid to leave during the thunder and lightning.

"Da and my brothers hauled kegs of his medicines there. I took the bottle with me and filled it." She shivered, and a soft look came into her eyes. "The names you mentioned

belong to my father and brothers. They died at Antietam."
She shrugged, a small, delicate movement. "Maybe their
ghosts came up with me. Jack gets angry when I talk about
ghosts, and I really don't know. I've never seen any ghosts, but
sometimes it's like I feel a presence. That's one of the reasons I
insisted on staying here in this valley.

"I live—*we* lived here," she said, opening her arms as if to
embrace the whole valley, "because my father, Colonel Micah
Angus McAllister loved this little piece of paradise.

"My father and his five sons emigrated here from
Scotland after his first wife died. Micah and the boys settled in
Philadelphia, where Micah met my mother, Lillian Fitzmartin.
He told us he honed in on her like a bee to honeysuckle." She
giggled and her eyes sparkled with remembrance. "My da
was a great storyteller."

Her dark lashes threw shadows across her cheeks. "My
mother adored him. She told me everyone who knew my father
joked that he could sell horse manure to the Army. She said he
could have married any girl he wanted, but ..." She arched her
eyebrows. "My grandmother tells the story a little dif-fer-ent-
ly. Grammie claimed he cast a spell over my mother."

Summer shook her head and took on a crotchety old
voice. "'Your mother went wild over that crazy Highlander."'
She wiggled an admonishing finger. "'Mind you, young
missy, keep your head about you where men are concerned.
Your mother disobeyed us and married him. He charmed all
the sense out of her.'"

Summer giggled at the memory and Daniel watched
thoughts tickle behind her eyes.

"Micah was a lot older than my mother, and he had five sons. The oldest, William, was fourteen. Mother was nineteen." A log shifted and a great swell of embers floated into the night sky. "Grammie especially didn't like those almost grown-up sons.

"After they eloped, my grandfather forgave them. Granddad even took my father into the family business. All the boys loved my mother. But yellow fever swept through the city the summer before I was born. Micah's two youngest sons, Martin and Ian, died. They were only seven and eight years old. The Fitzmartins had a summer place near Gwynedd where they went to escape the heat and the fever ravaging Philadelphia, but after the two boys died, Gwynedd wasn't far enough away from the city for Micah."

Daniel took advantage of the moment, leaning in to fill her coffee cup. He still didn't feel quite right, and his leg hurt like a son of a gun, but there was nowhere else on earth he'd rather be than sitting on this hard dirt, listening to Summer Rose. She smiled thanks at him and blew on the hot coffee.

"One of my grandfather's businesses was a large lumber yard, and my father worked for him as a lumber merchant. He traveled all over Pennsylvania and as far away as Michigan and Maine buying timber rights, hiring loggers, and seeing the logs floated to a railhead. He bought these thousand acres, everything you can see from here. He bought this land for himself."

She tried a sip, winced, and set the tin cup down again to let it cool. Her face glowed red-gold in the light from the fire. "My first winter, so I was told, four of us lived in a one room log and mud hut. William and Colin were off to school in Lancaster, so my parents, Jack, and I stayed in that little room. I use it now as a shed for a few goats and a dozen or so chickens. On very cold nights I drag Benjamin in there. I can't imagine how we lived in such a tiny place." She arched her eyebrows, her face giving the illusion that she was no older than twelve. "If you had ever met my genteel mother, you'd understand."

Hal stood and added wood to the fire. "Benjamin?"

"The donkey. He's stubborn. I'll give you a tour and introduce you when you're better. Anyway, when the war started, Micah and his three sons all joined up. Micah was charismatic. He had military experience and a good reputation from Scotland. He also knew people from all over the state." She snapped her fingers. "He raised a regiment quickly. His three sons, William, Colin, and Jack became officers. William and Colin were captains, Jack a lieutenant. He's a captain now. They were proud as anything to fight for their new country. Ezra, our neighbor, took Mother and me to see them off."

She sighed. "You know what it was like then. No one expected the war to last more than a month. Bull Run changed our thinking. My father and his two oldest sons died within seconds of each other at Antietam, mowed down like a row of corn." Her voice quivered, her eyes glistened. "Jack brought them home in a cart." She sipped at her coffee and her eyes grew wider and wetter. She lifted her face to the wide ribbon of the Milky Way. "The Germans took care of us. They made the coffins and helped us bury them. Their graves are up on the mountain."

Daniel passed her the canteen. She took a long sip. "A month later my mother became ill with a fever, and I feared she was dying. I ran to the Germans again and they raced to town to send a telegram to Jack. My grandparents were too old to travel. A doctor came out, but he couldn't help. When he left, Ezra, my neighbor, stayed with me." She choked a little. "So I wouldn't be alone when … Anyway, Jack came up from Washington on the train. When he arrived, she'd already died." She took an involuntary gulp of air.

"Jack wanted me to live with my grandparents, but I refused. I told him I'd run away. I needed to stay here. Ezra and Margie promised to watch out for me, and they do. My decision was a good one. I've cried almost as much as I can and I feel strong now. I've learned how to take care of myself." She sat up, still petting the dogs. "How did you hear their names?"

Daniel breathed deeply then shrugged. "Like I said, they came to me in a dream that felt incredibly real."

Hal tossed a stick into the fire. "Remember when you came to us as Kip? You told us the names of your father and brothers, as well as their ranks." He turned to Daniel. "Perhaps you remembered from then."

Daniel shrugged. "Seemed real. It wasn't frightening. In fact …" He let out a loud breath. "I'd love to see a ghost. It might help me believe in God again."

For a few minutes no one spoke. They studied the coals of the fire. A fish jumped close to shore, sending slow circles edging toward them. Summer Rose yawned. Her eyes kept closing and drooping, and she seemed to be losing the battle to keep them open. Among all the clotheslines, Hal found enough somewhat dry blankets for the three of them. While he banked the fire, Daniel stood and worked the stiffness out of his leg, then fixed her a bedroll and tucked the blanket around her.

She touched his face and told him to put more salve on his leg. "I'll check it in the morning." Her hand fell away, those big eyes closed, and she dropped into sleep.

The touch of her fingers on his cheek sent heat and chills racing through him. He wanted to lie down beside her, hold her, comfort her. Nothing else, he told himself. The dogs, not trusting him an inch, nudged between him and the girl, then showed their teeth and growled. Although curled beside her, their foxy noses resting on their tails, the dogs' golden eyes followed his every move. Daniel held his hands palm out. "Honest, boys. My intentions are honorable."

Growls rumbled through their throats until he returned to the fire.

Hal and Daniel refilled their cups then Daniel sat on the big rock. He checked his leg and applied more of the thick potion while Hal made sure the girl slept. The dogs growled at him, too. With a shrug, he headed back and added more wood to the fire.

"I met her half-brother a couple of months ago," Hal said quietly. "Captain Jack McAllister. He's a sad case. Nerves appear to be shot, so someone assigned him a desk job in the War Office. Lincoln's taken to talking with him while he checks the flimsies. Jack's thin as a tent pole, thinner than I am, and his body does a crazy tick. I also remember seeing him at one of the brothels. I doubt he'd remember me. He was in a corner, nursing a drink. The worst of Hooker's gang treated him like a pet. You and I need to contact our fathers soon about buying this land, to protect her if nothing else."

Daniel froze. "What is your purpose?"

"Easy, Danny," Hal said, holding up one hand. "I know we always seem to hone in on the same girl, but I got your message. You're serious. I'm just saying if you want the girl, you'd better own the land. My guess is someone will steal it out from under this Jack McAllister as soon as the war ends. And you and I both have the money."

"Yes, well, answer my question. What is your purpose?"

Hal sighed and shook his head. He didn't raise his voice, but its edge cut through the night air. "Aside from the fact that you're my best friend, and you'll no doubt be murdered for your arrogance and poor attitude one day, I'm impressed with this land. After the war, I'd like to settle in this valley. Maybe not all the time, but it would make a great retreat, like the Blairs and the Biddles have. A hell of a fishing and hunting camp. For Christ's sake, Daniel, I'm your friend. You're damn lucky." He nodded to the girl. "She's one in a million. Dressed in style, with that face and figure, she'd stop a regiment on Pennsylvania Avenue. And I see her eyes follow you. I'm not sure she knows it yet, but she wants you as much as you want her." Hal tossed a stick in the fire.

Daniel stretched out on his back, stared into the stars. "Sorry. I'm being a ... I really don't understand why I'm acting like this." His eyes drifted to the girl and he chuckled. "Am I crazy?"

Hal snorted. "You're crazy if you *don't* want her. Let me know if that's the case."

CHAPTER 7

MINT AND MIST AND
BLACKBERRY

Overnight, a heavy fog rolled into the valley. Before first light Summer Rose had navigated the canoe by sound toward the smaller of the two waterfalls, leaving the men asleep. All the talk about her brothers and father had brought back nightmares of war, of losing them and her mother. Even though almost a year had passed since her mother had died, Summer Rose missed her so much her chest ached. When she thought about her mother, like she did now, a dry sob stuck in her throat, and hot tears seared behind her eyelids.

The night before, she'd told the soldiers she'd cried as much as she could, that now she was strong, but she hadn't been a hundred percent honest. At least now she wasn't blubbering all the time, but the loss of her mother still cut like a pick thrust into her heart. She wanted to ask her so many questions; right now she wanted to ask her about the feelings curling inside her. This morning she needed time alone, time to renew.

From experience, she knew the trout. This season and early in the morning, they liked to gather in the lower stream of spring water at Forty Foot Falls, just below where she'd directed the men to bathe. She set out two rods, and within a half hour she'd caught a nice basket of trout. She filled another with blackberries. To navigate the return trip through the fog, she'd planned to whistle for Nip and Tuck and aim toward their yapping. Instead, she smelled coffee and wood smoke, and pointed the canoe toward the aromas.

Fog smothered the island. Daniel awoke as she left, worried about her. He was about to shake Hal's shoulder when he heard her paddle slice through the water. He rolled his pant legs to his knees and waded toward the sound. When she came into view, he walked the canoe to the beach, then lifted her from it, taking advantage of the position and cradling her against his chest.

She giggled and held the creel by its strap. "Six gorgeous trout. Do you know how to clean them?"

He noticed her bare feet and the way her breath tickled the side of his neck when she laughed, then reluctantly deposited her on the damp sand. "I'll clean the fish, but please don't go off again without telling us. You gave me a scare."

She dangled the basket of fish out in front of him, tilting her head to one side and smiling.

"How do you navigate in this fog?" he asked, his voice a little sharp.

"With ease."

Her voice, high-pitched and smooth, sounded like music. Her innocent demeanor drew him like a magnet, and yet she wore a mantle of agelessness, of knowing something he didn't. He could see how her brother might allow her to live alone. On the other hand, Daniel wanted to shake him, wounded war hero or not, for allowing such a thing. Here she stood in front of him, her neck as delicate as a flower stem, achingly beautiful, and cheerfully telling him about listening for the falls and returning by the smell of coffee.

Waves of mist thickened about them, and her blue-green eyes twinkled devilishly. "You should trust me a little, you know. I did fine before you showed up."

The white ruffle of her skirt brushed against the sand clinging to her feet. Still holding the basket away from her, she smoothed her skirt, stuck her hand in her pocket, and pulled out a compass. She held it up and he saw imps dance in her eyes. "If I found myself in trouble, I would have used this."

He shook his head and took the fish from her. Every inch of his body pulled towards her, wanting to sweep her against him, hold her in his arms. Still leaning down at the water's edge, he set the basket in the water then looked up at her.

"You are absolutely right. Somehow I mistook you for a helpless girl. I apologize. You're obviously far from helpless."

He stood and reached for her hands, holding both of them in one of his. Grinning, he stepped across the line her toe had drawn in the sand. Daniel loved to flirt, and he knew he was good at it. A general's wife had once told him when he smiled, her toes curled. He wasn't exactly sure what he did, but he did it now, sending all of his heart sailing through the mist to this girl.

She flushed and inhaled through her nose, smelling his breath, smelling him. His pale eyes seemed to laugh without sound. When his voice gentled further, it seemed to surprise him almost as much as it did her.

"Sweet Summer Rose," he said, "do you have any idea what I want to do right now?"

A new woman burst from the chrysalis inside her. Heat flooded her face and spread through her body, and her heart downright pounded. Blinking slowly, she lifted her head and cocked it to one side.

"Clean the fish?" she whispered.

He lowered his head and kissed her lips, tasting mint and mist and blackberry. When she didn't pull away, he leaned into her. With his one hand still holding both of hers, he brought his other around and touched her cheek and neck. His tongue brushed, ever so lightly, just under the center of her upper lip. A quiver rippled through her, like a puff of air on water, and the movement vibrated to every cell in his body. He ran his thumb across her cheek and deepened the kiss. Her body jerked at first, then softened, folding into him.

He broke the kiss but didn't pull away. His face smoothed, and he took a slow, shaky breath. His heart, already in his throat, calmed a little and he swallowed. After a second, he lifted her hands to his mouth and brushed her knuckles against his lips. The fingertips of his other hand still touched her face.

His voice came out soft. "You are lovely, Summer, and very much a surprise. You are more, more, than I ever …" He stopped, not having the slightest idea of how to word his feelings. One corner of his mouth curled and he stepped away from her, his chest constricting wonderfully at the sight of her bewildered expression. "I better see to the trout."

After breakfast, Summer Rose asked the men to carry a load of gear to the shore. She seemed to have regained her composure and confidence. "We have so much here I think it'll take two trips. I want to show you the house and my garden, and our animals need attention. I'm sure your horses will be happy to see you, and you need to rest, Daniel. When you feel well enough, I'll show you the valley." The words tripped through her lips, as if she needed to fill the air with syllables. "The waterfalls are spectacular, and we have seven springs." Her hand swept the still foggy sky. "The mist will clear in about an hour."

She handed Daniel her compass and her fingers rested on his palm a split second longer than they needed. "Go exact east, and you'll end up at the meadow where your horses are hobbled. You'll hear them. Right now I need a good scrub." She picked up a towel, a bar of soap, and a sack. "Would you come back for me in about an hour?"

They nodded and she tapped the side of her leg. Nip and Tuck were there immediately, following her across the island.

When they returned, she directed them on a short tour. The property impressed the men more than they could have imagined. The mountains, with their sheer granite cliffs, protected a good three hundred and thirty degrees of the thousand acre valley, and the entrance to the valley crossed a swift stream only expert horsemen on strong horses would attempt. Summer Rose told them her father and half-brothers had built the stone bridge just wide enough for a single wagon. She explained how they transplanted laurel and pines, training ivy to camouflage the structure.

The house, hidden among the pines, allowed a good view of the entrance and the lake. The flock of white geese she kept took to honking and nipping as they approached the house. "They're more of a deterrent than the dogs," she said. A wicked grin snuck onto her face. "They're insurance, too. If I have a bad winter, I pick the nastiest, and ..." She made a wringing motion with her hands. "Ezra and Margie gave them to me. Watch-geese, he calls them."

Well built of stone and log, with a wide porch on two sides, the downstairs of the house boasted two bedrooms, a kitchen, and a large living room with a beautiful stone fireplace. Upstairs there was a sleeping loft. The refinement surprised both of the men.

Hal bent at the knees and examined how the sluice cut through the wall below the stone sink. He stood in the center of the kitchen and studied its features, then ran his hand along the sink and touched the faucet. "Your father designed this? I'm very impressed."

"We have three springs close to the house. When you go outside, take a look at the pipes and cisterns, and the windmill. The Germans helped my father with most of it. They're very clever."

Turning, she motioned around the room. Fitted out with a utilitarian wood stove and work benches, the kitchen was cozy and neat. Pots, pans, and utensils hung along one wall, and shelves holding dishes and jars of spices hung on another. In the center stood a marble topped table with a fifty pound bag of flour beneath it.

Daniel made an exaggerated motion, rubbing his stomach. His eyes twinkled. "I love pie."

"Do you like sour cherry?" Her eyes teased right back.

"My favorite."

"I'll make one while you're here."

He grinned. "Be careful, Summer. I may never leave."

She lowered her eyes but couldn't quite hide the color filling her cheeks. Then she moved toward the door, motioning for the men to follow. The steps beyond the back door led to her garden, and Daniel thought right away that she had every right to be proud of it. Rows of vegetables, manicured and lush, stretched to a small fenced paddock and shed. Five dark-eyed goats and a dozen chickens rushed out to greet them. The donkey stayed in the shade leaning against the shed and chewing hay. Beside the steps grew several pots of herbs, in which Daniel recognized mint and parsley. Vines of deep green leaves with trumpet-like flowers clung to the weathered logs of the shed. He motioned questioningly toward them.

She shrugged. "Gourds. My neighbor grew them last year. Margie gave me the seeds. When they're dried, they're useful as tools and birdhouses." She grinned. "It's one thing the goats won't eat."

CHAPTER 8

TOMATO SANDWICHES

The living room was both comfortable and elegant, with an upholstered sofa and two chairs, small tables, a beautiful bench covered in needlepoint all lit by oil lamps with jewel-colored glass shades. A good oriental rug stretched under their feet. Against the wall stood an upright piano and a big green fern. Daniel studied the many books on the shelves beside the stone fireplace and was impressed by the eclectic variety: *Homer* in Greek, *Cicero and Caesar* in Latin, Chaucer, Erasmus, a great deal of Shakespeare, Locke, Defoe, Austin, Cooper, Hawthorne, Poe, and a dozen or so of Dickens' books, plus journals and pamphlets. Copies of recent works by Thoreau, Emerson, Darwin, and Harriett Beecher Stowe lay on a lower shelf.

He raised his eyebrows. "You've read …?"

She stepped closer and picked up *Pride and Prejudice*, then leafed fondly through the pages. "All of them. My grandmother believes fiercely in education, and not just for men. She hired tutors for my mother. Some were professors from a local boy's school. My father attended university in Scotland. The boys attended college, and our parents tutored all of us. They made sure we all read both Greek and Latin. We spoke only French at dinner."

"Where did your brothers go to school?" asked Hal.

"They went to Franklin and Marshall in Lancaster, just when the two schools merged. Our parents worked hard to educate us. My da probably did it so Grammie would stop yelling at him. Da taught us mathematics, astronomy, geometry, Latin, and Greek." She ticked off the subjects on her fingers. "My mother taught literature, music, history, and geography. I'm not an expert in anything, but I know a little about a lot of subjects." She touched the piano keys. "I also play the piano and swim like a fish." She smiled with a teasing light in her eyes. "Oh, and you've seen how good I am with a knife. I always beat my brothers."

Daniel's pale eyes never left her face. "I'm sure you did."

"Da taught me that I'm a McAllister, and even though I'm a girl, I can be as good as my brothers at just about anything." She set *Pride and Prejudice* back on the shelf and handed him *Walden Pond*.

"Grammie always reminded my father that he'd dragged away her only daughter, her only child, into the wilderness. She couldn't stand the thought of our not having what she envisioned as essential, so she had the furniture, the rugs, the dishes, and the piano all shipped to us. They have lots of money and didn't mind spending it on us."

The men leaned forward, fascinated. She never seemed to run out of stories, but neither of them tired of her voice.

"She sometimes sent my mother and me crates of books and journals. In the crates she included soap and a ribbon or a new comb for me, those thick candles, seed packets, sheet music, paprika, wine, talcum powder that smelled like roses, sometimes a new blouse for me.

"She always sends toothbrushes." She grinned at Daniel and let out a giggle. "Do you need one? I have extras." She sighed, still smiling. "I write her every week, but I'll avoid visiting. If I did, someone would make me live there. I want to stay here."

She slowly surveyed the room. "We were very happy. I miss them all." She took a deep breath then seemed to remember she wasn't alone. "You may put your things in the large bedroom. Mine is the smaller room."

As if she couldn't bear to settle for even a moment, she motioned with her hands for them to leave. "Excuse me, gentlemen. I need to set some dough to rise, and start that cherry pie. Daniel, why don't you give your leg a rest? Just lay down on the bed or on the porch swing." She nodded toward the book she'd given him. "Have you read Thoreau? Oh, and take these dogs with you, would you? They're always underfoot."

For three days he rested, reading and watching from the porch swing as Hal mended the gate, carved shingles for the roof of the shed, chopped firewood, or tramped all over the valley providing rabbits and pheasants for their meals. Summer Rose, when she wasn't smiling at Hal or raving about his expertise with a hammer or a shotgun, spent hours with Daniel, doing little things that suddenly meant so much more to him. She sat beside him, mending their clothes, pitting cherries, shelling peas, snapping beans, knitting socks. Her hands never idled. Between them, they talked of books and poetry, discovering they both liked Shakespeare's *Julius Caesar* and *Macbeth*, as well as Dickens and Poe, especially *The Raven*. They were both well versed in guns and horses, and she spent time admiring his LeMat pistol and Spencer repeating rifle. She said Chester with his chestnut coat and flaxen mane was by far the most gorgeous horse she'd ever seen.

She never said anything about it, but he knew she remembered their kiss, for its sweet quiver still hovered over them like a haunting melody. He no more could have excised that memory from his mind—not that he wanted to—than he could forget her face.

On the fourth day, she handed walking sticks to both men and touched Daniel's arm. "I believe you're strong enough for a short hike." She wore tan belted trousers, a long sleeved blue shirt, her bulky vest, and sturdy boots. Shouldering her knapsack, she led them up into the mountains as high as they could go without ropes or picks.

Partway up the mountain, the wind took her hat. Daniel snatched it from the air, but didn't hand it back. "I like your hair blowing loose." He folded the beat-up hat and tucked it in her pack. She shrugged easily and kept on, leading them halfway to the top of Switch Back Falls, where they stopped to survey the valley.

Hal knew enough about law to ask. "Jack inherited the land?"

She nodded. "He knows I love this valley. I'm sure he's hoping I'll fall for some fellow and run off, maybe to California or Brazil or—" Her eyes flashed with laughter. "Maybe Zanzibar, but I won't." She tossed her hair over her shoulder. "My home is here. I belong here."

In addition to her beauty, Daniel appreciated Summer Rose's ease around men, which he supposed came from growing up with three brothers. For another, she was practical. Each morning and evening, she checked Daniel's wound, applying more salve. They devised a routine where he wrapped himself up in a blanket before he dressed or just after he undressed, and she checked the wound.

Now, as they climbed, Summer eyed Daniel's leg every so often. When he tired, she stopped them high above the valley where the view of the patchwork quilt of fields and lake spread before them. They sat beside the tumbling water, and she pulled hardboiled eggs from her pack and tossed them each one, then spread a kitchen towel on the grass, setting several more eggs there. Next came a small board from her knapsack as well as the knife from the side of her boot, and she set about slicing bread, onions, white radishes, and tomatoes.

His hands peeled the egg, but his eyes locked on her, and his heart beat like a drum just below his collarbone. If he swallowed too hard, he feared it might smash through his chest. His hands ached to touch her. She saw him watching her through his lashes and her face glowed pink. When her eyes met his, he could tell her breath caught. Over and over, their kiss came to mind.

To cool his thoughts, he surveyed the fields, forests, and the lake, but his good intentions lasted less than two minutes. He watched her pull a salt shaker from a vest pocket.

"I love tomatoes," she said. "Some say they're poisonous, but they aren't. Sprinkled with a little salt, they're the best thing on earth."

She layered her fresh buttered bread with tomato and paper thin slices of onion. The tip of her tongue peeked from her mouth as she salted the concoction. She handed a sandwich to each of them, then fixed one for herself and took a bite. Juice ran down her chin, and she giggled, wiping her mouth on her sleeve.

"Pretend you didn't see that. My mother would have a conniption. She did *try* to make a lady out of me."

His heart did a little stutter. Inside his mind he whispered, *Don't change a thing, darling girl. Stay just as you are.*

Daniel missed nothing. He especially didn't miss that Hal watched her, too.

She led them along a narrow trail, where they easily ducked under the spill from a narrow section of falls, and walked along the side of a mountain. She pointed toward an enormous nest. "That's a bald eagle nest. It's been here as long as I've lived here. I wouldn't dare walk by here in early spring. They're huge, and fiercely protective of their babies."

Moving down a steep incline, under a cluster of circling hawks, Daniel stopped, giving himself a rest, and asked about a sled and snowshoes hanging in a tree. He was finding walking downhill more difficult than going uphill.

"I shoot a couple of deer over the winter and trade the Germans for ham, bacon, and lard." She nodded toward the sled and snowshoes. "I only hunt when there's snow. I gut the deer where it drops, then use the sled to take the carcass down the mountain. I use the shoes if the snow's deep."

Down in the valley she showed them a beaver colony. Long-legged cranes and a few blue herons stood on the dams. "Last winter I ran a trap line through here. I cured fox, beaver, otter, and mink, then traded my skins for most of my supplies. I couldn't get coffee this year because of the war."

When they arrived back at the house, Daniel rested on the swing again while Hal borrowed her shotgun and walked down to the meadow where it bordered a marsh. Within twenty minutes, he'd brought down two wild turkeys, then hung them by the shed.

"This land is a hunter's paradise," he said.

Once the birds were plucked and cleaned, the men stood beside her in the kitchen, learning her cooking methods. As she prepared the birds with bacon and spices, Hal asked, "What's that?"

She crushed the fresh green leaves between her oily fingers and held out her palms for the soldiers to smell. "Sage and rosemary, I press it under the skin and put a whole onion inside each bird."

Daniel and Hal roasted the birds over an open fire while new potatoes were dropped in a three legged pot, ready to boil over the coals. As they sat together, shelling peas, she asked more about them. "What did you do before the war?"

"We were students at PMC, the Pennsylvania Military College, in Chester," Hal said. "It's just south of Philadelphia. We and most of our class volunteered right after Ft. Sumter fell."

She nodded. "Franklin and Marshall emptied out, too. I think the boys just wanted the excitement."

Hal arched his thick eyebrows. "We heard those early drums and almost drowned in our arrogance. I find it difficult to believe I was so ignorant."

"We all were. How many did we lose at Gettysburg?"

They both shrugged. "Thousands and thousands. I'd guess at least a third of each army wounded and killed."

"Such a waste," she muttered.

Daniel leaned forward and dumped a napkin full of peas into the main pot. "Maybe forty to fifty thousand, if you count both sides, lest we forget we're all Americans. I can't even imagine that many peas, let alone that many men."

She studied the pot of peas. "I can't imagine it, either. How long can it go on?"

From the springhouse she'd pulled a bottle of red wine. "This bottle has been here since the year before the war. We went to Philadelphia for Christmas and brought two cases home with us. Before the war we used to go a few places. We took the train to New York and went to the opera, even ate at a restaurant.

"Before that we went to Washington. I remember eating oysters, raw and cooked every which way. Oh, and the mud." She wrinkled her nose. "I didn't like the mud. But I loved the oysters."

She set the table on the porch with blue and white china plates, and again they dined by candlelight. This time she put the candles inside glass chimneys. "It's a treat for me to use the china," she said, touching the dishes. "I haven't used it since Mother died."

Later they sat on the porch drinking coffee, devouring sour cherry pie, and watching fireflies. It was hard to believe great armies maneuvered somewhere on the other side of the mountains.

Daniel wanted very much to know how old she was, but a shyness held him back. Fortunately, not a timid bone existed in Hal. He came right out and asked. The dim light from the candles played on the well-defined bones of her cheeks, the clear line of her jaw, the long column of her throat. Both men's eyes focused on her.

"I'll be nineteen in September. If I were a man, I'd be one of your soldiers." She didn't smile. "Consider that, gentlemen, when you think I shouldn't live here alone. How old are you?"

"We're both twenty-three," answered Daniel. "We'll turn twenty-four in December, though I feel a hell of a lot older."

"You weren't much older than I am when you went to war." She smiled sadly. "None of us are very young, are we?"

CHAPTER 9

BEGINNINGS

Dressed in their clean and mended uniforms, swords gleaming, tack smelling of saddle soap, and their boots glowing with polish, they exchanged addresses and gave her all their coffee supply, as well as Daniel's Spencer repeating carbine and ammunition. He didn't tell her the rifle had been a gift from his father or that the army didn't fit out its cavalrymen with expensive guns. He insisted she take it.

"I can get another in Gettysburg. There must be hundreds available. I'll sleep easier knowing you have a repeating rifle here."

He'd enjoyed showing her how to load it, site it, and clean it. He also enjoyed her delight at its quick fire capabilities. How many girls would appreciate a rifle? Not many he knew could even hold a gun steady.

Hal irritated him when he jumped in and hammered pegs in the kitchen wall so she could hang the carbine where it would be handy. Daniel had been the one to suggest hanging it there, and he let Hal know by his scowl that he didn't like his friend bumping in where he didn't belong. Hal got the message, and Daniel walked her alone to the meadow for target practice. She caught on quickly, as he'd known she would. In fact, she was a crack shot. He discovered the top of her head came right to his ear and her hair smelled of lemon. The smooth hollow at the back of her neck made him long to plant a kiss there. He touched her waist to steady her aim, and guessed his hands would span it.

Now he sat in the kitchen, packing their saddlebags with the food she'd prepared: two dozen hardboiled eggs, a big chunk of sharp cheese, two loaves of bread, small jars of goat cheese and jam, a jar of peaches, oatmeal cookies, all the tomatoes and cucumbers in her garden, and a side of bacon.

When the time to leave arrived, she walked them to the stone bridge. Although the sun had just risen, the day promised blistering heat. Hal kissed her cheek and she hugged him, leaning her face against his shoulder. "Take care of yourself, Slim," she said.

"You called me Slim last night." Hal chuckled and brushed a tear from her cheek. "Only my mother sheds tears for me. Thank you."

She laughed a little. "I don't like goodbyes."

He mounted and gave her a salute. "I'm sure we'll meet again."

Hal had no sooner turned his back and nudged Dulcey toward the bridge, when Daniel's hand touched her shoulder. His fingers found the hollow, the one that had been driving him frantic. Not wanting to frighten her, he paused, but she leaned into him, her thick eyelashes brushing the soft skin beneath her eyes. He kissed her forehead, then beneath each eye, then her lips. For a long time he held her with his cheek against hers.

His mind told him she'd be safe there. *She's more capable than most men I know,* he reasoned. But the pain of riding away ... *Good Lord, I don't want to leave her.* His chest, his heart, ached, and he felt her breath catch.

The sound loosed the wild, longing which had been bubbling inside him, and he kissed her with a consuming passion. His hands covered her back, feathered the sides of her breasts, he pressed every willing inch of her tight against him then kissed the softness of her throat. When he backed away, he all but dove into those blue-green depths. His voice came out hoarse and awkward, but his hands were steady as they cupped the sides of her face.

"You know I don't want to leave you. I think I'm in love." He brushed his hands through her hair, its silkiness soothing him as he struggled to unearth all his svelte phrases, his sophisticated chatter. They'd all flown from his grasp and he felt as awkward as a colt. "God, I didn't know I could feel this way. I've wanted to kiss you since we left the island."

She nuzzled against his neck, kissing the skin at his collar, and he felt her smile against him. "I wish you had. I haven't thought of much else."

He chuckled. "I was afraid I wouldn't be able to stop once I started." He kissed the patch of skin by her temple, then her nose, and finally her lips again.

When he lifted his head, she said, "I don't want you to stop."

He gulped and cupped her chin in his hand. A laugh, dangerously close to a giggle, bubbled out of him and he shook his head. "You're no help whatsoever. I think, if your parents were here, they would object. Trust me, darling. I know when I should stop."

On the far side of the bridge, Dulcey stomped and snorted, a clear hint from Hal. Daniel ignored the message. His lips lingered on her forehead, drinking in the lemony scent of her.

"I'll find a way to spend my life with you here in this valley," he promised, discovering with relief that his confident smile had returned.

She reached up and brushed her fingers along his moustache, along his freshly shaved cheek. Then she stood on her tiptoes and kissed him with her lips open.

"I want you here." She took a deep breath and blinked quickly. "Don't worry about me, Daniel. I'm safe. And I'll be waiting when you come back. There's something ... I feel something powerful when you kiss me. So please. You take care of yourself, Daniel. Come back to me."

The way she said his name almost destroyed his honorable intentions. To save them both, he vaulted onto Chester's back, leaned down, and kissed her again. Chester followed his urging and cantered toward Dulcey and Hal. Both men turned and waved. Even from a distance, Daniel saw tears glisten in her eyes. His own vision blurred.

Hal turned to him. "You're lucky she left the dogs in the house. Did she tell you why her brothers named them Nip and Tuck?"

Daniel lifted his eyebrows. "She told me her mother named them."

"No. Her brothers did."

"I suppose you're about to tell me."

Hal nodded. "Given the proper signal, or if provoked, Nip nips off your balls while Tuck tucks into what's left. She said they're very well trained."

"She didn't say balls."

Hal threw back his head and laughed. "All joking aside, Danny, she's one in a million. If the courthouse in Gettysburg is open for business, I'll check on the deed and write to our fathers. I think part of the land might be in Franklin County."

"Why are you doing all this?"

Hal's crystal blue eyes narrowed, his weathered face cracked into a grin. "Oh, Danny boy, you've been bitten badly. I told you. I fell in love with the valley and half in love with your girl. When Mary's brothers kill you, I'll step in and save sweet Summer Rose."

"How reassuring."

"I thought so."

CHAPTER 10

PROMOTIONS

U pon entering General Buford's camp, even before Daniel dismounted, he was inundated with questions and complaints from half a dozen soldiers. One sergeant didn't like where he'd been directed to place the tents. Another had four soldiers sick with dysentery, which he blamed on the cook, while others blamed the location of Kilpatrick's latrines. Another soldier said his mare had just foaled and he didn't want to kill the colt. Several complained about the food.

Daniel wondered how one minute soldiers could fight to the death for their comrades and squabble like schoolboys in the next. As an officer, he found ninety percent of his time was spent managing disagreements and solving problems. Hal, also still mounted, appeared swamped with detail as well.

Daniel surveyed the swollen Potomac, Lee's breastworks and trenches. His wounded army, safe behind their fortifications, waited for pontoons to arrive.

Captain Myles Keogh spotted Daniel and approached on his chestnut gelding. Daniel knew Keogh well, and despite his pomposity, he admired him. He and Hal had learned many subtleties of command from this Irish soldier of fortune. Keogh, professional and unflappable to the core, wasn't the usual Irish immigrant. His family was landed gentry in Ireland. He'd gained military experience in Italy during the Papal Wars, fighting for the pope. He'd come to America, offering his services to the Federals, and ended up as General Buford's aide. The man was fine-looking, ramrod straight, and always impeccably fitted out in his tailor made and skin tight uniforms. The gold medal presented to him by the pope shone from a chain at his neck. When he waved, Hal and Daniel rode over to him.

"Lee's waiting for pontoon bridges to be brought up. Where in the hell have you two been?" Keogh grinned. "Knowing you, Goose, a woman must be involved."

Daniel's senses jumped to alert when he heard Keogh call Hal "Goose". This meant the two must have gallivanted together more than he'd realized. He nudged Chester between the two men and butted into the conversation, not about to let Hal mention Summer Rose or her valley. Especially not to a rogue like Myles Keogh.

"Hal usually is checking out girls, but I've been wretched since the incident of the head. He's been taking care of me." He grimaced for effect. "Then we were sent on a merry chase of misinformation to find you. We should ask where the hell you were. Both our horses needed new shoes. I also picked up some supplies in Gettysburg."

Keogh raised his eyebrows.

Daniel forced a laugh. "Clothes. My trousers were shredded." He refrained from mentioning the time he'd spent hunting for another Spencer carbine.

Keogh shuddered. "Horrid business, that head. You're lucky a bone fragment didn't sever an artery." He nodded to the hill overlooking the Potomac. "The general's up there. No wonder you had trouble finding us. We've been all over Maryland and Pennsylvania."

After he'd saluted and rode off, Daniel caught Dulcey's bridle and pulled Hal around to face him. "I'm dead serious about Summer. Not a word out of you about her. Understand?"

Hal nodded, then glanced up to the hillside. Generals Buford and Kilpatrick sat on horseback on a bluff. When Buford tipped his hat, Daniel waved back. Kilpatrick's eyes locked on them for a long moment, but he sat still as a stone.

"As much as I respect General Buford, I don't think I'd like to spend much time with Kilpatrick. Have you ever met him?" asked Daniel.

Hal cleared his throat and muttered. "You can tell a lot by how a man wears his hat. It's hard not to laugh at him. His men call him Kill-Cavalry behind his back. He's West Point, graduated in Custer's class. He's tough on his troops and his horses. I hate what he does to horses. He's not too kind to whores, either."

Both men ducked as a *minié* ball whistled over Hal's head. He pulled Dulcey into a copse of trees and Daniel followed with Chester as another ball hummed over his shoulder.

"What the hell? Damn the British and French for selling the rebs scopes. "

If sharpshooters were firing at them, they must be hiding something. Lee's army didn't have lead to waste. Daniel noticed Chester's ears perk up, and the coat along his pale mane quivered. Using binoculars, Daniel scanned in the same direction as Chester, studying a small stream spilling into the Potomac on the far side of the bluff. The water turned around a bend and ran right below Buford and Kilpatrick's perch.

Any cavalryman knew fresh water for horses was strategic. Daniel handed the glasses to Hal, who took a moment to study where Daniel indicated. He trusted that Hal understood. The soldiers were like that, not needing a lot of words, almost reading each other's mind. In the past, General Buford had accused them of being married.

"Go around to the left," Daniel murmured. "I'll take my men around the far side. We'll corral them as they get out of the water. They're right under Buford's nose, working along the shadows as the sun moves. They've muffled their tack, but Chester knows they're there."

Orders whispered down the chain of command and, in a matter of fifteen minutes, twenty of their men came up on the rearguard of a Confederate cavalry battalion. Before the rebels even knew what had hit them, Hal's and Daniel's men surrounded five hundred of the enemy without firing a shot. Buford and Kilpatrick rode down the hill when they heard the commotion, and Captain Keogh cantered over. They reined their horses together while Daniel ordered the prisoners' arms collected.

Buford shook his head, stopping his mount beside Dulcey. He nodded toward the prisoners, looking impressed. "I've missed you two. Welcome back."

Kilpatrick and Keogh rode to where the Confederate officers, now prisoners, stood beside their horses. General Buford lingered with his two captains. John Buford was a gentleman to the core and hailed from Kentucky and Illinois. Like many officers, he knew the opposing officer corps from when he'd been a student at West Point or served with them in the U.S. Army prior to this conflict. Buford's grandfather had fought in the revolution with Robert E. Lee's father. He was also a fourth cousin to General Jubal Early, one of Lee's lieutenants, and his current opponent. To General Buford the war was personal.

He gave Daniel a wry grin. "I knew you were too tough to kill. Heard about the head."

He indicated the captured Confederate prisoners filing by. "Well done. Gentlemen, come over to headquarters later, bring their battle flags. I'll add them to my collection."

"Before you go, I have a personal question to ask you, Sir," Daniel asked. "Did you know Colonel Micah McAllister?"

General Buford looked slightly surprised, but nodded. "Knew him well. Fine officer. Knew his sons, too. Why do you ask?"

Daniel shrugged, but Hal grinned from ear to ear. "Our Danny has fallen like a stone for his daughter, Sir. Can you believe it?"

John Buford nodded. "Actually, I can. I knew her mother. She was a kind friend to my Pattie. If she's anything like Lillian, you should marry the girl right away, Danny."

After dark, a corporal came for them, sent to escort them to Buford's command tent. As they walked along the river, they could see Lee's fires and hear the rebels singing. The corporal followed behind them, leading Chester and Dulcey in case they might need their mounts. Just outside the tent, Buford saluted them, then smiled. They nudged past General Kilpatrick and Captain Keogh, who stood just under the tent fly, deep in conversation. Keogh acknowledged their presence with a nod. Kilpatrick did not.

General Buford cleared his throat and laid a hand on each of their shoulders. "Your shoulder straps appear a little worse for wear. How about swapping them for these?" He nodded to Captain Keogh.

"Your service on the first day at Gettysburg merits a medal," Keogh said. "You helped hold the ground until General Reynolds came up. Unfortunately, the best I can do is a promotion. Thank you both for your valiant actions."

Their shoulder straps were exchanged for those bearing gold oak leaves, thus ending the non-ceremony. Unlike the others, Kilpatrick did not congratulate the two soldiers. "Don't go letting your heads swell," he said. "We lost three majors this morning. Stick your fist in a bucket of water. See the hole it makes? That's how important you are. Remember. You are replaceable."

Daniel wrote to Summer Rose that night. He told her about General Buford knowing her mother and what he'd said.

He told me I should marry you right away. I replied that was my intention, if she will have me. Will you?

In mid August, he received the first of her letters. He read it at least a hundred times.

I can't quit thinking of you, Daniel, or your kisses. They awakened a new part of me.

He carried the note in his breast pocket next to his heart. When Hal noticed, he teased him at every opportunity. "Your eyes are starting to droop just like General Meade's. Must be all that reading and writing and mooning over your girl."

In October, just north of the Rappahannock, Hal took a sniper's *minié* ball in his upper left arm. He lost a great deal of blood. Daniel found him in the hospital, talked the surgeon out of amputating, and led Hal's stretcher bearers to his own headquarters.

"I'll see to your men," he told Hal. "And I'll telegraph your parents. Just rest." He turned to Sergeant Abrams. "Make him some of that tea I brought back with me. And send someone over for his sergeant and Lieutenant Fisher." He dashed off orders and a telegram, then handed both to Sergeant Abrams.

He nursed Hal all night, forcing him to drink the foul-smelling tea. He found the bottle of Micah's medicine, which Summer Rose had sent with them, and poured some under Hal's bandages. When Hal slept, Daniel sat at his field desk and wrote to her, telling all about how he'd used her father's medicine and forced the foul-tasting tea down Hal's throat.

Two days later Daniel found Hal and his sergeant a berth on the train at Harper's Ferry. The arduous journey through Baltimore to Philly was full of delays. It took two days.

Hal spent the latter part of October 1863 and the first week of November at his home, west of Philadelphia. At Hal's insistence, a clerk in his father's office did the legwork involved in purchasing the thousand acres in Adams and Franklin Counties, and Hal assisted his father in preparing the paperwork. Harvey St. Clair was a meticulous lawyer and very good teacher.

Hal possessed a marvelous mind. While he recuperated, he put it to work. His father brought home crates of law books and piled them in the library at Thornwood, and Hal set about reading the law. In the evenings, he and his father discussed cases.

CHAPTER 11

FANNY

After a month of skirmishes along the Rappahannock and because of Virginia's mud—mud which a year before had scraped the hair off the legs of General Burnside's horses and mired both armies in mud to their axles—General Lee, in mid-November, took his army to his old winter headquarters between Richmond and Staunton. Much to President Lincoln's annoyance, Meade scattered his men north of the Rappahannock. Both armies seemed content to rest and sit out the bad weather, guarding their respective capitals, keeping a wary eye on their opponent.

Daniel, with an agenda in mind, took a few days leave and traveled home to Philadelphia via train. After spending the morning with his father he rode the few miles to the St. Clair farm, which sprawled along the Schuylkill River west of the city.

A groom who remembered Chester's name materialized from the shadows of the stable and took the horse. Daniel headed toward the house, where Mr. Stone, who had been the butler for the St. Clairs for as long as Daniel could remember, opened the door. He was tall, with thick gray hair, a stiff British accent, and an even stiffer moustache. Tears of happiness filled the old man's eyes as he embraced Daniel.

Daniel asked about his son, Ray. Six years older than Hal or Daniel, Ray had been a hero to both boys growing up. Harvey and Amelia, Hal's parents, had recognized the genius in Stone's son. They had sent him to the University of Pennsylvania, where he'd obtained a medical degree.

Mr. Stone sniffed, still unable to speak.

"Ray is with Grant at Vicksburg, right? Have you heard from him?"

Mr. Stone's voice came out hoarse. "Even better, Daniel. He's home on leave. He is now a surgeon with General Phil Sheridan. We're very proud of him. And he was married last week."

Daniel touched Mr. Stone's shoulder. "That's terrific. Give him my congratulations, and pass along my best wishes to his bride. I hope I meet up with him while I'm here in Philadelphia." He chuckled. "Not on the battlefield. Would I know the bride?"

"I doubt it. She's from St. Louis. Miss Grace Bradford, a wonderful girl."

Mr. Stone led him toward the library on the east side of the house. Hal's mother, Mrs. Amelia St. Clair, spotted him from the upstairs hall.

"Daniel!" Amelia St. Clair, dressed in brown velvet and blonde lace, floated down the stairs and hugged him, twirling him around then hugging him again. She was almost as tall as Daniel, and she pressed her cheek against his, wetting his face with her tears.

Amelia St. Clair was the oldest child of Sidney Waterman, an itinerant artist who'd earned his living painting portraits of prosperous rural farmers and merchants. She'd spent her childhood summers traveling in a wagon, mothering her three sisters and three brothers while her father painted third rate oils along the length of Lancaster Pike, going as far north as Lewistown and Lock Haven. Her mother had run off with a drummer. Amelia's family's rung on the ladder of Philadelphia society rested only a touch above the gypsies.

However, Harvey St. Clair, son of Philadelphia lawyers who dated back to the time of the first William Penn, fell in love first with her paintings, then with her. Amelia Waterman painted enchanting little watercolors of Philadelphia street corners, portraying street vendors pushing carts of colorful flowers, depicting rows of chestnut trees or a charming wrought iron fence. Her brush produced magic with light and rain and her artwork became quite popular in the city. Harvey first saw the paintings in a little gallery near his office. Then he met Amelia, and, to the astonishment of the people who counted in Philadelphia society, he married her. At first, Amelia was ostracized by the grand families. That came to a stop when Daniel Charteris' grandmother discovered Amelia was delightful. Mrs. Charlotte Charteris welcomed her into their home and heart.

Now Amelia held Daniel's shoulders and hugged him again, kissing both his cheeks. She'd always treated him as her third child, and loved him like one, too. Daniel's mother, Flora Charteris, had little natural inclination toward mothering, and had left Charlotte largely responsible for her grandson's upbringing. Charlotte, known as Nan to her grandchildren, had encouraged his and Hal's friendship since before they could walk. It was his grandmother's kindness that made Daniel special. White-blond, with devilish ways, sharp cheekbones and cookie-sized, polar green eyes, he was already an accomplished flirt by the age of four.

"Good grief," she exclaimed, her voice like silver bells. "You are more handsome than ever. I think you've grown." She shook her head, looking amazed. "I find it difficult to believe you're old enough to grow a moustache, let alone be a major. Isn't it a sad state of affairs? Our soldiers are still growing." Her amber eyes filled with tears and she took his arm and turned away, leading him toward the library. "I'm so glad you're safe and whole. You know, they blinded Martin West, and Cal Shuman lost both legs. No one expects him to live very long. My God. Both legs, can you imagine?"

He nodded, looking somber. "Jimmy Rhodes and Bob Winter are missing and presumed dead. I find it difficult to talk about the losses."

He stopped at the window and nodded toward a young girl standing outside at an easel. Her French blue cloak snapped like wash on a line, and dry leaves flew in a dervish about her. The whirling leaves brought him back to another hillside, where he'd held a young boy whose guts slowly bled out of him.

"Is she a friend of Emily's?" Emily was Hal's younger sister, and best friend to Daniel's sister, Abbey.

Amelia squeezed his arm. "Daniel, Daniel! Does a pretty girl ever escape your notice?"

He smiled. "I hope not!" He nodded toward the girl on the hillside, thinking she was pretty, but no Summer Rose. "It's just that I don't know her."

Amelia raised an eyebrow. "She is Fanny Leboutyn. Her mother was my cousin. Fanny is staying here for the winter, perhaps longer." She smoothed her skirt and gazed fondly out at Fanny. "She has become a student of mine. Remarkable girl. She is American, but she's spent most of her life in France with her grandparents. Her father is a famous engineer who has built canals, dams, bridges, and buildings all over Europe. Fanny lived an unusual life in Paris. She's very talented, very attractive, and very French." Amelia beamed at him. "Hal finds her fascinating. Can you imagine? She has a seventeen inch waist! He's helping her Americanize her English."

Daniel lifted his eyebrows but didn't bother responding. He knew Hal.

Amelia, her attention now diverted to Mr. Stone and the noisy drinks cart, took Daniel's arm and followed Mr. Stone into the library. She whispered, "Hal told me of Summer Rose. Is it true you asked for her hand?"

"Not exactly, but I will ask her." He lowered his voice. "… and, Amelia, I *will* marry her. You must help me. My mother will never forgive me for not marrying Mary. I know she's Abbey's best friend, and her father is a great friend of Father's. But Amelia, if I wed Mary, I'll be miserable all my life."

"Does this girl really disguise herself as a boy? Hal said she hunts and traps and lives alone." Amelia wrinkled her nose as if she could smell the curing hides. "I don't know if you should marry her, Danny. In Philadelphia, women can be very cruel. I know firsthand."

"Her manners are fine. Wait until you meet her. Just wait. Rough edges? She has none. Even if she did, I have no intention of living in Philadelphia." His eyes glittered. "Amelia, just wait. You'll see. She's absolutely the most wonderful girl in the world."

Hal stood as they entered the library and moved to embrace his friend. "I told you, Mother. He's been bitten."

The girls brought trays of coffee and hors d'oeuvres. Mr. Stone scooted them out to the hall then fixed drinks for the men and coffee for Amelia. Daniel and Amelia sat by the fire, welcomed by waves of warmth.

Amelia petted Daniel's knee. "So you're set on this country girl?"

"Tell her, Hal."

Hal picked up his whiskey glass and stood before the fire. "She's special, Mother. Unspoiled, beautiful, intelligent, possessing a natural grace." A corner of Hal's mouth lifted in a smile. "Actually, she reminds me of you. She has no conceit and needs none." A blast of November wind rattled the window and he closed his eyes. "The land is magnificent. If Daniel hadn't claimed her first, I'd court her for the land alone." He sipped his whiskey and his blue eyes sparkled. "I believe you might know her mother, Lillian Fitzmartin."

Amelia's chin jerked up. "Lillian Fitzmartin? Why is she living out in the middle of nowhere?"

"Lillian Fitzmartin died a year ago. It's a long, convoluted story."

Amelia took a quick breath. "I didn't know her, but I knew *of* her. I held her in awe. She came into my father's gallery and admired my little paintings. She bought one, and because she was popular, I sold a number to her friends." Amelia leaned forward and added a large dollop of brandy to her coffee. "And you know how that ended up. I married your father."

She shifted her attention to Daniel. "How are you going to break off with poor Mary?"

Daniel took a drink of his bourbon. "A letter ..." He drained his glass then shrugged. "How do I tell her she's nice, but not enough? And my mother—"

A spear of lightning crashed not fifty yards away, and the windows rattled. Fanny, the girl-woman-child, ran into the library and burrowed her face in Hal's coat. "I hate storms." Her small shoulders heaved.

Daniel and Amelia exchanged a bemused glance as Hal took her cape and led her to a large wing chair in the corner. He knelt in front of her and pulled a crisp linen handkerchief from his sling, using it to wipe her tears. Daniel couldn't hear what Hal said, but he watched as she nodded then patted her disheveled hair. Hal lent her his comb and tucked a loose golden strand in her chignon. When the storm moved on, he led her back to the fireplace.

"Daniel, may I present Eleanor Frances Leboutyn, better known as Fanny. She is from France and is wicked at chess. She's also a promising artist." He squeezed the girl's hand. "Fanny, I want you to meet my best friend, Major Daniel Wallace Charteris, better known as Danny. He is by far the most dangerous man in the Army of the Potomac— dangerous to women, that is. He's useless in battle. Never stay alone in a room with him. Your reputation will be destroyed."

Daniel bowed and took her hand, kissing it as gallantly as any Frenchman. "Don't believe a word Hal says. He lies.

His reputation is far worse than mine, and he's the one who is useless on a battlefield." He winked. "He has been known to hide under his horse."

Amelia stepped in. "Pay no attention to these two. Come, sit down, Fanny. Perhaps you could help us with a little problem."

Fanny sat on the sofa as Amelia explained Daniel's desire to break off with a girl to whom he was almost engaged. The girl graced them all with a bright smile.

"Ah. I am very good at this. I have—what is the word?—dissolved two engagements."

"Two?" Hal exclaimed, sitting beside her.

Amelia sat on the other side of her, looking surprised. "You don't look old enough to have been engaged once, let alone twice."

Daniel watched, amazed by the realization that he didn't want to flirt with Fanny. He couldn't remember the last time he'd been this close to a desirable girl, especially one Hal obviously wanted, and had felt nothing. But since Summer, not a single girl had turned his head.

Her deep dimples flirted. "Oh, gentlemen, I just appear young. Promise not to tell anyone. I am seventeen, almost eighteen." The fire crackled and reflected across her face, catching her hair so that it flared orange-red. "The first betrothal was one of those childhood things. The boy next door and I promised each other when we were nine." Her eyes dipped and her red-gold lashes fluttered. "At the time, we both were heartsick. The second wasn't silly at all. Why do you think I am here in America? Jean-Paul and I tried to elope. We made it all the way to Calais." She rolled her big blue eyes and made a chopping motion with her hand. "My father put a stop to that nonsense." She brushed a curl behind her ear. "It's Mary McGill, isn't it?"

Daniel nodded, feeling like a heel. He was well aware Mary deserved an explanation.

Suddenly the tiny girl jumped to her feet, placed her hands on Daniel's cheeks, and kissed him squarely on the lips, not once, but four times. And they were long, sensuous kisses. Her lips were locked on his. Over her shoulder, Daniel could see Hal and his mother, faces frozen, mouths ajar.

She pulled away and settled again between Hal and Amelia. Grinning from ear to ear, she said, "Now I won't be fibbing when I tell Emily I kissed the infamous Major Charteris, and more than once." Her bright eyes danced. "You have a reputation, Sir. And Emily will tell your sister, who will be furious with you. And Abbey then will run and tell Mary. By tomorrow, you will receive a note from Mary."

She dismissed Mary with a wave of her hand. "She's been making eyes at Captain Hathaway. I overheard her tell Emily she was tired of waiting around for you, so Danny—" She laughed again. "You don't mind if I exaggerate a little about the kissing, do you?" She turned her head. "You don't mind, do you, Hal?"

Amelia smoothed her skirts and looked away, hiding a smile. Hal shrugged, but Daniel noticed the vein, bloated like a worm, at his temple.

Daniel stood, winked at Amelia, then bent and kissed the little redhead's hand. "You are absolutely amazing. Exaggerate all you want. I would never have thought to turn it around and arrange Mary breaking up with me. You are very clever."

She nodded.

"Well, Summer and I both thank you." He grinned at Hal's scowl. "You have a treasure here, Hal, an absolutely delightful treasure."

Fanny blushed and tucked her arm beneath Hal's, leaning her cheek on his shoulder.

CHAPTER 12

THE BEST LAID PLANS

Fanny's subterfuge worked. By nine o'clock the following morning Daniel's agenda was completed. Mary wrote:

Dear Daniel, I wanted you to be the first to know that I've accepted Captain Hathaway's proposal. We plan to be married before Christmas. Please send me your best wishes. Fondly, Mary McGill.

He dashed off a note of congratulations to Mary and avoided all contact with his mother, who fortunately had back-to back engagements with her varied political and social groups. He spent another necessary hour with his father going over finances, and managed to be slapped by Abbey, his teenage sister, for kissing that little French tart.

All in all, he felt his visit a success.

With his cheek still stinging, he turned Chester and pressed the horse to a full gallop as he ducked through the stable door. The ride to the St. Clair farm helped clear his mind. Racing along the river, he spotted Fanny's bright blue, hooded cloak rippling in the wind, and halted Chester beside her. Hal stood with her, a hand on her shoulder. Daniel dismounted and grabbed Fanny, swinging her in the air.

"I owe you. I owe you my life."

Hal threw his good arm around Daniel's neck and chuckled. "Your life may not be very long. Mother heard the McGill boys want a duel."

"Hell! No one duels anymore. They're illegal."

"No one needs to duel. We have a war going on where killing is legal." He shook his head.

"I've been busy, Danny-boy. We're catching the Washington train later today to finalize the sale of the land with Summer Rose's brother. From Washington, we'll catch the train to Gettysburg, register the deed, then hear the President's speech at the cemetery there on the 19th. I told Captain Keogh we'd be there."

I'm marrying her," Daniel said. "No long engagement. No one will prevent me." He laughed. "I'll beg forgiveness after the deed is done."

Fanny's cloak crackled like a flag, making Chester snort and prance. She raised one tiny hand. "We want you safe and happy." She leaned into Hal, her face aglow with adoration. "Listen to Hal."

Hal slapped his friend's back. "Come to Washington with me. Then I'll go with you to Summer Rose's lake."

"Where are we meeting him?"

"Willard's. In the lobby. Everyone in Washington meets at Willard's. He's bringing his attorney. I'll deal with him."

"You're not a lawyer. Do we need a lawyer?"

"Dad and your father went over every possible scenario. Wait until the deal is signed, then ask for her hand in marriage. I, personally, don't think you should ask."

"I want it right for her, Hal."

"Okay. Just wait till the deal is signed. We've agreed on a price, which includes the house, outbuildings, and the lake."

In the comfortable atmosphere of Willard's, Summer's brother sighed heavily. "I wish you much happiness, Major. Me, personally, I feel as if the weight of Atlas has been removed from my shoulders. I'm glad to have both the land and my sister settled. You have no idea how I worry about her."

At least three times every half hour, Jack's neck twisted involuntarily and a great spasm trembled through his twisted body. *I guess standing right beside your father and brothers when they're killed could do that to you,* thought Daniel.

As they parted, they shook hands, and Jack McAllister asked, "When you met Summer, was she dressed as a boy or a girl?"

Daniel didn't feel comfortable telling her brother that he'd seen her in her ruffled underwear.

Fortunately, Hal spoke up. "Both."

"Then you'll understand how odd it all is. She rarely acts like a girl. I send her money, but she'd rather cure hides and sell eggs. Runs about pretending to be a boy." He made a face. "I wanted her to go to her grandmother's, but she refused. Stomped her foot and refused."

Daniel watched her brother's head jerk to the right followed by a shudder ripping down his left side. "My father and our oldest brother spoiled the girl rotten. Now, she claims her grandparents are senile, rattling around in that old mansion up near Chestnut Hill. I thought she'd be safe there. She refused. She's a handful, Major Charteris. Best of luck."

CHAPTER 13

DIAMONDS, FISTS, AND KISSES

While they waited to board the Baltimore train, they shopped at the stores around Center Market in the heart of Washington. They bought oranges and lemons, chocolates, and coffee. On a whim, something entirely unnatural for Hal, for Hal did not part with cash easily, he bought Fanny a pair of beautiful, blue kid gloves made in France, and an entire bolt of lovely Irish wool for his mother. He asked the merchant to wrap the packages and post them to the house in Washington.

Daniel bought two bottles of champagne then went off by himself. When he returned, he dragged Hal to the jeweler and showed him the ring he wanted for Summer: three huge diamonds, embedded in a platinum filigree basket, the center stone at least two carats.

"Good Lord, Danny. Sure you don't want something cheaper?" He steered Daniel toward less expensive rings, but eventually gave up. Nodding to the jeweler, Hal asked, "May

I use your loupe?" He studied the stones and negotiated a better price.

As they boarded the boxcar, Daniel asked, "How do you know so much about diamonds?"

"I don't. I read a little, and I bullshit a lot. I'm good at asking questions and understanding money. Stick with me. Once we get this war out of the way, we're going to build an empire."

They traveled, along with their horses, in the chilly boxcar, playing poker with Pinkerton agents. Baltimore, which was usually a madhouse, went smoothly, but Hanover Junction promised a long delay. They decided to ride the rest of the way to Gettysburg.

Although the day was damp and overcast with a blackening sky, Gettysburg's streets filled with somber-faced politicians from all over the North. Military officers, all solemn, milled about. Parents, soldiers of every rank, with raw grief written on their faces, etched in the slant of their spines, walked about in a daze.

Daniel and Hal stopped at the courthouse, where they registered the deed. They planned to stay overnight in Gettysburg with men from their regiment and attend the dedication of the Soldier's Cemetery tomorrow. Right after the speech, they'd head for Camelann. They wanted to hear their president speak. Even more importantly, they wanted to honor their comrades.

As they turned left at the bottom of the back steps of the courthouse, a solid punch landed on Daniel's jaw. He went down like a rock, and before Hal or he knew what happened, a boot kicked him in his midsection. He looked up to see Mary's brother about to kick him again. All reason left Daniel. He grabbed Richie McGill's foot and, using his tremendous strength, twisted. Richie howled and stumbled like a wounded bear.

While Richie regained his balance, Daniel jerked to his feet, swiping the blood from his jaw. Anger surged, flooding him. He'd always had a temper, and in battle it kept him alive. He used the rage now. In his peripheral vision he saw Richie's brother, Bob, equally as big as Richie, in the shadows of the alley. As he and Richie jockeyed for position, Daniel unhooked his belt, which held the holster for his prized Baby LeMat pistol, then peeled off his jacket and handed both to Hal.

Hal took the belt and weapon and nodded toward Bob, who took his brother's belt in turn. Then he shoved Daniel's LeMat alongside his Remington and glared pointedly at Bob. The four of them, actors in an ageless and macabre play, took their positions.

Hal had a formidable reputation. Daniel knew he'd only have to contend with Richie, though he was enough. Mary's brother was a good inch taller than Daniel, and Daniel knew Richie boxed. He could tell by the muscles in his forearms, and by his footwork. They'd played together as children, and before this minute Daniel bore him no ill will. But now …

Daniel had boxed at PMC and taken the senior prize. Wrestling and kicking weren't allowed there, and they were confined to three-minute rounds, gloves, and the ten second count for a downed fighter. At this particular moment, Daniel wasn't planning to abide by any rules. He'd been attacked, his anger was alive, and his temper had escaped. This fight, although between officers and gentlemen, would be down-in-the dirt street fighting, like the New York boys fought.

His knee came up and slammed Richie's groin. As Richie buckled, Daniel pummeled his kidneys then pounded another knee into the big man's face at the same time his fists smashed into Richie's ears. The bones of Richie's nose crumbled like gravel crunching. Bright blood arched toward Daniel and sprayed down his front. Daniel leaned in again for the body blows, and Richie's face, sodden with sweat and blood, red with pulverized flesh, lost resistance.

But Daniel couldn't stop. He hammered the bigger man, kicked the side of Richie's knee, fell on him, rolled with him, his fists still pounding.

Hal's pistol fired. Richie was out. Hal grabbed Daniel's arm, breaking his momentum, and pulled him off the unconscious Richie.

"I hear horses, Danny. Let's skedaddle."

As Daniel gathered Chester's reins, Bob knelt beside his brother. He lifted his face to Daniel, his expression twisted between fear and fury. "You're an animal, Charteris. You didn't need to damn near kill him."

Daniel lunged toward Bob, but Hal yanked him back. "Easy, Danny."

"He started it," Danny growled, then spat. "Keep that son of a bitch away from me." He mounted Chester, wiping his bloodied hands on his thighs. "I mean it, Bob. Keep him away from me." Chester pranced, inches from the McGill's boy unconscious form. "I'm sorry it didn't work out with Mary, but I didn't deserve to be blindsided by you two."

They changed plans and headed to Camelann. Daniel told Hal not to tell Summer about his temper.

Hal snorted. "She wouldn't believe me, anyway. I doubt you could do anything wrong in her estimation."

Tears glistened in her eyes when she saw him. "Oh, Daniel."

Just seeing her melted the hardness inside him. Despite the pain, he hugged her tight against him, then pulled away so he could see her, and brushed a strand of hair back from her face. She tried to touch his face, but he gently blocked her hand. His teeth moved in their sockets on the lower side of his right jaw, and he could sense half his face swelling into a darkening mass as big as one of her birdhouse gourds.

She brushed away a tear on her cheek. "I can help you. Oh Daniel, does it hurt terribly?"

He nodded, and she led him to the big soft chair which he assumed had been her father's chair. The fire's warmth swept over him.

"Here. Let me have your coat." She folded it over her arm and helped him sit down. "I have a special tea. It helps dull the pain."

A wave of nausea filled him when he remembered the tea.

"I know it's not your favorite, but let me fix a pot. It goes down easier if it's mixed with whiskey." She blinked innocently, but her smile hinted at mischief. "Would either of you happen to have any whiskey?"

Hal patted his chest. "I always have a flask."

She lifted Daniel's feet to an ottoman and deftly removed his boots, tucking a wool throw over his legs. When she returned with the tea, she urged him to down it. She then made a poultice of dark waxy leaves and added the salve that had cured his leg. She ground it in a mortar, then spread the green paste on a thin cloth, and tied it around his head. Hal made some comment about a jack-o-lantern with a diaper, which he didn't think was funny at all. She sat on the ottoman, massaging Daniel's feet, helping him fall asleep. He slept fitfully, interrupted every couple of hours when she or Hal changed the poultice.

When pearly light filtered in through the windows, he felt tentatively around his face, and was impressed when he discovered the swelling was down, his teeth were intact, and the pain was minimal.

Summer gently touched his face and held up a hand mirror. "I see a few bruises, but most soldiers show bruises." She leaned forward and carefully kissed the edge of his mouth. "Hal still wants to attend the ceremony, so I laid out a clean shirt for you. Hurry. He insists we go with him. I put some warm water on the washstand in my room. Your kit's there, too." She stood and twirled, smiling like a young girl. "See? I'm all dressed up."

She wore a split skirt of black corduroy with a matching short jacket, layered over a ruffled white blouse with jabot. Hal walked into the house just as Daniel tried to whistle and failed. Hal finished it for him and they all laughed, though Daniel didn't smile.

He glanced in the mirror, studying his beat up face. The sight brought both anger and shame. Richie must be a mess. *When, Daniel, will you learn to control that temper?* But without his temper, Daniel was well aware he probably wouldn't be alive. His quickness to fight gave him an edge and had saved him countless times. He just had to be careful when he used it.

He patted his breast coat pocket for reassurance then smiled when he felt the diamond ring. With great care, he brushed his teeth, washed, shaved, and changed his shirt, then found Hal outside and told him to go ahead.

"We'll catch up with you." Again he patted his breast coat pocket.

To Daniel's surprise, Hal shook his head. "I know you, Danny. I'll wait. Ten minutes. That's all. We'll stop for breakfast in Gettysburg. Chester's already fed and saddled."

"What the hell's gotten into you?" His voice snapped. "Fine then. Let's go. I'll propose to her tonight."

His anger dissipated once she was riding behind him, her soft curves pressing against his back, the lemony scent of her drifting to him.

The dedication was everything he'd hoped it would be: poignant and patriotic, sad and solemn. The black cloud of remorse still hung about him. Too many had paid the ultimate price.

"Four score and seven years ago," Lincoln said, *"our fathers brought forth on this continent a new nation, conceived in Liberty, and dedicated to the proposition that all men are created equal."*

President Lincoln voiced the thoughts Daniel couldn't put into words. Two of his great grandfathers had served as captains under Washington. As Daniel listened to Lincoln speak, he felt Summer Rose's warm fingers find their way between his. She'd lost her father and brothers. Her loss touched him. He squeezed her warm hand, unaccountably pleased they shared this moment. As the speech continued, her attention, like his, was on the president, but her palm grew damp with emotion. He fought an urge to gather her to him, comfort her as best as he could.

"... that we here highly resolve that these dead shall not have died in vain ... that this nation, under God, shall have a new birth of freedom ... and that government of the people, by the people, for the people, shall not perish from the earth."

On the ride home, with only the stars lighting the road, he whispered to her over his shoulder. "Dulcey's no match for Chester. Hold tight."

Urging Chester into a loping gallop, he lost Hal, then slowed to a smooth canter, and rode to the foot of the switchback waterfall. In the starlight the water thundered, the mist like a veil of liquid lace studded with diamonds. He pulled her around so she sat on his lap, her legs dangling to one side, and snuggled his coat around them both. As he kissed her, Chester shook his great head and Daniel chuckled to himself. *Even the horse keeps me honorable.*

As the huge moon inched over the mountains, Daniel held up the ring. The diamonds dazzled like white fire. He had a speech all prepared, but his words came out all choppy, not at all like he'd planned.

"I love you. I've loved you from the first moment I saw you," he blurted, then swallowed hard. His hand gentled her cheek. "Will you marry me, Summer? Be my wife? The mother of our children? Allow me to share your life forever?"

Tears filled her eyes, and she nodded, mute.

He slipped the heavy ring on her finger. "I asked your brother for your hand. He said okay, and Hal and I purchased all of Camelann from him. Your home will always be here for you." He glanced down at the ground, then back at her. "I'll get on my knees, if you'd like."

She wiped her tears on her sleeve and peered down. The moon silvered the puddles and mud. She shook her head then leaned against his shoulder. "Chester's back is perfect. No sense ruining those trousers, too."

Her eyes shimmered in the moonlight, as did the ring when she held her hand up. "I didn't know diamonds could sparkle like the stars." She sighed, and he thought he might drown in her gaze. "I am honored to marry you, Daniel. You've made my dreams come true." Her voice caught and trembled. "You bought the land?"

He nodded. "Hal and I did. We plan to buy more, too."

"I'm the luckiest girl in the world."

"I'm the lucky one." He kissed her a dozen or so times then stopped, squirming a little in the saddle and rearranging her on his lap. He hugged her tight against his chest, sure she could feel his heart beating under his shirt. "You've learned quickly."

She giggled, touching the back of his neck, running her fingers through his hair, along his jaw line. "I like your kisses," she whispered as she outlined his lips with her little finger. "My insides are all squiggly, and I'm hot as if it's July, not November." Her voice turned husky. "I'd like you to kiss me all night."

He swallowed hard. "I'd like nothing better than to kiss you all night, but right now I'm going to take you home before something like that happens."

CHAPTER 14

DEARLY BELOVED

"Who is he arguing with?"

"I think he's the chaplain," said Hal.

They stood just outside the pine bower before the tent chapel at Gettysburg. "The chaplain looks pink, and Daniel looks angry."

Hal nodded. "Daniel has a temper, but he usually gets what he wants."

Two minutes later, Daniel and the weary chaplain approached her. The man's pinkness had receded, and he smiled at her through the fringe of ginger-colored hair. He motioned for a young woman to come with him.

The chaplain took the hands of both women. "Miss McAllister, I'm Chaplain Anders, and this is Miss Irene Wood." He turned to the petite and pretty blonde. "Would you, Miss Wood, please take Miss McAllister to the nurses' tent and help her dress? It appears a wedding is in order." He turned on his heel, facing the men. "Major, come with me. We're not used to weddings here."

Summer, her eyes big as a spaniel's, glanced over her shoulder at Daniel and Hal as Irene led her to a large tent. The nurse directed her past a row of iron cots to a washstand and copper tub, curtained off by a screen.

"I'll send in some hot water," Irene said. She nodded toward a washstand. "Soap, clean towels, and a wash cloth are underneath." She set Summer Rose's valise on the end cot, dug inside, and held up a skirt and blouse. "These are lovely." Irene ran her hands over the pale gray skirt of heavy silk, trimmed at the waist and hem with black velvet, and the high necked blouse of white Spanish lace.

"They belonged to my mother. I have a mantilla, too, of matching lace."

Irene dug further into the bag and pulled out the shawl. "I'll press these." She reached over and squeezed Summer Rose's forearm, grinning. "You have no idea how much we need a happy event around here. I'll be right back."

Forty-five minutes later, Irene helped her into her things, buttoning all the pearl buttons that ran down the back of the lace blouse, tucking in the shirttails, and fastening the skirt's hooks at the waist. Summer Rose sat as directed, feeling as if she were in a dream. Her braid came undone and Irene brushed the loose tresses until electricity crackled and Summer's hair flew about her head. Both women giggled as Irene knotted her hair into a loose chignon, expertly sticking combs here and pins there, pulling out strands and curling them with her finger. At last she draped the shawl over Summer's shoulders. She turned Summer Rose around slowly, dabbed rouge on her cheeks and touched her lips with beeswax.

Irene nodded and held up the mirror. "You're beautiful, darling. I can understand why your dashing major made no bones about how much he wanted to marry you." She giggled. "I heard him. He told our dear chaplain that if he couldn't marry you today, he'd hold him responsible for … your virtue."

Summer felt her cheeks flush. She wasn't sure how she was supposed to feel about what he had in mind, but the thought made her heart race.

They had both been surprised when Hal insisted they marry with haste. "I don't want to sit around here watching you two make cow eyes all day," he said. "I'm not a very good chaperone. Is there any reason you can't get married tomorrow?"

"I didn't want to rush her."

"No reason to wait, Daniel."

"Then tomorrow it is."

Summer Rose looked up at Irene, as the nurse said, "I suggest, dear girl, that you just let your handsome major have his way with you. He'll have you one way or another." She giggled again. "I certainly wouldn't advise fighting him."

Hal and a convalescing officer who had lost a leg in July stood up for them. While Daniel bathed and donned his dress uniform, Hal and the one-legged colonel hunted for flowers along the main street of Gettysburg. Hal's arm was still in the sling and Colonel English, on his new prosthesis, thumped beside him, using a cane for balance.

Gettysburg in November 1863 spoke poignantly of the price of war. When they finally came upon a small enclosed garden, Hal knocked on the door. "My best friend is getting married," he explained, "and we want a small bouquet for his bride. Do you mind if we take some flowers from your garden?"

She smiled. "Wonder we haven't lost them to frost already. Wait here a moment."

She stepped inside and returned a moment later, wearing a shawl, and holding scissors and a handful of ribbons. "Here. Cut what you want." She followed him about. "A wedding? Wonderful to have something happy around here. Allow me to help, Major. What's the bride's name?"

"Summer Rose."

"Ah. How perfect! A few of my neighbor's roses are still in bloom." She took the scissors and reached over the fence, cutting several late autumn roses and fitting them in with the rest of the bouquet. "Come sit on the steps," she said, scraping off the thorns with sure movements. "I'm good at this."

Hal, Colonel English, and the woman sat on the stoop. She stripped all the thorns then intertwined some snapdragons, laurel leaves, and baby's breath, eventually wrapping a rainbow of pastel ribbons around the stems. She held up the sweet posy, letting it trail with long ends of ribbons. "Give her my best wishes."

Chaplain Anders found a young trooper who played *Aura Lea* on his guitar and sang in a rumbling baritone:

When the mistletoe was green,
Midst the winter's snows,
Sunshine in thy face was seen,
Kissing lips of rose.
Aura Lea, Aura Lea,
Take my golden ring;
Love and light return with thee,
And swallows with the spring.

A few soldiers congregated in the chapel, and, as Hal walked her toward Daniel, those soldiers who could, stood. Daniel, his dress uniform brushed and polished, belted and sashed, appeared magnificent. He beamed as brilliantly as did his brass buttons. But no one noticed him. They saw only Summer Rose.

"Dearly beloved, we are assembled here in the presence of God ..."

After the ceremony, the chaplain, Hal, Colonel English, Daniel and Summer walked to a tavern near the garden where he'd picked her flowers. Summer Rose stopped and kissed the woman when she came outside. Townspeople lined the street and waved as she walked by.

"I knew your father, Mrs. Charteris." Colonel English told her as they sat down to lunch.

Mrs. Charteris. Her face lit with a grin, and she held in a giggle. She loved the sound of her new name. It was hard to believe it was true. Her Lochinvar had found her.

So daring in love, and so dauntless in war,
Have ye e'er heard of gallant like young Lochinvar?

Now, sitting beside her new husband in the small, low-ceilinged tavern, Summer took a sip of wine. A crackling flame in the fireplace cast a golden glow over her face as she spoke. "He knew a great number of people, Colonel English," she said. "Did you know him before or during the war?"

Beneath the table, Daniel laced his fingers with hers. The room grew dim, her eyes starry. She wondered if it was the wine. Maybe it was just too much happiness, or perhaps simply his touch. His thumb brushed over her knuckles, and she leaned into his arm, surprised at how difficult it had become to think.

"Both. Truly, an honorable man. Your father was one of a kind. I worked for the railroad before the war and purchased lumber from him. The soldiers, the railroad men, the lumbermen ... they all loved him. He knew the first name of every man in his regiment, their hometown, and their mother's name."

The waitress brought their lunch, and they all tucked into the shepherd's pie.

"That was delicious," said Colonel English afterwards. "I wish the army cooks made something like that. My mother did, and oh, her pies ... Tell me, Major Charteris, are you able to manage a honeymoon?"

Daniel shook his head. "I feel lucky to get a few days' leave. Speaking of which, Mrs. Charteris, are you ready? We've a long ride ahead of us."

He had wanted to get a room in town, but Summer had insisted they return home for their wedding night.

Hal stood and took Summer Rose's arm. "Allow me, Mrs. Charteris. I have two presents for you." He led her through the dark tavern, and as they stepped into the cold afternoon air, he slipped his army coat over her shoulders. "I can get another right down the street," he told her, which wasn't at all true. Hal's coat had been tailor-made from fine Scottish wool, not the shoddy stuff sold to the army. He walked her over to Dulcey, the sweet mare he'd ridden from Bull Run to Fredericksburg, through Antietam and Gettysburg. "I'm taking the train home. Take care of Dulcey for me. She's earned a rest."

He moved to kiss her on the lips, but at the last minute pressed a kiss to her forehead. He winked at Daniel, coming up from behind. "Easy, Danny boy. You're a lucky man." He helped her mount and handed up her saddle bags.

She leaned down and kissed his cheek. "The bouquet is beautiful." She patted the saddlebag. "Thank you for the coat and the horse, for everything. Take care of yourself, Slim."

CHAPTER 15

A LIFETIME OF NIGHTS

They arrived home at twilight. The geese honked and nipped and beat their great wings. The dogs, howling like banshees, ran circles around Summer Rose and Daniel as if they'd been gone for weeks rather than a day. He lifted Summer from Dulcey and carried her up the porch steps, his spurs jingling with every step. When he stopped before the door, he kissed her and tickled her throat with his breath, which steamed in the November air. She giggled as she opened the latch. He carried her inside, twirled her around then set her down. He hung their great coats on pegs by the door, along with the mantle of lace.

A strand of her sable hair fell loose, and he tucked it behind her ear then kissed her with tenderness. No giggles this time. Her eyes sparkled like jewels and his stomach tightened a little. Responsibility, like the shadow of some prehistoric bird, hovered around him. *I'm all she has now, except for Jack.* Her father's words from the dream came to mind. *"Make sure you deserve her trust."*

"I'll see to the horses and bring in some wood and our bags. I won't be long."

While he was gone, she spun through the house, lighting the kitchen stove and the fireplace and filling the teapot. She'd fixed a tray with her mother's china, silver, and linen napkins before they'd left. Now, in a whirl, she set the bread to toast and the potato soup to warm. Cold ham, cheese, tomatoes, and crunchy pickles came out of the larder. She'd laid the fires and planned their wedding supper this morning before they'd left for Gettysburg. She wanted everything to be perfect. Her hands flew and her heart raced.

The sound of wood being stacked on the hearth came from the living room, and she heard Daniel talking to the dogs. He entered the kitchen without his jacket, the collar of his white shirt open. He'd rolled up his sleeves and his arms looked strong and hard. Now he stood in his stocking feet with two bottles of champagne, showing her he'd planned ahead as well.

She fixed him a bowl of warm water, where he washed his hands while she prepared two plates of toasted sandwiches. She cut them in triangles and arranged pickles and pickled beets in little dishes, along with cups of warm potato soup, sprinkled with paprika. She was aware of his eyes following her every move, and heat burned in her cheeks. He dried his hands on a towel she laid beside the sink, and smiled.

He picked up the tray and asked. "Where do you want this?"

She moved to open the door, and he followed, setting down the tray as she pulled a small table in front of the couch. They worked as a team. She lit the oil lamps and the candles; he popped the champagne cork and poured two glasses. As they sat, the sides of their thighs touched and the fire growled, shooting sparks up the chimney. They both smiled nervously, sipping champagne, eating small triangular sandwiches, and trying desperately to think of something to say.

Surprisingly, Daniel felt shy. Experienced women were his usual fare, and most often he was reacting to some lonely widow. Never before had he had all the responsibility. He popped the last sandwich triangle in his mouth and leaned back on the sofa, folding his big hands across his chest. The sap in the logs crackled, the fire hissed and roared. He looked at his wife and his breath became shallow. He'd never wanted a girl as much as he wanted her. Part of him was a stallion on the scent of a filly, and part was the mare protecting her foal. The firelight reflected on the pearl tipped pins in her hair and the pearl buttons of her blouse. The back of her neck still fascinated him. He reached over and pulled one hairpin loose.

"Do you mind?" He placed it on the tray. She'd told him the pins had belonged to her mother, and he knew they were precious. "I want to see your hair loose." His fingers ached to run through the rich mass of it.

She rushed to remove all the pins, but he took her trembling hands and laid them in her lap. "Allow me."

He unfastened one button, the one at the back of the high collar, and ran one finger along the lace. The pulse in her neck throbbed like a sparrow's heart. He wasn't sure exactly what she knew about marriage. Her life had been so solitary. She'd never gone to school, had no sisters or girlfriends, and her mother was gone. He cringed at the thought of the rough old man from his dream telling her anything about this.

His cheek brushed hers, and his voice came out a gravelly whisper. "Do you know what happens between a husband and wife?" He wanted everything right for her. Some sense, an instinct, warned him tonight was more important than his desires. Tonight set the stage for twenty thousand nights, a lifetime of nights.

She lowered her eyelids, and the firelight threw the shadows of her lashes across her cheeks. "Irene told me a little. She said you'd have me one way or another. I think I know what she meant." Her blue-green eyes opened wide. "The animals ..." She swallowed hard and sipped more champagne. Color deepened in her cheeks. "I understand the mechanics." The lights in her eyes danced. "I hope you're gentler than the goat." One side of her mouth curled. "He bites."

Enormous blue eyes held his, and he caught his breath as warmth flooded his chest. Good God, she was a surprise. A wonderful surprise. Her attempt at a joke, her sweetness touched his heart. He pressed her cheek against his chest and kissed her hair.

"Oh, sweetheart, I promise I won't bite."

He eased the pins from her hair and undid another pearl button. His fingers combed through the rich strands and brushed her cheek. "I love your hair, your skin." He lowered his head and kissed the back of her neck with his open mouth. "Your skin is unbelievably soft."

His left arm wrapped around her chest, his hand splayed over the swell of her breast, over her heart. It pounded, stirring something deep in his core. Something vibrated in the bones guarding his heart. When a shudder trembled through her, he slowed his breathing. He knew she shivered with expectation, fear, and, he hoped, desire. As if she read his mind, she pressed her hands to his neck, touched the skin at his open collar, and kissed the hollow of his throat. A soft moan purred from him and the band around his chest tightened, squeezing tears into his eyes. He'd had no idea he could feel so full of love. His very center soared way past lust, beyond even what he'd considered what love might be. Every part of him longed for her, screamed for her, but some sense, a knowing, held him back.

She lay below him on the sofa, her shining hair a dark fan against the wine red fabric of the cushion. He knelt on the floor beside her. "I won't surprise you," he whispered. "I'll tell you everything I'm about to do."

He kissed her eyelids, her cheeks, then dropped kisses over the creamy skin of her throat. His hands spanned her waist, and he unfastened the last of the pearl buttons while he kissed the side of her neck where it sloped to her shoulder. The lace slipped low, and he eased her blouse off, laying it on the arm of the sofa. All the time, her huge eyes watched him.

Still on his knees, he framed her face with his hands then slid them down the sides of her neck, across her shoulders and arms. Above the lace of her corset and chemise, the gorgeous skin of her full breasts gleamed golden and red in the firelight. He couldn't help himself.

"I'm going to kiss you here," he said as he lowered his head. His experienced hands reached beneath her and unlaced her corset.

At last, he eased it off and placed it by her blouse. His other hand moved lower, unfastening the hooks at her waistband, loosening it. His fingers slid beneath the fabric and inched across her belly. He lifted his head and his eyes met hers.

"I'll touch you here, too." In that instant, her body arched to him, her sweet mouth opened in surprise then she smiled. Desire crashed in a crescendo through his resolve and filled his every cell. In one swift movement he lifted her, cradling her in his arms. His legs felt both weak and unbelievably powerful; he wanted to devour her. Her skin paled, her eyes glazed, and he feared she might faint.

He smiled and bounced her twice in his arms as if she were weightless, a child's doll. He wanted to show off his muscles and ease a little of the tension. He raised his eyebrows and growled, and she giggled.

"My God. Do you have any idea how lovely you are?" He kissed her mouth, freeing the hunger that consumed him. He carried her toward the bedroom and kicked open the door. "You smell delicious."

CHAPTER 16

AWAKENINGS

He awakened to the smell of coffee, bacon, fresh bread, and her, but when he opened his eyes, she wasn't there. Beside him lay a robe of dark green wool flannel along with a pair of deerskin moccasins. Across the room, steam rose from the pitcher on the washstand. He stood and stretched, reaching high over his head, then washed himself, brushed his teeth, and put on the robe and slippers. He ran a hand down the sides of the robe, noting the French seams and the softness of the fabric. The slippers fit, too. He shaved and trimmed his moustache, then made his way through the living room, to the sounds and scents coming from the kitchen. To his wife.

She stood by the sink, gazing out at the snow, which moved in great swirls across the lake. A neat, dark braid fell down the middle of her back. He came up from behind, slipped his arms around her, and nuzzled her neck. Her robe was made of the same soft wool as his. She turned in his arms, her body pressed into his, awakening all his senses. Nibbling kisses exploded into hungry ones.

She drew back, gasping for a breath. "I want you to trust me." She pointed to a stack of blankets and towels on one of the kitchen chairs. "Come for a swim."

"You're joking."

Her face stretched into a wide grin, and she planted a quick kiss on the corner of his mouth. With a thrill, he suspected more facets of his new wife might exist than those he'd discovered last night.

"Trust me. You'll be surprised." She picked up the linens, took his hand, and led him outside to the lake.

He chuckled and pulled her into his arms, kissing her again. The snow blew inside his sleeves and under the hem of his robe. "This is a ploy to cool me down. Right?"

She gulped a little air and lowered her eyes for a moment then lifted them. "Last night you asked me to trust you." A corner of her mouth curled. "And I did." She pulled in a deep breath and took his hand. "Now, I ask for you to trust me."

The snow swirled and danced around them. She placed the towels on the stone bench and shrugged her robe from her shoulders, then stepped from her slippers and walked onto the wooden dock.

He dropped his robe on the bench. Tiny pins of cold pricked his skin. He looked up to a raven scolding him and breathed in the crisp, almost harsh, scent of pine and winter. Last night, in the warm glow of the candles, her body had seemed like that of a goddess. He'd told her, too. Now, in the gray mist of morning, with the snowflakes dancing around her, she seemed even lovelier. The cleft of her spine was deep, her bottom smooth and tight, and her legs were long, strong, and sleek. He smiled and decided her legs were now tied with the back of her neck as his favorite part of her body. She dove into the water; he kicked off his slippers, already moving toward her. *I must be in love or crazy,* he thought as he raced toward the dock.

He braced for the freezing water, gave a wild Yankee yell, and dove into an embracing warmth. As he surfaced she swam toward him and wrapped her arms around his neck. Diamonds of water droplets sparkled on her thick eyelashes.

"What is this?" he asked, his hands dropping to her waist as he found footing on a large rock ledge deep beneath the surface.

"I told you. The water stays the same the year around. In summer the lake feels cool, in winter it's warm. It's the contrast. My father said there must be thermal springs. Some spots are warmer than others, but this pocket is one of the warmest. I believe it's why my parents built the house here." Her face grew serious and devilish at the same time. "Isn't it wonderful?" She kissed his nose. "It never freezes. Micah warned us that we must never tell anyone about our lake, or we'd be overrun with bathers. We're fortunate our valley is difficult to find."

She bobbed under the water and soaked her hair again, then handed him the sponge and the bar of soap from the string bag she'd attached to her wrist. "Would you please help me with my hair?"

She turned and pressed her naked back to his chest.

After loosening her braid and lathering up the sponge, he soaped her hair, her back, her bottom, and everywhere else.

He took his time. A pair of eagles careened in the morning sky, screeching and sending echoes through the valley. He cupped her breasts, which filled his big hands, rubbing his thumbs over the nipples; he felt her intake of breath, and decided there might be a third contender for favorite part of her body.

She retrieved the sponge and turned, her eyes twinkling, and washed him all over. Last night had cured her of any shyness. She kissed the frost off his moustache and pulled him low in the water, her strong legs tightening around him. She grinned as he shivered, knowing it wasn't the cold that caused the response.

Her voice came out low and throaty. "Kiss me again like you kissed me last night. I have so much to learn."

Her tongue flickered across her lips and he kissed her, producing the same effect he had last night. She kissed him back, using her tongue like he'd taught her. She'd figured out how to move her body all by herself. He finally stopped and held her close. His voice came out hoarse and low.

"You're going to find yourself in trouble."

Her lips brushed the skin below his ear. "You told me that last night. I like your kind of trouble, Major Charteris." She moved her body, brushing against him in all the right places. Her eyes widened. So much trust lay in them. "Do you like that?"

Desire, hot and furious, slammed through him. He couldn't speak.

"I want you to teach me everything," she whispered.

"Good Lord, Rosie, you are full of surprises." He'd taken to calling her Rosie sometime during the night—about the same time he'd fallen hopelessly in love with her. "I think you may teach me."

CHAPTER 17

PROMISES

They warmed up on the kitchen floor amid blankets and towels. After breakfast they made love on the couch, then again in the bedroom. Later, sprawled on the bed, entangled and limp as the crumpled sheets, their hands still explored. The snow had stopped, and the sun flowed through the bedroom window, warming them. Her cheek pressed against his chest; he combed her tangled, still damp hair with his fingers.

"You've exhausted me," he said. "I think I'd better dress and tend to the animals. Come with me?"

She shook her head. "I need to fix my …"

He chuckled. "Have you noticed Chester's mane? His tail? I'm an expert at braiding."

She peppered kisses up his chest to his mouth. "You'd braid my hair? You are too good to be true."

He swung his legs off the bed. "Just you wait."

After they dressed, he combed and French braided her hair, then together they saddled the horses and galloped around the lake. Nip and Tuck came for the run. They slowed the horses to a walk as they neared Forty Foot Falls. Snow lingered in patches on the north side of the rocks, and a fan of ice collected by the foot of the cascade. The horses drew close together and Summer and Daniel sat sideways in their saddles, facing each other. He braced his boots on Dulcey's saddle, one leg on each side of his bride; she hooked one knee beneath her and leaned against his leg. They'd already developed a rhythm as if they were dancing. Daniel touched her cheek; the curve of her shoulder filled his hand. One side of her mouth curled; the other side of his responded. Their breath caught at the same instants, and their hearts drummed the same beat. He couldn't get enough of touching her. Every time he looked at her, she seemed more beautiful.

The story of breaking up with Mary spilled out of him, even the part about Fanny kissing him in front of Hal and his mother. "Hal wasn't happy. You'll love Fanny. She's clever, and I can tell she cares about him. I hope he has enough sense to marry her. He needs to settle down."

Daniel paused and kissed her, and somehow she ended up on his lap. Chester didn't seem to mind the extra weight. "Do you mind me telling you about Mary? It's just that I don't want any secrets between us. Ever. I'll never lie to you."

He babbled on about how Mary and his sister were friends, and how her father and his father were also friends. "We all grew up together. It was her brother who damn near broke my jaw."

He considered telling her about beating Richie, but didn't know where to begin. Plus, he didn't want her to think of him that way. He fleetingly wondered if not telling her constituted a lie. He touched her face again and felt emotions fill him and spill over.

"God, Rosie. I look at you, and I forget to breathe. I want my family to meet you, but I'm afraid they'll hurt you, because they'll be furious with me.

"My parents aren't like Hal's parents," he said. "To my family, marriage is a merger of proper blood and old money." A sardonic chuckle slipped out. "Or maybe it's old blood and proper money." He shrugged. "My mother had the guest list all ready for my marriage to Mary. She may never forgive me. It's okay if she makes mean comments to me, but I don't know what I'd do if she or Abbey hurt you.

"I didn't know someone could become so important to me. I've never talked so much in my life."

She ran a finger along his moustache and smiled. "I don't mind. I love it."

He kissed her finger. "I know I must leave you. Too soon, I'll have to go back to the war. It's ironic, you know? I'm a major in the army, responsible for hundreds of men." He pulled her into the crook of his arm. "But the thought of leaving you paralyzes me."

She placed her hands on his cheeks. "Daniel, I was here alone for over a year." Her lip curled in a wry smile. "You saw me with the Spencer. I'm as good a shot as you are, and I carry a knife in my boot." She moved to pull it out of its sheath. "I'll show you that killing the snake was no fluke."

He shook his head. "I know it wasn't." He shuddered as he remembered the snake. "Your accuracy is uncanny, unbelievable."

"I'll be fine. I can take care of myself. You. I want you, my love, to worry about taking care of you. Bullets are flying around where you'll be. I want you safe."

All he could think about was how to protect her. He couldn't just leave her here alone. Her brother might have been able to abandon her, but he couldn't. A solution materialized in his head.

"You'll love Hal's mother." *If Amelia comes to Washington,* he thought, *I can leave Summer Rose there.* "Amelia is wonderful. She's an artist." He suddenly remembered. "Oh, and she met your mother once."

He told her the story about her mother coming into the gallery, how she'd bought one of Amelia's paintings, and how the purchase had led to Amelia's paintings becoming popular. Because of their popularity, Amelia met Harvey and they fell in love.

"Hal can thank your mother for his existence."

Summer cupped his face with both her hands and kissed him with her newfound passion. "I won't allow anyone to hurt me or anyone I love." She growled, making his heart pick up its pace again. "I'm like my father, Daniel. I'm fierce. You think I'm a kitten because I'm a girl, but I'm more like a mountain lion. My father told me my skin was thicker than that of the boys. I can be very stubborn, too.

"Daniel, I love how you love me. I never knew I could feel like I do for anyone like I feel for you. I want you to understand something. Nothing will ever separate us. Nothing. I ... I would kill to keep you safe."

CHAPTER 18

CHANGES

Two days later, Summer and Daniel rode to the Zimmerman farm. She introduced him to Ezra and Margie Zimmerman and their nine children, who ranged in age from fourteen to a baby. Seven boys and two girls. Margie, dark blonde and round, with a little white hat perched on her hair, and Ezra, lean, bald, with a grand, shaggy beard, shook hands with Daniel, and hugged Summer Rose. Neither of them had ever seen a ring like the one Daniel had given her. They stood by the paddock fence, admiring Ezra's new bull, and visited for a time.

Daniel charmed Ezra, Margie, and their children like he'd charmed her. The little girls, Jill and Hannah, ages eight and three, hung all over Summer Rose. Jill hid her face in Summer Rose's skirt every time he glanced at her; the older boys ogled Daniel's uniform. None of them had ever seen an officer up close. He removed the bullets from his revolver, then knelt, letting each of them site it. Somehow he remembered all the names of the boys, even the baby's name. When Sam and

Jimmy asked to see his sword, he removed it from where it hung below his left stirrup and showed it to them all.

"A great deal of practice is required in order to walk and sit with a sword, let alone fight with one," he told the boys. "Chairs can be tricky. You can get in all kinds of trouble."

He rubbed Steve's head. The sword was as tall as the boy. "You'll need to grow some in order to wear it."

Daniel slipped it on his own army belt. Right away the sword stuck in his boot, then tangled between his legs, caught in the hem of his jacket from behind, and tripped him. He swung around and the sword caught in his wife's skirt, lifting it to her knee. He scrunched his eyebrows like blond caterpillars and whispered, "You can get in a lot of trouble lifting ladies' skirts." When he sat on a bench, it stuck out between his legs. He had all of them laughing, even the little girls. He winked at Jill, who hid her face in Summer Rose's skirt.

Ezra promised to deliver hay and oats. "I just butchered a steer and a hog. Would you like a couple of steaks and some chops? I'll wrap them and put them in the spring house for you."

"That would be wonderful. Please stack the hay and oats in the shed. I'm taking Daniel to Morgan's Corner. He needs to send a few telegrams, and we'll wait for replies. We might not be back until after dark."

As Daniel settled accounts with Ezra, he asked, "Would the older boys like to earn a little money by taking care of the animals? We may need to go to Washington."

Big smiles erupted on Joe and Matt's faces.

As they left the Zimmerman property, Summer Rose jerked her chin toward his sword. "Have you ever killed a man with it?"

He nodded. "But I've actually used it more to roast steaks than to kill anyone."

"I'm serious. How many?"

"I didn't keep track."

He knew she sensed his discomfort, but she asked anyway. "How can you kill a man?"

His eyebrows jerked up. "It isn't difficult when they're trying to kill you. You said you'd kill to keep me safe."

She nodded. "You know what I mean. How do you prepare for killing?"

"I close all the other parts of my mind."

He'd asked himself that same question so many times, and had come around to that answer a long time before. He could tell she didn't understand, so he tapped his head and ran a hand down his body.

"Think of a train. I'm the engine. You're in the first car, my friends and family in the second, various acquaintances in the third. My commanders, fellow officers, and my soldiers take up the rest of the train. I unhook the cars containing you, my family, and friends, and put those cars on a siding, then I hook on the cars containing my men, and we barrel full-throttle into battle. I've bonded with my men and they with me. Most will fight to the death for each other. Training takes over. And anyone who tells you they aren't afraid is either a liar, a pompous fool, or an idiot."

His pale green eyes twinkled. "When it's over, I shall come back to the siding and find you. And days later, after ravishing you many, many times, I'll be human enough to see other people."

An impish grin slid across her face. "Daniel, be careful what you say. I may stop these horses and drag you into the bushes just so I can see what this ravishing is about."

It ended up they did need the boys' help. Hal's return telegram said General Buford was dangerously ill with a fever. He'd relinquished his command on the Rappahannock and wasn't expected to live long. The ever-faithful Irishman, Captain Keogh, accompanied the general to Washington, to General Stoneman's home. Many of his staff, summoned by Captain Keogh, had gathered at his bedside.

In the telegram, Hal further hinted at a surprise. He suggested they stay at the house on 18th Street, the one kept by their fathers' firm, Charteris & St. Clair. Daniel telegraphed back and asked Hal to convince his mother to come to Washington. He was counting on Amelia to solve a number of his problems.

Hal's return telegraph read: "Mother will arrive in Washington the day after tomorrow."

CHAPTER 19

A JOURNEY

"I can stay here and take care of the animals."

He shook his head. The thought of being away from her once the spring campaigns started made his stomach turn. A separation right now was impossible to even consider. He opened a small valise.

"Put necessities in here and pack what you wore for our wedding. That'll be perfect until we can fix you up like a major's wife. Enroute wear your Kip attire and pretend you're a boy again." He grinned and shook his head. "You certainly made a convincing Kip."

When she asked where they'd stay, he explained how the law office of his father and Hal's father owned a house in Washington. "They have clients in Washington, and they argue in front of the high court. They use it then, but most of the time it's empty. A couple of clerks might live on the third floor. Hal and I have often stayed there."

He noticed her upper lip wobbling and wondered what was going on. In a small voice, she said, "Nip and Tuck, they can't stay here. They'd starve."

He paused for a moment, looking down at her pale face. All her heart seemed to be there in her trembling mouth. The pulse in her neck throbbed. He knew, especially Mr. Stone, would have a conniption, and he had no idea how Harvey or Amelia might react to two dogs landing uninvited on their doorstep, but he knew, too, the dogs would not eat a bite without her signal.

He smiled, one side of his mouth curving up. "They'll come with us. What can anyone say?"

She jumped up, hugging him, plastering his face with kisses. "I knew you'd understand."

He bought a mule, named Chauncey, from Ezra and planned to ride Chester and Dulcey to Washington, using the mule to haul gear and grain for the animals. The trains to Washington were slow and sporadic at best, unsafe too often. "We'll pack our greatcoats and my dress uniform with the tent. They're too bulky for a long ride." He noted her confused expression and kissed the tip of her nose. He loved her more today than he had yesterday. "We'll take it slow for the dogs."

They left early the next day, stopping in Gettysburg, where Daniel reported to the post commander. They then went to the Quartermaster, where he procured mess kits, ponchos, and extra blankets for both of them. They stood in the warehouse, gazing around at the vast stores of clothing.

"Rank has its privileges," he told her.

From the shelves, he pulled down a wide-brimmed felt hat, a warm jacket of navy wool, new long boots, chaps, and gloves. After securing the chaps, he helped her into the jacket, then pulled her collar up by the edges of the material and drew her close.

"You make a very convincing boy. You have the walk down perfect." Their faces were an inch apart and he sucked in a deep breath. "Good Lord, I want to kiss you in the worst way."

Just then, several soldiers stepped through the door. She grinned. "I don't think that would be a good idea."

He frowned. "Stay close to me, a step behind. I'll tell anyone who asks that you're my brother, Kip." He did up the top button of her shirt and tucked a strand of hair inside her hat. "Kip, Rosie, Summer Rose, Mrs. Charteris, you've a gamut of names. By the way, my love, no one but me, not even Hal, may ever call you Rosie. You are my Rosie, and only mine. I'm not too happy about Hal calling you Kip either."

At the tent chapel, he asked about Chaplain Anders and Colonel English, but couldn't find them. As they were leaving town, they ran into Irene Wood, who was hurrying toward the ambulance wagons. She slowed when she saw Daniel and stopped when he asked her about Chaplain Anders and the colonel.

"Colonel English went home to Boston, and Chaplain Anders left for Washington last week."

"My brother, Kip, and I are on our way to Washington. Have you heard any news of General Buford?"

Irene peeked around Daniel, glanced at the dogs and looked directly at the boy. "You don't fool me at all, Summer Rose. I'd recognize those eyes anywhere." She hugged her. "I'm leaving for Washington now. I heard that Captain Keogh took him to General Stoneman's house. I'll be nursing at

Harewood Hospital. From what I understand, Harewood's full." She hugged them both. "Wonderful to see you. I must be off now."

Daniel and Summer took two days to get to Washington. Nip and Tuck had no trouble keeping up with them and were a great help in keeping Chauncey moving. The first night, they pitched the tent at an isolated spot a couple of miles upstream from the Army encampment at Pipe Creek. They made a fire, buried potatoes and onions in the coals, and cooked the steaks on a makeshift grill. The dogs feasted on the leftovers.

Summer surveyed the clear sky. "Let's sleep outside."

Daniel looked up. The new moon gave the stars and the Milky Way center stage. "Okay. Sleep in your clothes. We'll sleep back to back." Traveling with a woman was different. Especially this woman. He moved her into a shadow and kissed her nose, then kissed her more thoroughly. "I was told they cleared all the Confederates out of these parts, but you can never be positive, and I wouldn't trust a number of our own men. I'm glad we have the dogs. However, it's best if no one suspects you're a girl. Understand?"

She nodded and kissed him, pressing her entire body tight against his.

He laughed and held her at arm's length. "You aren't convincing me."

They awoke in the middle of the night, both nearly naked, wrapped around each other.

"Hell, I'm not very good at listening to my own orders, am I?" he mumbled, then pulled a blanket over their heads. "Come here."

She wiggled out of her remaining clothes and rolled into his arms. "Sometimes, when I'm with you, I feel like a wild woman."

"I like you wild."

CHAPTER 20

WASHINGTON D.C.

A s a herd of cattle pushed down Pennsylvania Avenue, Daniel used his knee to nudge Summer to a side street. She leaned into him, relishing his touch. In the fading light, the city was every bit as busy and noisy as Daniel had described. Summer glanced at everything at once, noting the half-finished capitol dome and the half-finished obelisk to Washington. A mass of animals and humanity teemed about them. Hammers rang from scaffolding which swarmed with black bodies. Soldiers with guns drilled to the cadence of their sergeant's voice. A black boy darted across the street with a squealing pig slung over his shoulders.

She had been only nine when she'd come to the capital with her family in '54, and the city had been little more than a large village. She'd seen her first Negro slave on that trip. In fact, she'd been shocked to see men and women chained and auctioned in Georgetown. Now the city bustled with teamsters and hucksters, shouting, cracking whips, all their sounds mixing with the noise of the cattle.

Daniel whistled for the dogs and edged her to a side street as the herd of cattle rumbled by. The smells of yeast, fish, beer, and cattle mixed unpleasantly, and she was relieved when he leaned over and tied a handkerchief around her face, smiling his crooked grin. Their clothing, stiff with caked mud, was the gray of statues and monuments.

"I've never seen a girl so dirty." He chucked her under the chin. "You're a tough trooper, Rosie. Every day you surprise me."

He pointed south toward the Executive Mansion. "Just the other side is a rough section called Murder Bay. Stay out of there. It's full of thieves, prostitutes, and worse."

They arrived at the house as a lamplighter walked by, lighting the gaslights along 18th Street. Becca and Ned Hostettler, a young German couple who had worked for the St. Clairs in Philadelphia since the war began, and who had traveled with Amelia to care for this house as well, came out and helped them unload.

Daniel made a quick introduction. The Hostettlers, both strong-boned and blond, with ruddy pink faces and pale blue eyes, could pass more for brother and sister than husband and wife. Ned still had a strong German accent, but Becca spoke as clearly as any American.

"Ned will run the horses and mule to the livery," Becca said, sending a sly wink to Summer Rose. "Don't worry so, Daniel. Chester loves Ned. He'll take good care of him."

She petted the big horse's neck then snapped her fingers and whistled. "Nip and Tuck are you? I hope you're good watch dogs. Daniel, put your saddlebags, equipment, and guns in the basement, and your boots at the bottom of the stairs."

She took their outer coats and hats and held them away from her, wrinkling her nose "These clothes are foul. Daniel, bring her up through the kitchen. I have coffee or tea ready. And I just made vegetable soup. Maybe some warm soup would taste good." She patted her thigh. I have some leftover chicken. Do you like chicken, boys?"

Summer Rose smiled. "They love chicken."

In a workroom off the kitchen, she gave Daniel and Summer Rose long white robes and slippers and instructed them to strip out of their filthy clothes.

"I want your socks and smalls, too."

When they were in the robes, she gave them steaming towels to wipe their hands, arms, and faces. Summer Rose tied her hair back with a black ribbon, pleased to be somewhat clean again.

After the dogs wolfed down the chicken and curled at Summer's feet, Becca served large bowls of vegetable soup and toasted cheese bread to Summer and Daniel. "Ned fired up the boiler." She scowled at Daniel. "You made this lovely girl ride a horse all the way from Gettysburg?"

He bit into the cheese toast. "I wanted to take the train, Becca. She insisted we ride. I'm finding my bride very bossy."

He bent forward and slipped one hand beneath his wife's chin, and she sank into the delicious warmth of his palm. He pulled her toward him, his other hand still holding toast in the air, while they kissed.

That was how Amelia first saw Summer Rose, sitting at the kitchen table in a white cotton robe, her dark hair damp and curling, her face glowing with the love Daniel spilled on her and with two dogs that resembled wild red wolves curled at her feet.

Becca saved the moment. "Mrs. St. Clair, do you believe our Danny made his bride ride all the way from Gettysburg? You could hardly tell she was a girl, and the mud ... I hope it was mud. I'm heating water for baths."

Daniel stood, his blond chest hair curling out from the neck of his white robe, the devil of a smile all over his face, and embraced Amelia. "Amelia, may I present my wife, Summer Rose McAllister Charteris. Darling, this is Hal's mother, Amelia St. Clair. She knew your mother."

Summer Rose stood and took both of Amelia's hands. "Daniel and Hal have spoken so kindly of you I almost feel I know you." She lowered her eyes, aware of their robes. "Mrs. Hostettler took our muddy clothes before we could track miles of dirt through the house. Thank you for your hospitality." She lifted her chin. "I'm very much looking forward to knowing you. I'd love to hear about my mother, and Daniel tells me you're an artist. I look forward to seeing your paintings." She dropped her gaze to Nip and Tuck. "I hope the dogs are not too much trouble."

In that moment, Amelia understood all the gymnastics Daniel had gone through to marry this girl. Her face, her figure, the way she held herself, the timbre of her voice, everything he and Hal had said rang true. Amelia stepped around the dogs then sat and pulled the girl down beside her, still holding her hands.

"We need a good watchdog. I found two soldiers asleep in our shed. Becca, that soup smells delicious. Would you fix me a bowl, too?" She turned to Summer and lifted the girl's hand. "Tell me about your wedding. Your ring is lovely."

"Thank you," Summer held the ring to the light. "I have never seen anything like it. And our wedding was perfect."

As she finished telling all about it, Summer hooked her arm beneath Daniel's and leaned her cheek against his shoulder. "Daniel and your son were all kitted out in their dress uniforms. The nurses just about swooned."

Daniel chuckled. His big fingers rested on her arm, and he squeezed. "Were we at the same wedding? I only saw you." He picked up his wife's hand and kissed it. "I need to clean up and go over to where General Buford is. Are you all right here without me? I don't like to leave you alone so soon, but I should go."

"I'll be fine. Mrs. St. Clair will take good care of me. Do what you need to do."

Daniel turned to Amelia. "I have a favor to ask. Summer Rose needs new clothes: everyday things, all that fluff that goes underneath, and at least one formal dress, probably two. Whatever you think she needs." He winked at his wife. "Buy whatever you want. Amelia knows how you'll be expected to dress. Would you help her, Amelia? I'm not sure how or where women procure clothing. Make sure it's billed to me, not my father."

Amelia clapped her hands. "What fun, Daniel. I may bankrupt you. Go take your bath while I plan with your lovely bride."

Amelia and Summer were still sitting at the kitchen table a half hour later when Daniel, groomed and polished, came to say goodbye. He looked the epitome of the handsome warrior, with his sword and sash and gleaming leather.

As he stood there with hat in hand, Ray and Grace Stone came through the kitchen and more introductions were made. Son of the St. Clair's butler, Ray Stone was a major and a surgeon, a serious man with silver blond hair, a small square beard, and startling blue eyes. Decked out as formally as Daniel, except he wore the bright green sash of the Medical Corps, he was one of the small herd of doctors trying to keep General Buford alive. Daniel and Ray decided to walk over to General Stoneman's house together.

Grace unpinned her hat and handed it to Becca. Petite, with dark hair and eyes, Grace smiled with her lips tight, for her teeth went every which way. She sat on the other side of Summer Rose.

"I am so pleased to finally meet your husband. Ray's father told me so much about Daniel, and his n-name is always in the p-papers." Her last words stammered, and she blushed. "Mr. Stone has known him since he was a baby. I'm glad to meet him at last. You too, Summer." She turned to Amelia. "Thank you so much for inviting us here."

Becca came into the kitchen, dropping a towel over one arm. "Your bath is ready. Miss. Ruthie will help you."

Amelia got to her feet. "I'll take her up, Becca. What room did you give them?"

"The Rose Room. Where else would I put a girl named Summer Rose? And even though it's almost winter, Daniel likes that upstairs porch." She nodded to Summer Rose. "I unpacked your bag and laid some things out for you."

Amelia smiled. "Our bride looks exhausted. We'll dine informally this evening, since the men are away. Come, my dears. Becca, send up a tea tray to Summer's room, please. What room are you staying in, Grace?"

"The one with the red wallpaper."

Amusement danced in Amelia's smile. She lowered her voice. "Ah. The ladies call that the Red Room. The men secretly dubbed it the Passion Room."

Grace linked her fingers and propped them under her chin. "Oh, I hope it works for Ray. I want a baby so terribly. My father offered a hundred dollar gold piece to my sister or me, to whomever produces the first grandchild." She rolled her eyes. "I want that gold piece!"

Amelia coughed. "Change into a comfortable wrapper, Grace, and come over to Summer's room. We'll have tea while she bathes."

CHAPTER 21

THE ROSE ROOM

Tea proved not to be the nightmare Summer envisioned. The Rose Room consisted of a bedroom painted a warm rose color with a small sitting alcove and a large dressing room. A door led from the sitting room onto an upstairs porch. In the dressing room sat a huge porcelain tub, steaming behind a canvas curtain, which kept the fragrant warmth inside the tent-like affair. She shed her robe and sank into the foamy hot water.

Amelia set a teacup, also steaming, on the windowsill. "Be careful, Summer, I put a little brandy in the tea to help relax you."

Summer Rose nodded and leaned into the sudsy warm water which caressed every sore inch of her body. She closed her eyes becoming conscious only of the warmth and sounds: the click of latches and rustling of skirts, the fire crackling. She sank deeper, only half listening to the conversation, until Grace mentioned someone sleeping with someone who wasn't her husband. Summer Rose sat still, straining to listen.

"My sister heard she's a hussy, goes after any man in uniform," said Grace.

The maid left and Becca's rosy face peered around the canvas curtain. "Feel better, *liebchen*?"

More hot water filled the tub, and rose-scented salts permeated the room. Summer rolled her head back as Becca lathered her hair and rinsed it with more of the lush smelling water. All her aches seemed to disappear. When the time came to step out of the tub, Becca wrapped her in towels and guided her to a little dressing table.

She picked up the cotton nightgown that Summer had brought with her. "Did you make this?" Summer Rose nodded, and Becca pursed her lips with admiration. "The pleats and the stitching are beautiful. I love the little band of roses you embroidered. Here, let me help. I have a clean robe." She pointed to a jar of cream. "Rub that into your elbows and heels."

A robe of rich red, quilted velvet cocooned Summer's body. She suspected it was one of Amelia's. Becca whispered, "Washington bleeds gossip. Take everything you hear with a grain of salt." Then louder, she added, "Come out and sit by the fire. I'll comb your hair."

Summer touched Becca's hand. "I haven't felt so pampered since before my mother died. *Vielen dank.*"

Becca shook her head, smiling mischievously. "I think that young husband of yours pampers you a bit. He's besotted, *liebchen*, besotted. I've known Daniel since he first came to Washington, and every mother dragged her daughter here to see him. Never has he treated a woman like he treats you.

And how he looks at you? Oh, he melts my heart when he looks at you."

Summer Rose giggled. "He melts mine, too." She held a finger to her lips. "Don't tell anyone. We don't want that tidbit to bleed all over Washington, do we?"

Becca arched her pale eyebrows. "Smart cookie."

The sofa of dark blue damask stood by the fire, and Summer set her feet on a fringed, round ottoman while Becca dried and combed her hair. Amelia fixed plates of tea sandwiches and angel cake, iced with coconut and candied pineapple. "Did you make this cake, Becca?"

Becca nodded.

"May I have the recipe?"

She fell asleep amid gossip about Delores Baldwin, who had gotten sick at Mrs. Blair's soirée, and Pamela Kaufman, who had slapped her sister in public; then Melanie Somebody who had a black eye and claimed her baby hit her.

"You know it's that husband of hers," she heard Amelia say.

"I heard she deserved it. Daddy said it's a wonder he didn't shoot her. She'd gone way past flirting with that young lieutenant of artillery. You know. The one all the girls fussed over last week."

"Do you really believe she deserved a beating?"

Grace laughed an unkind laugh then whispered. "My father certainly would think so. Her husband found her naked with the lieutenant."

Summer's young husband found her asleep on the sofa. He touched her arm and she blinked awake. When she saw him there, she sat up and stretched. "Oh, Daniel, I meant to stay awake for you. What time is it? How is your general?"

The dogs had come upstairs with him and curled in front of the fire. "I took them outside and thought it best if they stay here with us tonight. Mr. Stone did not look happy. Don't look so worried. He'll come around."

Daniel had removed his jacket and now sat on the other end of the sofa, slipping out of his boots. He seemed very tired. "It's after midnight, and General Buford is dying. His fever keeps coming back. He sinks in and out of delirium. He recognized me, but he's fading quickly. The scene was about as bad as you can imagine."

He shook his head, looking terribly sad. "I don't know which is worse, wasting away or having your head blown off on a battlefield. He's only thirty-eight. Pattie, his wife, and their children are too ill to travel. They'll never see each other again. I can't even think about it." He dropped his chin to his chest. "I heard talk that they'll promote him to Major General, a death bed promotion. I think that will please him."

He stood with his boots in hand and his shirttail hanging loose. "I do have happy news, though. Hal and Fanny are here. I told you about Fanny. Well, they're married; they eloped. Hal came over to General Stoneman's house about ten, and I walked back with him. She's pregnant. Amelia is furious, and his father doesn't know, so pretend I've said nothing."

He took his boots to the door and set them in the hall, then hung his coat in the closet. He returned, dressed only in a loose robe of embroidered black silk. He fixed himself a drink from the bottle of bourbon Amelia had left on the sofa table, then came and sat beside Summer. He put his feet on the ottoman, and she wriggled close to him, resting her head against his shoulder when his arm came around her back. He gave her a sip from his glass and smiled when she made a face.

"It's an acquired taste." He squeezed her hand. "Can't be as bad as that tea you forced down my throat."

She rubbed her cheek like a kitten against his shoulder, and they sat for a long time in silence while the flames danced and cavorted, telling stories in their brilliant ashes.

He finished his drink. "Hal seems happy, but he can't be as happy as I am. Come to bed, Rosie. I'm exhausted. One thing about this house I especially like is that the sheets are crisp and stiff and smell wonderful."

He flung the black silk robe over the foot of the bed, and climbed in behind her. He sank his nose into the side of her neck and inhaled. "You smell delicious. What is that?"

"Becca doused me with rose-scented water."

"Ask her to do that again." He turned down the lamp until only the light from the fireplace lit the room. He didn't speak for a moment, and she intuitively took his hand. "The sadness is so very hard. To see the general fading is difficult," he said, then sighed deeply and pulled her close and rubbed a possessive hand over her hip. "Snuggle your bottom against me. I love having you next to me at night. I wake up and know you're right beside me." He lips found her temple, and he kissed her there. "I love, too that you're the easiest person to talk to I have ever met. We need to sleep. We're meeting your brother for lunch tomorrow at Willard's. Smell the sheets. So fresh and crisp. If you keep wiggling like that you're going to get yourself in trouble."

She wiggled again. "Daniel, that threat is no longer effective. I told you before, I like your kind of trouble." She turned and kissed the side of his mouth. Her young, *besotted* husband was already sound asleep. She nestled up like a spoon inside his arms and whispered into the pillow. "Da, William, and Colin, please take care of him. I love him. He is my heart. Take good care of his general, too. He may come to you soon."

PART TWO

MURDER BAY

CHAPTER 22

A DIAMOND AND RUBY BRACELET

Daniel swore under his breath when he recognized his error. The bar at Willard's was packed. *Good Lord, they're three deep. I should have brought her in the Pennsylvania Avenue entrance.* A woman smelling of whiskey brushed against him; the bar vibrated with chatter. The men and women openly leered at Summer Rose. Although he understood she looked lovely, he didn't want her exposed to this element. Daniel nodded, oozed diplomacy, and used his strong body to shield her as he moved toward the lobby. He spotted Henry Willard, one of the hotel's owners, and steered her in his direction.

Henry led them through the kitchen to the lobby. "Yes, yes, I know. He's over here near the palm tree." Henry bowed, kissed her hand. "Oh, Daniel, your father has a reservation at one o'clock."

Daniel nodded as her brother, much like a box turtle, popped his head out from behind the palm tree. He felt her shoulders jerk and watched her eyes brim with tears, as Jack McAllister, her brother, hugged her.

"Congratulations, Summer. Daniel tells me you're married." He held her at arm's length and turned her around, then kissed her cheek. "You're all grown up and beautiful. Where did the little girl go?" He took Daniel's hand. "Excellent work, Daniel." He chuckled, looking again at his little sister, taking in her tailored dress of black wool with the exquisite lace jabot, and oval cameo. "She's cleaned up nicely."

They all but crept, for Jack grimaced with each step, into the noisy, but elegant dining room. He seemed happy to see her and pleased that she was married to Daniel.

Daniel ordered champagne, and they all decided on snapper soup, chicken salad, and fried oysters. Jack seemed uncomfortable. His neck kept twisting as if he wanted to see behind him.

Finally, Daniel asked, "Do you want to change seats?"

He did. Jack seemed to relax when he could see the room's entrance.

Summer told Jack how Daniel had taught her to shoot a Spencer rifle and about their wedding. "We're just waiting now for General Buford's health to improve."

Jack's face contorted, and he coughed, his body twisting. When he settled, he nodded toward Daniel's new shoulder straps, "Congratulations, I heard you were promoted."

Daniel shook his head. "It's embarrassing. Both Hal and I now are colonels. Not because of merit. I think we're filling up space on someone's chart." He shrugged. "I have brand new eagles on my shoulders and nowhere to go." His fingers softly drummed against the white linen tablecloth. "Do you know where I'm going?"

Jack's shoulder jerked and he squirmed in his seat then straightened up. "I can't tell you exactly where you're headed, but I can tell you a little. Not much will happen until a commander is chosen to lead the Army of the Potomac. Enjoy the reprieve."

He took a sip of coffee and Summer was vaguely surprised to see he held the cup steady.

"I also can tell you the generals won't decide this time. President Lincoln's hand is at the helm now. We've had great success out west. Grant, Sherman, and Sheridan are the rising stars at the moment."

After lunch they walked toward the lobby, and Jack told them both, "I'm very relieved to no longer have the responsibility of either the property or you, little sister." He faced Daniel and his left eye gave a small tic. "I know you'll take good care of her."

As they neared the door, Louis Woodward Charteris barged up to them. He was almost as tall as his son, with abundant dark hair and tanned skin. He took Summer Rose's hand, kissed it, and bowed with old world charm. Except for the odd pale green of their eyes and a similar intensity, father and son shared little resemblance. He straightened, but continued to hold her hand. The Willard's lobby buzzed with almost as much activity as the bar.

"You do not need to introduce your wife, Daniel. She's the picture of her mother, whom I had the honor to know quite well.

"Welcome to our family, my dear."

Summer bowed slightly. "I'm pleased to meet you, Mr. Charteris." She turned and included Jack in their circle. "May I present my half-brother, Major Jack McAllister."

As Louie took Jack's hand, he kept hold of Summer Rose's. He told them he'd first met Lillian Fitzmartin at the Christmas Ball, the year of her debut. "I was an old married man by then, but for a few moments I fell madly in love with her. So beautiful, truly she was the belle of the ball." He turned to Jack and continued. "However, your father, Major McAllister, quite literally, swept her off her feet. No one else ever had a chance.

"Micah McAllister was a Renaissance man. He arrived in our city with his good name, a thick brogue, and thicker shoulders, and could charm any girl he wanted. He chose Lillian Fitzmartin. They were a popular couple. He was handsome, intelligent, and well-spoken. A magnificent dancer." He glanced at his new daughter-in-law and said, "Your mother was gracious and eloquent. Then his small sons died so tragically, and they left." He shook his head sadly. "One day they were here, the next they were gone. I heard they were living in the wilds. The two of you certainly don't seem the worse for it. Daniel tells me you lost your parents and your two older brothers. I'm sincerely saddened for you both."

"Thank you, Mr. Charteris," said Jack. "We had a good life in 'the wilds', as you call it. I wouldn't have traded those years for the world." He bowed slightly. "I must get back. Thank you for lunch, Daniel. Good to meet you Mr. Charteris." He bent and kissed his sister's cheek. "Stay in touch."

Louis led his son and Summer Rose to a small grouping of chairs in a corner of the lobby and hailed a waiter. "Champagne, please. It's not every day my son is married and promoted to colonel." While they waited for their beverages, they spoke of Daniel's mother and sister, Hal's marriage, the deaths and wounding of several friends.

"Father, when you go back to Philadelphia I'd appreciate you looking into something for Summer. Her grandparents, Ralph and Martha Fitzmartin, live near Chestnut Hill. They're in a bad way. Both are ill. It's heartbreaking. They have a competent housekeeper watching over them, who Summer writes to constantly." He glanced at his wife. "We both would feel better if you'd send someone from your office to look out for them. I can't take the time to go there, and I don't want Summer traveling by herself. She's their only relative. Would you contact Girard Bank and just check them out?" He turned to his wife. "What was the name on the letter?"

"George Crenshaw."

Approaching lightening flashed in the windows as huge raindrops splattered against the glass.

"I'll check myself. I knew Ralph Fitzmartin years ago. What a shame. This war …" As the waiter poured the champagne, Louis looked at his son. "Did you walk?"

Daniel nodded.

Daniel's father directed the waiter. "See that my carriage is brought round." He raised his glass.

"A quick toast, I'm afraid. I'm meeting Governor Curtin in a few minutes, and it's pouring. Please make use of my carriage." He stood glass in hand. "Best wishes and congratulations. Stay safe, Son." He took a sip of champagne then bent and kissed Summer Rose's cheek. "You are lovely, my dear."

Although his carriage waited under a portico, a doorman held an umbrella for them. As they settled into the plush interior, Summer spotted something sparkly tucked in the seat cushion. Her small fingers plucked out a diamond and ruby bracelet. She held it out to Daniel. "Your mother's?"

Daniel arched an eyebrow. "Not likely. I'll run this inside."

CHAPTER 23

BREAKFAST AND PLASTER DUST

During the following fortnight, the weather turned truly wintry. Now snow pelted the windows and an inviting coal fire burned in their sitting alcove fireplace as Daniel and Summer dressed for another funeral, again at the Presbyterian Church on Thirteenth and "H" Streets. General Buford's heartbreaking funeral was held there two days ago. The losses just didn't stop.

Summer looked longingly at the sofa, "I'd like to curl up here with a book all day."

Daniel, with bits of lather still on his face and his suspenders hanging loose, glanced at the freshly made bed and grinned. "I'd like nothing better than to curl up with you—not to read, mind you. However, duty calls."

Making a grand effort to ignore him, she stood in front of the mirror to put the final touches on another new outfit, a dark green, almost black suit. Black seemed to be the color of choice these days and even this forest green suit seemed bright. Amelia had assured her the green was the perfect thing for this funeral. For warmth, she had donned all her crinolines, all were white but one was trimmed with a delicate lavender ribbon. She swished the skirt to check that not too much color showed. Daniel came up behind her and wrapped his arms around her.

He kissed the back of her neck. "You, my darling girl, look wonderful. No one will notice that touch of lavender, and I'll enjoy knowing what's beneath the somber green."

She sighed and gave up resisting his allure. She found something exciting about being embraced by her half-naked husband while she was dressed up. "Oh Daniel, I have to be the luckiest girl in the world." She turned in his arms, spread her hands, and raked through the blond hair on his chest, brushing the soft curls about her fingers; her eyes, all serious and big, looked up at him. The pheasant feather on her hat bobbed near his eye, and her tongue flicked over her lips. Her words squeezed out between breaths. "Kiss me ... please."

His wide mouth curled at the corners. "I'd be honored, my lady, but first ..." he said as he removed her hat and set it on the little table by the door. "That feather's a weapon." He bent and kissed her deeply and tenderly then abruptly turned her around and gave her bottom a gentle swat. His other hand rested on the doorknob. "Get yourself out of here before I throw up your skirts and pin you to the wall." He yanked open the door only to discover Grace and a maid standing there, each with an ear pressed to where the door had been.

Grace let out a little gasp then smiled as she bent over searching for something. "Oh, Danny, be a dear, check for my garnet earring. Did it per chance roll under your door?"

Unable to speak and with his mouth ajar, Daniel glanced about the floor and shook his head then closed the door and clicked the lock. He turned around, his look of shock replaced by a grin. He whispered. "They're still out there. I can hear them giggling. Should we give them something worthy of eavesdropping?"

She smiled with all her imp laughing in her eyes, then spoke in a voice both sultry and loud. "I like it better, darling, when you pin me to the mattress."

She turned and heaved herself onto the middle of the freshly made bed, her green velvet skirt and crinolines ruffled around her like the petals of a pansy. The big brass bed as well as the floor boards squeaked and complained.

He landed next to her, making the bed thump against the wall and the springs squeal even louder. His hands, at the same time, dug into the mounds of lace. He had no intention of missing this opportunity. "A yelp or two from you," he whispered, "will give them plenty to talk about." He rocked the bed, which produced suggestive noises. His hands, at the same time, moved with the intent of creating similar rhythmic squeals from his wife.

She let out a fake yelp as his hands burrowed amid the mountain of velvet and lace; she giggled and pulled him close. "If you keep that up, I won't have to pretend."

At breakfast Summer couldn't miss Grace Stone's smirk at their late appearance. The serving maids giggled, too, and Summer suspected the entire household knew all the details of their private lives as she suddenly realized their bedroom sat directly above the dining room. She swallowed hard and somehow kept from blushing. She hoped plaster dust hadn't sprinkled down on Becca's lovely breakfast. As she smiled a good morning around the table, she watched her husband pull his earlobe. His pale green eyes latched onto Grace's garnet earrings. "In whose keyhole did you find it?"

She turned away to hide her grin as a crimson tide inched from Grace's chin to the roots of hair. How she wished she had Daniel's ability to turn a phrase.

Harvey St. Clair, Amelia's husband, stood and pulled out her chair. Harvey had arrived in Washington the previous evening. He planned to escort his wife to this weekend's Christmas Ball. Now, Summer appreciated his courtly manners. If he noticed the tension between Grace and Daniel, he ignored it, and if he'd heard the thumping and squeaking of the big brass bed, no one would ever know it.

As he pushed her chair in, he said, "I understand, young lady, you are a crack shot with a Spencer carbine. The President and Congress recently approved the purchase of 13,000 Spencer rifles and carbines for our soldiers. That's quite a story," he said as he took his seat and snapped open his napkin. "I happened to be there that day. Young Christopher Spencer, the inventor—he's only 30—sauntered into the Executive Mansion, past the bodyguards, carrying the rifle and ammunition—thank heavens, he wasn't a rebel—then he convinced Lincoln, Secretary Stanton, and me to come shooting with him out by Washington's monument."

Harvey nodded with appreciation. "That did the trick. President Lincoln is a very good marksman. He approved purchase on the spot. Now a lot of our boys will have repeating rifles. Louie and I already knew how good Christopher's guns were. That's why we purchased them for our boys last spring."

Again Summer swallowed hard, just now understanding what Daniel had done when he'd given her his rifle. "I'm learning, Sir. I'm not quite as good as your son, but—" Her eyes danced. "I'm a touch better than Daniel. I handle a knife best of all, Mr. St. Clair. My father made sure I could take care of myself."

Hal bounded downstairs, disheveled and yawning, and asked Becca to help him fix a tray. He sighed, his smile tight. "Fanny was up most of the night. She asked for some tea and toast, and I may as well take up a plate for myself."

He walked around the table and kissed his mother, then Grace. When he came to Summer Rose, he grinned. "Not black? You look lovely, Kip. The green becomes you." To the table, he added. "I wish you could have seen her coming out of the pines, dressed as a boy with three pheasants all ready to cook on a thick stick. Danny and I were about ready to gnaw on our arms. We'd eaten nothing but jerky and wormy hardtack for days. We had no idea Kip was a girl." His eyes narrowed. "How did we miss that?" He shook his head. "I'm not sure we would have cared. Once we saw those hens, we noticed nothing else. And this Kip wanted to trade them for mere coffee!" He chuckled and winked at Daniel. "If we'd been out of coffee, we might have shot you for those hens."

Daniel wiped his mouth with measured slowness and placed his napkin beside his plate. "I beg to differ, Hal," he said, laying his hand over hers. He didn't like Hal's attitude, and Hal had regurgitated this story at least six times since they came to Washington. "I knew that night she was a girl.

I also knew better than to tell you." He smiled around the table. "Notice, I'm the lucky man she married."

He meant it to be funny, but no one laughed. Hal reddened and Becca handed him a tray. Along with the breakfast, a hothouse gardenia floated in a little glass bowl.

Hal bent to sniff the gardenia. "Thanks, Becca. Poor Fanny feels miserable. She'll love the flower." As he lifted the tray, he muttered to Daniel. "You did not know she was a girl."

CHAPTER 24

FIRST DANCE

Hal and Daniel met in the upstairs hall, decked out in their dress uniforms, ready to attend the Christmas Ball. As they started down the stairs, Hal said, "Sorry about the other morning. Fanny was up all night. So was I. Regardless, I shouldn't have gone on about Summer being a girl. I see her all dressed up and am surprised every time at how …." He glanced sideways at Daniel and didn't finish. "I have my own problems, but at least, I don't have yours. Do you know your mother's in town?"

Daniel lifted an eyebrow.

"And Mary was married three days ago to Emmett Hathaway. He's artillery with Hancock. Tall, red-haired, he went to Germantown then West Point, long sideburns. He's friends with her brothers. Decent chap. Mary bawled all through the wedding."

Daniel grimaced.

"That's the good news." They continued down, side by side on the wide staircase. "I understand Captain and

Mrs. Hathaway will be at the ball tonight. Your mother accompanied them on the train along with Mary's parents the day before yesterday. They all are staying at Willard's. Your mother thought it would be awkward for Mary if they stayed here."

Daniel jerked. He understood Mary not staying here, but his own mother had made no effort to meet Summer Rose or let him know she was in Washington?

"Pay no attention to her, Daniel. Flora must be furious about your marriage. She's just grinding in the knife." He shrugged and shook his head. "Ray and I will keep our eyes open."

Ten minutes later, the girls gathered in the large upstairs hall while Amelia assembled the men and the servants at the foot of the stairs. Earlier in the afternoon, Amelia, no debutante herself, had crammed years of training into a few hours. Amelia had whooped and done a little dance when Summer told her, "I love to dance. My father loved to dance. He taught all of us."

Other important lessons were emphasized: how to sit, how to walk and curtsey, how to enter and exit a carriage while wearing a hoop, how to balance a tea cup.

"It's best if you just don't eat or drink anything, and for heaven's sake, don't stick out your pinky."

Now as Daniel stood at the foot of the stairs, all thoughts of his mother's rudeness evaporated. He hoped heaven existed just so her parents and brothers could look down and see her tonight. He wondered if Jack planned to attend the dance. He hoped so.

Grace, in peacock feathers and blue taffeta, and Fanny in butter-colored silk and tulle, shimmered and rustled. They were beautiful. But he only noticed his wife. Her dress of rich, cocoa-colored velvet draped beautifully over her stunning figure and picked up the creamy color of her skin and the rich brown of her sable hair. Silk petticoats and trimmings, all the way down to the ruffles on her pantaloons, foamed like whipped cream on hot chocolate. She wore her mother's earrings and pearls. And her hairpins. He smiled. He remembered her hairpins.

When she took his arm, he bent and kissed her, so proud he couldn't stop smiling. He whispered. "You taste of sugar and spice and look gorgeous. Be warned, I may drag you into a coat closet and ravish you."

She grinned and leaned into his shoulder. "Oh Daniel, getting past the layers of clothing would cool your ardor. I'm trussed up like a turkey. Two French ladies made this new corset. I wonder if their great grandmothers learned their trade during the Inquisition?"

Becca helped her with her cloak and gloves and handed her a fan from which dangled a little dance card. As they walked to the carriage, Daniel wrote his name diagonally across all the lines.

"Now the most beautiful girl in the world must dance every dance with me," he said as he handed her the fan and card. He lowered his voice. "Trust me, I'll find a way beneath the guardian layers."

Wise Mr. Stone had ordered two large carriages. Two couples to a carriage allowed room for the hoops and crinolines, and Amelia's practice sessions produced perfectly executed entrances. The girls backed into the carriages, and the men stuffed their skirts in behind them, producing much laughter.

The wait in the line of carriages in front of the hotel, the walk to the entrance, checking their coats, their announcement, everything moved at a crawl. While they waited, Grace, who had attended the Russian Ball in November, went on and on about how grand that affair had been, and Ray entertained them with behind the scene stories of drunken generals and rude heads of state. They all grew impatient, but Grace did so with little elegance.

Finally their turn came, and Summer's hand slipped into his; and, even through the double layer of their gloves, he felt her warmth. She squeezed tight as they entered the anterooms and faced the antagonistic stares of his mother, Mary, and the McGills. A silence filled any leftover space in the room, as if everyone forgot to breathe. Daniel spotted a healthy-looking Richie and sighed with relief. He wondered how much Mary and her mother knew of their ugly fight. He was disappointed when he couldn't find any evidence of his father. He nodded hello to the group across the lobby.

No one blinked. Then Emmett nodded and Daniel acknowledged the gesture. He hoped Mary would find happiness. His mother, blonde and regal in black satin and diamonds, turned her back to them. The strains of a mazurka beckoned from the ballroom, and Amelia herded their party to the floor. The four couples made up a quadrille. For most of the evening they dominated a corner of the floor as one set followed another. The orchestra played a waltz, then a polka. Daniel and Hal, who had taken endless dancing lessons, demonstrated the steps, and the group caught on so well that spectators gathered and applauded. They swirled and dipped and stomped, twirling with wild abandon. The music ended to applause and a mad rush for champagne and oysters. Poor Fanny turned green at the sight of a raw oyster.

Just before midnight, Daniel spotted his mother leading a small entourage across the dance floor: Mr. and Mrs. McGill, the newly-wedded Captain and Mrs. Hathaway, and two couples he didn't know rode in her wake. Very glad he'd consumed a stiff whiskey and with a sense of duty, he embraced his mother and led her toward Summer Rose. He made introductions, exchanged Christmas greetings, congratulated the newlyweds, even kissed Mary's cheek. He noticed her upper lip twitch. Emmett noticed, too. The strains of another polka reached them, and Emmett asked him to show him the steps. As he demonstrated, he watched Summer speak with Mary and his mother. Graciousness became her. Mary smiled. Summer Rose touched her arm. They laughed. His mother touched her cheek. He gave a silent thanks for his decision to marry her, a lump rose in his throat.

When his mother's entourage left and Mary and Emmett whisked off to try the polka Daniel whispered, "What on earth did you say to Mary? My Mother?"

Summer smiled smugly. "I just told Mary I thought her lucky, that Emmet seemed both kind and handsome." She smiled again. "I told her, too I could tell Emmett was besotted with her. She liked that. And I just smiled a lot at your mother and agreed with her."

He kissed her, dancing her toward the entrance. "Thank you. Leave your hoop with Amelia. It folds up, doesn't it? We'll walk home."

They moved toward the hall leading to the coatroom, her arm tucked in his. "I liked Mary." She said. "She's nice and pretty."

"Would I pick any other kind of girl?"

She wrinkled her nose. "Your taste is impeccable, but does she know the first thing about digging out a bullet or stitching a wound? You definitely made the best choice."

He couldn't help but grin at her. "You expect me to need a lot of stitching?"

"Indeed, I do. You *are* a soldier."

He stopped and kissed her right there in the entrance. "You are the best thing to ever happen to me. Now you just wait here. I'll find Amelia and ask her to help with that hoop then I'll fetch our coats."

CHAPTER 25

BLACKJACK

While Daniel retrieved their coats, Amelia helped Summer Rose remove the hoop and tuck up the excess material of the skirt. Hooks and eyes had been sewn into the back of the waist and seams of the dress for just that purpose.

"Harvey is deep into politics," Amelia muttered, then kissed them both. "If he wasn't, I'd go home with you. But he wants me to stay."

As he stepped outside, Daniel took his wife's hand. Fog, thick and unmoving, shrouded the streets. From the river near Foggy Bottom, someone set off fireworks, and they stood for a moment watching the bursts of lights over the Executive Mansion. She leaned into his arm as firecrackers sparked across the street.

At Pennsylvania Avenue he turned and headed toward 17th Street. Two soldiers patrolling on horseback trotted by, followed by a loud carriage of partygoers. As they strolled past Lafayette Park, Daniel pointed across the street to the President's House, barely visible in the mist.

"Hal and I dined there once, when we first came to Washington. We stopped Mrs. Lincoln's carriage when her horse bolted, so we were rewarded with an invitation. Dinner was okay, but nothing special. The dining room ceiling leaked. Mrs. Lincoln and Edwin Stanton were there as well as John Hay, one of the President's secretaries. Lincoln entertained us with his stories."

He relaxed a little as he led her by Blair House and Admiral Lee's House, then another park where more firecrackers popped and crackled, and acrid smoke blended with the mist. Three men staggered through the ornate iron gates and passed them.

A second too late, Daniel jerked alert, aware of their sobriety as the men swung around and came up from behind. One grabbed Summer Rose and dragged her into the park, as the other two came at him. In the dim gaslight he saw the glint of brass knuckles on one man's fist, and a lethal blackjack in the hand of the other. He grabbed Brass Knuckles by his shoulders, spun him around, and shoved him into the other boy. Reaching beneath his coat, Daniel pulled out his revolver and fired two shots into the air, but they did nothing to frighten away the attackers. Brass Knuckles swung at him and Blackjack moved to go behind him, but Daniel fired again. The round ripped into Brass Knuckles' jaw, jerking his head back, taking off a huge chunk. He staggered and wheeled, then fell face down, blood pooling in the snow. Daniel swung sideways with his pistol aimed at Blackjack, who dropped to his knees and held out the blackjack like an offering to the gods. Daniel grabbed it and smashed it across the boy's face. He had not stayed alive in countless bloody battles by not knowing how to fight.

Halfway up a little hill strewn with boulders and scrawny cedar trees, he made out Summer Rose, struggling with her attacker. He ran toward her, sliding in the snow. When he reached her she stood alone, still as a rock. One hand gripped her black cape tight to her chest, while her other held her knife at her side. Blood dripped from the blade and trailed into the rocks and pines. Daniel grabbed Summer and held her tightly against him. Seconds later, Jack McAllister, gun in hand, jumped from a cab and ran to them.

"Help her into the carriage." Jack ordered. "Go. Quickly. I'll take care of this." He motioned with his gun toward the still bodies of the hooligans and the trail of blood. Daniel did as he asked. "No questions. Get her out of here. I'll stop by the house later."

He closed the door behind them and rapped the side of the carriage. The driver's whip cracked, and the carriage lurched down the street.

Daniel fell to his knees before her, unsure of where to put his hands. "Where are you cut?"

He watched her swallow hard. A wide smear of blood ran across one cheek, widening as her tears reached it. She wiped the blade on one of her gloves, then lifted her skirt and returned her knife to its sheath. Splatters of blood and mud slashed her crinolines. Her breath came fast, her shoulders heaved.

She met his eyes. "I cut him. Daniel, it was so fast. I cut open his cheek, and I got him in the shoulder." She started to cry. "He had his hand between my legs. It's h-his blood all over me. I … I wasn't hurt. I will never-ever forget his face!"

Her cape fell open and his breathing stopped. The front of her gown had been sliced open from neck to pelvis, the skirt and crinolines shredded. She spread her arms and the layers of clothing, fell open. Her pretty corset had been sliced from top to bottom, every stitch of the front seam laid open, and her lace pantaloons hung, ripped half-off. The only thing covering her upper body was a thin, now bloody, chemise. She reached down and yanked off the pantaloons, which she dropped and stomped on. "I can't stand the smell."

"Blood gushed from him. I got him from his eye to his jaw." Her finger mimicked the slash.

Daniel stuffed the gloves and pantaloons in his pocket then he grabbed her hands, holding them for a moment. With his own hands shaking, he pulled her cape together. Her fingers closed over the edges, holding it in place now that the buttons were gone.

She stared into his eyes. "Da trained me, Daniel. I had my knife out, and I sliced him before he … He'll need someone to sew him up. I didn't even think. I meant for his throat. You believe me, don't you?"

Daniel sat up and sank back against th seat, letting out a loud breath. His voice came out a whisper. "Of course I believe you." His hands wouldn't quit shaking. He pulled out his handkerchief again and gently wiped her face, clearing away the remnants of the blood. "Thank God Jack arrived when he did. How the hell did he get there so fast?"

Daniel sat up quickly, a frown making deep furrows across his face. He glanced out the window as Jack's carriage pulled up to the house on 18th Street. He was confused. He hadn't heard Jack give the address. A tall man in a dark coat, hat, and black leather gloves opened the door and lowered the step. Daniel nodded thanks, stepped out of the carriage, then turned and helped Summer. He held her tight against his left side as the coachman moved ahead of them, up the porch steps. Racing hooves thundered down the street. Daniel's right hand still held his revolver. He led her to the stairs and inside. The first man, the one who had opened the carriage door, said, "I'll wait outside and watch the house until Major McAllister arrives." He bowed slightly. "I work for Allan Pinkerton."

Daniel nodded as things fell into place. He knew who Pinkerton was. A Scotsman by birth, Pinkerton was a private detective from Chicago who worked closely and secretly with President Lincoln. He'd rocketed to a position of power in wartime Washington.

Daniel walked Summer upstairs and met Becca on the landing. She rushed ahead, opening the door to their rooms. Summer walked silently into the room and sat on the edge of the bed, still clutching her coat.

Daniel holstered his revolver and kept his voice calm. "Becca, have Ned check all the windows and doors on the first floor. Make sure everything is locked up tight. Also, ask him to heat the boiler. And please bring up a few glasses and ice. Summer Rose's brother, Major McAllister, will be here shortly. You or Mr. Stone, please escort him here. Thanks Becca."

Becca, wide-eyed, glanced at Summer Rose and ran from the room.

"Would you help me, Daniel?"

He removed her cloak and folded it on the bed beside her. Without it, the enormity of the attack hit them, and he felt sick with both rage and relief. He stood behind her, helping her peel off the ruined dress, the slashed corset, and the bloody chemise. Nausea rose in his throat, and he tossed the mess onto the closet floor. Her ruined slippers, her stockings, and the gloves and pantaloons from his pocket followed. As he removed her pearls, he couldn't help staring at her thigh, where four claw marks spread across the skin along the outside of her knee.

She unstrapped the knife and sheath, placing them on the dressing table. So sweet, so lethal. He picked up the corset again and eyed the clean cut. The knife had been razor sharp.

"God, Rosie. He could have killed you."

He pulled a clean robe from its hanger and draped it over his arm, trying not to notice the pink water in the basin. He held the fresh wrapper and, as she found the sleeves, his arms slid around her. She turned around and reached beneath his great coat and jacket, laying her cheek against his shirt. "I still want a bath, but I wanted his blood off me. Hold me, please, for just a moment."

He held her tight to his chest, kissing the top of her head. After a minute, she backed up. He slipped the blackjack into his trouser pocket and dropped the corset on the closet floor.

Her eyes narrowed. "Daniel, that man had sliced open corsets before. His face … He knew exactly what to do. He just didn't expect to run into Micah McAllister's daughter."

A tap sounded at the door. Daniel pulled the door to the closet closed. When he opened the door to the hall, he took the drink tray from Becca as she barged past him, running to Summer Rose. "What happened? There's blood on the stairs."

Summer hugged Becca, backing her away from the closet. She kissed her cheek. "Yes, Becca, but we're safe. My brother will be here shortly. And now I'm absolutely starved," she said, hoping to distract her. She maneuvered Becca toward the door. "I'm going to take a quick bath. I can manage myself. Would you make us a little tray of those open-faced bacon, onion, and melted cheese sandwiches you make?"

"Where are the others?"

"Still at the hotel. When they return, Amelia will ask about us."

Daniel made a motion as if to seal his lips. "Just tell her we're back. We don't need everyone running in here asking a million questions. Ask Mr. Stone to do the same. You know how this house is a cauldron of gossip."

As Daniel fixed two drinks, he said, "You can see we're both fine, but precautions are necessary. I'm counting on you, Becca. I don't want the others upset tonight. And I don't want our names in the headlines of tomorrow's papers."

CHAPTER 26

THE BLOODY CORSET

Half an hour later they heard laughter, thumping, boisterous voices, and giggles on the stairs, then doors opening and closing. A calm Becca knocked and carried in a plate of small sandwiches and another of cookies. She set the plates beside the drinks tray.

"Your brother is here, too. I took him into the kitchen." She nodded toward the sandwiches. "I'll bring him up as soon as I'm sure the others are settled. No one saw him except Mr. Stone and Ned. The other man left." She opened the door then glanced back over her shoulder. "Your brother's a gentleman. He warned me about the gossip, too."

Daniel had cleaned and reloaded his revolver while Summer bathed. Now he laid it with the blackjack beside his glass of bourbon on the mantle. He knelt before her with his back to the fire, examining her thigh and dressing the wound with a tincture of iodine and her father's ointment.

"Watch that. Don't let it fester. Leave it open for tonight. I'll ask Ray to check it tomorrow." He nodded toward the drink he'd fixed her. "Drink some. It's medicine."

"You're bossy."

A little of the tension left him. "This is paybacks for that god-awful tea you made me drink?" He touched her cheek. "You look lovely despite all of this and smell heavenly."

Her ice blue, silk peignoir fell in soft folds as she picked up the glass. "Thank you." She sipped the dark liquid then sniffed it. "Is this a different kind of whiskey? It's not so bad."

She took another tentative sip and patted his hand. "I'm less upset than you might expect. I killed a bear once. With a knife. You know it isn't hard to kill a man when he's trying to kill you. You told me that. Tonight was no different. I knew what he was after. His hand ..." She took another quick sip. "I had no qualms about slashing him. I'd have killed him, too."

A soft tap sounded. Daniel said. "Come in."

Jack entered with Nip and Tuck. The dogs yipped and howled and made a beeline to their mistress. Summer stared at Jack as they settled, confused. Her brother, still tall and lean, now stood straight and displayed no ticks or head bobs. What happened?

He came around the end of the sofa, shook hands with Daniel, then sat beside her. He squeezed her hand, and unexpected tears filled her eyes. The back of her throat ached. His hand jerked as if burned, and he motioned to her drink.

"Would you mind fixing me one of those, Daniel? It has been quite a night." He crossed an ankle over his knee. "I'm so grateful you were there to protect my sister. Keeping your revolver handy is a good idea." He picked her hand up again and held it. This time no rush of emotion came, but his voice was hushed. "Thank heavens you're okay. We lost his trail. I'm sorry. I have men guarding the house."

Daniel handed a drink to Jack and set the tray of sandwiches on a small table in front of the couch. "Protect her? I may need protection *from* her. She killed a bear?"

Jack let go of her hand and settled into the sofa. "Slit the poor beast's throat. Caught him right under his jaw." He swept his fingers across his own throat in demonstration. "She was covered with blood. Da took off her boots and threw her, kicking and screaming, into the lake." He shook his head, his lips curled at the memory. "Good Lord, were you angry." He squinted at Daniel. "I take it you haven't yet seen her temper."

Daniel straddled a wooden chair next to Summer, and he leaned his forearms across its back. A slow smile played across his face. "I look forward to it, as long as she isn't angry with me.

"Now Major, I'm curious about something. How did you manage to be Johnny-on-the-Spot tonight?" He reached over and took her hand, squeezing it once. "Oh, and by the way, I slashed that man."

She stiffened.

His eyes flashed a warning.

But Jack wasn't stupid. "You're wise. I planned to suggest that you did the damage." Jack patted her knee. "No sense sharing your skill with a knife with the world, or, for that matter, letting the world know you were even attacked."

He turned to Daniel. "The one you shot is dead. We have the one you clobbered. He's in Capitol Prison. The other one, the one Summer slashed got away. We know a little about him. His name is Hobbs, Carlton Hobbs. His uncle was once Lieutenant Governor of Maryland; however, his mother's people came from South Carolina. He's a rebel to the core. We've been watching him for the last six months."

Jack chose another sandwich from the tray and ate it in one bite. His eyes flicked toward his sister. "I can see the questions lining up in your eyes, Summer."

He settled back and cleared his throat. "You must admit, Summer, you're unusual. We both are. There's no point in trying to explain our odd family to anyone who hasn't seen the valley, heard the stories about our parents." He nodded to Daniel. "How many girls do you know who receive a knife for their fourth birthday? How many can load a shotgun by the time they're five?

"If people hear about tonight, someone, somehow, will construe that you brought this attack upon yourself." He sipped his drink and sighed. "Your dress was cut too low or too short. You didn't conduct yourself with propriety. Who knows? Neither your husband nor I want you held up to public scrutiny. Washington may not burn its women at the stake, but this city can cut you off at the knees both socially and politically. Trust me. Your husband's career could be ruined as well as your reputation."

Jack continued. "Hobbs is up to his eyeballs in blood sports: cock fighting, dog fighting, and every other vice the city offers. He doesn't just gamble, he organizes the fights, breeds the dogs, make the fights spectacular. It's truly sick. People pay to watch the killing of mangled animals." Jack reached down and petted the dogs. "At the beginning of the war he operated in the District of Columbia. Recently he moved all the blood sports except the cock fighting into Virginia."

He ticked off the details on his fingers. "We know he's in cahoots with several of the brothels, procuring girls. His weapon of choice is a knife, and he's been known to undress women with one." His eyes drilled into his sister. "Did he slit your clothing?"

She bit her lip and nodded.

"May I see your things?"

She went to the closet and brought back the corset and the dress, still rolled in a ball. He shook out both articles, then looked at Daniel. "Our father was the best knifeman I've ever known. He trained all of us. Colin and William were good." He pointed to his sister. "But she's the best of the four of us." He held up the cream-colored corset, embroidered with dainty pink roses, and now stiffening with drying blood. "I'd never attempt this. Do you have something I could stuff this into?"

She headed out to the hall linen closet, returned with a pillowcase, and gave it to Jack.

"Did he violate you?"

Daniel stood abruptly; his wooden chair toppled over. "No, he did not. Do you need to know all this?"

"Easy, Colonel." Jack held up his hands while Daniel righted the chair and sat back down, still seething. "The thing is, we haven't made this public knowledge, but we know of twenty-seven girls and women who have been raped since the war started. Some were murdered. All were poor women who lived in Murder Bay: whores, serving girls, scullery maids, young, homeless widows. Some weren't yet fourteen years old. We found a sixteen-year-old girl last month in the

Haymarket, gutted like a fish and buried in a manure pile. The horrors make the hair on the back of my neck stand up." He took a sip of his drink and turned to his sister. "You know about Murder Bay, don't you?"

"Yes, Daniel warned me, and so did Harvey and Ray."

Jack said, "Murder Bay houses 450 brothels. You know what a brothel is, don't you?"

Her big eyes grew enormous. "Yes, Daniel explained that term, too."

"We estimate there are about 7500 whores housed in that area. A few brothels are quite elegant, the rest are ... they range from functional shelters to tarpaper shacks to abandoned crates."

He took another sip of his drink. "Hobbs' fingers are everywhere from cockfights to providing girls for certain officers' private parties. He moves in interesting circles."

Jack inched to the edge of the couch, his words came faster, and his voice cracked. "In late November, an eight-year-old girl was abducted, the daughter of a sergeant in the Home Guard. She was an exceptionally beautiful child. We suspect the same gang. Good sources reported someone bid in the thousands for her at a midnight auction held aboard a yacht anchored off Alexandria." His eyes slid to Summer and he swallowed hard. "They bid, you understand, for ..." He snapped his fingers. "She's gone. Evaporated."

Summer sucked in through her teeth, but Jack's voice stayed calm. "They're not finished with you, Summer. Carlton Hobbs will demand revenge for tonight. We followed his blood for a block. Where did you slice him?"

She made a slashing motion with her hand from her eye to ear then sunk the imaginary blade into her shoulder.

Jack nodded and patted her knee. "One of our snitches heard your name on the street. That's why I followed you. But I never imagined they'd touch a colonel's wife."

Daniel jumped to his feet, horrified, catching the chair before it toppled. "You used her as *bait*? Why in hell didn't you at least tell me? I'd never have walked home ... Christ, Jack!"

Jack put up his hand again. "I didn't think he'd attack. You're right. I'm sorry. But I also knew she could take care of herself."

"Don't even consider such a thing again. "Who in the hell do you work for?"

Jack's spine stiffened. "Washington is a cesspool. Most of the magistrates, the marshals, the police are Confederate sympathizers. And the influx of soldiers and former slaves into the city has overwhelmed them. I represent the army. My immediate commander is General Heintzelman. I work with Allan Pinkerton. And President Lincoln."

Daniel refilled Jack's glass then handed it back to him. He didn't resume his seat, but studied the fire for a long moment. Finally he turned, one hand still on the mantle. "Who funds this evil? Who paid the money? Who pockets a commission? Who owns the yacht?

"What was her name?" he asked quietly.

Jack head bobbed up. "Who?"

"The little girl? The sergeant's daughter?"

"Elizabeth Darling. Her parents called her Liza." He took a sip of whiskey, but his words came out raspy. "I hope she's dead."

Daniel set his glass down with a thunk. The ice rattled. "If they spent that much money on her, I guarantee you she's not dead."

No one spoke for a long moment. Finally, Summer asked, "They'll sell her over and over, won't they?"

Jack nodded and stood, then leaned down and kissed her cheek. "Take care, little sister. Keep these beasts nearby. I posted guards." He picked up the pillowcase with its bloody contents and shook hands with Daniel. "You still don't have orders?"

"No, neither does Hal."

"I'll let myself out. I'll be back in the morning."

CHAPTER 27

LATE NIGHT AT THE WAR DEPARTMENT

Jack crossed Pennsylvania Avenue to the War Department Building. The fog swirled eerily around the gaslights. The guard opened both doors as Jack wiped his boots on the wire mat. He then hung his coat on one of the hooks inside the door. At the far end of the cavernous area he made out President Lincoln, standing at the entrance to the cipher room where he could just see. John Hay, one of Lincoln's secretaries, and Secretary of War, Edwin Stanton. They huddled over a table by the telegraphs. He was not surprised. None of these men slept much. Lincoln checked the telegram flimsies several times a day. Jack waved to the men.

Lincoln raised his long arm. He flicked his wrist and motioned Jack over to the table. "Hello Jack. You're just the man we need. Would you be so kind as to key in a message? Archie stepped out for a minute, and none of us can figure out this new contraption."

Jack nodded to each of the men, laid the pillowcase on the floor at his feet, and took the paper from the President's hand. He said, "It's another dispatch to Major General Grant in Chattanooga."

As Jack set about concentrating on the device, John Hay spotted the blood on the pillowcase, picked it up, and dumped the contents of the bag on another table. He lifted up the corset. "Ooh-la-la. To what gorgeous creature does this piece of apparel belong?" He noticed the knife cut and blood. "Good God, is she okay?"

Stanton shook out the mutilated and bloody dress. All three heads turned to Jack.

"Give me a minute to send this and I'll explain." He flashed a sardonic grin. "I'm not an axe murderer. Those are my sister's things. She was attacked only a few blocks from here."

Lincoln took the corset from his secretary. He ran a long boney finger down the center seam that had been sliced open. "Is this the sister who lived by herself after your parents and brothers died? The one who hunts and throws a knife so well? What's her name?"

Jack nodded. "Summer—Summer Rose. Just a minute, Sir." The click of the telegraph echoed eerily with the President's footsteps as he paced about the room.

While Jack worked the key, the President took the dress from Edwin Stanton and examined it, too, shaking his head.

Jack keyed in the last line and signed it A. Lincoln. He turned in his swivel chair, he suddenly felt as if his bones had turned to mush. Exhausted, too weak to stand, he looked up at the three men. He started to force himself to rise, but

Lincoln patted his shoulder and pulled up a chair opposite him. He folded his long frame into it. "Take your time, Jack. Summer Rose is your only living relative, isn't she? Is she okay? What a pretty name."

Jack nodded. President Lincoln was the closest thing he'd had to a father since Antietam. His kindness, now, threatened to overwhelm Jack. He felt close to tears, but would rather die a thousand deaths than cry in front of these men. He took a deep breath and told them about the attack on Summer.

"She's married now to Colonel Charteris, one of Buford's cavalry officers. They live over on 18th Street. He killed one of them, wounded the other one, a third is still at large."

Lincoln nodded. So did Stanton. Lincoln said, "He and his friend, St. Clair, I believe, stopped Mother's carriage at the start of the war. They came to dinner. Big fellow. Remember him Edwin? They were great conversationalists. Well spoken. Mother liked both of them."

Stanton scowled. "St. Clair and Charteris. Conversationalists? They should be. Their fathers are Philadelphia lawyers. I've fought court battles with them—too many times to count."

John Hay, who made no bones about his frequent visits to the brothels nodded. "Hal St. Clair, I know him, ran-in to him at Maggie Hall's. He's quite the poker player. The ladies like him."

Jack felt better now. "I planned to ask you, Sir, if I could use—borrow them, so to speak, on that matter we're working on, with the girl. Since his wife was attacked Colonel Charteris is very motivated to apprehend these rapists and with General Buford's death they're at loose ends."

One corner of Mr. Lincoln's mouth curled up and an eyebrow arched. "You want to borrow a couple of cavalry colonels?"

In the background, the Secretary of War's eyes bulged.

Jack nodded to both men. A smile crossed his lips. "I'll give them back in the spring."

Lincoln chuckled. "Please don't let General Pleasanton hear you use the term 'borrowing'. He's very possessive of his colonels."

John Hay picked up the corset. "We should invite them to dinner again. I'm sure Mrs. Charteris is a fascinating conversationalist, too."

Lincoln eyed the corset, his forefinger gingerly touched the embroidered roses. "I'm sure we'd all give her our rapt attention."

At the 18th Street House, Daniel took the dogs downstairs when he went to check the doors and windows. He spoke with the guards and allowed the dogs the run of the house. He brought up a bucketful of coal when he returned to their room. Once upstairs, he changed into his black silk robe and banked the fire for a slow burn. He slid his revolver under the sofa and lay down with his head in his wife's lap. She ran her fingers through his hair and massaged his forehead and temples.

"That feels wonderful. I should be massaging your forehead, though."

"Shush. Just enjoy it."

He closed his eyes and let his body, coiled as tight as a clock spring, relax under her touch. The warmth of the fire lulled him into a half sleep, then dropped him into a nightmare. In his mind's eye, her bloody corset fell open, except instead of the corset it was her chest, slashed open like the carcass of a lamb. His heart slammed against his ribs and he jerked awake.

He rolled onto one side, facing the fire, and stared at the orange-red coals. Fear, raw and ugly, sent cold sweat to his skin. He slipped one arm beneath her knees and closed his eyes, resting his lips on the ice blue silk draped over her legs, trying to banish the flashing images.

Blood didn't frighten him. That she came inches from being raped and killed choked him.

Sex was never far from Daniel's mind, though he rarely thought about it. Desire, lust, sat behind a valve of some sort; he could turn it on or off, but it was always there. He understood the driving force. He understood, too, its power, how sex fueled invention, competition, and ambition. Everything from a nail to a howitzer spoke of sex. However, Hal and he, even as wild and thoughtless as they had been, were always in control. What kind of man needs sex so badly they could hurt a child? What possesses a man to throw a woman down in the snow, then rape and kill her? Hide her body in a manure pile?

He'd never considered these questions before. He'd unconsciously known the power of sex. Like the tide, or sap running in the trees, it simply *was*, and nobody stopped it. He lay with his head in her lap, and the irony that his body ached for her didn't escape him.

He roughly pulled her down beside him and kissed her, then rolled to the floor, cushioning and crushing her at the same time. He kissed her with the consuming need that had built all evening. The thought of losing her filled him with fear, and desire shot through him like a roaring stream. Her body arched, fitted against him, tried to keep pace with his passion but failed.

Spent, he lay in the firelight, naked and breathless. He kissed the hollow of her shoulder, his mind a puddle. He didn't know how their robes had come off. His was under her, but his fingers found her peignoir and he snapped it open. The silk fluttered over them, soft as a gossamer blue mist, sending fresh shivers through his skin. He rested his cheek against her breasts and breathed in the scent of her as her heart pounded beneath his ear. With great care, he spread his body over hers and holding both her hands in one of his, stretched her arms above her head. He kissed one breast, tasting it, savoring it then did the same with the other. She whimpered and shuddered and half-heartedly tried to break free. Ever so slowly he moved. The fire hissed and crackled, glazed their bodies in red-gold light. The pale blue silk of her peignoir flowed over them like a silent waterfall.

"This," he said as he ran his tongue along her collarbone to the hollow of her throat and moved his body with painstaking slowness, "is for you." Three times, with control, which surprised even him, he took her to the edge, each time muffling her cries with his mouth. Even when she shook and bit his shoulder, he held back. Only when she voiced unladylike expletives and *serious* threats of what her Bowie knife could do, did he let loose all his pent up passion.

Beneath him, glistening with a fine sheen of sweat, she jerked and screamed into his throat. He smiled and kissed her again.

After a long moment, he said, "I love you more than you can ever imagine. You're my sun and my moon and all the stars."

She kissed his neck, and the logs on the fire shifted and crackled. "You'll never love me as much as I love you."

He hugged her tightly. "Oh Rosie, I wouldn't take any wagers on that."

Later, in bed, he held her most of the night and slept very little. Once he knew she was deeply asleep, he checked the house again. He stepped onto the upstairs porch and spoke to the guards, who assured him all was quiet. He brought the dogs back to the room.

At daylight, when he heard rustling throughout the house, he and Summer knocked on Harvey and Amelia's door. The couple sat by a table near the fire, drinking coffee. Harvey wore a red silk robe that matched his velvet slippers. Amelia, fresh and crisp like always, poured them coffee—only she would have china cups ready for guests at this hour. Harvey looked over a newspaper, spectacles on the end of his nose.

Daniel pulled two more chairs to their table and glanced at Summer. Jack had advised them to not disclose Summer's part, but earlier they decided to hold nothing back from Amelia and Harvey. The couple exchanged dismayed glances and Amelia took Summer Rose's hand, holding it tightly in her own.

"Oh my dear! Are you all right?"

Summer nodded. "I am now. My brother's an army major who works with Allan Pinkerton," she said. "He posted guards around the house overnight. He helped us and plans to stop by around ten this morning. Would you like to speak with him?"

Harvey lowered his chin. His great shaggy eyebrows pushed toward the center of his forehead. "I would. I appreciate the guards. The two girls who come in daily?" He glanced at Amelia. "Perhaps we should see if they can stay here. Let us know when he returns."

Amelia reached across the table and touched Daniel's arm. "You know, none of this can get out. They'd ruin her. You, too."

Jack arrived at ten sharp and met with Harvey, Amelia, Daniel, Summer, Hal, and Ray in the library. Mr. Stone had lit the sconces and started a crackling blaze in the fireplace.

"We'll keep the guards here indefinitely," Jack said. "and I'll see that the daily maids are moved into the house. I think you're wise, Sir, and ..." He glanced around the room, meeting the eyes of all the men. "The women should have an escort at all times when they leave the house. Sergeant Roth is very capable. He'll arrange it." He pointed to his sister. "I want you to stay inside for the next week or so. Don't give them a target."

Harvey winked at Summer Rose. "We must give the city's criminal element a fighting chance." He reached across the table and squeezed her hand. "I'm very glad you're okay."

CHAPTER 28

OLD CAPITOL PRISON

When all except Hal, Daniel, and Summer Rose left the library, Jack told them the gist of his conversation with the President. He knew better than to mention that the President or anyone even saw the corset. To the group at the library table, he said, "Trust me, gentlemen, while inspecting brothels is not even remotely pleasant, it's much better duty than inventorying boxes of firing pins or patrolling along the Rappahannock in the dead of winter. Come with me now. I'm on my way over to Capitol Prison to question the one you hit with the blackjack."

As the group dispersed, Daniel nodded. "Let me get my coat and send Ned to fetch Chester and Dulcey. Come on Hal."

When they left, Jack eased into a chair beside his sister.

"Keep him safe. He's my heart, Jack."

Jack took her hands. "I'll make a bargain with you. You take care of yourself. I'll watch over him. You're the only relative I have. I don't ever want to be as frightened as I was last night when I saw you holding that knife with the blood dripping off the blade. I thought…I thought it was your blood…my God, Summer, you're all I have left."

Capitol Prison had been built in 1814 after the British burned the original Capitol Building during the War of 1812. Used for about ten years as the Capitol until the original building could be rebuilt, the red brick structure now housed the usual assortment of thieves, murderers, and prostitutes, along with insubordinate Yankees, Confederate spies, the likes of Belle Boyd, Antonio Ford, and Rose Greenhow. Daniel and Hal had ridden by the prison countless times, but now was the first time they'd stepped inside. Dark, damp, smelling of wet straw, unwashed bodies, both animal and human waste, the building gave them shivers. They'd brought the boy to them hooded, and, even hooded and manacled with his hands splayed on the tabletop and his feet shackled to the floor, he wore a chip the size of Ohio on his shoulder. The three men stood in the shadows across from the boy. Jerry Cox was his real name, only nineteen years old and already well-known in Washington's prison system. Captain Fish, one of the wardens of Capitol Prison, had told them as he led them to the interrogation room, "He's a tough little nut, slippery as an eel, and mean. Keep him in chains."

Daniel stepped forward and took the interrogator's seat. They'd spoken with Jack, and, in addition to Daniel's rage at Summer's assault, he and Hal had more experienced extracting information from Confederate spies than either cared to claim.

Daniel withdrew from his pocket the blackjack, a seven inch baton, this one a flexible mesh leather stick packed with fine gauge buckshot, made to fit easily into a man's hand. Used with strength it could dent a skull with a single blow. Daniel motioned for Hal to stand behind the prisoner. When situated Daniel nodded. Hal whipped off the hood. The boy's eyes were slits and surrounded by green-black flesh, his face splotched with dried blood. He took a minute to adjust to the light then squinted up at Daniel. From the look that flashed on his face, he recognized him, but he managed a brazen shrug.

Daniel pressed a knuckle between the boy's eyes, all the time bouncing the blackjack in his other hand. Hal held Jerry's head still. Daniel said, "Must hurt like hell." In a swift one-two move, Daniel brought the blackjack down on the first joint of Jerry's right thumb, crunching the bones, then swung it up so it smashed a glancing blow to his already damaged nose.

The boy screamed.

Jack did too, "Jesus Christ, Daniel. Don't kill him."

The words hissed out of Daniel's mouth. "The only reason this vermin isn't dead is he has information I want. My wife came within inches of being raped and sliced open last night. Give me a reason not to kill you."

Blood streamed from the boy's face, dripped down his chin, and onto his mangled thumb. Tears, which must have burned like hell, made white streaks down his cheeks. Daniel swung the blackjack again, this time smashing the other thumb.

The boy screamed again.

"You have eight more fingers, ten toes, and a mouthful of teeth, and I have all day. Talk you little worm."

He stood, nodded to Jack, and stepped partially into the shadows.

Black clouds rolled over the city as they rode by the address Jerry Cox had given them. The high-class brothel, which housed, according to Jerry, expensive whores, and boys and girls who brought top dollar in the world of child prostitution, was not in Murder Bay, but in an out-of-the-way little known section of the city bordering Georgetown. The three story stone mansion sat on a hill surrounded by a couple acres of woods and lawns. The madam, Pearl Mason, Jerry told them, was the premier courtesan of the city with a few select clients.

The three of them reconnoitered the area noting access by both the street and alley.

"We need a plan. I don't want anything to slip thru my fingers," said Jack. "Go home, get some rest. We not only need to take care of Mrs. Mason, we have 450 brothels in Murder Bay to inspect. I'll come by the house tomorrow at 8:00 in the morning. I want to explain to the women what you'll be doing."

Hal snorted then said, "This I want to hear."

Jack's talk went surprisingly well. No one fainted or screeched outrage, but at breakfast two days later, Grace, out of nowhere, asked the men. "How are the brothel rooms decorated? Is it true they have crystal chandeliers in the bedrooms?"

Every one of the men apparently felt a need to butter their toast at that moment, concentrating hard on getting it exactly right. The drone of whispers from the kitchen ceased. Not so much as a pot banged.

Grace went on. "We know what you're doing and we're all curious. I think at the very least you could tell us what those places are like."

Hal put down his napkin and cleared his throat. "Some have crystal chandeliers. However, Maggie Hall's place is more like a men's club: leather chairs, mahogany tables, dark walls, an elegant, marble staircase."

Daniel had only been inspecting brothels for two days and he hoped to never see another one. He remembered not only the elegant houses, but also the sex cribs that serviced the troops with regimental precision. Twenty-some cots lined along a wall, each separated by a filthy blanket or sheet, girls taking on five boys an hour, beefy bouncers prodding the slow or timid.

"Are they open … for business … in the morning?" asked Grace.

Daniel asked for someone to pass the jam. Harvey studied his soft-boiled egg. Amelia looked excessively pale.

"What do the women wear?" asked Summer.

Hal snorted. "Clothes. Most of the time.

Summer ignored him and fired off more questions. "Do they serve food? How many *girls* are housed at the Blue Goose? How many at Madame Russell's Bake Oven? And who on earth made up those names?"

"Is there entertainment? I mean other than ..." asked Amelia.

--➤≫≪⋖--

That night in their room, Summer sat on the edge of the bed, watching Daniel undress. "Do they make big eyes and beckon you to them?" She let no emotion at all show in her voice, but he saw, even in the dim light from the candles, a flare of jealousy spark in her expression.

His eyes teased. "I tear their arms off me, and smile back at them and tell them I have the most gorgeous, sensuous woman in America for my wife, and if they're not careful, she'll find them and cut out their hearts with her Bowie knife. Maybe their tongues. I tell them you strap it to your calf when you're not holding it in your teeth."

He folded her into his arms and rolled across the bed. "Oh, sweetheart, some of the women do offer themselves, but you can't imagine how vile the cheap brothels are." He told her of the sex cribs, the filthy curtains, the rancid smells. "The soldiers, kids, old men, crusty sergeants, waiting, lined up all the way down the stairs and around the house. Fifty-cent whores, they're called. It's all about money. The girls are exhausted. I doubt any would look at us cross-eyed without first establishing the price."

The following morning Amelia said, "I heard John Hay frequents those places. You'd think the President's secretary would be uncomfortable if he were to meet the congressmen and senators he works with during daylight hours in Maggie Hall's house after hours."

"You'd think so," said Daniel. "But in the better houses, the atmosphere is much like a club. I think many go there to rub elbows with the powerful. Some men simply stay downstairs, have a drink, a plate of oysters, or pâté and crackers, then leave. You can order a steak or chops or a cup of snapper soup. Piper-Heidsieck champagne corks are always popping. They drink French wines and Scotch whiskey. Maggie Hall employs a chef. You want an appropriation or a promotion, some kind of deal, Maggie's is the place to make it."

He nodded to Hal. "Some have roulette tables, and there's always a card game. We hold Hal back."

"Do they change the sheets between sessions?" Fanny asked.

Daniel shrugged. He doubted the sex cribs even used sheets.

Jack found out—from John Hay of all people—that on the 22nd of December, Mrs. Mason planned a discreet, invitation-only, reception from 8:00 to 11:00 in the evening. "I cannot attend. My reputation precedes me, but you two are not only unknown you're the type she'd like as clients: young, good looking, and rich. John has finagled invitations for you both and will meet you at Pennsylvania and K Street at 9:00 o'clock."

"I'm not stepping into a whorehouse reception, no matter how elegant or important, without telling Summer Rose. Don't ask me to deceive her that way."

"Good Lord. My sister married a man with scruples. Let me talk to her."

Jack found her alone in the kitchen copying recipes and apprised her of the situation.

Surprisingly she agreed. "I trust Daniel. He knows where I am." She smiled with all her imp in action. "He can't get better," she whispered, "… there." With a very serious face, she continued, "I've found if one gives anything full concentration, one becomes very skilled at whatever it is, whether it's throwing a knife, knitting, or what happens between the sheets with your husband."

Jack blushed to his collar. He was so very glad she was married.

After dinner of the 22nd, Summer lit the library fireplace and curled up on the leather sofa with *Les Miserable*. A pot of tea and teacup sat on the end table. When Daniel, decked out in his dress uniform with sword and sash, came to say goodbye, she stood up and kissed his cheek. "Don't sit down and ruin those knife edge creases in your trousers. You know how hard Becca worked to get them there."

He chucked her under the chin and kissed her forehead. "Remember, I love you."

The minute the door to the courtyard closed, she ran to the window and looked down on them mounting their horses; she wished she'd kissed him hard and said something less inane than the comment about his trousers.

CHAPTER 29

THE HOUSE ON THE HILL AT HAMMER ROAD

John Hay, in evening clothes and high spirits, met them at the appointed time; they rode the few blocks to the house on Hammer Road. Chester took an immediate dislike to the groom so Daniel sent Hal and John Hay ahead into the house and walked Chester along the fine gravel path to the stone stable. He found a young black boy Chester did like who showed them to a stall. Commodore, his father's horse, stood in a stall two down from Chester.

He wasn't surprised that his father was here, but he felt awkward. How does one greet their father at a whorehouse? *I'm certainly not here for sex. Perhaps he has other reasons, too.* "What the hell," he muttered as he made his way to the house. "I hope the whiskey's good."

It was. And the infamous Mrs. Mason was stunning and lush as the room surrounding her. She stood near the blazing fireplace while the room hummed with chatter and glittered with the light of hundreds of candles. A towering Christmas tree stood in one corner, a bar in another. At least fifty men in evening clothes or dress blues surrounded her, all like gulls in the wind pointing to the prize. Before stepping down into the large octagonal room, Daniel paused in the archway. A silence hushed the room, and she motioned him over as if he were an old friend, and led him to the Christmas tree.

The exotic scent of spices and tropical flowers drifted about her; her skin glowed the color of coffee with cream and a hint of pale pink. Her enormous chatoyant eyes shone silver, her thick, dark hair was drawn back into a mass of curls at the nape of her neck. She was beautiful. Dressed in a heavy ivory silk dress with a triple strand of pearls, she smiled at him, made him feel a little lightheaded. The points of her breasts pressed against the taut material of her bodice. Whores, the good ones, he'd learned in just two days, knew exactly how to smile and what to say, how to make a man feel like a prince. She was lovely, as gracious as Amelia. She extended her hand, and the diamond and ruby bracelet—the one Summer had found in his father's carriage —slid to her wrist.

He took her hand and bowed slightly, not kissing it. The bracelet had been as effective as a bucket of ice water. "I am Daniel Charteris, but I believe you know that already."

She half smiled, her eyes twinkling and still holding his hand, she responded. "I'm Pearl Mason, and I believe you know that, also." Her speech held just a tinge of the deep South, and her laughter tinkled like silver coins spinning on marble.

His stomach turned over, remembering what Jerry Cox had told them. *She runs a dozen top-dollar girls through her house, but always keeps a kid or two for the truly sick. Charges a fortune for them, too. Gold. Always gold for the kiddies. She looks real sweet, acts like a lady, but she's evil. She trains the kids—boys and girls—good on how to please a man. Or a woman. Calls them her little golden geese. When their peachy smooth skin grows hair she ships them over to Murder Bay to the crib joints. She owns a number of those. By then the girls are addicts. The boys...become whatever they can to survive.*

A waiter brought him a glass of bourbon neat on a silver tray. He took it and saluted her. "I noticed my father's horse in your stable. Is he here?"

"He was." She turned and surveyed the room. Her wide mouth held the hint of a smile. "He may have left." She shrugged coyly. "Does it matter?"

She looked up; his attention followed. "He may be upstairs. A number of pleasures await a man up there." The eight-sided room soared three stories with circling balustrades, open hallways, and dozens of closed doors. Liza was probably behind one of those doors. Finding the girl would not be easy, and with a sudden sickness in his gut, he knew it would not be tonight.

He set his glass down on a little side table and said, "Excuse me, Mrs. Mason I must speak with Hal."

Anger flashed in her silver eyes. She was not used to being dismissed.

He found Hal near the bar. John Hay nodded to him then resumed his conversation with a Vermont businessman. Daniel looked about the room. He knew at least half the faces, the princes of the city. To Hal Daniel whispered, "I'm leaving. If I stay, I'll either get drunk or smack someone or both. Coming with me?"

Hal slowly shook his head. "I thought I'd try my luck at roulette, and the lady invited me for a private party later."

For a moment Daniel was speechless. "How in the hell did you managed that? You've only been here forty-five minutes."

Hal shrugged, arching his shaggy eyebrows. "Danny boy, my reputation or the size of my ..." he paused and then smiled, "bank account must have preceded me. And I brought gold."

"Christ Hal. I thought you quit the whores?" whispered Daniel as he grabbed another shot of bourbon from a passing waiter. He drank it in one swallow.

"Don't go getting righteous on me, Danny. My sweet little wife has been sick every evening since we've been married. I'm not blaming Fanny, but I'm no monk. He took another swallow of his drink. "It is what it is ... but then I'm not married to Summer Rose." Hal knocked back all of his drink.

Daniel turned and walked out of the room. He wanted to choke Hal. He was in the stable before he could take a deep breath.. While the stable boy saddled Chester, he walked over to Commodore. He ran his hand down the white forelock, fed him a sugar cube from his pocket. His anger toward Hal dissipated. He remembered his own reaction to Pearl Mason. Lust had grabbed hold of him until he saw the diamond bracelet. Who was he to judge?

The boy brought Chester over. He tipped him, then mounted and made his way through the city to his wife.

Sergeant Roth took Chester's bridle and nodded toward the stairs. He whispered, "She's been there since you left, Sir."

Summer was waiting for him, wrapped up in two shawls, with her dogs curled beside her. When he walked up to her, she stood, folded her arms around him, and kissed him about as passionately as one body could kiss another body. He swung her into his arms cradling her. "I want you, a bath, and a drink, and I'm not sure in what order. Let me shed these clothes—get the stink of that place off me—and I'll tell you about my evening. You must be cold." He looked at Nip and Tuck. "Come on boys, I know you'll want to hear this too."

They lay naked on the high bed. Hal, liquid and in a stupor, stretched and grinned. Beside him, Pearl smiled as well. She'd made all the right moves and had earned her hefty charge.

He touched her face. "You're very beautiful."

He noticed her peeking sideways at him. He knew women well enough to know Pearl had been surprised. She rolled over and leaned on her elbows, her eyes drifting appreciatively over his chest and lower. He felt his interest return.

She noticed, too. "I can tell you enjoy sex. Do you have a favorite … type?"

Hal gave her a lazy smile then sat so he could take a slow drink of brandy. "I don't have a type, so to speak." He weighted one of her breasts in his hand. "Gorgeous, sensuous brunettes who know how to move and please a man do just fine." His eyes surveyed her body, and he shrugged, knowing she wanted more of an answer. "Occasionally I appreciate a little diversity."

"Men? Boys?"

He laughed, spluttering a little of his Remy Martin. When he recovered, he dipped his finger in the brandy and outlined her lips. "Not my proclivity exactly. I like women, girls, blondes, brunettes, redheads, young gorgeous girls."

"A variety?" Her smile was wide. "I'm available, of course, but I can provide whatever you want. If I don't have it, I can find it for you."

"Expensive?"

"Depends." She slid on top of him and straddled his thighs, still fondling him.

"Tempt me."

"I have a little blond angel. Very young. Very delicious. Would you like a little rosebud?"

He flashed his eyes a little wider, but he didn't say anything. He grabbed her hips, lifted her and lowered her body onto his. "Time's a-flying, Miss Pearl. Less talk. I'd rather not think."

Daniel spent the night in his wife's arms. Silver moonlight, bright as sunlight, streamed through the curtains. Her skin melded into his, warm and silken; he couldn't touch her enough. Even now, her body still soft from their lovemaking and pressed along the length of him, he wanted her again. It amazed him. The honeymoon was over, and yet every time he touched her, brushed against her, he wanted her. He pressed his lips into the crook of her neck and shoulder, drinking in her scent as he fell asleep.

In the morning, everyone in the house knew Hal hadn't come home. Fanny came downstairs in her robe with swollen eyes, disheveled hair, and a sodden handkerchief. She checked all four levels of the house, and every time a horse rattled down the street, she ran to the window.

The big clock in the hall had just chimed nine when a note from Jack arrived. When Fanny saw it, the anxiety on her face melted like hot candle wax203

Happy at last, she dropped the note in the fireplace and trudged back up the stairs. "I need to sleep. I was so worried I don't think I slept a wink."

A lump of guilt settled in Daniel's stomach. He hated the lies, the games. He slipped his arm around Summer Rose's waist. "Would you like to spend the day with me?"

"Of course."

"Come upstairs and dress in your new culottes. I want you close to me. All day."

"Jack will fuss."

"I outrank him."

CHAPTER 30

NOT AS THEY SEEM

"She needs to get out of the house," he explained. "She'll be safe here."

Jack fluttered his hand. "Sit by the stove. Just stay out of trouble, Summer. I know you don't look for it, but trouble finds you."

She surveyed the room. It was basic, its raw wood walls and floor housing just three desks, three chairs, and a potbellied stove. She'd brought an extra saddle blanket, and now doubled it, using it as a cushion as she leaned against the wall near the stove. Snow had drifted, filling the lower corners of the windowpane. Through it, she could see downhill, toward the road.

After removing her black leather gloves, she opened her haversack and pulled out *Les Miserable*. She had just about finished it. Daniel brought over another saddle blanket to cover her legs. She looked up to thank him, and from the corner of her eye she noticed Jack's scowl. She wanted to stick her tongue out at him, but didn't.

Daniel and Jack conferred over ledgers and stacks of paper. She stayed in her nest until lunchtime, when Daniel unpacked Becca's ham and cheese sandwiches and pulled Hal's chair up to his desk. A trooper brought around a fresh pot of coffee.

Around two, she heard whistling and saw Hal hitch Dulcey beside Chester in the long lean-to. He sauntered, still whistling, into the room. A gust of icy wind blasted up a corner of her blanket and she shivered. As Hal closed the door, he spotted her and the whistling stopped. He appeared about as happy as Jack to see her. She smiled and pointed to the book.

"Just pretend I'm not here."

He dragged his chair to the other side of Daniel's desk and spent a good bit of time sketching in pencil, using a ruler. The two of them talked and pointed. Jack leaned into the conversation; she sat still, her nose buried in Dickens now that she finished *Les Miserable*, trying not to listen. But words snuck through. She heard *gold* and *eight o'clock* and *Liza*. After that, she couldn't help straining to listen. Then she heard her name, and Daniel let out an emphatic "No!"

Her brother said, "She'd be good with the girl, Daniel."

Jack motioned for her to come to Daniel's desk.

"We may have found Liza Darling. Hal, um, made arrangements to buy her for a few hours. You know what I mean, don't you?"

She nodded.

"Eight o'clock tonight. He's the first scheduled for her. Hal will go into the house and plans to pay two hundred in gold for two hours with the child. Hal's funding this transaction."

He cleared his throat. "When the opportunity is right, he'll either walk out the door with her or signal us with a gunshot. Daniel and I, and our soldiers, if necessary, will be prepared to go in and get her. One of us will carry the child outside to you. I think it is best to give her to a woman. You'll bring her back here, accompanied by two troopers, where Ray will meet you and examine the girl. We'll need to make several arrests."

He took a deep breath. "This operation is pure army. Liza is the daughter of an army sergeant, and I'm keeping the Pinkerton men out of it. The President wants it that way. I'm hoping she can see her parents tonight."

"Do you want a carriage or a horse?" asked Hal.

"She'll ride Chester," said Daniel, acquiescing to the plan. "He's fast, big, and sure-footed." His eyes riveted onto hers. "If you don't think you're able to do this, tell us now."

She shook her head. "I can do it. I agree. I think she'd be better with a woman, too."

Two sketches of the interior of a house lay on the table, and she picked them up, studying them closely. One was marked First Floor and the other, Second Floor. The drawings were detailed, showing entrances, staircases, beds, dressers, closets, bathrooms, windows, doorways, fireplaces, all done with meticulous care in Hal's perfect printing. The drawings were good. He must have some of Amelia's talent.

"This looks quite elegant."

Hal leaned forward, nodding. "It is. Oriental rugs, silk draperies, very much like an upper class home. I'm trying to figure out where a secret room might be."

Her eyes met Daniel's, and she knew in that instant that Hal had been nowhere near a bear baiting pit last night.

She smoothed her face and slid the papers back onto the desk. "Daniel, would you send a trooper for my long cloak? Is that possible? And Hal, consider wearing your great coat tonight. The cape is detachable. You could wrap the child in it."

Daniel swallowed hard and nodded. "I'll send Joe Roth. Is there anything else you'd like?"

"Yes. Please tell him to ask Becca for a pair of my socks."

He slipped an arm around her. "Right now, I'd like to ride with you over to Hammer Road, where the house is located. It's not far. I want you to see the lay of the land in the daylight."

He sent the sergeant on his mission and borrowed two horses from the soldiers. "We won't be close enough for anyone to recognize me, but someone might recognize big old Chester."

Her voice came out cold. "He was with that woman last night, wasn't he? The one selling the child? He wasn't hunting down a bear pit or whatever. Did you know where he was this morning when Jack sent that note?"

A blast of fine snow made its way up his sleeves and sent shivers down his spine. He didn't answer her until they crossed a large, snow-swept field, and came to a fence beside Pennsylvania Avenue, which, despite the blowing snow, was busy with traffic

"I knew last night."

Her face paled. "Oh, Daniel, I'm not sophisticated enough for all this intrigue. Would you do that? Would you sleep with a whore? Would you lie to me so blatantly, or have your friends deceive me?"

He removed his gloves and reached across the small space, touching her face. His thumb stroked her cheek. "I've been asking myself the same questions all day. I promised you I would never lie to you. The truth is, I don't know. I don't think I would or could." He laughed lightly and shook his head. "I couldn't stand that place last night."

She didn't smile as he dismounted and handed her his reins. The drifted snow was nearly to his knees. He placed his big hand on her boot. "This business is complicated. A little girl's life is at stake. I felt physically sick when Hal told me she was scheduled for two patrons tonight. They drug the child. What in the hell do they do with her for two hours? Christ, it makes me sick. She's Jill's age."

Despite the cold, her cheeks and neck burned, and she felt as if she couldn't breathe. She had wondered much the same thing—what did they do with the child—but he just didn't understand. The snow swirled around them.

"It won't happen, Rosie. Never." He lifted the top rail of the fence, set it aside, and turned to lead her horse across the fence row. "But …" He frowned. "If it did, would you want me to tell you?"

"*If it did?* You can stand there and say, 'It won't happen', then ask, 'If it did'?" She stood in the stirrups and dove headfirst at him, knocking him over into the deep snow. His hat flew off and he landed hard on his back, knocking the wind out of him as her teeth hit his brow. Blood trickled from her lip. She didn't seem to notice. She sat on his chest, her small-gloved fists pounded him, flying so fast he couldn't catch them. She stopped for a second, smeared the back of one hand on her cheek. He caught her hands.

Tears mingled with the blood. "Would I mind? Are you crazy? You are damned right I'd mind." A shadow fell over them.

"Colonel Charteris?" asked John Hay, his walrus moustache immediately identifying him. "Do you need some help?"

Still holding her wrists, Daniel sat up. Wet snow slid down the back of his neck and blood blinded his one eye. With his good eye, he looked at his wife. Her hat leaned to one side, the blasted pheasant feather threatening him. Red blotches bloomed on her cheeks, and blood still seeped from the corner of her mouth, which looked as if it was about to bite him. He feared letting go of her hands. "We may. One or both of us appear to be bleeding."

A tall figure bent over offering a snowy handkerchief. "I believe you both are bleeding."

He watched the President doff his top hat and offer his other hand to Summer.

For perhaps three seconds, she appeared dazed. However, that didn't last.

Looking up through his good eye, Daniel watched flabbergasted as she took the President's hand and with a ballerina's grace stepped over him, smiling at President Lincoln.

"An accident?" the president asked with his eyes twinkling,

John Hay offered Daniel his hand and helped him to his feet and brushed snow off the back of him.

Summer Rose nodded. Her big eyes glowed bright blue-green, so brilliant against the blacks and whites of the wintry landscape. "Yes, oh yes, of course, Sir, an accident. My horse ... "

Mr. Lincoln grinned and bent over cupping her chin in his big hand and dabbed at her lip. "I think you'll be fine." He cocked his head and studied Daniel, who now stood beside her. "You husband may need a few stitches. Come, into the carriage. We'll drive you to Harewood." His hand held her elbow as he directed her. "I've wanted to meet you, Mrs. Charteris. I work with your brother, Major McAllister. Here, keep my handkerchief."

John Hay opened the carriage door and helped them both up the step. "I'm John Hay. I know your brother, too." He glanced at Daniel. "You are really bleeding, Sir." He turned back to Summer." Excuse me, I'll get his hat." The President held the bridle of her horse while the driver chased Daniel's.

They sat beside each other on the rear-facing bench. She turned to her husband and dabbed at his eyebrow and whispered. "I told you you'd need lots of stitches."

His voice still low, snapped. "I never dreamed that marrying you would present such … opportunities for … stitches."

"Are you sorry?"

"That I married you?" He let out a low chortle. "Oh. No. Never. How many women could manage to have the President of the United States holding her horse while she mops up her husband's face with the President's handkerchief? Only someone demented would pass up such a woman?"

He lowered his voice. The hint of a smile creased his face, and he squeezed her knee, "Rest assured, Rosie, I have no regrets. However, in the future, I'll take more care in my choice of words."

She whispered, "That would be wise."

Just then the carriage dipped and Mr. Lincoln sat opposite them. His eyes still twinkled.

John Hay jumped on board and slammed the door. He handed Daniel his wet hat then smiled at Summer, pointing out the big stone house on the hill. "That's Mrs. Mason's place. I was just showing the President where it is." He paled. "Oops. Was I not to mention that?"

"It's okay, Mr. Hay." She turned to her husband. "Tell them the plans." She bent forward and touched the President's arm. "You're the President. He can tell you, can't he, Sir?"

CHAPTER 31

LIZA

Without giving an explanation, Hal declined Mrs. Mason's offer to take his great coat. He knew she wouldn't question him. Besides being extremely pleasant, the trial run last night had been worth the high cost. In addition to surveying the premises, he'd let Pearl Mason know who was in charge.

Pearl ushered him upstairs to a different room, one that overlooked the street. The bedcovers had been turned down, the many pillows fluffed, and a doll had been placed on the bed. He wondered vaguely if she was reminding him that Liza was a child. As if he needed a reminder. He hated being seen, even by this whore, as someone who would hurt a child.

He removed his great coat and laid it over the arm of a chair.

"May I fix you a brandy, Colonel St. Clair?" asked Mrs. Mason. "We have more of that Remy Martin Napoleon you liked so much." She sat on the sofa beside him, her leg pressed against his thigh. Tonight, she wore a red satin dress with a wide gold belt and some exotic perfume with a hint of cinnamon. "Have you ever been with a child?"

He didn't answer. He couldn't.

"No?" Her honey voice possessed a musical quality. "Take your time, Colonel, there's no rush. She likes to be fondled, petted. She's very sweet and will do anything you ask." She giggled. "Make it a game. I told her about your wild goose. She'll love it. She likes to play. We've placed silk ropes on the bed, so you can restrain her if need be. However, if you're patient and kind, she cooperates very well."

The Remy Martin backed up in his throat.

Pearl picked up the black velvet bag he'd placed on the table in front of the couch. The coins jingled.

"There are jars of creams and ointments beside the bed. I'm sure you can figure that out, or, if you'd like, Cal or I can stay with you and assist. If you run into trouble, there's a bell pull beside the bed. I'm sure you understand. It's important to us that our patrons don't hurt the girl." She stroked the velvet bag of coins. "She's our little golden goose."

Pictures he didn't want to see materialized in his head and he nodded stiffly, still afraid to speak. He took another drink of the brandy and cleared his throat, thinking about the money.

"I suggest you leave the gold on the table until we complete our transaction. I've shown my intentions." He grinned, and it wasn't a pleasant expression. "Now I need to see yours. Where's this angel you praise so highly?"

She rose and tugged the bell pull. A few minutes later, the largest and blackest man Hal had ever seen entered the room. Carried in his massive arms, dressed in a blur of pink silk, was a child, eyes closed. Her blond hair hung halfway to the floor, so silky straight it appeared to have been ironed. Pain arched in Hal's chest. The child was heartrendingly beautiful, and so, so vulnerable.

Hal glanced up at the man. Hal stood six foot, two inches and thin as a nail. This bruiser towered over him and quadrupled Hal's mass. What caught his attention, however, wasn't just his size or his purple-black skin, or even his tailored tuxedo, but the man's ingratiating expression. It held no softness, no tenderness at all. He stopped in front of Hal and bowed, offering the girl as if she were a tray of desserts. *Take this little Crepe Suzette! Or perhaps the Warm Cherry Tart!* The man showed not a smidgen, not a speck of remorse or protectiveness toward the child.

"Lay her on the bed, Calvin," said Mrs. Mason then smiled at Hal. "Unless you want me to stay, we shall leave you now." She backed out of the room.

As the door closed he stuffed the gold inside his tunic, dug the socks out of his coat pocket, and walked to the bed. He sat gently beside the child.

This girl was what? Eight? Nine? Now she looked up, her pupils large and black as Spanish olives. They followed his every move.

He used his softest voice. "I'm going to put these warm socks on your feet."

It took some doing, for her feet flopped about like half-dead carp, numbed by the drugs. She was obedient and sat up when he wrapped the cape around her shoulders. "I'm going to pick you up and hold you over my shoulder. It's very important that you stay quiet. Can you do that, Liza?"

She nodded as if she understood agreement was expected of her. He fitted her over his left shoulder and opened the door an inch and peered out. He expanded the inch and surveyed the upstairs hall. Gas sconces cast shadows along the open stairwell, but no one was in sight. He heard only a thump from the floor above. So far, so good, he thought. He felt the girl's head pop up, and he patted her back with the hand that held her.

"Keep your head down, sweetheart," he whispered. He stepped into the hall, keeping his back to the wall, barely daring to breath. Gently, he closed the door behind him and approached the stairs.

From his left, Calvin burst out of a doorway. Hal shot him between the eyes and the girl screamed. The stairwell filled with the earsplitting boom of his Remington pistol. Hal had made the decision to shoot Calvin the minute the big man had bent before him, offering the girl. Now the giant crumpled and fell backwards through the banister, careening through the air. His huge arms stretched out, and the sounds of wood splintering and glass breaking saturated the open space to the room below. A sickening thud jarred the house as his body landed. Liza stopped screaming and buried her head in his neck. From the third floor a male voice let out a string of expletives and a door slammed hard.

Another latch clicked as Mrs. Mason slipped into the hallway, her expression furious. Her eyes, manic, locked onto his. She swung both arms up and pointed a two bullet derringer at him.

"Put the girl down." Her breath came in ragged heaves and shook her shoulders. "Take your Yankee gold, you son of a bitch. I'll kill her before I let you take her." Her beautiful face contorted into something evil, her voice softened. "You see, Colonel, she's my little golden goose. Come to Mama, darling."

The child turned, stretching her arms toward the woman. Hal saw a shadow move along the wall behind her and breathed easier.

"Your little golden goose, Mrs. Mason, is going to cook yours. You know, I was almost thinking of you as human until I saw all those jars and creams." Something raw opened inside him and the urge to kill her roared through him. His breath sucked with a rasp. "How could you? She's a child."

Pearl spit at Hal, and her breath came in short little bursts. Her voice reverted to its deep Southern accent. "You frequent brothels, pay for women, and you need to ask? *How could I?* You know nothing, Sir." Spittle sprayed his face. "What has happened to this child is nothing. You … you have no idea."

So consumed by rage, Pearl didn't see Daniel slide in behind her. As he inched the last few steps, Pearl screamed, "I said put her down, you son of a bitch!"

Daniel reached around and slammed her wrist against the wall, then trapped her arm against her body, immobilizing her. He pressed his revolver into her spine and her tiny gun thudded onto the carpet. He kicked it behind him.

"You broke my wrist!" she screamed.

Jack and a sergeant, who had been waiting out of sight, thundered up the stairs, handcuffs ready. They dragged her, fighting and screaming, down to the landing. When she saw Daniel's face, she snarled.

"You! You have no idea what you have unleashed."

Daniel turned toward the little girl. She'd hid her face in Hal's collar; terrified sobs shook her small body. He softened his voice. "Take her down to Summer Rose, Hal. She's waiting just outside the service entrance. Use the kitchen stairs. This child doesn't need to see this." He motioned to the sergeant and nodded toward Mrs. Mason. "Find her a cloak. The prison's cold."

Daniel ordered troopers to the top floors to quiet the prostitutes and patrons. He sent others to check every room.

Laughing horribly, Pearl Mason plopped down on a step. She glared at Hal, then Jack, then back to Daniel. She hissed. "Your father won't like this, Danny. He'll be disappointed in you."

An iron ball settled in his gut and he tasted rust in his mouth. As a soldier he'd learned how to concentrate on the minute, and he did so now. Thoughts of his father and the extent of his possible involvement he buried deep in his mind. He ignored Mrs. Mason. She turned to Hal, glaring at him as he stepped cautiously past her.

Her upper lip curled. "I curse you, Hal St. Clair. You will die and I'll spit on your bones, you bastard."

Still reeling from the comment about his father, Daniel almost lost control. He wanted to knock her into next week. He knew how to hurt her. "Any spitting you do won't be at Hal, Mrs. Mason. The guards at the prison are men in Liza's father's company."

Her face collapsed, and she glared at him. "I was just making a living."

"Selling children? I hope you rot in Capitol Prison."

"I won't rot for long. You'd be surprised at the people I know in high places."

Summer Rose, already mounted on Chester, waited just outside the kitchen door. Hal stepped into the frigid air and carefully managed the porch steps. The snow crunched beneath his boots. He lifted the girl off his shoulder then kissed the top of Liza's head.

"You're safe, honey."

He handed her up to Summer, who settled the girl in front of her. She tucked the girl inside her cape, tight against her body then pulled the hood up over her own head. She fitted one of the small saddle blankets around the girl's legs. She looked down at Hal, her face radiant. The girl was safe.

"I see you used the socks."

Hal nodded, unable to speak. Summer Rose looked back toward the house and Hal's gaze followed hers. The door was open, and they watched the sergeant force Pearl, dressed in her red satin dress with a black cape over her shoulders, into a kitchen chair. She glared at Summer Rose.

CHAPTER 32

ENDINGS AND BEGINNINGS

Daniel found them several hours later, snug in the middle of two pulled-together cots at Harewood Hospital. Ray had directed him after telling him the girl would be fine, at least physically. Daniel removed his shirt, boots, and holster, and stuffed them under the bed. He lay down, curling his body alongside his wife. He fixed the covers and leaned over Summer's shoulder and touched the child's arm.

His throat ached with the knowledge of what he'd seen. They'd found the secret room. It wasn't a room at all, but rather a drawer in a trunk in a storage room. He couldn't imagine this little girl stuffed in that drawer, though undeniable evidence gave them reason to suspect it. Inside the drawer was a small blanket and pillow, with a few strands of long golden hair on it. They found scratch marks, cut by her fingernails, around the inside of the lock, and a small dirty doll in the back of the drawer. He took the doll out of his trouser pocket and placed it on the bed at Liza's fingertips.

People like Pearl Mason must have something missing or broken in their brain. He hoped they'd keep her locked up for years. In the drawer above Liza's little prison, they'd found Pearl's bookkeeping: several small, passport-size notebooks, each with a name on the cover: Jenny, Naomi, Ruby, Jimmy, Camilla, Joe-boy, Teddy, Liza. Jack had handed him the one with LIZA printed in neat black letters on the cover. Daniel spent a long time studying it, figuring out what the numbers and notations revealed. Pearl had paid $2000 for the child. A hefty price, but the return had been significant.

In meticulous columns, Pearl showed how she'd made $6600 in gold from this golden goose. "Add it up," Jack said. "Eight years old and she's been used by, at the very least, thirty-three men."

After each $200 entry were initials. Daniel made a decision not to look at them, terrified he might recognize some of them. Pearl knew a lot of damaging information, but he couldn't handle thinking about that tonight.

Jack scooped the other notebooks into a briefcase. He picked up one and pointed to the date on the outside of the cover. "Other children, long gone, dead, or grownup." Daniel heard him suck in a chest full of air. "The curse of childhood: growing up."

Irene Wood found clean clothing for Liza, dressing her in a pretty calico dress with a wine red corduroy jumper and a long warm coat of navy wool. Before eight o'clock in the morning of Christmas Eve, Liza's parents came with a closed carriage and took her home.

Overnight, warm air had pushed out the frigid temperatures. Now the sky misted and spit, the ground becoming a mass of melting snow and mud. They all stood outside the barracks and waved goodbye, so happy she could be a little girl on Christmas Eve with her family tonight. Jack rode up at the last minute and pulled Daniel aside.

"The President sends his thanks. He's grateful." He handed an envelope to Daniel. "I wanted to let you know that General Grant will be given the command of the entire Union Army. He's on his way to Washington shortly. You and Hal will be assigned to General Sheridan in his Army of the Shenandoah and posted near Harper's Ferry.

"Phil Sheridan is a good commander. He's a little wild, but all good cavalrymen are wild." He snorted. "Look at you and Hal. You're both crazy. You'll learn from General Sheridan. If the war lasts long enough, and you don't do something stupid, you'll probably end up with a star.

"I've made some arrangement for you and Hal to give recruitment speeches while you wait for specific orders. I'm sending you out toward Harrisburg; I've made up a schedule. Three year enlistments are up this spring and our ranks will be depleted. I'll write you the details."

His gaze travelled to his sister, who was laughing with Irene, looking lovelier than ever. "Take Summer home to Camelann as soon as possible. She likes to plan her garden and plant onions early. She starts seeds in jars on the windowsills, too. Da always meant to build her a little greenhouse. Let her fix up the place for Fanny. Also, I wanted to let you know a number of nearby farms are for sale. You and Hal should take a look at them. The war won't last forever. Veterans will want to marry, and they'll make good tenants." He nodded. "Summer Rose has some gold, but don't pay over two dollars an acre."

Hal rode up and dismounted, and Jack handed him an envelope as well. "Your orders. I know Fanny can't travel yet, so I ask that you stay here until she can. I could use the help. Ray told me she should be feeling better in a few weeks."

He saluted both men. Summer Rose strolled toward them and tucked her arm through Daniel's. He turned and kissed the top of her head.

"I have a horse you can have, Summer," said Jack. "You'll love her. She's a fine little mare named Matilda. Her markings are unique. I'll bring her by the house."

Jack put one foot in the stirrup and was about to swing himself into the saddle when Daniel put a hand on his shoulder. "Who the hell are you, Jack McAllister?"

Jack smiled the damnedest smile. "I'm many things. I am, as far as you are concerned, Summer's brother. Take good care of her. She's the only family I have."

PART THREE

SUMMER'S VALLEY

CHAPTER 33

HOME SWEET HOME

Because Fanny caught a miserable cold and Summer stayed to care for her, they didn't leave Washington until a few days before Valentine's Day. As they boarded the Lancaster train, Daniel told her, "Your brother has me giving recruitment speeches throughout south central Pennsylvania for the rest of February and into March."

"What do you say?"

He grimaced. "God, country, duty, honor. Rally round the flag boys in some variation or another. I try to emphasize that while the war is about ending slavery, it is also about saving our country, the one for which our grandfathers put their necks on the line. My grandfathers, Hal's too, were captains under Washington. Nan Charlotte's older brother died at Yorktown. Secretary Stanton tells me I'm good at it. Every day the boys look younger. God, I want this war to end."

To avoid the wretched Hanover Line, Joe and Stephen met them at the Lancaster station with a wagon and took

246 | *Caroline Hartman*

care of the luggage and the dogs. The sun felt deliciously hot and the exercise invigorating as Summer and Daniel took the horses cross country and arrived at the lake late in the day, where they met Ezra.

As Summer prepared a tray and started coffee, she overheard Daniel speaking. "We'd like to put a greenhouse on the south face of a new barn."

Ezra led them to the end of the road, where snow lingered in the shadow of the hemlocks. "Here. Extend the road a hundred yards and build the barn on the far side of the hill. We'll bank it so you have a big loft for straw and hay, and plenty of room for the animals on the ground floor." He rubbed his hands together. "We'll clear the road and build a shell in a week, then finish it by spring." He pointed uphill. "We can pipe water in from the spring. A stone springhouse would be nice for cold storage. You'll probably get a cow come winter." He turned to Summer, just carrying out the tray of coffee. "I'll have your greenhouse finished by the first of April. I'll order the glass from Pittsburgh. Special artisans from France make the sheet glass now."

Telegrams sizzled back and forth between Hal and Daniel. Without digging into Summer's treasure of gold, they bought four farms, bringing their total acreage to about 3500. Hal suggested Summer keep her gold.

"Now isn't the time to sell. Your father showed good sense in leaving you gold. The price is okay now, but it'll go up closer to the elections. Wait to sell."

Hal made a whirlwind visit, then he and Daniel rode to Gettysburg to finalize the transactions. He stayed two nights at the lake, visiting each farm with Daniel between recruitment rallies. In the first week in March, Ezra sent Matthew to Hanover to pick up Hal and Fanny. Jimmy followed with a wagon for the trunks.

As the buggy pulled up to the house, Summer could tell by Fanny's wrinkled expression that she wasn't impressed by their log cabin. Summer and Daniel gave them the large bedroom. It didn't matter to them. She and Daniel slept as tight and entwined as newborn kittens wherever they were.

She knew Hal loved the valley. The first day, he and the dogs walked the paths that laced through the mountains. At sunset, as the birds flew to their roosts, he brought down a string of pheasants. He hung them in the shed and told Summer he'd clean them later. When Fanny, in all innocence, asked if he cleaned them with soap and water, she noticed Daniel choke back a chuckle.

"Fanny does try," she whispered to Daniel later as they snuggled in bed. "She loves walking around the lake with the dogs, and she likes to sit in the sun on the stone wall and watch the Germans building the barn."

Instead of responding, he disposed of her nightgown and ran his rough hands down her spine. "I love your skin. Why do you bother putting on a nightgown?"

She sighed as she rolled against him. "Because I love when you take it off." Her hands moved over his chest. "Fanny sews beautifully. She makes little nightshirts and dresses out of flannels and lace her grandmother sends from France, materials we can't get here. Honestly, Daniel, she could sell them in expensive shops in New York or Philadelphia. They're exquisite."

His big hands pulled her tight to him, making thinking difficult for both of them, but she felt she had to stand up for Fanny. "She does help in the kitchen. Her pie crusts are marvelous. Even Ezra said so, and you know how good Margie's pies are."

"Hal seems more content," he said, kissing her throat. "Having him content is important. Otherwise, he'll—"

She sat up with a jerk. "Here? They have brothels here? Are you joking?"

He tugged her back down, holding her body tight. "Not every man has a wife like you." He chuckled, tickling her neck with his breath. "I've heard some women don't like when their husbands make love to them." He kissed her hard and long. "Can you imagine?"

She wrapped her legs tight around him and giggled. "Not every girl has you."

In the evenings, Daniel, Hal and the girls played bridge and discussed their plans. Fanny drew sketches of the valley and the compound as they imagined it, filling sheets with various renditions. They talked about the details of the houses they wanted to build. From little tidbits of conversation, Daniel and Summer understood that while Fanny felt the valley might be a nice place to spend the summers, she had no intention of living in the wilderness the entire year. Hal didn't seem to mind her attitude. They both possessed a level of sophistication neither Daniel nor Summer desired.

One evening Daniel said, "I could care less if I miss the opera season. When the cranes whoop across the lake is close enough to opera for me." He winked at his wife. "Of course, every once in a while we'll have to go to New York or Philadelphia to shop and let you get all gussied up and eat your fill of oysters. One opera and a play or two might be fun."

After Hal and Fanny went to bed, Daniel and Summer swam in the warm lake. When the weather moderated, they piled the tent and blankets into the canoe and spent nights on the island. After a while they just left the tent set up. Those few weeks, while the carpenters' hammers rang through the valley and buttercups blanketed the ground around the lake, Summer Rose and Daniel found magic.

Hal, in his own way, found happiness. He slept little, choosing to spend his nights devouring the crate of law books he'd brought along. He heard Daniel and Summer tiptoe out to the lake and suspected their intentions, but never said a word. During the day he accompanied Daniel to rallies or rode alone through the surrounding towns, introducing himself to mayors, judges, church leaders, people Jack had suggested they get to know. When Hal returned, whistling and looking smug, Daniel hoped his friend had stayed out of the bawdy houses. Every town seemed to have them, and Hal found them, but he also found tenants, all veterans, for the four new farms. He helped them get settled and decide on the crops to plant. Horses, scarce because of the war, were expensive, so he convinced them to share the draft horses for plowing and planting. He'd return often with a string of rabbits or a half dozen pheasants and always with a saddlebag of newspapers.

Sword shaking filled the newspapers. The presidential election loomed in November and vast amounts of political venom made its way into the papers. Both sides threw ugly accusations at each other, the ugliest being that of 'miscegenation'. *The New York World,* one of the papers backing the Democrat nominee, George McClellan, for president, coined the new word inside an anonymous pamphlet called, *Miscegenation: The Theory of Blending the Races.* The authors claimed the Republicans wanted to mix the races, and the campaign got uglier by the day. The President was referred to as the Widowmaker. The papers said Abraham Africanus the First, the Widowmaker, had killed a half-million white men, and now he promoted black men marrying white women.

Three year enlistments of soldiers ended that spring, and enticements to reenlist filled the papers. Opinions about anything to do with the war, the drafts, the riots filled the editorial columns. As Jack had predicted, Grant was given command of the Army, and Generals Sheridan and Sherman were his rising stars. All of them read the editorials, applauding Grant's tough attitude and criticizing his ruthless use of troops.

March 21st, the day before the men were to leave, came all too quickly. While they spit-polished their leather and shined their brass, Summer brushed their uniforms and ironed their shirts. Fanny helped her fill their saddlebags with a two day supply of food.

That night Summer Rose and Daniel took the canoe out to the island. They lay in each other's arms, cushioned by distant thunder and the soft air coming off the mountains.

"I want you to kiss me all night," she whispered against his neck.

"You keep doing what you're doing, and I guarantee you'll be kissed all night."

Naked, wrapped in quilts and wool blankets, they clung to each other, listening to the rain patter against the surface of the lake and the canvas walls of the tent. Thunder rumbled and the air smelled lush with spring. Heartbeats of lightning from beyond the mountains filled the interior of the tent with flashes of brilliant orange light, then counterpoints of blackness.

His strong, rough hands massaged her back. "I love all of you, but I especially like the back of your neck. I always have." He planted a kiss there, sending a shiver down her spine. As the storm moved nearer, the flashes of light increased their tempo, and the air crackled between them. "And your back is a deep valley." He pressed slow, hot kisses down the cleft of her spine and pretended to bite her bottom. "I'd like to take your bottom with me as a pillow."

"Oh, Daniel, if you took me with you, you'd never get any soldiering done. I'd wear you out every night. Your general would send me away. Banish me." She rolled over and held his face to her breasts, kissing his hair, his forehead. "The only consolation I have is that you'll miss me as much as I miss you."

He gathered her against him, studying her face and tracing his fingers along the contours as if trying to memorize it by touch.

"You have no idea what you are to me," he murmured, his voice cracking slightly. "I don't know if I could live without you. You keep all the blackness at bay. You're my talisman, my anchor, my hope."

They delayed returning to the house until the small hours of the morning. "Leave the tent," she said. "When it's dry I'll put it away, ready for when you come back."

She helped him saddle Chester and Dulcey then walked beside him, leading Dulcey with one hand, holding his hand in the other. He took the reins and tied the horses to the hitching post.

As he dressed, she lay on the bed with her heart in her throat. Her entire body ached from holding back tears. The bed moved as he sat to put on his boots; she heard his spurs. Then it moved again when he stood, and her eyes opened as he pulled on his blue shirt. Its matching brass buttons marched in columns from his wide shoulders to his narrow waist. The belt, the yellow sash, the revolver, each had its place. He tucked his gloves in his belt. She stared at him, her handsome, powerful soldier, stunning in Union blue. As much as she admired him, when she saw him in the uniform, it made him suddenly vulnerable, filling her with dread.

Holding hands, they moved into the living room, where Fanny and Hal were saying their own farewells. She smelled clean leather, damp wool, heard spurs and boots as her senses melded with the night noises and smells from the open window and the pines beyond.

"If you could get a picture taken, one of those photographs, I'd love it," Fanny said, glowing with adoration for Hal. "I'd like one of you both and one of just Hal."

Summer Rose wanted to ask for a photograph too, but she dared not speak. She feared if she let loose one fragment of fear, she'd melt into a puddle of emotion. If she let one tear escape, a torrent would follow. Her heart beat so fast it hurt.

Daniel didn't speak either. His big hands pulled her out to the porch where he held her for a long time. All the love, the fear, and the hope spoke in the pressure of their bodies against each other, then he kissed her one last time and rode away.

She and Fanny stood on the porch with the sky just graying enough to see the lake and the outline of the trees. They held each other until they no longer could hear the horses' hoof beats.

Finally, in the lonely silence, Fanny yawned. "I'm going back to bed."

Summer took the lantern and walked the other way, toward the new greenhouse, with Nip and Tuck scampering alongside her. "Take care of him, Da," she whispered. "He is my heart, my life."

She'd planned to start planting seeds, but stopped dead in her tracks as soon as she spotted the potting table. Daniel must have known she'd go there first, because he'd left her a letter. Just seeing the envelope waiting there for her, marked with his firm, round script, made her heart race. She set the lantern on the bench and dropped to the slate floor, the dogs curling alongside her. Her heart beat strong and hard as she tore the envelope open and read his words.

My Beloved, I miss you already

CHAPTER 34

HARPER'S FERRY

Daniel cleared his throat and Hal, standing beside him, shuffled then coughed. The colonel sighed deeply, moved a stack of papers to another section of his desk, and lifted his chin. Cropped gray hair, steel-rimmed glasses, tired blue eyes. Daniel estimated he was no more than forty. He didn't bother to stand.

Daniel surveyed the tent. A six foot board, suspended off the ground by bricks, spanned the back wall, its length filled with haphazard stacks of paper. Chairs held even more paper. Along an adjacent canvas wall leaned boxes and crates of ammunition, bandages, fuses, as well as a roll of wire. Daniel mused that if the colonel could find anything it would be a miracle. Beside him, he could sense the neat and orderly Hal cringing.

The colonel eventually nodded. "Bill Banion. Got a letter about you two from a Major … somebody … McAllister. Here it is." He studied the men as if they were sides of beef and Daniel fought back the urge to laugh. Now he understood his wife's anger when men ogled her. "Which one of you is St. Clair?"

"I am, Sir."

The colonel bellowed. "Sergeant Major Landon! Here's your gift from God." He turned back to Hal and laughed unexpectedly. "That's what your major called you." He snapped the paper with his finger. "We have a hundred and five warehouses spread from here to Winchester and Charleston, brim full. We need to know what's in them." He snapped the letter again. "This major says you're good at organizing."

The sergeant major, a man of middle height, and built like a brick wall, walked into the office and gave a sharp salute.

"Pleased to meet both of you."

To Daniel the sergeant said, "I like that horse you rode in on. General Sheridan is expecting you. Unfortunately, he's away right now. Yesterday we received 4000 horses from Nebraska. They need to be evaluated, sorted, broken, and trained. He thought you might organize that." He pointed uphill. "They're corralled near Bolivar. If you'd follow me, gentlemen."

The three of them saluted Colonel Banion, who didn't bother to return the salute. As they exited the tent, Daniel asked, "Where can we put our gear? We need to take care of our horses."

The sergeant led them to a tent beside the river, in the shadow of Maryland Heights. It was a little off by itself and close to a guard post.

Sergeant Landon pointed to the towering cliffs on all sides of the town. "It's a little like living in a well. Anyone controlling the heights controls Harper's Ferry. We make sure our guns are up there."

Closer, he indicated the tent. "You'll be getting regiments soon. Until then I have to put you here."

He motioned for an orderly to take their horses, but Daniel shook his head. "I take care of my own horse when we're in a new place." He ran his hand down the pale mane. "After they rest I'll see to the new shipment. I'm sure I'll find 4000 horses. They'd be difficult to hide."

One hundred and five warehouses and 4000 horses later, after countless rides along the steep trails of the Blue Ridge, and after much jiggling of the structure of the war machine, Daniel and Hal received regiments. Because of the warehouses and horses, they missed fighting in the Wilderness and at Cold Harbor, two horrors that had the North, even Mrs. Lincoln, calling Grant, "That Butcher." In the Wilderness, the injured burned to death; at Cold Harbor both commanding generals refused to surrender for four days, allowing the wounded to scream and suffer among the rotting dead on the field.

The evening Daniel and Hal received their commands, they stood to the rear of the command headquarters, near Winchester, twenty-five miles from Harpers Ferry. It was the same place where they had first encountered Generals Grant and Sheridan close up. Except for a determined squint in his clear blue eyes, Grant's short, round-shouldered demeanor didn't impress them at first. However, despite his dirty boots and dusty uniform, the more he talked, the more they listened. His sharp eyes appeared to miss nothing.

Sheridan, bandy-legged with long arms, was even shorter than Grant. Daniel picked up the gossip that Lincoln described Sheridan as "that brown, chunky little chap, with a long body, short legs, not enough neck to hang him, and such long arms that if his ankles itch he can scratch them without stooping."

The rapport between Grant and Sheridan as they stood over their maps intrigued Daniel. They pointed and grunted, then nodded and grunted again. Sheridan's finger drew a wide circle around Virginia, then stabbed at the place marked Richmond.

"I'll cut all his communication with his capital."

Two days later, they thundered south in the valley along with seven thousand troopers. Daniel wrote to Summer Rose from the field.

My darling Rosie,

I hope my letter finds you healthy. While I miss you more than you can imagine, I am enjoying commanding troops again. We're working hard to shape up our regiments. I have three excellent sergeants who are teaching the green lieutenants which end of a horse to move forward, and I'm relieved to say most have gotten the gist of it. We rode out of Harper's Ferry last week, and they're learning fast.

Virginia appears picked dry by vultures, both the feathered variety and the Yankees, rebels, and flimflam artists. The women and children are gaunt, and I feel sorry for them. The few cows we came across were pathetically thin. Their pastures are hardscrabble. The cows, however, fare well compared to the former slaves who stayed on the plantations. I've seen slave quarters before, but now you cannot imagine how deplorable they are. Our horses live better. So do your goats. Their clothing may as well be paper. What will happen to them in cold weather I cannot imagine. They tell us of whippings and the rape of girls as young as five. It's good we're fighting this war.

However, our mission is to destroy Lee's army and level Virginia. We crossed the North Anna and struck the Virginia Central Railroad, then tore up miles of the railway. We destroyed its rolling stock, 1,500,000 rations, and burned a railroad bridge over the Rapidan. At a salt lick in the middle of nowhere, we found 400 half-starved Union soldiers who had been captured by the rebels. We released them.

We're moving in a large circle around Richmond, destroying the railroad and any stores we find. Richmond, however, is too well fortified for cavalry to take.

Have I told you yet in this letter how much I miss you? I long to have you next to me, though you probably wouldn't want to be near me, just yet. I need a good soaping and a long swim in the lake.

Yesterday rumor ripped through the camp that General J.E.B. Stuart had been killed. Few are ill-mannered enough to throw their hat in the air and whoop, but a lot of us are glad not to fight him again. You have read about his plumes and his exploits with the ladies, but he was, first of all, a tough fighter. His men would have ridden through hell for him and often did. Sheridan called for a moment of silence in memory of Stuart. They had both been at West Point at the same time.

Hal and I have gotten to know Phil Sheridan. He is by far the finest commander I've ever served under. At first glance, he seems odd, even funny looking. I don't think he's as tall as you, but he's tough, doesn't miss a trick, and is one of the most intelligent officers I've ever met. And he's only thirty-three. Also, despite his odd countenance, he has a dignity about him, always seems to know the right thing to say or do. You would like him.

I miss you more than you can imagine. Hal and I put in for leave next weekend, though it's just three days. I'm excited for Amelia and Harvey's visit to Camelann, but most of all I long for a swim with you. With all my heart and my love,

Daniel.

Sheridan left for Washington to attend a conference with Grant. Hal and Daniel took their troops back to Harper's Ferry; they left in the early hours, riding for Camelann.

CHAPTER 35

A WILDCAT

Daniel and Summer gave Hal's parents their room, only too happy to escape to the island. Fanny and Hal's new house was under roof and their excitement was palpable as they walked Harvey and Amelia through the framed rooms. Summer's hopes lifted, seeing how Amelia loved the valley. While the men took horses to survey the new properties, Summer led Amelia out for a swim, wearing the stylish swimsuits Amelia had brought with her. They were the latest in fashion: two piece bathing costumes consisting of a loose fitting, navy blue cotton jacket and trousers. As they neared the shore, Summer hauled herself onto the floating dock Ezra and his older boys had fashioned from scrap lumber and empty barrels, then helped Amelia onto the dock as Fanny brought the rowboat out.

Fanny tied up to the floating dock and giggled. "The baby's too big. I'll save the swimming costume for next summer. You both are adorable. Grandmamma wrote and said the suits are the rage in England and France."

After their swim, Amelia and Summer helped each other wash their hair with water from the rain barrel, then they changed into clean chemises and sat on a blanket in the shade by the shoreline with Fanny, letting their hair hang loose to dry in the breeze. Amelia and Summer pitted sour cherries for pies. Fanny was surprised at how adept Amelia was at seeding the cherries and told her so.

Amelia laughed, sending the sound of tinkling bells over the lake. "Who do you think cooked for my brothers and sisters when my mother ran off with a drummer?"

Fanny's eyes grew huge. "Your mother left her children?"

Amelia laughed her silvery laugh. "My mother produced seven children in twelve years. Even as a child I thought she birthed them painlessly. But she didn't enjoy the day to day demands of children. She said it was like being pecked to death by ducklings." Amelia shrugged. "She just didn't have the temperament." She smiled brightly. "I, on the other hand, loved caring for children." She eyed Fanny's swollen belly. "I'd love to help with the baby. I'll bring Becca, too." She winked at Summer. "When you start a family, I'll come help you, too."

Summer swallowed hard, battling the tears which lurked right behind her eyelids. Being with Amelia had stirred up bittersweet memories of her mother. Amelia had become a mother to them both, though stronger toward Fanny because of the baby. A pang of jealousy dug its teeth into Summer Rose. They'd been married since November, making it seven months, and still no baby.

Amelia must have sensed her sadness, for she reached over and hugged Summer. "In good time, sweetie. There's no hurry. Many would say you're lucky to have this time together, alone with Daniel."

Summer stood and lifted the heavy yellow bowl of cherries. "I'll sugar these up and put them in the pie shells, then pop them in the oven. We'd better get dressed. The men should be back soon."

After sliding the pies into the oven, she took her fresh clothes into the kitchen to give Amelia privacy, and was just slipping on a clean chemise when Daniel and Hal walked into the kitchen. She turned quickly and Hal did too, but he couldn't avoid getting an eyeful of lovely female form and flesh.

Daniel frowned but attempted a joke. "Familiarity breeds contempt."

"... and children," Hal muttered as he left the kitchen.

Daniel walked over and picked up her corset, helping her with the laces. "I'm usually *undoing* these. This isn't nearly as much fun. I'll be very glad when their house is finished and I can have you all to myself." He kissed the back of her neck.

She giggled. "I love our island, though." She slipped on her blouse and stepped into her skirt. "Did you have a good day?"

He hitched up the hooks at the back of her waist. "Profitable. Harvey suggested we buy the Feed and Seed store in Morgan's Corner and advised us to expand the store to include machinery and tools. Harvey knows what's developing at the Patent Office. Hal already has tenants for the farms. How were the swimsuits?"

"Not as good as birthday suits, but I love Amelia. Having her around is so comfortable. We took a long swim and sat under the trees and pitted cherries. She helped prepare dinner."

"You have no idea how wonderful it is to be here." He kissed her then lifted his head and sniffed the air. "Is that sour cherry pie?"

She nodded, and he nibbled her lip. The lines around his eyes crinkled. "I'm starved and I don't mean just for pie."

The soldiers left Sunday evening.

Just after midnight, a bloodcurdling screech had Summer sitting straight up in bed. The sound came from right above Fanny's bedroom window, and Summer's heart thundered. Last week two hens had disappeared. Summer sprang to the kitchen, grabbed the rifle, and flew out the front door. The starlight provided just enough light for her to site the mountain lion midway up the tree. She made two quick shots, a third, then the big cat plummeted to the ground. At the sound, Amelia, Harvey, and Fanny materialized on the front porch.

Harvey let out a huge Indian war whoop. "My God, girl, Grant should enlist you as a sharpshooter. Excellent shooting! Just look at the size of that cat! He's huge."

Summer walked over to the still animal and gazed sadly at it. She knelt and petted the gorgeous tawny coat. "I don't like killing them. They're so beautiful. But I can't allow him to get so close to the house. He was after my goats, and he'd kill them in no time. He could hurt Fanny or the dogs. I just can't let that happen."

She decided, rather than risk ruining Harvey's lovely red slippers, to wait until the workman came in the morning to dispose of the body. She snapped her fingers, and the dogs went back to the porch. "I hope you can all go back to sleep."

Fanny wrote to Hal and told him what Harvey had said about Summer's shooting skills, and Hal told their fellow officers about Daniel's wife, the sharpshooter. Word even got to Sheridan, then to Grant. Daniel took a great deal of teasing and pretended to be upset, but secretly he was proud of her. *Just wait until these laughing cavalrymen get an eyeful of her. They won't think at all about how she shoots a gun."*

Amelia and Harvey returned to sweltering Philadelphia. After a week of the heat, Amelia took Emily and Abbey to Cape May. Two weeks later, facing out over the sea from the porch of Mrs. Joshua Hamilton's Guest House in Cape May, she received the telegram that Fanny had produced Amelia's first grandchild, a beautiful baby boy she'd named Henry Andover St. Clair. She'd already nicknamed him Hank. Six days behind the telegram came Summer Rose's letter.

Dear Amelia,

You must come and see your fat and happy new grandson. Surprisingly, Fanny had an easy labor. I expected her to have trouble since she is so tiny, but apparently she's built for motherhood. Everything happened so quickly. I sent one of the workmen for old Doc Kent, but he didn't get here until after Ezra had delivered the baby. Thankfully, we made a good team. Ezra was here, working on the new house, and he knew exactly what to do.

Your grandson is absolutely beautiful and healthy. He howls loudly and is growing. Hal made a whirlwind trip here yesterday to see his son and little Hank stole his daddy's heart. Hal is pleased as Punch. Daniel didn't accompany Hal because General Sheridan took him to a strategy session with Grant at the Executive Mansion. Can you imagine? He's meeting with Mr. Lincoln and General Grant. Hal said I should be proud of him. He's done very well. I think Hal is afraid Daniel will get a star before he does. You know how competitive they are. Hal is crowing about being a father before Daniel.

Come as soon as you can.

Love, Summer Rose

P.S. I want a baby just like your grandson!

Amelia was unable to come for another three months, because Emily came down with typhoid.

In August Daniel wrote his wife:

My darling Summer Rose,

I hope this finds you well. I traveled to City Point with General Sheridan in early August. Grant gave him exact instructions. "Push up the valley. It is desirable that nothing should be left to invite the enemy to return. Take all provisions, all forage, and stock wanted for use in your command. Such as cannot be consumed, destroy. Bear in mind, the object is to drive the enemy south, and to do this you want to keep him always in sight. Be guided in your course by the course he takes."

On the surface, Rosie, Grant's orders appear easy. March up the Shenandoah Valley, take what you need for your army and destroy everything else. Make it so a vulture flying over the valley needs to pack a lunch. However, darling, nothing about Grant's orders will be easy.

The valley is bordered by thick mountains which shelter the raiders. (We call them raiders; the renegade soldiers like to be called rangers.) Northerners consider raiders outlaws; southerners think their rangers are heroes. The raiding parties are not large, maybe up to 100 men and boys. Most are a few men causing havoc. After all, they're farmers about to have their crops and barns burnt, their animals confiscated or destroyed. Their motivation to stop the Union Army comes from a powerful source. These farms are not only their livelihood, they are the legacy of their fathers, the future of their children. These Raiders farm by day and raid by night.

One of the worst is Mosby. Ten years ago he was expelled from the University of Virginia and jailed for shooting a classmate. He studied law in prison, received a pardon, and set up a practice of law. At the beginning of the war, he'd served as a scout for Jeb Stuart, then he raised a guerilla company with the Confederate Government's blessing. Around March of last year—you may remember it—he became famous by grabbing Union General George Crook and his subordinate General Kelley, right out of their beds in a Cumberland, Maryland hotel room. They tied the generals to their waiting horses and whisked them through our lines to Libby Prison in Richmond. They eventually were freed, but there were a lot of red-faced Yankees, and the stage was set for hard tactics on both sides. Sheridan, hearing these stories, asked Grant for permission to deal harshly with the partisans. Grant said, "When any of Mosby's men are caught, hang them without trial."

I, personally, don't agree. Feelings of hatred and revenge run raw and rampant on both sides. I would not want to see any of my men hanged. I did put in my two cents, but Sheridan sent word to his subordinates, and Custer, you know how hot under the collar he can get (I know I should not throw stones), caught six of Mosby's men. He shot three. Another, a seventeen year old, was dragged through the streets until someone shot him. Then he hanged another two and placed a placard around one neck: "This is The Fate of Mosby and All His Men." Two weeks later another of Mosby's men was similarly captured, hanged, and placarded, this time by Bill Powell, another hot head.

I live for your letters. I carry them all tied up with a blue ribbon in my saddle bag, and reread them when I can. Stay well, my love. We ride south and west tomorrow toward Front Royal. I'm tired. I need a bath. I need you.

Love, Daniel.

CHAPTER 36

A PRIVATE WAR

The last of the sunlight slanted at an angle, and Daniel could make out the dust and bugs, the lavender light. No noise except their own horses snorting and flapping their ears, and the air didn't seem to move at all. Daniel knew the raiders were out there, just on the other side of the gully. He sensed them. He knew, too, they were Mosby's men. Mosby hadn't been nicknamed the Ghost without reason.

He waited, listening, his arm raised. Just as the last of the sun dropped behind the mountains, they came over the rise at a gallop. They dipped into the gully then shot up and out, whipping their mounts, screaming their god-awful rebel yell. Daniel kept his arm raised, kept looking directly at Mosby, who thundered toward him, silhouetted against the dying light like the devil himself.

Daniel had met the Ghost on the battlefield many times. Mosby didn't like him any more than Daniel liked Mosby. Beneath him, Chester strained, anxious to charge. He nodded toward the bugler just as he cut the air with his arm and pulled his LeMat, nine-shot pistol from its holster. The bugle blared and Chester leapt into action. Daniel's men gave their own Yankee yell and roared forward. Some fired their revolvers, some used carbines, others liked short-barreled shotguns. His men were a formidable force. The battle, a hacking, bloody brawl, raged for a good twenty minutes.

Just as they were about to rout the rebels, a horse shoved into Chester. Daniel's faithful warhorse slipped in an odd patch of gravel and lost his footing, spilling them both downhill. Daniel rolled clear and Chester seemed okay, so he swung himself back into the saddle, but two rebels appeared out of nowhere. One grabbed the horse's bridle while the other expertly lassoed and dragged him off Chester while the first rebel took his prized LeMat revolver and clobbered him with it.

When he awoke, he was confused, blindfolded, shoeless, his shirt in tatters, with his hands bound behind his back. He assumed he was on the way to a prison camp. In the trees behind him, he heard Chester snorting and pawing the ground. No stranger would ever ride him. He was a one man horse. Because of this, Chester more than likely would end up butchered and served to the troops.

Daniel leaned against the ancient oak and searched beneath him for a rough edge. The aroma of coffee—he suspected it had come from his own saddlebags—drifted toward him. While they enjoyed his coffee, Daniel found the sharp edge of a root. He whittled and scraped at the cheap twine binding his wrists. When he freed them, he took a chance and used one hand to slip the blindfold slightly askew. A half-dozen rebels, lean, rough men, rested around the fire. Chester lowered his big head and pressed his velvet muzzle on the side of Daniel's neck. He could see someone had already confiscated his saddle.

He kept his hands behind his back and slumped against the tree. Sentries exchanged positions. From the small window below his blindfold, he studied the rebels as they lowered themselves around the fire.

Just before light, he stood and backed into the woods, taking Chester with him. Free of the other horses, he vaulted onto Chester's back. Someone shouted and Daniel pressed Chester to a full gallop, plastering his body along Chester's spine. Just as he thought he'd made it, the lash of a lariat again slapped against him. The sound of two sets of hooves pounded close behind him. Knowing he had little chance of escape, Daniel leaned forward and slipped the bridle from Chester's head just as the rope knotted around his shoulders and yanked him violently through the air.

He awoke in what he thought might be an old schoolhouse. Stars peeked through the roof. His hands were tied, as were his feet. In the dim light, he could make out the meaty, filthy guards. They had hung a noose over the beam along with the placard made by Custer's men: THIS IS THE FATE OF MOSBY AND ALL HIS MEN. Daniel counted twenty-five or so Yankees sprawled on the rough floor.

One of the guards noticed he was awake. He tapped the sign. "Guess what we have in mind for you, big boy? Eye for an eye."

Mosby had captured over seven hundred Union soldiers. He sent all except these twenty-seven south to Libby Prison in Richmond. These men were Custer's men, or so it was rumored. "Let their names leak out to the Yankees," he told his men. "I'm doing this in the name of justice, not revenge. An Eye for an Eye. For the seven Custer executed."

On Friday, the three guards stood them against the wall and sliced the ropes binding their hands. As Daniel worked the numbness from his fingers, he noticed one guard filling a well-worn kepi hat with folded pieces of paper. The big guard, the one with a dirty beard dipping toward his belly, hollered in a deep Mississippi accent, "Y'all, each take one of these here slips of paper."

The skinny, choirboy-faced guard passed the kepi. "Open 'em up. If you got a mark on your paper, stand over here."

Six men and the drummer boy moved to the front of the room. The young rebel snorted, looking nothing like a choirboy now, and pointed to the smooth-cheeked drummer boy. "You'll take a long time to croak."

Daniel's stomach dropped at the thought of the kid hanging. Custer's men had shot a seventeen-year-old, a brutal and senseless killing. Mosby must have felt a pang of moral rectitude, for another lottery was held among the remaining twenty. Daniel received the unlucky lot and stepped into the drummer boy's place.

Rumors leaked across the picket lines. A rebel picket told a Yankee picket that Daniel was being held at Front Royal. Four hours later, another picket said Daniel and six other men had been hanged by Mosby. Chester, his mane and tail matted and full of briars, thundered into Sheridan's camp. Sergeant Major Landon spotted him and cleaned the horse himself. A patrol from the area around Front Royal found his diary, a packet of letters, and a picture of Summer Rose. A smart sergeant delivered them directly to General Sheridan's headquarters and the telegraph wires sang. When Hal came in from patrol, his sergeant told him.

Hal rode straight to Sheridan's headquarters and barged up the porch steps. In the distance, by the waiting locomotive, he saw Tom West, a correspondent for the *Washington Chronicle*, talking to Sheridan.

"Keep those goddamn correspondents away from the telegraphs," he roared at Sergeant Boyle. "God forbid she reads it in the papers, and I don't want her to hear from anyone else, either."

His eyes dropped to the corner of the sergeant's desk where someone had left Daniel's diary, Summer Rose's letters, and her picture on top of a stack of mail. Nausea gripped Hal and he doubled over. His legs suddenly lost all strength, and for a moment he couldn't breathe. Only the desk held him up. To lose Daniel was to lose an enormous part of himself.

"Sir?" asked the sergeant.

Hal, with difficulty, straightened. He slid the packet of letters and the diary into his tunic. "I'll give these to his … I have a seven hour ride. Do you understand the importance of this not making the headlines? Tell the general. He'll understand."

Twilight had just snuck under the pines when Summer heard hooves pounding over the bridge. All ready for bed in her nightgown and robe, she was about to dash for the rifle when she heard Dulcey's whinny. Her heart sank. How could Hal know already? Fanny had just left this morning.

Summer sat back in the chair and snuggled Hank tight to her chest. Fanny had left her bottles with nipples, and Hal's son seemed to be doing okay on goat's milk. But how Fanny could just leave her three-month-old baby, Summer didn't know.

She'd used every argument she knew in an attempt to convince Fanny to stay, but Fanny was adamant. "You don't know everything, Summer. Hal and I aren't like you and Daniel. He's never loved me. Not like Daniel loves you. I even suspect he sees ..." Fanny burst into tears. "I can't talk about it."

She heard footsteps run across the porch and hugged the baby closer. Hal burst into the room and Summer lifted her eyes to the mantle. Hal, his skin a horrid, moldy clay color, leaned against the wall and Summer pointed sadly to the mantle.

"She left you a note."

He snatched it, read it then fell to his knees beside her chair. He lifted Hank, kissed his tiny forehead, and held him while tears welled in his own eyes. After a moment he stood and placed his son in the cradle, rocked him until he settled, then knelt by Summer. He took her hands.

"I'm so sorry, Hal. She—"

"Summer, I don't know how to tell you ..."

Her pulse suddenly raced. He hadn't come about Fanny. From the look on his face, he'd had not understood her letter.

"Danny's dead," he said, his voice cracking with grief. "Mosby hanged him in retaliation for what Custer ...."

She stared at him, saying nothing, she couldn't breathe.

He reached in his tunic and pulled out the packet of her letters, Daniel's diary, her picture, and she adjusted her stare so it focused on the little treasures.

She felt nothing. Heard nothing. A numbness crept through her hands and feet, grasping for her heart. With her little finger she touched the pale blue ribbon—it was one of her hair ribbons. She remembered the night he'd taken it. "To tie up your letters," he had said. Her eyes blurred. She didn't blink, didn't move. Her mouth opened and closed, opened again, like a dying fish gasping for life.

"No-o-o."

The letters spilled onto the floor, and she crumbled with them, attempting to gather them up, but her hands didn't work. She collapsed into a heap and didn't move. It was as if a knife had stuck her. She quieted and he picked her up, her breath warm on his cheek. He carried her to the bed she shared with Daniel and arranged her on the quilt. He scooped up the letters and set them on the rocking chair, then removed her slippers. She startled, curled into a ball, then started to shake and sob. Hal sat next to her, rubbing her back. After a moment, he ran outside, returning with his jacket and a flask. He uncorked the bottle and held it to her lips. She spluttered and coughed but took a long draught. All the while, he stroked her arm, talked to her. His voice was soothing, so he kept talking. She took another long swig of whiskey.

"That's a girl," he said. "We're a pair aren't we?" He laughed derisively. "I'm not really surprised Fanny left me." He took a drink and handed her the flask. "You know what surprises me? She didn't take Hank."

Summer Rose sat up, and he pulled out a handkerchief to wipe her tears. She slumped against him and sobbed while his hand rubbed circles on her back. She leaned into his shirt and cried harder. Every inch of her trembled and she couldn't speak. He held out the flask. She took it.

"I came as soon as I could. I didn't want you to read it in the papers. The correspondents are right there at headquarters ... Danny's death will be big news. They wire their stories, and I know Ezra brings over the papers early." Tears slid down his face and he choked. She felt it shudder through him. "Danny. Not Danny. I can't believe it."

Her sobs were tight little convulsions now. He took the flask, drank, corked it, then laid it down beside her.

"I never deserved Fanny. I just didn't love her enough to keep her." He shook his head. "I never saw a man love a woman like Daniel loved you."

CHAPTER 37

BETRAYAL

Hal hated himself, but his thoughts leapt to months, even a year or so, down the road. He'd ask Summer Rose to marry him. Guilt at his disloyalty to Danny rolled over him, but the thoughts came anyway. Fanny was the farthest thing from his mind.

Summer took his handkerchief, sat up for a moment and blew her nose, then took another drink of the whiskey and slid back down into the crook of his arm. She tried to speak, but couldn't. The words were swallowed up by sobs as they started up again. He rubbed her arm and let his lips rest in her hair. She didn't notice.

Daniel stumbled into the picket line. What was left of his uniform was in shreds and hung off him like rags. The sleeves and shoulder straps had been ripped off, his trousers were in tatters, and his bare and bloody feet resembled raw meat.

A Yankee guard backed him up against a tree and stuck a rifle in his gut. Daniel didn't know the password. It had been changed.

Another guard walked over. "Colonel Charteris?" He helped Daniel sit on the tailgate of a cart. "Your horse came in by himself earlier, Sir. Good to see you, Sir." Another soldier threw a blanket over Daniel's shoulders.

Daniel had managed to pick loose the ropes binding his hands, but his wrists bled and burned. He had no idea how far he'd run through the forest.

"Sir, we heard Mosby hanged you."

His breath came out in ragged lungfuls. "Damned near did. He sure as hell tried," he managed to say. "The rain came down so hard ... helped me get away from the dogs. I slipped off the horse and ran into the woods. The rain covered my trail. Can you help me mount a horse? I need to get to headquarters."

General Sheridan's sergeant woke him. The general took one look at Daniel and sent for Ray. He sat Daniel at his dining room table and went over the map, inch by inch. While Daniel told of the horrors of Mosby's camp, Ray cleaned up his feet and the rope burns on his wrists. Gravel was embedded in his ankle.

"I slid down an embankment," he explained. "They shot Love and Rhodes. The other twenty prisoners are already on their way to Libby or Andersonville. While I hid in the water, I overheard them say one other man escaped. I didn't hear his name. They said Mosby was glad we'd escaped. We'd frighten the rest of the Yankees with our stories."

Daniel looked around. "Where's Hal?"

"Sergeant Boyle said he went to tell your wife. Left a few hours ago," said Colonel Banion.

Daniel turned to General Sheridan. "Sir, I must go. I'll be back tomorrow. I can't let her think I'm dead."

Ray chuckled and so did some of the others. "You'd better let him go, General. He'll take French leave if you don't."

Sheridan nodded. "Eat something first." To Colonel Banion he said, "Wake up George and have him fix Danny one of those good steaks and some eggs, and some of his bread. Pack some food for him, too." He apprised the room. "Would a couple of you go to his quarters and get this man another uniform? Go to supply for some boots. He needs a sidearm, too."

"I suppose you want Chester. That horse came back to our stables a few nights ago. Sergeant Landon cleaned him up." Sheridan smiled at the expression on Daniel's face. Most cavalrymen loved horses. Chester was a favorite. "That horse probably knows the way home." He smiled at Daniel. "You'd better shave, too. Don't want to scare that pretty little girl of yours anymore than she's already been scared."

An hour later, fed, dressed, armed, shaved, and somewhat clean, Daniel rode north, pressing Chester hard.

How long he slept, he didn't know. He awoke into a half-sleep, holding Summer Rose, who still jerked with heart-wrenching sobs. The enormity of Fanny's departure had started to sink into his brain. *How am I going to manage a baby by myself?* The very first second he'd held his son, Hal's heart had opened like a flower. Everything he'd ever wanted, good or bad, weighed against this child. He might not be the best soldier in the Union Army, he definitely wasn't the best husband, but he knew he'd be a wonderful father. His ambition soared. He promised himself he'd clean up his life. No more wild women or reckless antics.

Hal closed his eyes. In his mind, he reread Fanny's long letter. He'd always possessed an eidetic mind, able to memorize long passages with ease. He'd been too dazed with the news about Daniel to really pay attention to it, but now guilt clutched at his core. *She thinks I'm a bastard. Well, I am a bastard I can't even count all the times I've cheated on her.*

His mind's eye again saw the heavy blue vellum and the ink smeared from her tears. In the letter, Fanny had said she couldn't stay here. She'd die of hurt. "We weren't married by a priest. I don't even have the blessing of the church. I don't feel married." He could hear her sobs as she wrote. "I miss Paris and Papa. I'm afraid my grandmamma will die."

Summer shook against his chest, still not awake. He closed his eyes and brought the blue vellum, puckered with Fanny's tears, back into his mind again. "I am not ready to be a mother," she'd written. "You'll be a better father than I a mother. I can't manage a baby all the way to Europe." He cringed as his mind read the final paragraph. The puckers and smears increased. "I saw, Hal, how you followed her with your eyes. You murmured her name in your sleep. If you just once looked at me like you looked at Summer Rose, maybe I could bear it." Further down in a post script she'd written. "Hal, for your own good, take your son, and get away from her. She's Daniel's wife. I've never seen her do a thing to encourage you. She's my friend; Daniel is yours. She only loves him."

He pulled Summer closer. How many friends and classmates had died? The loss of Danny tore out his heart. The thought of leaving Summer ripped a hole deeper into his chest and tears came to his eyes. As if he'd spoken, Summer turned in his arms. Her lush body pressed into his, and her hand brushed his wet cheek. He kissed her palm.

"I'm so sorry about Fanny," she croaked.

Fanny barely crossed his mind. The idea of leaving Summer Rose threatened to suck out his heart. Her hair had come loose and now fell across his arm. He brushed it away from her face. She hiccoughed loudly and asked for another drink of whiskey. He handed it to her; she emptied the flask. He reached into his jacket pocket and uncorked another.

Blackness surrounded her; the pit loomed, bottomless. A wave of heat swept over her and she threw off the covers, rolling onto her stomach. She couldn't imagine living without Daniel; she didn't want to live without him. *He is my heart, my life,* repeated over and over in her mind, like a Gregorian chant. *He is my heart, my life. He is my heart …*

She must have fallen asleep, because when she awoke, soft lips kissed her. The kisses comforted. They stopped the shudders and the horrible gasps. They even stopped the bed from spinning. The heat … God, she'd die from the heat. Their skin sought and found each other. His hands on her naked skin … so good … so cool.

CHAPTER 38

ON THE ISLAND

Daniel found them naked.

She sensed him more than saw him, but once she opened her swollen eyes she flew to him, still unaware of where she was or what was happening around her. She threw her arms around his neck, overcome by the rush of emotion. She couldn't speak.

But Daniel untangled her arms roughly and shoved her so that she slammed back against Hal, then he left.

Why did he do that? Where's he going?

She glanced down at her body, then at Hal. He was as naked as she was. The reality of the situation struck her as if she'd been slapped. She grabbed her nightgown, stumbling after Daniel, pulling the simple white cotton gown over her head as she ran. The moon was full and high; huge, silver clipper ship clouds barreled across the night sky. She saw him through the kitchen window as he stepped into the canoe.

Behind her, Hal hopped into the kitchen, pulling on his trousers. "Let me talk to him. I know Daniel. He might ..."

She could see the canoe plowing toward the island. Each stroke of the paddle lifted the tip of the canoe out of the water. Her head ached and whirled. "You stay with Hank. Oh God, Hal! How? How did my clothes come off? Did I do that?"

She leaned over a bucket and threw up. Hal handed her water, but his eyes didn't meet hers. She rinsed her mouth, spit into the bucket, then gulped the water and wiped her mouth on a towel. Her heart beat wildly. "Tell me we didn't do anything ... anything else."

He shook his head. "Christ, Summer. I don't know. I'm still drunk."

She leaned over the bucket again and threw up. She lifted her head. "Stay with the baby. You might have to milk the goat."

"How in the hell do you milk a goat?"

"You're a grown man. Figure it out."

She ran out the door and through the garden. She dove into the cool, fresh water. Her fast, even strokes raced to the island

He beached the canoe and collapsed on a patch of dry grass. Rage boiled inside his head; his heart pounded, deafening as battle drums. His hands ached to grab Hal, to bash his face to a pulp. He dropped his head into his hands, his elbows resting on his knees, wishing he could think. The picture of them in the bed wouldn't leave his mind. His breath came in ragged lungfuls, and his feet hurt. He pulled off his boots and his bloody socks, then unbuckled his belt and holster and put both beside his boots. When he fell back, the moonlight flooded over him, the lake, the island. He closed his eyes and felt exhaustion and rage swamp inside him; his chest threatened to explode. Somewhere in his mind he thought if he slept he might be able to handle his rage.

He heard a splash and sat up with a jerk. She emerged from the water, looking more sensual than she ever had before. Moonlight lit her; the wet white cloth clung to her body, hiding nothing. She was a goddess. His voice snapped, hoarse and hard, and he held both his hands up, palms out. "Stop. This island isn't big enough for us both. Go back."

She crumpled at his feet, sobbing. "He told me you were dead. Oh God, Daniel. I went out of my mind. Hal comforted me. I was so frightened … I got drunk. I wanted to die. I didn't know what to do. You are my life, Daniel."

His voice dripped with fury. "You could have fooled me. Go back."

"Daniel, he gave me your diary, my letters. He told me John Mosby hanged you. Fanny left Hal." Her voice lifted an octave. "She's on her w-way to Paris and she left the baby here. I must have fallen asleep. I was drunk. He's devastated."

Daniel's voice roared and she cringed, squeezing her eyes shut. "The only goddamn thing Hal is devastated about is that I walked into that room."

Each word slammed her like a punch, and worse, a fear coiled in her belly. Nausea rose in her throat again and she looked down. She noticed his bloody feet and gasped, reaching for him.

He held up one hand. "Don't touch me."

She dropped her hand onto his ankle and he grabbed her like a mountain lion might grab one of her goats. This man wasn't Daniel; he was some wild beast. She'd always known of his strength, but she'd never experienced it used against her. He ripped off her little white nightgown, shredding it in one powerful movement, then slammed her beneath him, knocking the wind out of her, hurting her, driving his body into hers. The suddenness and the force frightened her, took her breath away.

When he finished, he collapsed like a man drugged, pinning her to the dry grass. She was unable to move; his brass buttons cut into her skin, but it was her insides that felt torn open. She squeezed hot tears out of her eyes.

She could tell by the rhythm of his breathing that he slept. More sobs threatened as pain twisted and burned inside her. She willed the sobs away and concentrated on not throwing up, watching the great clouds sail across the sky. She listened to the flutter of the owls' wings as they hunted, the rhythm of Daniel's breath.

Somehow she ignored the pain. Here was Daniel, her beloved Daniel. An hour before, she had thought he was dead. *Oh God, thank you for returning him to me.* The steady thump of his heart beat against her chest and a shudder rippled through her. She squirmed and wiggled, freeing an arm, which she wrapped around his shoulder. She kissed his neck. His rough beard scraped her face. Tears ran from the corners of her eyes. Eventually, even with his buttons biting into her skin, she fell asleep.

→»«←

He shifted his weight off her, and she shivered in the chill and dampness of morning. The sky, pink and pale yellow, reflected in the lake. A lone eagle, his enormous wings dipping and gliding, circled low over the water, then screeched and plummeted for a fish. Daniel looked down at her body and ran a finger over one of the marks where his buttons had dug into her flesh. His gaze shifted to the shredded nightgown, and he stood in the pearly light so he could remove his blue shirt. He threw it at her and she jumped a little.

"Put it on." His tone was curt, hard like it had been last night, and it sliced into her heart. He picked up his revolver, holster, and boots, then stuffed his socks in them and put everything in the canoe.

Tears streamed down her face. That he'd hurt her was one thing; that he cared so little for her feelings hurt far more. She didn't know how to react to his anger. A shudder ran through her. Her nightgown lay where he'd thrown it, and she picked it up, her hand trembling. Never before had she seen anyone so angry. Holes made by his fingers spoke of the strength he'd used to rip it from her. She pressed the torn, wet material to her chest, keeping her head down, and her face turned away to hide her tears.

He walked to the canoe and shoved it into the water just as the sun burst through the trees, slashing light across the lake. He rotated his shoulders as if to loosen his joints, then turned toward her. With his upper body naked, she could see the muscles of his chest and arms distended with rage.

"Sit up front." His voice snapped like a hard slap.

She did as he said and sat facing forward with her eyes closed, her hands clutching the gunnels. Her head throbbed.

With a lurch, he pushed off from the shore. Every powerful thrust of the paddle reminded her of his strength. Her chest tightened, and she forced herself to turn around.

She wiped her face with the tattered material, looked at him, and held her eyes steady. "Daniel, I don't deserve this treatment."

His pale green eyes drilled into her. His look could have shattered foot thick ice. He laid the paddle across the gunnels.

"Let us review, sweetheart."

Each word, clipped and tight with sarcasm, flew like bullets into her heart. She tasted fear.

"I am almost hanged. I escape as they throw the rope over the tree limb. I run. I run miles in my bare feet. I hide in a cold stream while they hunt me with bloodhounds. I hear the dogs sniffing at my footprints. Then I ride for seven hours, almost ruining a horse I dearly love, so you wouldn't think I'd been killed. Instead, I find you and Hal, drunk and naked in bed. What do you think you deserve?"

He took a two dollar gold piece out of his pocket and tossed it to her. She picked it up and stared at him, confused.

"I think that covers what a whore costs."

With a jarring thud, the canoe rammed the shore. He stood, took his boots and gear, and stepped out of the canoe, swinging it around so it rested on the grass. Hal was nowhere in sight. Daniel limped past the cooing baby, not even glancing at Hal's son. He banged into the house then banged out a minute later with clean socks. He sat on the steps and pulled on his socks and boots.

She flinched at the rawness of his feet.

"I'm going to see to Chester." He nodded toward her. "I need my shirt."

There was something in the way he said it—*I need my shirt.* His tone, the slope of his shoulders, something, and it infuriated her. She climbed out of the canoe and marched up the stairs, pounding her bare feet with every step. Still not understanding what had kindled her anger, she lit the stove and slammed the iron door closed. Out of habit, she filled the kettle with fresh water and thumped it down on the burner, then stomped into the bedroom, which told a tale she didn't want to hear.

Hal's dirty socks and his belt hung on the footboard. Two whiskey flasks sat empty on the floor. The sheets, pillows, and quilt lay sprawled all over the place, as did her letters to Daniel. Through the fog of whiskey, she couldn't remember what had happened. All she felt was a horrible void, a black pit that threatened to swallow her when she'd thought Daniel was dead.

She walked past a mirror, noticing the tunic only covered her to mid-thigh. Her hair was wild. *Good lord, I'm a wreck.* She grabbed her hairbrush and turned her head upside down, brushing the tangles from her hair, and thought about Hal. She'd clobber him so hard his head would spin. She'd put a rock in her fist, just like Colin had taught her.

Daniel's face from last night flashed in her mind. *I'll bash him, too.* The picture of her torn nightgown returned and she shuddered. She reached in the pocket of Daniel's tunic and found the gold piece he'd thrown at her. *How dare he throw money at me? How could he be so cruel?* She wanted to shove the gold piece down his throat. He had to realize it was all a horrible mistake. She'd no memory of what had happened.

I thought you were dead, Daniel. I would never want Hal. I don't understand what happened. I love you, Daniel. You are my heart. She pictured his face as he'd flipped her the coin and tears streamed down her face. She slammed the gold piece on the dresser. "Damn you."

She heard loud voices and ran to the porch, her heart flooding with fear. Daniel, bare-chested and bloody-fisted, loomed over Hal. Hal tried to stand up but fell down. She rushed back inside to the kitchen, grabbed her rifle, and ran onto the porch. She raced down the steps and to the paddock yard, her hair flying wild. She fired two quick shots, which thudded into the fence behind the men.

Daniel glared at her. "I'm going to kill him."

"Back up, Daniel. If anyone is going to be killed, I'll do it."

He moved toward Hal and she let loose another shot. The lead whizzed inches from his bare chest and thudded into the fence behind them. He fell back and swore at her.

She yelled, "Hal, get on Dulcey and get out of here."

Daniel started to move but the mouth of the rifle was aimed directly at him.

"I'll take off your ear, Daniel. You know I can do it. Let him go." She motioned with the rifle for Hal to move then yelled at Daniel. Tears threatened again. "I don't want you hanged. I just about died last night thinking you were dead. Go on. Get out of here, Hal."

Hal stood as if frozen, wobbling back and forth. They all turned at the sound of hooves pounding over the bridge, and stared in disbelief as Jack galloped into the yard on a sweat-soaked horse. He skidded to a stop and dropped to the ground, looking as winded as his horse. He held both hands up and slowly walked toward his sister.

"I was told Mosby hanged Daniel. I see they were mistaken."

She motioned with the rifle. "Help Hal onto his horse. No questions, Jack. Just do it."

He did as she requested. It took time because Hal had difficulty standing, let alone getting on the horse and sitting straight. Then Jack insisted on refilling Hal's canteen. While she waited, the sun beat down on her, and she wiped sweat off her face with the torn nightgown. She stuffed it in the tunic pocket and glared at Daniel. As each minute ticked by, her anger grew like a wildfire.

When Hal rode off, Jack asked, "Anyone want to tell me what's going on?"

In unison they yelled, "No."

Summer Rose motioned with the gun. "Take Daniel up on the porch and take off his boots. His feet are raw. He could lose his feet if you don't clean him up. There's a bottle of Da's salve in the kitchen. Use it."

"I need my shirt," Daniel yelled.

She threw the rifle to Jack. "Cover him."

Never in her entire life had such rage consumed her. She glared at Daniel, looking as if he might be crazy. "You want your shirt?" She whipped off the shirt, holding it by a sleeve, then whirled it around her head like a lariat, and flung it with all her might at Daniel.

Both men stared, their faces set as if in stone. Daniel didn't even lift his hands to catch the shirt. It thudded against his chest and slid to the ground.

"Take your goddamn shirt."

Tears ran down her face and she threw back her head, her hands on her hips and her hair whipping about. She marched toward the house, gorgeous as a Greek goddess and just as naked. Neither Jack nor Daniel moved, not even when they heard the door bang shut.

CHAPTER 39

A PLAN

Muttering and swearing under her breath, she took a pitcher of hot water into the bedroom and gave herself a wash. She dressed in an old blue shirt of Daniel's, and pulled on Kip's ragged pants. She managed to stop crying, but her hands wouldn't quit shaking as she braided her hair. They continued to shake as she changed the sheets and straightened the bedroom. When she'd finished, she crumpled onto the bed, exhausted, sick, and miserable. Lying there, she could hear their voices through the open window, but couldn't make out what they were saying. Eventually she heard Jack banging around in the kitchen, getting water and rags. He knocked on her door and asked for clean socks for Daniel, acting as if nothing were wrong. She pointed to the top drawer of the bureau.

She wanted Daniel to come to her, to tell her he was sorry for hurting her, for his mean words, but he didn't. Around noon she heard him leave. When Chester's hooves pounded over the bridge, she raced through the kitchen to the porch, getting there just in time to see him galloping away. Her legs gave way and she collapsed as if she'd been punched in the stomach. Only the porch railing kept her upright.

Jack supported her to the kitchen and sat her down at the table. He pressed his hands against her shoulders and massaged her neck. After a few minutes, he puttered about, making coffee, toast, and scrambled eggs. She ate slowly, chewing each bite with deliberation. Her hands shook so the silverware clattered against the plate. When she finished, she leaned back in her chair, her hands still shaking.

"He's still angry with me, isn't he?"

Jack nodded. His voice came out shy. "He said he found you in bed with Hal. Where in the hell is your head, Summer? Did you—"

The tears came again. "I don't know, Jack! I was drunk. I was out of mind with grief. Hal had a flask, two, and I drank. A lot. I honestly don't know what happened. Did he tell you what he did?"

Jack shook his head. "It's a wonder he didn't kill you."

She breathed a sigh of relief. She didn't want anyone to know what he'd done. She was strangely ashamed of him and of herself for what had happened on the island.

"Jack, I'm not going to just let him go." Her eyes, big and wet, closed, and she felt an unutterable sense of comfort when his hand grabbed hers. "I have to do something," she said, her voice cracking. "Will you help me?"

He leaned his chair back on its rear legs. "What do you have in mind?"

As she told him, he drummed his fingers on the table, then sat up with a jerk, all four legs of the chair slammed down.

He narrowed his eyes and nodded slowly. "It's doable. And it might just be the thing to teach you not to get so emotional." He continued tapping the table. "You could get yourself in a lot of trouble, even killed. I do know Phil Sheridan, though. I might be able to use my influence. He all but worshiped our father. He met Da that year he was on probation from West Point. But I'm not sure. I don't want you to go off halfcocked. Tell me again."

He took mental notes as she talked, and made several suggestions. They needed to stop while she fed Hank and changed his diaper.

"By the way," he said when she was finished, "I do have good news. Fanny wired Amelia, who is on her way here to take the baby. They should be here by dark. Harvey sent a telegram."

She nodded. Her mind started a list. "I'll get Amelia settled. I can't just leave her with the baby the minute she walks in the house. There are some old uniforms in the trunk in the loft. I'll have to take one in and shorten the sleeves and trousers."

She stood suddenly, the tears all gone and replaced with determination. "I'm going to cut my hair."

"Aw, honey, do you have to do that? Daniel loves your hair."

She shot him a glance. "Understand something right now, Jack McAllister. I want him back, but he'd better like a lot more than my long hair. I gave him my heart. I'd die for him. He knows that if anything happened with Hal, it was a mistake, a stupid mistake. If he had an ounce of sense, he'd know that."

Jack swallowed.

She stood and retrieved the scissors, then moved toward the door to the porch. "Once it's cut, I've crossed the Rubicon."

He swallowed hard again. "I'll help you. Fetch a sheet."

The rescue team found Summer Rose wrapped in a sheet, her long braid lying on the floor of the porch. Amelia put her hand over her mouth and her amber eyes widened to the size of small apples.

Becca jumped out of the carriage before it stopped, then ran up the steps to take the scissors from Jack. "I'm good at this, Major McAllister. Let me take over."

"Happily." He moved gingerly down the steps and helped Amelia from the carriage. "Thank you for your telegram this morning and for coming."

"I couldn't stay away. When Harvey told me Mosby ... then the telegram from Fanny ... and then ... we heard Danny was okay. But I can't believe she left the baby."

Amelia ran up the steps to the porch and pulled a chair beside the cradle. She reached for the baby and nested him in her arms. He started to fuss, then snuggled back to sleep. Amelia's face held the smuggest of smiles. "Oh, he is gorgeous."

Becca repaired Summer Rose's hair, producing a ragged boy cut, with spikes shooting out in all directions. She held a hand mirror up. "Maybe when you wash it?"

Summer shrugged. "I'll jam it under a cap. I'm going up to the loft to find that old uniform now."

When she left, Amelia asked. "What happened? Something happened."

Jack gave them an edited rendition. "She and Daniel had a tiff, a serious one. You know newlyweds. She's off to make amends."

In Jack's mind, both men had behaved less than honorable, as had his sister, and the fewer people who knew, the better. He knew loss, how it ripped you apart, crushed you, and he'd do anything to help Summer. On the other hand, while he wanted to rattle both Daniel and Hal, he'd do what he could to help them, too.

Amelia cooed at the baby, and Jack shook his head with confusion. How could such a sweet woman produce such an arrogant bastard as Hal? Yet he knew the good side of Hal, too. Hal, without any reservation, had put up the gold to free Liza. He'd also been the first anonymous donor to the nurses' cab fare fund. His father had contributed too, along with many grateful soldiers. But Jack had noticed long before this happened, how Hal would brush against Summer, of his covert peeks at her. And Summer? He didn't even try to understand women. Daniel, well, he had a suspicion of what Daniel had done.

Most people loved Daniel, and he was just as guilty as the next person. Daniel oozed charm. Just about everyone, from the rawest recruit to Grant, even Lincoln, gravitated to him. And yet he'd seen the torn nightgown when she'd wiped her face, and he'd heard rumors of Daniel's temper. He put two and two together, but he knew better than to interfere. Not yet, anyway.

Summer returned, waving the uniform. Jack took it from her and handed it to Becca. "We'll fix this later." He led Summer by the elbow across the porch. "Someone better watch out for you. Those dark circles under your eyes would make a raccoon jealous. I want you to rest."

As they moved into the house, tears welled in her eyes. "Jack, don't be kind. I'll cry again. Tell me how stupid I was. Do you think he'll ever want me back?"

He chuckled. "He must have had some reason to nearly kill Hal." He fluffed the pillow, and she sat on the edge of the bed. "Lie down, Summer. I want you to rest. We have a whole team here to help now." He covered her with a blanket, bent, and kissed her forehead. "We'll work through this. Rest now.

Two days later, high above Harper's Ferry with the Potomac and Shenandoah Rivers roaring below them, Jack mounted his horse. His heart did a little sputter every time he glanced at his half-sister. Even dressed in Colin's leftover uniform, which Becca had altered, Summer still looked too much like a girl. She fiddled over the small fire, roasting coffee beans and boiling water. Her hair stuck out every which way.

A couple of days before, while they were still at Camelann, Becca had baked a cake to celebrate Summer's twentieth birthday. Jack, from his lofty age of thirty, watched and ached for her. She was too young for such problems, but the war had torn all their lives asunder. Later, with just the two of them at the table, she made a little ritual of cutting a long string of rawhide and removing her wedding ring. She slipped her ring on the rawhide and knotted it tightly on the string, then hung it around her neck. Her voice threatened to crack.

"I'll wear this next to my heart until Daniel puts it back on my finger."

Now, she gazed down at the confluence of the Shenandoah and Potomac Rivers, and the village of Harper's Ferry, which was situated at the bottom of a narrow gorge, bordered by sheer granite walls. The enormous Union Army arsenal and its immense stores sat below her. Opposite her, and uphill at Bolivar, stood another military compound. Sheridan's Army of the Shenandoah appeared vast. Not all of it was there, but a great mass of the North's power was spread over the hillside opposite her. She could see thousands of tents, wagons, sheds and storehouses, as well as horses, mules, caissons, pontoon bridges, and enormous stacks of supplies.

Not quite autumn, the air blew brisk and carried a bite. She poured herself a cup of coffee, then panned the valley with her father's binoculars. She'd read somewhere that Jefferson said this expanse of water and rock was worth crossing the Atlantic to see, and she agreed. The view of the rivers as they broke through the Blue Ridge Mountains took her breath away. She imagined that in some prehistoric age, rocks larger than houses must have spewed about, as if left in a war of titans. Trees were sparse.

After only five minutes, she spotted Daniel's flag. Her heart did a little flip when she saw big old Chester about halfway up the hill, standing across the river and opposite her. She loved that horse almost as much as Daniel did. Someone, not Daniel, stood by the horse, grooming him.

Then she saw Daniel duck out of his tent. Tears burned and her heart raced, but she wiped her face with her hand and didn't make a sound. He stopped and talked to Chester, then walked toward the long rows of tents, melting into thousands of men and horses. She lay still for a long time, watching Chester, hoping to get another glimpse of Daniel. Finally, she put the glasses down and reached in her pocket for the gold piece. She tossed it over and over, watching it spin and catch the light. Up and down, spinning and flipping, like the thoughts racing through her mind.

The spirit of her oldest brother sat beside her, though Will didn't speak for a long time. He just let his presence fill her. The memory of his face formed in her mind: his elaborate moustache, the one dimple, the sweet smile. He, of all her brothers, had been her hero. He had been her ideal for a good man. He'd kissed away her tears and bruises, fixed her scrapes, told her stories.

When she was little, to keep her away from the road or the lake, he'd spun elaborate tales of evil trolls lurking under the bridge, of an army of tiny, wart-crusted dragons living beneath the lake that would pop up, breathing fire and snapping their long teeth if she ventured too close. She remembered the day he'd left for war. He'd sat beside her on the piano bench and played the bugle calls, then told her how beautiful and brave she was, and how she'd need to be strong for all of them. He'd left a sweetheart, who he'd planned to marry. She still exchanged letters with Molly Mehard.

She wasn't surprised to hear his voice.

I want you to know, he said inside her head, *I'll be here with you every step of the way. I'll be the voice in your ear, telling you how to fit out your gear, how to maneuver your mount. And Summer, when I tell you to duck, for heaven's sake, duck. I'll cover your back. You shoot that Spencer better than anyone down there, and no one is as good as you are with a knife. Listen to me, Sweetpea. We—Da, Colin, and I—have been watching over you, and your Daniel, too. I'm madder than hell at him, but I like him. He'll come round.*

He shook his head and anger spoke in the lines of his face. His voice was just as strong as if he sat beside her. *Sweetpea, that gold piece was a cheap shot, like kicking a man when he's down. If I were you, I'd frame it and hang it where he'll see it every day, to remind him for the rest of his life of what a bastard he can be."*

He examined her critically. *"Dirty up your face and neck. Gives the allusion of whiskers. What name did you decide on?"*

She leaned back. "Samuel Ross. Sam. I sort of like it."

"Why not Kip?"

"Daniel first met me as Kip."

Will nodded. *"Don't be surprised if you see him with a black eye. I may give him one."*

She grinned, the first genuine expression popped onto her face since before Fanny had left. She gave the coin a high flip. "Don't hurt him too much. I kind of like the way he looks. Do you think he'll ever forgive me?"

"Oh, Sweetpea, if he has an ounce of sense he will. You sure you want him back? I still don't like how he hurt you."

Color rose high on her cheeks, and she let out a deep breath. "I love him, Will. I don't ever want to be hurt like that

302 | *Caroline Hartman*

again, but I keep reminding myself of what must have gone through his mind when he found me with Hal." She sighed. "The worst thing is, I still don't know if anything happened or not. Hal kept giving me whiskey, and I kept drinking it. I was out of my mind. Doesn't Daniel realize that? Oh, I should never have allowed Hal near me."

Tears threatened and she shook her head, forbidding them. "I want to be the one that decides what I want. Do you know what I mean?"

She awoke with a start. For a second a feeling, so true and strong, she could have sworn William sat right beside her. Then a coldness, the kind of chill brought by fear, fell over her. She remembered Will leaving Molly, how he'd bent from his horse and kissed her hard, tears running down both their faces. A knot tightened inside her chest as she remembered how he'd come back from Antietam—on a cart, under a blanket.

PART FOUR

SHENANDOAH

CHAPTER 40

THE GENERAL'S DOG

After Daniel saw to Chester's care, he closed himself in his command tent. He stripped, washed himself, and shaved. Once he was dressed in a clean uniform he headed for his troops. Pity the poor trooper with a dirty horse or, for that matter, dirty boots. Aware that his temper balanced precariously on a razor thin edge, he made a mental note to pause before reacting. God knows he regretted not pausing the other night. Still, he couldn't erase the picture burned in his mind. That picture of Hal and Summer Rose in bed. He just hoped Hal had the sense to stay away from him.

Once in a while, other pictures flashed through his mind: her body emerging from the water with the white cloth clinging to her, her shocked expression when he'd tossed her the coin. He shook his head and a smile came to his face as he remembered her defiantly whipping off his shirt and marching buck naked into the house. It all came back: the smell of her, the feel of her skin. He was still furious at her, but he also raged at himself. His dark side told him the little bitch deserved to hurt, but the softer side felt a deep, burning shame.

--→≫≪←--

The sun sank into a kaleidoscope of purple and gold, ribboned by streaks of red and pink. Summer Rose spotted Jack riding up the trail with two soldiers, and stood as they neared. She noticed right off that the general appeared to be shorter than she was. She also noticed that his uniform was meticulous. His posture was West Point to the core. Rather than a cap, he wore an odd little flat hat. His black eyes darted, surveying her, the trail, the view, all with lightning speed.

He said, "At ease."

The sergeant led the horses to a wooded area and tied them to a tree. She asked them all if they wanted coffee. Everyone did, and she scrambled around for cups.

While she passed coffee around, Jack spoke. "General Sheridan, Sergeant Landon, I'd like you to meet my sister." He slid one arm around Summer. "Micah McAllister's daughter and Colonel Charteris' wife. She's our Summer Rose."

She started to object, but Jack pinched the underside of her upper arm, and she bit back the words.

General Sheridan squinted his black eyes and studied her, nose to toes. He took in her oversized uniform, her hacked off hair, and the dirt smeared on her face. He liked how she didn't try to win him with an easy smile, but stood straight, her shoulders square, her unusual eyes unblinking.

"At ease, Ma'am. Let's sit down and discuss what you have in mind. I want you to know right up front that if I didn't respect your father so much, and owe him my life, I wouldn't even consider your proposal. I don't want a goddamn—excuse me, Ma'am—I don't want a woman killed or worse under my command. First, I want to know what the hell—excuse me—what you have in mind. What damn good is playing soldier going to do for you?"

For a long moment they sat in silence while she looked up at the changing sky. Finally she spoke. "Daniel and I were married less than a year ago. I know I sound like a romantic fool, but General Sheridan, Sir, he and I are like bacon and eggs, bread and butter, salt and pepper, even Lewis and Clark. We belong together. He's my life, my heart. I know I'm important to him, too." Her voice cracked, but her eyes stayed dry. "We're magic together, and we had a … misunderstanding. A serious one. I was at fault. I don't have any chance of winning him back if I sit at home and cry, making myself sick. What if he were killed, and I never have another chance? I'm just hoping if I can be near him, I might win him back. I can do most anything a boy or a man can do, and I've had experience masquerading as a boy."

Jack's eyes followed her and she could tell he hid a smile, trying to look gruff. "Sir, I can ride a horse and throw a knife as well as Daniel. Actually, I'm better than he is. I killed a bear with nothing but a knife. And I'm much better with a rifle than he ever was. I just want another chance. I promise I won't be any trouble. I'll make a fine soldier. General, I come from a family of soldiers. None of us play at soldiering, Sir. We take it very seriously." Her brilliant eyes drilled into him. "And it's not only that. I love this country too, Sir. My father and two brothers died for it. I heard what Mr. Lincoln said at the cemetery. I want to keep this country undivided as much as you do."

Phil Sheridan took off his strange hat and ran his fingers through his dark hair. "Do you have any ideas, Sergeant Landon?"

The sergeant had a lot of stripes on his sleeves. He wasn't particularly tall, a couple of inches taller than she was, but he was wide shouldered, with a thick neck, and hard muscled all over. Sergeant Landon coughed and cleared his throat.

"We could have a little fun with this situation, General. Nothing like a little humor to build camaraderie and heighten morale, Sir. We really need some of that right now. I can fix her up so even her husband won't recognize her. Who cut your hair?"

Jack grunted.

"Okay," said the sergeant, giving a half smile. "We'll fix the hair." He asked her to stand and turn around. "I'll put you in a brevet lieutenant's uniform a couple of sizes too big for you, pad you in a few places to minimize your shape. I have some eyeglasses, those tinted ones. You say you can ride a horse. Can you really ride? Do you use one of those sidesaddles?"

One corner of her mouth curled up. She liked this sergeant. "I've never ridden a sidesaddle."

"Rumor has it you're a crack shot. Are you?"

As if they'd practiced for a lifetime, Jack tossed her the rifle then threw three pieces of shale in quick succession into the vast expanse over the river. Her brothers had always teased her unmercifully, but she was well aware they were proud of her skill. She wheeled to one knee, pulled off three rounds, and three little puffs of gravel dotted the sky. The shots echoed across the valley.

"Will that do?"

The sergeant didn't react. "Do you know the bugle calls?"

Jack piped in. "My older brother taught her on the piano when the war was heating up."

"How would you like her as a dog, General? Give me a couple of days to train her. She could sleep in the storage room at Headquarters. She'd be safe there."

Summer Rose crinkled her nose. "A dog? What do you mean by a dog, Sir? My purpose is to be near Daniel, to see him, be close to him."

General Sheridan grinned. His black eyes danced. "Oh, you'll see plenty of him. A general's dog is our slang for aide. A dog does all the unpleasant tasks no one else wants to do. I'll make sure you spend lots of time near your husband. I'll have you running messages back and forth between my command and his, day and night." Sheridan shook his head. "He used to be one of my better officers. He hasn't been back a week, and I've already had complaints from six of his junior officers. Since he returned he's been a heartless son of bitch. Everyone's blaming Mosby, but I suspect it's you who has his dander up. If he isn't careful, one of his own men will shoot him." He saw her expression change, and corrected himself. "I'm exaggerating. He's not that damn bad yet."

He blew out both sides of his mouth and tossed out his coffee grounds. "Hell, Ma'am, you're just going to have to put up with my cussing. I swear like a cavalryman." He glanced at Jack and nodded. "Between Sergeant Landon and me, we should be able to keep her safe." He frowned. "How big was the bear?"

"Three hundred pounds."

General Sheridan lifted one eyebrow and eyed her appreciatively. "I have a suspicion keeping you out of trouble may be a challenge."

Like a sudden shift in the wind, his face lost all humor. "I have two more questions. First, if I ask you to do something you absolutely do not want to do, will you do it without question? You can't have a mind of your own if you're to work for me. You must trust that Sergeant Landon and I know what we're doing."

She thought for a long moment. Jack cleared his throat. "Yes, Sir. I think I can do that, as long as it doesn't hurt Daniel."

He grinned at the expression on her face. "I won't ask you to bayonet him. Maybe shoot him, but never will I ask you to bayonet him."

She nodded, her expression looking very much as if she'd swallowed a cricket.

"The second question is: Does this trouble have to do with Colonel St. Clair?"

Her eyes widened and she swallowed again. "Yes, Sir."

"I thought it might. They used to work together like a well-trained team of horses, now they're about as cooperative as a pair of jackasses."

Summer Rose's blue-green eyes sparkled. "Jackasses? That sounds about right."

CHAPTER 41

COLONELS AND GENERALS AT PLAY

Within two days Summer commiserated with every dog in the world. She'd been close to tears several times, but then she'd think of her goal, and her tears would dry up. Sergeant Landon was a tough taskmaster. And Jack had said he'd stick around to give moral support, but, thought Summer, his definition of moral support must be different than mine.

Sergeant Landon had managed miracles with her appearance. General Sheridan had sent over his own barber, George, a tall skinny black man with wiry gray hair, who doubled as General Sheridan's private cook. He just about scalped her. She doubted if any hair on her head was an inch long.

While Sergeant Landon spent an afternoon teaching her to salute, how to stand, as well as the protocol of her duties for the general, he sent Jack to town with a shopping list. Jack returned with several packages, one of which held a full body corset. Sergeant Landon eyed it against her body then proceeded to cut off the bodice. He held out a stack of flannel towels.

"Start with two, Sum—I mean Sam. Start with just two, and see how it works. Wrap these towels next to your skin around your body from above your bosoms to your hips." He demonstrated on himself then handed her a card of safety pins. "Secure 'em with these." He held up the altered corset. "Strap this contraption upside down and over the padding— lace it up the front—then put your blouse over it. Our objective is to flatten you out. I don't want any bumps, lumps or dents. We're not looking for a wasp waist." He pointed to Jack. "I want you straight up and down like your brother, or a little plumper. Understand? Go in the storage closet and put yourself together. Holler for Major McAllister if you need help."

She managed without any help and the two men agreed the result resembled a chubby boy—who still look liked Summer Rose. Sergeant Landon sat her down in his desk chair and plucked her eyebrows into nonexistence.

"Your brother picked up some theatrical makeup in town along with this mirror." He opened one of the small jars and dabbed a smidgen of black grease on his little finger. "We've a little theater company downtown. Smudge a little black cream below each eye and on your eyelids, and a little streak on each side of your mouth, then blend it in. Use your little finger." He chuckled and dabbed his ring finger with white paint, using it to mark her forehead and chin. "Blend the white, too. It changes the contours of your face." Last, he glued on a small moustache. "I have more of these.

"My wife was on stage when I first met her." He held Summer Rose's face steady with his thumb and forefinger. When he was satisfied, he held up the mirror. "See how your face changed? It takes a little of the prettiness out of you." From his shirt pocket he pulled glasses, wire-framed with lenses tinted a medium blue shade, and slipped them on her nose.

He spun her around to face Jack. "Now Major McAllister, do you recognize your sister?"

Jack grinned and ruffled what hair she had. "You look good, kid. That moustache is perfect."

Sergeant Landon had shoulder straps with brevet lieutenant bars sewn on her shirt. She fitted her forage cap and picked up her rifle, then saluted the sergeant sharply.

"I'm sending Matilda with your brother, and I procured you a mare from our stables. Your husband would have spotted Matilda a mile away. This horse is gray with black stockings and a white blaze. Someone named her Rabbit. You can change her name if you want."

He stood. "General Sheridan is back. Let's introduce you to Rabbit, and the general to his new dog." His eyes twinkled. "Grab a couple of sugar cubes from my desk."

Rabbit looked as worn as Summer Rose felt, and she immediately loved the ragged mare. She fed her a sugar cube and nuzzled her neck. "I'll clean you up tomorrow, and we'll become great friends."

They met General Sheridan on the lawn in front of the post headquarters. He motioned for her to turn around;

he beamed. "By damn, you've done it, Sergeant. Her father wouldn't recognize her. You removed the girl and damned near wiped out the prettiness."

Summer Rose bit her tongue, not sure she'd wanted *all* of it taken away.

Sheridan's black eyes just about pierced her skin. "Have you ever bowled?"

She shook her head.

"Sergeant, show our new lieutenant the ten pin game I devised. Get that other wet-behind-the-ears lieutenant out here. We'll need two dogs."

Sergeant Landon held the empty cannonball in his meaty paw. Even empty it appeared to have a nice weight to it.

"General Sheridan devised this game. He named it 'Dutch Ten Pins.'"

The cannonball hung from a rope, suspended between two elms in the front yard of headquarters. On a board between the elms sat ten pins.

"The object of the game is to wipe out the pins by swinging the cannonball in such a way that it misses the pins on the forward throw. Watch. As the cannonball swings back, it wipes out the pins." He showed them how to set up the pins. "Your jobs, gentlemen," for he included Lieutenant Timmons, "will be to set the pins up every time they are knocked down. One of you will set the pins, and the other will run the ball to the next player. Take turns. Think you can handle that, gentlemen?"

The lieutenants snapped to attention, saluted. "Yes, Sir."

Sergeant Landon took her aside. "The general has invited all of his senior officers for games and dinner. We'll see if Colonel Charteris recognizes you."

Her heart raced as she stood at attention near the front of the parade ground while the brass rode up. She and Bob Timmons took the reins as the generals and colonels dismounted, taking turns leading the horses to the stable, where grooms took them. She noted right off that only stars and eagles had been invited. She recognized Generals Devin, Torbert, Wilson, Rosecrans, and Custer. Tom Devin stared at her a little funny, then handed her the reins to his horse. Last fall, he'd sat beside her at Amelia's dinner party. He'd flirted with her, all the time winking at Daniel. General Devin was one of the few generals she liked. Several of the colonels were familiar, too. She knew Julian Bells, David Wood, and Charlie Wilder.

Daniel arrived on Chester. Her heart thumped out of control, sending heat to flood her face. For a moment, Daniel paused to rub his hand over Chester's neck, but she was sure he didn't recognize her. In fact, he barely noticed her as he handed her the reins. The horse, however, knew her right away. He gave his signature snort, shook his big head, and pressed his velvet muzzle to her neck, almost bringing tears to her eyes. She whispered to him all the way to the grooms.

Five minutes later, Hal rode up. Lieutenant Timmons took Dulcey. Hal didn't even glance in her direction. Dulcey nickered as Lieutenant Timmons led her away, and Hal walked to the opposite side of the yard from where Daniel stood.

Waiters took drink orders and offered selections of oysters, pâté, and cheeses. A few newspaper correspondents moved among the officers. Everyone visited for a short time then General Sheridan started his game. He gave them a demonstration and Summer noted how he flicked his wrist to make the cannonball spin, giving the ball the necessary lift to loop up and around then plow down the pins on the back swing. Her job was to either run the ball to the officers or set the pins. When she ran the ball, she stood out of the way, waiting beside the officer while he let fly the cannonball.

All the general officers took a turn. As she started to run the ball to Colonel Bells, General Sheridan raised his hand, halting play. He clamped his cigar between his teeth, took a drag, then pointed to Daniel. "Start with Daniel. Pretend, Colonel Charteris, that Mosby's head is swinging on that wire. We're all anxious to see what you'll do with the Ghost's head."

Ripples of laughter moved through the men. Summer didn't flinch, but ran the ball straight to him. She understood the general's maneuvers. He'd set Daniel up on purpose.

Daniel grinned and warmed his knuckles on his chest, oozing charm. No one, she thought, is better at charming than Daniel—when he wants to be charming. A few of the men made comments. She heard someone yell: "Put your wife's face on it!"

Her stomach dropped as his grin faded. Someone must have heard he wasn't on the best of terms with his wife. She kept her face hard as stone and added another notch to the list to which Hal would have to answer.

Daniel frowned down at her when he took the ball, but she didn't look away. She was extremely grateful for the cover of the blue-tinted eyeglasses. "You're new, aren't you?"

"Yes, Sir," she said, lowering her voice slightly.

"You have a name, Lieutenant?"

She snapped her best salute. "Yes, Sir. Lieutenant Samuel Ross, Sir."

"At ease, Lieutenant. Now, Sam, what's the trick to this game?"

She leaned toward him. "It's in the wrist, Sir. Next time General Sheridan takes a turn, notice how he moves his wrist."

"Thank you, Lieutenant Ross. When you get to know me better, you'll realize I'm very observant."

She kept her face smooth. *Observant, my foot! You have no idea who I am!*

He threw the ball and she held her breath as it soared past the pins, sweeping them clean on the return. A few clapped, several swore, one or two laughed.

They played for at least another hour. She ran the ball to Daniel three more times, standing near enough to smell him. Once her fingers brushed his, and a knife of pain shot through her chest. She longed to fall into their easy rapport.

When dinner was served, she and Lieutenant Timmons stood at attention near the front door. The aromas of beef steak, good hearth bread, and onions drifting from the dining room made her mouth water and temporarily took her mind off Daniel.

After cigars and cognac, Sergeant Landon approached them. "Lieutenant Ross, follow me."

He walked her toward the elms. "Colonel Charteris' fellow officers have set up a joke for him, a trick of which General Sheridan doesn't entirely approve.

"Somehow, your boy's fellow officers got wind that he's on the outs with his wife." His brown eyes twinkled. "How he could ever do that, I do not know. I heard she's a sweetheart. He must be either stupid or crazy. Or both." He cleared his throat. "Anyway, General Sheridan wants to dampen their powder, take the fun out of their joke, so he's playing a trick on the tricksters. Are you aware that your husband hates snakes?"

"Yes, Sir."

"Do you?"

"I don't like them, but growing up with three mean, older brothers cured any fear of reptiles, bugs, or such."

"Your brother said the same thing. I have a burlap bag with a six foot Black Snake in it. I double bagged him. I'd advise you to walk the creature over to your colonel's command tent, untie the bag, and leave it under his cot."

"I wouldn't want to hurt him, Sergeant."

Sergeant Landon cleared his throat. "It seems his fellow officers bought your colonel a present. They all chipped in and paid for a whore."

Her eyes popped wide.

"She's going to be escorted to his tent," he pulled out his pocket watch and frowned at it. "In about an hour."

"Thank you, Sir. Where's this bag you spoke of?"

She caught a whiff of pungent smoke, and General Sheridan's impish face materialized, glowing gold as he inhaled on his cigar.

"I'll show you where it is, Sam. I wouldn't miss this for the world. I'm glad you're a decent sport." He walked beside her. "Now tell me. How are you getting along?"

"Better than expected, Sir."

With the roar of the river beside them and the rough road lit by torchlight, the three maneuvered the steep streets of the army post, heading downhill toward Daniel's command tent. "Did our George fix your hair?"

She bowed and swept off her hat. "I must say, it's easy to care for. I believe my hair is shorter than either of yours."

They walked down the rutted gravel road to a small tent which possessed a good view of Daniel's headquarters. Several chairs were set up under the open fly. Sergeant Landon ducked inside and came back with a burlap bag, which he handed to her. He walked ahead of her and called Daniel's sergeant to the side of his tent. Summer slipped inside, knowing this was the blind obedience General Sheridan had demanded. If it stopped the ridiculous prank the others had planned, then that was just fine. Besides, the snake wasn't poisonous. In the dim light from the torches outside, she cut the tie on the bag, and shoved it under Daniel's cot. She touched the blanket on his bed, wanting to curl up on it, snake or no snake.

She crossed the street and the general indicated she should sit in the camp chair beside him. The smell of his cigar brought comfort and she smiled when Jack joined them. He squeezed her shoulder as he sat in the chair behind her and beside Sergeant Landon.

Around ten o'clock, Chester clomped by, turning his big head right toward her. She heard Daniel dismount and murmur to the big horse, then speak to the groom. Watching Daniel do familiar things hurt, made her heart ache. She followed his shadow as he moved about his tent, lighting lanterns and candles, then he sat at his field desk. General Sheridan reached over and touched her hand.

"Your brother said you could handle this. Is he right?"

She nodded. "I don't promise to like what happens."

Just then they heard the *clomp-clomp* of a pony pulling a two-wheeled wicker cart. On the side of the buggy bobbed a little red lantern. Behind the white-maned pony, they could hear the rustle of officers who had come to gawk. Many had consumed too much whiskey and were about as quiet as a dance troop. To Summer Rose, the entire scene became less funny by the minute. She didn't like seeing Daniel tricked. And she certainly didn't like the idea of a whore.

Jack, as if reading her mind, leaned forward and gripped her shoulder as the girl stepped out of the vehicle. Summer could smell her musky perfume. Daniel stuck his head out the tent flap, and the girl ducked inside without any invitation. Summer Rose willed her heart to slow.

Almost immediately, a piercing scream came from Daniel's tent, followed by several sharp retorts from a revolver. The crowd parted as the woman shot out of the tent and scrambled into the waiting buggy.

Daniel stepped out behind her. "Sergeant!" he yelled. "Get that goddamn snake out of my headquarters."

His fellow officers roared with laughter. Daniel didn't show good sportsmanship or even a sense of humor. There was certainly no charm. "The rest of you can get the hell out of here." He fired his revolver into the air. "If I want a woman, I'm quite capable of finding one."

Phil Sheridan slapped her on the back. The diminutive general bent over double, holding back laughter. She had a feeling he'd been watching for her reaction as much as Daniel's.

He stood. "You're not laughing, Lieutenant Ross."

She knew the effect her eyes could have on men, and George hadn't trimmed her eyelashes. She removed her glasses and allowed, even in the orange torchlight, the full blast of her blue-green eyes, with their lush lashes, to latch onto his face.

"Sir, it's hard to laugh when your heart is in your throat." She wanted to spit. Instead she asked, "May my brother and I stay here tonight? I'd like to be close to Daniel. I believe you understand by now that I know how to behave. I went along with your adolescent joke. I feel a need to watch out for him." Across the dirt road, his sergeant exited the tent with the obviously dead snake.

She didn't move, but was surprised when General Sheridan reached over and tugged the rawhide string from its hiding place around her neck. He palmed the ring and studied it for a moment, then tucked it back inside her shirt collar. His black gaze lingered on her. She glared back at him.

He made a dismissive motion with his hand. "You take care of the details. Just make sure you're at headquarters at seven. We ride to Charlestown and Winchester tomorrow. I have a meeting with General Grant. I'm taking your colonel with me, and I'd like you with us." His black eyes twinkled.

"Humor some old generals, my dear. Believe it or not, our lives are, for the most part, very colorless, at times downright boring." His voice sounded gravelly. "There will be a troop of about fifty or so men. Are you up for a thirty mile ride?"

She snapped to attention and saluted. "I look forward to it, Sir."

He nodded. "Good. Remember, we're making history here." He turned to her brother. "Major McAllister, I have a packet of documents for the President. Stop by my headquarters before you leave in the morning."

The entire evening came close to a nightmare for Daniel, and his desire to strangle Hal increased tenfold. Granted, the snake and the girl had unnerved him. He shuddered at the memory. He hated snakes. It wasn't just the snake, though. The girl, the smell of her alone, brought to mind Murder Bay and the brothels. He shook his head. Earlier, at the dinner party, he'd been out of sorts. Someone had let his comrades know of his difficulties with Summer, and that someone could only be his old friend. He was so angry he didn't trust himself to speak with Hal. Bashing his face to a pulp here would be inappropriate. He knew some rule existed that frowned on field grade officers groveling in the dirt while attempting to kill each other.

He shook his head again, but images of Summer Rose kept floating in and out of his consciousness: her, dripping wet in the moonlight, her, stomping naked into the house. In his head, a war battled. One side of him wanted to shake her. The other side longed to hold her tight. His body ached for her; his heart told him to jump on Chester, gallop to Camelann and tell her how sorry he was. No matter what she'd done—and there must be an explanation—what he had done was despicable, unforgivable.

I should have shot Hal. He reached inside his tunic and touched the remnant of her nightgown, which he'd found in his pocket. He remembered how he'd ripped it to shreds with his rage. A weariness crept into his shoulders and he sighed. The picture of her and Hal, naked, barged into his mind. Anger, blood red, and hot as hell, reared its ugly face.

CHAPTER 42

PURPLE-TOED SOCKS

Jack took her to the stables before first light. "Your horse needs a good grooming. I wanted to teach you how to fit out a U.S. Cavalry mount, but I have to get over to headquarters and catch the train. Take care, kiddo. Check out the other mounts. You'll figure it out."

As Jack walked uphill toward the depot, loneliness knifed through her. Only adrenalin kept her upright. All night she'd paced, then tossed and turned. She'd sat up, hugging her knees and staring at Daniel's shadow against the wall of the tent across the street. Her heart took up residence in her throat.

Last night Sergeant Landon had sent over her kit, and she'd cleaned herself as well as a girl could around thousands of men. She washed herself, never exposing as much as an inch of flesh below her neck. Becca had brought her a bottle of rosewater and she splashed a little on her body. She understood it wasn't exactly the right scent for a soldier, but she certainly smelled better with it than she did without it.

Now, at the stable, she cleaned Rabbit with sudsy water, then rinsed her, buffed her dry, and brushed her. She trimmed and combed her mane and tail, then cleaned and polished her hooves. During the entire grooming, Summer whispered to the horse, making friends. She left Rabbit with an extra measure in her feed bag, ran uphill to General Sheridan's mess, and talked gruff old George, the cook and part-time barber, out of a handful of carrots. On the way back from the mess, she checked out other cavalry mounts and fitted Rabbit out like them. When she was done, Rabbit looked pretty good, if she said so herself.

While she sat on a low wall near Rabbit, polishing her boots, she heard Daniel's voice, then Sergeant Landon's as they came round the corner of the barn with General Sheridan. Daniel glanced at her, then looked again at her sock, wearing a puzzled expression on his face. Damn. He'll guess. Jamming her foot in her boot, she jumped to attention and saluted.

She knitted all their socks, and she always did the toes in a purple yarn. It was her signature. Her mother had done the same. She doubted too many soldiers wore purple-toed socks. Daniel didn't say anything, but the question on his face remained.

Sergeant Landon must have sensed something awry for he turned to Daniel. "I want you to look at Chester's foot. I hope it's just a shoe."

Just then the general's groom brought Rienzi out of the barn. Summer Rose knew of Rienzi, knew he'd been named after Rienzi, Mississippi. She remembered Daniel telling her how the 2nd Michigan Cavalry had brought the Morgan stallion, Michigan born and bred, to Rienzi, Mississippi and presented him to General Sheridan. The papers caught the story and Rienzi became legend. Summer Rose's breath caught in her throat at the sight of the stallion: gorgeous, gleaming black, at least seventeen hands high.

Sergeant Landon approached, leading his bay gelding. He nodded, then whispered, "Rabbit shines." He sniffed. "I smell ... flowers?"

The rosewater had been a big mistake. She raised her face to the sky. The sun promised heat. She sniffed and shrugged. "I'll smell like a trooper in twenty minutes."

Sneezing from the dust, she thundered out of the village near the rear of a double column. Within five minutes, dust coated any exposed skin and her mouth felt gritty. She petted Rabbit's filthy neck. *Good grief,* she thought. *All my hard work on Rabbit is gone.*

The front of the column held Generals Sheridan, Devin, and Rosecrans. They were followed by buglers and color bearers, half a dozen more brigadier generals, and twice as many colonels. Daniel rode Chester at mid-column. Hal, on Dulcey, was there as well, but they weren't side by side. Like two magnets with their negative poles pushed together, they avoided each other.

She was surprised when she spotted the two good looking young officers, Jake Hunt and Ed Kincaid, who Daniel had brought home to lunch one day near Christmas when they lived in Washington. She remembered, too, that they'd been fresh out of West Point, lieutenants, headed out west to their first post, starved for a decent meal and female conversation. Somehow they'd ended up here and were already captains.

She almost waved and hollered. *Hello, remember me? I fed you imported ham and Christmas tarts. Remember?* Then she realized Christmas was a lifetime ago, she possessed no hair, and she was supposed to be a brand new second lieutenant.

Lieutenant Timmons, who rode beside her, also ate the dust of fifty-some horses. His know-it-all attitude irritated her, and she was glad the dust prevented his speaking. He only wanted to talk about the women on the camp's fringes, selling their wares. He acted like he knew a lot about women. She bit her tongue, because his lack of knowledge was obvious.

Thank heavens the horse soldiers stuck, for the most part, to a plain, straight forward, double-column canter. A couple of times the bugler rattled out Left or Right, and they wheeled into a wide turn, then back into a double column. Rabbit seemed to know exactly what to do. Once, too, they changed, slick as a dance step, from two abreast to four abreast, then into a straight wall of horse soldiers. Rabbit's gait was smooth. Summer Rose whispered to her constantly. In her head, she thanked Will for teaching her the bugle calls. *I'd have made a damn fine soldier.* As they swung back into a two-abreast column, Sergeant Landon's head kept turning back. Once he even nodded approval, eyebrows arched. She quelled the urge to stick her tongue out. The damned inverted corset hid her curves, but chafed her skin. Her armpits felt raw.

They rode through farmland lush with fat livestock and fatter barns. Unlike the rest of Virginia, the Shenandoah groaned with plenty. Small children waved, their mothers did not. The adults knew Sheridan's mission. He'd already started what they called "The Burning," and they hated him for it.

For a while the troops rode along the Shenandoah River, swollen with recent rains. The vistas, stretching one after another all the way into Maryland and Pennsylvania, took her breath away.

She knew the recent history. Lee had invaded the North through this valley twice, at Antietam and Gettysburg. Now Lee pushed Jubal Early north in order to draw the North's power away from Washington, and Grant maneuvered Phil Sheridan into the Confederate path to stop any movement toward the North. She realized how, below the rank of general, much of soldiering was just plain boring. Even Daniel, as a full colonel, was merely a pawn in a giant chess game. No one talked; they rode. A soldier had a lot of time to think. Daniel's broad back and wide shoulders made her fingers itch to reach out to him. The hair at his neck needed a trimming. She longed to care for him, to run her hands over his skin.

They stopped to water the horses at a spring near Charlestown. She knew the town had changed hands almost as often as Harper's Ferry had, and it was near here where they'd hanged John Brown. Right now, no one waved flags or offered cookies. Charleston definitely leaned toward the southern cause. The soldiers dismounted and stretched while Daniel talked with the two captains. Lieutenant Timmons came over and tried to talk to her. He'd heard about the trick played on Daniel and relayed it all over again. He thought it hilarious; she fantasized about cutting out his tongue. The bugler sounded, the soldiers remounted and cantered through the valley.

She rode into Winchester thirsty, sore, and covered with dust. The town was frayed like an old sofa, with rickety frame

330 | *Caroline Hartman*

houses and rusty wrought iron fences, both needing at least a coat of paint. Wash flapped on a line in a side yard. Two Negro women worked in a garden. An orange cat darted across the road. A little girl waved from an upstairs window until a woman dragged her inside and slammed down the sash.

The troops arrived in a big open field next to a sloping hillside of fruit trees. Off to the other side loomed a dark woods. From the opposite direction rode more Union troops and a big covered wagon. Harnesses creaked and rattled, horses snorted and snuffled as they all dismounted. Summer led Rabbit into the shade of some hardwood trees where a clear brook ran. The nerves along the entire length of her spine tingled. In the distance she watched General Sheridan walk up to General Grant.

She'd studied the papers Sergeant Landon had saved for her, and she'd listened to talk around campfires. The strategy was complicated and political. The officers in Sheridan's command talked of little else other than the importance of Lincoln's reelection. She knew a number of northerners were unhappy with the war. Even some of her neighbors had expressed discontent. Joshua, Ezra's brother, who lived on the next farm over, complained about the high cost in both men and money. General McClellan, the enlisted man's hero, never got around to sending them into battle. He was running against President Lincoln on the Democratic ticket. Just last night she'd overheard Sheridan saying how General Grant's losses at Cold Harbor and in the Wilderness had really hurt President Lincoln.

"What we need is a big victory. Thank heavens for Sherman," he said as he stood and threw out his coffee grounds. "At least he's had some success in Tennessee and Georgia."

CHAPTER 43

ROSES IN THE APPLE ORCHARD

The cooks set up a simple buffet and hot coffee under the trees, and Daniel helped himself to a plate of beef stew and biscuits, then took more coffee. Last night and this morning, he'd drunk so much coffee his blood felt rusty. He walked off by himself, feeling no desire to talk to anyone. He nodded to the two young captains. He'd spoken to them earlier, and they'd asked about Summer Rose. Artfully, he dodged their questions and disclosed nothing. Christmas was a lifetime ago.

Right now, he hated himself. The lieutenant, the one with the purple-toed sock, had caught his attention, and he felt oddly angry about the sock. Aware of how unreasonable his thinking was, nonetheless he'd always thought purple-toed socks belonged just to him. It had never occurred to him that someone else beside Summer might knit purple-toed socks. A picture of her materialized in his mind, haunting him. He ached for her. Then he'd yell at himself. His temper was on a very short leash.

Off to his left, Sheridan and Grant walked by. The rest of the brass milled about: some dozed in the shade, others smoked cigars or talked. At times like these, he and Hal would have stayed together. Now Hal stood with Bill Banion and a group of colonels.

Daniel's teeth clenched and he set off, ambling along a wagon track. Neat rows of fruit trees undulated across the hills and the vista, carrying a heavy fragrance of ripe apples, brought to mind Summer Rose's sweet valley. Nowhere else seemed quite so beautiful, so perfect. It was a little piece of paradise and his mind drifted to her, to sweet memories of her. He ended up at the horses where Chester whinnied for attention.

He fed Chester an apple and noticed the same young lieutenant brushing the gray horse. He remembered that horse. She'd been tagged for the knackers, and he'd personally countermanded that order. Now the lieutenant fed an apple to the gray. Trimmed and clean, the mare shook her head, proud of herself.

He complimented the new lieutenant. "I've seen that horse before. A good grooming makes a difference. What did you name her?"

He sniffed and caught a vague scent of roses. The lieutenant stood on the other side of the horse, bent over, fiddling with the stirrup. "Someone already named her Rabbit, Sir. Sergeant Landon said I could rename her, but I like Rabbit. Her coat reminds me of rabbit fur."

Lieutenant Timmons walked over. He sniffed. "What did you do? Feed her some roses?"

"She got into them all by herself."

Timmons nodded. "I had that nag for a day. She'll eat anything. Traded her. Now I got me a pretty little thing. She rides like a well-trained whore."

She noticed Daniel cringe. She knew he wouldn't like a horse to be compared to a whore. Her heart went out to him. *He's exhausted. Da, take care of him. I love him.*

Sheridan sat with Grant on a little bench in one of the apple orchards, where they were discovered by a cloud of gnats. Grant carefully peeled a yellow apple, letting the skin unravel in one long ribbon.

When Sheridan had finished unrolling the map of Virginia, he said, "I'm ready now." He pointed to the area in question. "I'll start moving supplies into the canyon at Berryville tomorrow. We'll sweep up the valley."

Grant speared a slice of apple and held it out to Sheridan. Phil took it. General Grant then pointed at the map with the blade of his pocket knife. "Drive Early south. Take his guns, his wagons, take as many prisoners as possible. Push him south. At the same time, take everything you need from the land, then destroy everything else. Burn the barns, the fields. Destroy any livestock you don't need. Run the Negroes off. I don't want them to be able to plant a thing. You'll probably have to send patrols up into the mountains because they'll try to hide their livestock. It's pretty difficult to hide large herds of animals. I know how hard it is for a cavalryman to kill horses, but it needs to be done. Lee's army must never refurbish itself here again. When do you think your supply lines will be in place?"

Sheridan studied the map as he fanned the determined gnats away from his face. Both generals swatted, but the insects kept coming back, darting at their eyes. "Monday, before daylight."

As they stood to walk back, Grant leaned over and picked up a handful of the soil, then let it sift through his fingers. "This soil will hold up well if we don't get a two day deluge. Watch for rain. I've seen mud destroy the best laid plans."

Chapter 44

GENERAL SHERIDAN'S SHOT OF WHISKEY

Summer Rose spotted Daniel's mother, then his father. She dashed into the warehouse and up the ladder before she remembered she wore a mustache and a soldier's uniform. She crouched in the loft's open window, her heart hammering like a hummingbird's. *What the devil are they doing there? Someone must have told them about me. Good Lord. They'll tell Daniel.*

Just then, Daniel rode in from patrol, covered in soot and looking bone tired. His head jerked up with surprise. He hadn't expected them, either. He dismounted, and the three of them stood right below her window.

Flora said, "Daniel, you're dirty!"

With a grin, he moved to kiss her cheek. She backed away, looking disgusted.

"We stopped at your wife's place," said Flora. Summer's eyes widened. "We almost missed it. Charming little cabin, but it's in the middle of nowhere."

Summer didn't need to see Mrs. Charteris' nostrils flare, she heard the sneer in her voice. "That German woman who works for Amelia told us your wife had ridden to a neighboring farm. She didn't remember which one. We saw Amelia later, but she wasn't any help at all. We did see Hal's darling baby. That's all Amelia could talk about. Are we going to get one of those soon?"

Summer Rose grimaced. Not likely.

"I wanted to go over a few things with you and Summer," Daniel's father said. "Her grandparents passed away within a week of each other. The bank took care of the funerals. We sent telegrams, but received no response. We couldn't ..." He cleared his throat. The dust at the intersection was fierce. "The house, the art, the businesses, the money from their sale, all the investments are to be held in trust for your sons. Girard has been very cooperative. Summer— well, actually, *you* will have a sizable yearly income from it. Daniel, I hope we can convince you to come back to Philadelphia. Fitzmartin Hall could be magnificent. It would take some money to fix it up, but you have plenty now. How can you stand this backwoods? All of it is so ... primitive."

Flora waved her hand in front of her face. "The smoke is so thick. And the odor." She puffed out air. "It smells ghastly. What on earth are they burning?"

Summer didn't hear any more. She sank onto the floor, her legs spread out, tears filled her eyes. After a time, she forced happy thoughts of her mother and grandparents into her mind, and more tears came. *At least they're together. At least they have each other.* She peeked out the window again. Daniel, leading Chester and walking between his parents, headed toward the hotel. Loneliness swamped her. *Keep him safe, Da. He's my heart.*

She heard Sergeant Landon calling her. She had socks to sort and stacks of underwear, trousers, and shirts to put away. Sergeant Landon didn't let her sit on her cot all day eating bonbons, which was too bad. She was losing weight and figured she could use a few bonbons. Army grub was truly disgusting. Almost every meal, when she smelled the food, she had to dash from the mess tent and throw up.

Sergeant Landon proved to be a great source of gossip. He relayed to her all the trouble her mother-in-law had created at Sheridan's headquarters. "She told Colonel Banion to clean up his papers, that he was a disgrace. She started to help him. You should have seen Colonel Banion splutter."

He laughed. "She advised the general to wear a wider brimmed hat because he was damaging his skin, and did he have to burn so close to camp?" He chuckled again. "She point blank told him Rienzi was too big for him. That he needed a smaller horse, perhaps a pony." The sergeant slapped his knee. "You should have seen the general's face."

When Daniel's parents left for Pittsburgh two days later, he told her General Sheridan had a shot of whiskey at seven in the morning to celebrate.

"Why are they going to Pittsburgh?"

"Your father-in-law is running for the Senate. Pittsburgh is full of all those iron masters making howitzers and cannons, becoming millionaires. Politicians and money, Sam, are like iron filings to a magnet."

Daniel didn't have time to celebrate his parents' departure. Every time Summer saw him his face was covered with soot.

All the soldiers returned to camp filthy and worn out. The sky above the valley blackened. Oily soot painted every blade of grass, every surface in the valley.

She didn't understand Sheridan's latest ploy, putting her on patrol with Daniel. Every morning she rode out at the end of his column, eating dust, and every evening she returned as dirty as the rest of them. All the burning, the killing of the animals made her sick. Fortunately, the two young captains, Kincaid and Hunt, protected her from the worst.

She suspected Sergeant Landon's hand in these orders. He made sure she was assigned to one or the other's company, and they made sure she held the reins of the other troopers' horses rather than set fire to the fields or the barns or kill the livestock. The smoke from the fat barns as they burned blackened her face and choked her heart.

Sledgehammers smashing the great stones of the mills to smithereens rang in her ears long after they'd done their damage. How would the mothers make bread?

She cringed when the soldiers shot the milk cows and killed hundreds of chickens. How would the mothers feed their children?

It took all her willpower not to stop and hug the crying children. Her own face smeared and blackened with soot and tears. She knew General Sheridan had rules, and Daniel and his officers for the most part followed them. However, hatred and vengeance ran deep. Custer and Daniel's troops knew who had raided with Mosby, and no mercy was given to their properties. She cringed, watching her husband's face harden as his men gave an eye for an eye.

They knew, too, what farms belonged to particularly vehement Southern politicians or Confederate officers. They leveled those farms. The soldiers knew every trick. If the silos were empty, they checked the walls of the houses for grain. If they found any, they burned the house. They discovered hidden cows and horses in out-of-the-way ravines in the mountains, and family valuables buried in the garden. Some soldiers tricked the farmers out of their savings, promising not to burn their barns, then taking their money and allowing another patrol to do the dirty work. Great clouds of smoke thickened the autumn haze as thousands upon thousands of acres burned, destroying millions of dollars of crops and property.

Feelings ran hard on both sides. Sergeant Landon told her Custer had executed a weak-minded boy he'd caught with a rifle. "The townspeople," he said, "begged Custer not to execute him. They said he was only squirrel hunting. You know Custer, hot tempered as usual. He saw a strapping boy with a rifle where prohibition of carrying arms had been posted. The boy was executed." He paused for a moment. "I can see his side. Early's troops, partisan bands, and bushwhackers nip at his troopers."

Summer cried all night when they found the body of the son of Quartermaster General Montgomery Meigs, head of the entire Union Army's supply. He'd been shot, his hands tied behind his back. Twenty-one year old Johnny Meigs had been blond, kind, always smiling. He'd graduated first in his class at West Point. Everyone admired and loved him, said he was a brilliant engineer. He'd been one of General Sheridan's favorite lieutenants. Summer Rose saw Sheridan ride up, dismount and cut loose the hands of the dead boy. The anger in his face rose like a flooding river. With a voice cold and hard as an Old Testament prophet, he ordered the fifteen mile radius from where Johnny's body was found to be leveled.

"Every house, every barn, every goddamn blade of grass. I want only bare dirt! I don't give a damn if they claim to be Yankees. They can claim they're Albanians for all I care. They didn't stop this. He was executed." The words hissed from between his teeth. "I want to lay my cheek on the dirt and not see anything higher than a pebble. Burn it black."

CHAPTER 45

SHERIDAN'S RIDE

On the evening of October 18th, Captains Jake Hunt and Ed Kincaid, and Daniel bent over a map spread on the tailgate of a supply wagon. Fresh from reconnaissance of the Valley, the captains reported to Colonel Charteris that General Jubal Early was building up his rebel forces. A zephyr ruffled the edge of the map, Daniel smoothed down the paper in an unending battle.

"He's planning on attacking, Sir," said Captain Hunt, smacking down the corner as a breeze picked it up again.

The three officers turned their heads when Lieutenant Ross walked by and nonchalantly placed two fist-sized rocks on the edges of the map.

Daniel stared at a rock for a second, then asked, "Lieutenant, is that fresh coffee I smell?"

"Would you like some, Sir?"

"Yes, please."

The lieutenant nodded and walked to the adjacent wagon. When Lieutenant Ross returned with the coffee, Daniel's gaze lingered on the hand wrapped around his cup. He frowned. For some strange reason whenever Lieutenant Ross appeared, he thought of purple-toed socks, then of Summer Rose.

"Phil Sheridan must like you," he said. "You aren't much bigger than he is. Lieutenant Ross, my captains tell me you're a crack shot with that repeating rifle of yours. Tomorrow, I'd like you up front near me. If you're as good as rumored, I may recommend you as a sharpshooter. In fact, get your gear and put it near my headquarters." He motioned to one of his sergeants. "Sergeant Bowman, Lieutenant Ross is riding up front with us tomorrow. Find him a spot near headquarters. Tomorrow, watch his accuracy."

He turned back to Kincaid and Hunt. "Captains, place your companies near us and bivouac them toward Fisher's Hill, behind my headquarters. I want to see the two of you first thing. Right now, walk over to General Custer's headquarters with me and tell him what you saw." He picked up his coffee cup and nodded to the lieutenant. "Thank you."

That same evening, Sheridan returned to Winchester via train from a strategy conference with Grant. From his comfortable bed in Winchester, he awakened at dawn to the din of distant guns. As George shaved him, he dismissed the cannonade as irregular and fitful. Then he frowned. "We shouldn't be able to hear guns from here, should we, George?"

—➤➤◄◄◄—

At breakfast, the guns continued to mutter, so he ordered his staff to saddle up. When he'd left for City Point on Sunday, his fine army sat encamped fifteen miles away. More than once, Grant had mentioned how important holding the

Shenandoah was. Sheridan wasn't about to let General Grant down. He climbed onto his beloved Rienzi and raced up the valley of the Shenandoah.

The first soldiers who met Sheridan hollered, "We've built breastworks, Sir. We're prepared for retreat."

Sheridan yelled back. "Retreat? Retreat? Hell! No one's retreating. We'll drive 'em back. We'll lick them right out of their boots."

As Sheridan approached the lines, the stragglers recognized Rienzi, if not Sheridan himself, and cheered. He shouted at them, waved his odd flat hat, smacked it against his thigh. He reached down and unsheathed his sword and lifted it high. "Damn you. Don't cheer me, you sons of bitches. If you love your country, come up to the front! We'll sleep in our own camps tonight or we'll sleep in hell!"

By the dozens, then hundreds, then thousands, then tens of thousands, they followed the little general on the big horse. He waved his saber high or swatted a straggler's rear end with it.

"Damn you! We'll send them back or to hell."

Behind the mass of soldiers ran a cheering line of horsemen, several miles wide, propelling any stragglers who hadn't been embarrassed enough by their general into marching toward the enemy. The sound of cheers, the roar of men, the thunder of tens of thousands of hooves, all mixed with the notes of the bugle, racing to reclaim what Jubal Early's troops had so recently taken.

Sheridan pranced Rienzi down the line, inspecting his regiments, making sure they were all in formation and at strength. The men cheered, and he hoped old Jubilee Early heard it. He'd been fighting that son of a bitch for close to a year. When he saw one of Gregg's captains standing with a company of prisoners, he stopped and questioned them from Rienzi's back. When he was convinced Lee hadn't sent General Longstreet to reinforce Early, he continued down the line, checking his troops.

He lined up all his regiments neatly, like his bowling pins, and waited until he was sure he could whip the enemy. Then, at four o'clock in the afternoon, as the autumn sun inched toward the horizon, he let them loose with a roar that scared the last crows out of the trees. The cavalry, Daniel and Hal's regiments, and dozens more rallied and slashed into Early's flanks. The clang of swords, the roar of carbines and artillery, the bitter smoke from the shells, filled the air. The horsemen dismounted and fired their rifles, chewing up Early's line, routing it. Summer Rose, involved for the first time in the actual fighting, became immersed in the heat of it. She lost her glasses, but not her accuracy.

From a distance, Daniel picked out the vague shape of his new lieutenant. With a trained eye he watched Lieutenant Ross take down a line of rebels. A wide line of Yankee horsemen continued to push stragglers forward, while the infantry rolled behind Sheridan, recapturing all the ground lost that morning. They freed at least a thousand Union troops who had been taken earlier, regained all their captured guns, and took twenty-five Confederate guns. Early's forces were routed, and the cavalry picked off most of their wagons, capturing at least 1300 more rebel prisoners.

Summer Rose mounted Rabbit and rode over to Captain Kincaid then glanced back through the dust to where Daniel rallied his troops. Her glasses, her hat were gone. She could imagine the mess her makeup was. She glanced down at her too thin body, knowing the corset now fitted poorly and the outline of the false bulk could be made out beneath her shirt. She wondered how much longer she could continue this masquerade.

She stood in Rabbit's stirrups, her hand shading her huge eyes and scanned the battlefield. A large part of her incredible accuracy was simply her eagle eye vision. She glanced at Captain Kincaid. Beneath his fringe of dark hair, now almost white with dust, he grinned and shook his head. She shrugged and held a finger to her lips.

For a moment the dust settled, and she almost choked when she recognized what she saw. Hobbs. Carlton Hobbs and a cohort thundered directly toward Daniel, reloading their rifles as they rode. Hobb's mutilated face, the one she herself had cut in the attack after the Christmas Ball, was so familiar, burned in her mind. She leaned forward, carbine in one hand, reins in the other, then nudged Rabbit with her knees and aimed the mare toward Daniel. She anchored the reins to the saddle and lifted the Spencer to her shoulder, balancing the barrel across her left arm as her right arm helped site through the billowing clouds of dust. She raced toward Hobbs and stood in her stirrups, firing, her strong legs guiding the horse toward Daniel. Firing again and again, she missed Hobbs, but unsaddled his comrade. Hobbs, holding the reins in his teeth, saw her as she raced toward him.

He yanked the reins out of his mouth, then threw his head back and laughed when he recognized her, taunting her and making an obscene motion with his arm and fist. His ghoulish face sent shivers to the pit of her stomach. Daniel turned, and she suspected he, too, recognized her, but it didn't matter, for all his attention was engaged in a fierce sword fight. She bent low, urging Rabbit forward. When they were only three feet apart, Hobbs' rifle jammed. He leered at her, his puckered, monster face laughing as he licked his lips, then he withdrew his sawed off shotgun and aimed it at Daniel.

Her heart froze. With her gun empty, and no time to reload or pull her knife, she swung with all her might, throwing the Spencer at Hobbs. It bounced off his shoulder, slowing him. At the same time she threw herself at Daniel, vaulting from Rabbit onto Chester's broad rump, grabbing at the back of Daniel's saddle.

She took the load of buckshot Hobbs had intended for Daniel. It landed smack in her back and backside. She rolled off Chester and hit the ground hard. From a small hill, Hal saw the young officer fall and spotted the rebel with the grossly scarred face, aiming a shotgun at Daniel. With a single round from his rifle he winged the rebel, then raced toward Daniel, followed by Captains Kincaid and Hunt.

Captains Kincaid and Hunt dismounted, positioning their horses to protect her, and Hal skidded Dulcey to a stop. Daniel jumped off Chester, landing beside Hal, who picked up her Spencer and stood back while Daniel knelt next to her. He looked down at the sprawled boy with the moustache, the oddly padded body and the boy haircut, and although a voice in his head told him it was Summer, he couldn't make his mind believe it. Then suddenly he couldn't breathe and he choked. He knew it was her. With his heart pounding, Daniel reached for the artery in her neck. The battle roared around them, but it seemed miles distant. For a heart-stopping second, he felt no pulse. He dared not breathe. Then, ever so soft, a faint thump came to life beneath his fingers.

"She has a heartbeat," he whispered. His hands slid down her limbs, then he turned her over and saw the bloody mess of mangled flesh made by the shotgun. "Christ!" He turned to Jake Hunt. "Commandeer a wagon, an ambulance, anything."

Ed Kincaid touched Daniel's arm. "Sir, she threw herself behind you. I saw it. She blocked that load of buckshot meant for you."

Jake Hunt came back with Sergeant Landon. Daniel stood, helpless, as the sergeant lifted her onto the wagon bed and laid her cheek against the wooden ledge. Daniel tore off his jacket and covered her wounds. He pressed one of his sleeves under her cheek, but she didn't so much as groan. The battle still roared; Daniel couldn't hear anything outside the circle of their little band on the hillside.

He watched Hal slide her rifle onto the wagon and his breath caught as Hal's hand grabbed his shoulder. "Take care of your wife. I'll see to your regiment." He watched, as if in a dream, as Hal tilted his head, signaling for Captains Kincaid and Hunt to follow him as soon as they'd tied Chester's and Rabbit's reins to the wagon.

He heard Hal say, "You know what to do, gentleman. Take care of his troops. We'll rally near Sheridan's headquarters just beyond the spring below Cedar Creek."

Daniel hopped onto the wagon and slid her across his lap to cushion the worst of the bumps. Some part of him could see the rebels retreating in the distance, another part concentrated only on her. He ran his finger along her hairline as Sergeant Landon pointed to the yellow flag of the medical corps flapping over the tents just coming into view.

"How's she holding up, Colonel? We have about another half mile."

He shrugged. Long ago he'd given up on God, but right now he prayed anyway. When they topped the hill and he saw the surgical tent, he let out a breath. Ambulances were already unloading the wounded.

At Belle Grove, Sheridan himself came over. "Ask Colonel Stone to come here," he told Sergeant Landon.

Ray, his apron crimson to his knees, his arms covered in even more blood, did a quick survey of her wounds then motioned with his elbow for Daniel to bring her inside the long surgical tent where lanterns hung from the tent poles. Ray rinsed his hands and arms then sluiced off an empty operating table with a bucket of water and a soapy sponge.

"Lay her face down. What happened?"

As Daniel told him, Ray sliced off her shirt and layers of padding. A few surgeons, two orderlies, and a half- dozen soldiers waited, gawking. Daniel shifted from side to side, trying to stand in everyone's way. He didn't like her exposed, wearing just her camisole and torn trousers. He wanted to protect her.

Ray held up the mangled corset. "This saved her life." He cut back her trousers and, with care, peeled back the bloody fabric. "She'll live, Danny boy. She's got a bloody backside full of buckshot, which will take hours to remove." He bent over and inspected her bottom closely. He mopped up some blood with a clean rag. "It all hit the fleshy part, none hit bone."

He lifted his head. "You have a couple of choices, Danny. I can't spare a surgeon for picking out buckshot." He glanced at Daniel, then at his orderlies, who were eyeing her backside with interest. "They could do it, or you could.. What do you think? I'll give you everything you need. It's not much more difficult than plucking a chicken. It just takes a lot of time. We'll swab her with iodine when you've finished. You've seen it done. You watched me take the gravel out of your leg." He stopped for a second and listened. "The battle, for the most part, is over."

Daniel appreciated the nonchalance of Ray and the other doctors, but he noted too, the eyes of the orderlies, stretcher bearers, and the other patients. Those not near death were all but drooling, ogling her body like a man eyes a girl.

General Sheridan walked into the tent at that moment, and overheard Ray's suggestion. He noticed the orderlies, chastised them with a finger snap and a wave of his hand. He approached the table and studied Summer's half-exposed back and shot-up rear end.

"Ouch!" He turned to Daniel. "I spoke with Hal and those young captains of yours. They have your regiment under control."

As General Sheridan shook out a sheet and covered her, he motioned to Sergeant Landon. "Find a decent sized tent, a table, and some lanterns. The girl needs privacy. Private Jennings, you are to protect this girl. You don't need to look at her to do so. Help Sergeant Landon set her up with a cot and some of those linens my aunt sent. You'd better get a telegram off to her brother, Sergeant."

Daniel picked up his coat, grabbed by warring emotions. Admiration for how the general was handling the details joined the churning pool of anger as his mind started to sort itself out. *Why am I the only person who seems surprised that she's in a uniform, trying to pass for a boy? That she's even here?* Fury gathered until his hands shook. He could do nothing to control either his hands or the rage.

He lowered his voice in hopes that it would stay even. "You've known all along, haven't you?" The volume increased on its own, though his voice cracked. "Jesus Christ, Sir. How the hell did you allow this to happen?"

"Calm down, Colonel." Sheridan's voice, while not loud, held a snap to it. "I was under the impression you wanted nothing to do with her." He snorted. "You know of her father, don't you? I admired him, and she ... well, she's one tenacious young woman. Did you know she killed a bear?"

His gaze drifted down to the rawhide string around her neck. Daniel shoved his hands in his pockets and paced the length of the tent. "Yes. And a mountain lion. And I just watched her take down a bunch of rebels. But she's a goddamn *girl*, General Sheridan. You should never—"

Sheridan lowered his voice, the words clipped through his teeth. "I should ... I should ... Protocol, Colonel. Carry on. I ... I trust you'll do a good job."

Daniel turned away. Very gently, Sheridan lifted her head and slipped the cord off her neck. For a long moment his black eyes hardened as if to bore through Daniel's back. At the same time, his hand snapped the ring into his fist. He'd give a lot to have a woman like this love him as much as she loved her colonel. His eyes softened. His voice didn't.

"By the way, Colonel, she's a marvelous goddamn girl."

Daniel turned, and the general held out the rawhide with the ring weighting the cord between them. Not a grunt, not a cough came from inside the surgery. The general's black eyes drilled into Daniel. "Put this back on her finger when you decide you deserve her. You certainly don't right now."

CHAPTER 46

BUCKSHOT AND BOTTOMS

Daniel spent two hours picking buckshot out of her bottom. After about the fortieth pellet, he regained control of his temper. After the sixtieth pellet he became adept at removing them. Around the seventy-fifth Ray came over with a big bottle of iodine and some cotton. "Swab this on her skin, thick, when you finish. It'll sting like hell and probably wake her up. You've done great. Go get yourself a cup of coffee. I'll check her out. Help me turn her over." As she turned, her breasts pushed at the thin material of her camisole and she groaned.

Ray said, "That's a good sign."

Daniel pulled the sheet to her chin.

"Get some food. Be back in ten minutes."

Daniel did as he'd suggested and brought back a plate for Ray. Summer was back on her stomach with her bottom, at least, covered by a sheet.

"How long will she be out?"

Ray took the plate and stood beside Daniel, eating. "Thanks. I forgot how hungry I was. This bread is great. And roast pork ... I'm starved. Where did you get this?"

Daniel growled. "Sheridan's mess. I just took it. I'm so angry at that ... I ... Did you know she was here?"

Ray nodded. "She came to me a few days ago with questions. I didn't mean to keep it from you. I've just been ... "

Daniel studied Ray for a moment. His apron, shirt, and pants reeked of blood and worse, his silver beard and hair held tiny flakes of dried blood. He looked exhausted.

"I'm literally buried in work, Daniel." He chuckled. "From what I know now, I think the entire army knew." He took a big spoonful of beans. "When you yelled at Sheridan, I thought for sure you'd end up in irons or be shot on the spot. Be careful, Danny. He's the best commander I've ever worked under, but he's quick to strike."

He turned toward Summer Rose. "Don't be too harsh, Danny. She's boosted the morale. All the burning, the killing horses, it's hard on some. The men love it: a girl officer, the wife of a colonel. Word spread about what a good shot she is. I just heard the boys in your regiment took bets on when you'd figure it out. Sheridan made his own legend today. If he hadn't, she probably would have. Did you see him rally the troops? I've never seen anything like it. He ensured Lincoln's reelection and gained himself a spot in the history books."

Ray glanced at the table. "She'll come around soon. She's grumbling and moving a little. You know she's pregnant, don't you?"

Daniel choked.

Ray chuckled. "Well, you know now. I wish you could see your face." He gazed down at her. "It'll be easier to remove that buckshot while she's still out of it. Remember the iodine." He stopped at the tent flap and stuck his head back in. "It's going to burn like hell, but we're finding it stops infection." He laughed again. "Hang in there, Daniel. You're as white as a truce flag."

A child.

Daniel stood for a moment studying her back. His heart hammered against the bones of his chest as if it might crack it open. Amidst all this death … a child. He bent and kissed the back of her neck and ran his hand down her spine. Even with all the bruises she was still a goddess, and even with all the questions spilling into his mind, he was surprised how much better he felt after he'd kissed her. *Will she ever forgive me?* His breath caught in his throat and he ran his hand through the short pelt of her hair. He shook his head and murmured, "Who the hell cut her hair?"

He felt an arm on his shoulder and turned to see Jack standing beside him. "She talked me into it. The President had a packet of material for Sheridan and I brought it on one of the locomotives. I'm going right back. I just saw Ray. He told me what happened and about the baby. Congratulations." He handed Daniel a bottle of Micah's salve.

Daniel nodded and pulled out the last few pellets, then pulled the sheet up to her waist. "Thanks. Do you have the formula for this stuff?"

Jack shrugged and held up one of the lanterns. "See how chafed she is under her arms? She bound herself up to hide her shape. Use that salve on the chafing, too. She may know where the recipe is. Eye of newt, toe of frog stuff. I don't know." He shrugged again. You have a small audience of waiting wounded outside, watching every shadow that flashes on the sides of the tent. They heard there's a girl in here." He shook his head. "There's something about soldiers. They can always tell when a pretty girl is around. What in hell prevented you from figuring it out? Half your regiment knew."

Daniel shrugged. He understood how stupid he'd been. He didn't need Jack reminding him.

Jack turned toward the cot, the one Private Jennings had made up, then bent and pulled down the top sheet and blanket. "Her hair, her uniform, everything you see she did for you." He stood and stretched. "When you douse the lanterns, stick your head out the fly and tell them she's fine. They've been waiting. I'll leave you now. She's about to wake up. I'll tell the President. Christ, Danny. *He* knew."

Before he applied the salve, Daniel dabbed all her spots with iodine. Thankful she didn't awaken, he took the warm water and washed most of the gunpowder and dirt off her face, neck, and hands. He carefully peeled off the fake moustache. She needed a swim in the lake, they both did, but he managed to clean her up a bit. He washed the dirt of battle off himself and removed his boots, tunic, and any buckles or belts that might hurt her. He slung his pistol holster and a canteen over the iron rim of the cot, and stood his rifle beside it. He took his time, rubbing her bruised and chafed spots with Micah's salve, then doused all the lights and stuck his head outside the tent.

"She will be fine, gentlemen."

Off to the side, he noticed Hal, who thumbed the corner of his wide-brimmed hat, then turned and walked away. He suspected Hal wasn't just there for Summer Rose.

Daniel carried her to the cot, wrapped in a sheet. He lay down with her, snuggled her half on top of him and half beside him, making sure her bottom felt no pressure. He pulled a crisp sheet that smelled of sunshine and lavender over them. The night was quiet. He could hear water running over rocks, a distant rifle retort, the low voices of guards and the wounded, and her breathing. Every muscle in his body relaxed for the first time since that horrible night, the night when he'd raped her. He pulled her closer, wondering if she wanted the baby. How could she after the way he'd treated her? He kissed the side of her face, and she made a smacking noise with her mouth.

He squeezed her gently and kissed her cheek again. "You awake?"

He felt her nod and helped her lean up, so as not to put pressure on her bottom. He held out the canteen.

"You gave me a scare," he whispered.

The interior of the tent let in a little light thrown by the torches and campfires outside. She stared at him a long time, so many emotions swimming through those large eyes. Finally she took the canteen and drank a lot.

"Thanks. I was so thirsty." She leaned her head against his shoulder. "Oh, Daniel, I've missed you."

He kissed the top of her head. "I've been inhuman without you."

"I heard rumors of such. Shouldn't you be with your regiment?"

"All taken care of. I'm right where I belong."

She wiggled her body to fit more beside him than on top and yawned. "If I go to sleep, will you be here when I wake up?"

"If I have to leave, I'll wake you."

They slept until reveille, when he untangled himself and dressed in the weak light. She rolled flat on her belly and snuggled into General Sheridan's linens. In the dim lantern light and through her thick lashes, she followed his every move as he washed and shaved, slipped into a clean shirt. Her heart filled and threatened to burst. As light inside the tent turned to gray, Little Phil stuck his head under the tent fly, coughed, and entered. The creak of leather and the clink of his spurs came with him. He hung a lantern on the center pole and she wondered, as she always did, how they managed to get his shirts so white. Even in the midst of battle she'd never seen him anything but perfectly groomed.

"I brought over some trousers and an old shirt," the general whispered, approaching the cot. "I'm happy to find someone shorter than me able to use them"

Daniel stood at attention. "Thank you, Sir."

The general smiled at her, then shifted his attention to Daniel. "At ease, Danny." Any animosity of the night before was gone. "I sent Custer and Wilson's divisions snapping at

General Early's heels. He's finished. Jubilee doesn't have the men to make another attempt. Those two captains of yours, Kincaid and Hunt, I promoted them to Lieutenant Colonels. Top notch officers. They're handling your regiment with much skill, and Hal is watching over them. When you're put together, you're in charge of my headquarters. Sergeant Landon is a great organizer." He pointed to Summer. "You may use my dog if you want. She's smart, but watch her. Trouble shadows her!"

He chuckled and sat down on the edge of the cot. Only her head and part of a shoulder peeked out of the bed linens. She turned on her side and studied him. Clean-shaven, he smelled of Bay Rum and soap. He tousled what little hair she had and his black eyes softened, deep lines forming at the corners.

"My dog looks a little beat. You have my permission to stay in bed today, Lieutenant Ross. Dr. Stone says you'll be fine. I'll send over breakfast for both of you. I believe you have accomplished your purpose." He bent and kissed her forehead. "I saw you standing in the stirrups, firing that Spencer as fine as any horse soldier I've ever had the privilege to command. You know, Mrs. Charteris, girls aren't supposed to be able to do such things. We'll be pushing south soon where we'll run Bobby Lee's Army into hell. We'll end this goddamn war. Are you coming with us? I could use a sharpshooter."

She smiled.

His face scrunched up, and he looked at the ceiling of the tent. "You'd think after yesterday, I'd be famous. I rallied the troops. I turned the day around. The Washington papers said

I not only knocked McClellan out of the race for president, but predicted I would knock the price of gold down below $200. Do I get any credit? No. You know who everyone is talking about? Rienzi! He's the hero of the day. A horse stole our thunder, Sam. No one will remember you or me. What would you think of my renaming Rienzi? I'm considering 'Winchester'. How does that sound?"

She nodded. "I think Winchester would be a fine name. I've changed my name a few times, and it's worked for me."

He stood and noticed the rawhide cord beneath Daniel's collar. He looked at her bare hand. "Daniel, she doesn't happen to have a sister, does she?"

"No, Sir, she does not."

CHAPTER 47

INDIAN SUMMER

Summer was still in bed, wearing an old shirt of Daniel's, with her bottom discreetly covered but pointed toward the ceiling, when Sergeant Landon handed her a telegram.

> GENERAL SHERIDAN:
> I TENDER TO YOU AND YOUR BRAVE ARMY THE THANKS OF A NATION AND MY OWN PERSONAL ADMIRATION AND GRATITUDE FOR THE MONTH'S OPERATION IN THE SHENANDOAH VALLEY, AND ESPECIALLY FOR THE SPLENDID WORK ON OCTOBER 19.
> A. LINCOLN.

"I'm so happy for him. He deserves it."

"What's more, Miss, is that Assistant Secretary of War, Charles Dana, arrived from Washington last night. We had to wake the general. Mr. Dana promoted him to major general in the regular army. No one can take that away from him after the war. Non-regular army commissions will revert to peacetime status after the war. He'll be a major general forever."

"Did he rename Rienzi?"

Sergeant Landon nodded. "Winchester. The local people love it. And there's a Pass and Review this afternoon." He handed her a package. "I picked these up in town for you. I guessed at the sizes."

She stood on her knees, opened the package, and fluffed out several petticoats and a tiered skirt of gauzy blue cotton. After fingering the material, she shook out the full skirt and spread it out on the cot. Each tier, trimmed with a taupe ribbon embroidered with daisies, darkened to a deeper hue of blue. The white blouse and blue sweater were also trimmed with the same taupe band of daisies. She crushed the skirt and blouse to her chest. "I love it. Thank you. To be a girl again ..." She giggled and held up the pantaloons. "You have remarkable taste, Sergeant."

"I told you I have two teenage daughters. I'd better."

"What about my hair?"

"I wouldn't worry about it. A number of the Southern ladies also chopped off their hair. You'll be surprised how many you'll see with scarves over their heads. The ladies, from what I understand, made a grand attempt to raise money for the Confederacy. They cut their hair and sent it to the European wig makers. I think they know now that our navy has their ports blocked. Nothing is getting in or out. You'll see lots of shorthaired ladies about. If I were you, I'd be proud of your cropped hair. Now get dressed. I'll send in some hot water and towels." He winked at her. "You can use that pretty smelling stuff you used when you first came."

"You knew?"

He chuckled. "I could smell you coming around a corner."

Indian Summer came to the Shenandoah and stayed for most of the autumn. A purple haze hung over the valley, sunny days with a bite, and crisp nights. Summer Rose stayed, also. General Sheridan teased her, saying, "Summer is staying with us. You must stay, too."

She, along with the soldiers, watched the great exodus from the valley. Sheridan's army had burned and destroyed all its substance. No food or fodder remained for Bobby Lee's army. None remained for the population, either.

Jack came to check on his sister and visited Hal. He told him to request leave so he could help his mother take his child to Philadelphia. Hal did so, then spent two days in Camelann, closing up the house, visiting the tenants, arranging for the care of the property and the animals.

Amelia, Becca, Ned, and Hal, along with baby Hank, took the train from Hanover. Hal delighted in holding Hank all the way to Philadelphia. The little boy could sit up now, and he smiled and giggled constantly. He loved to play peek-a-boo. Hal ran his fingers through the boy's golden-red hair, thinking his hair must come from Fanny, but those eyes were his. Hal hadn't imagined he could love anything as much as he loved Hank. He noticed Amelia's fingers wiggling, wanting to hold the baby, but he only laughed.

"You can hold him while I arrange for the carriage," he said. When Amelia's expression didn't change, he said, "Mother, quit fussing. You'll have him until the end of the war. I'll only have Hank for one more day."

"I'm just afraid his mother will show up and take him away from me."

"I wouldn't worry too much about Fanny. She didn't want him. She left him." Bitterness hardened his voice.

Amelia shook her head. "Hal! The girl is just sixteen. Few girls at sixteen have any idea what they want. Her father wrote me right after you were married and told me she'd lied about her age. He was very upset. He's rich and important. Who knows what he'll do? I live in terror of them showing up at my doorstep and taking Hank away. I want to hide him somewhere he'll be safe."

"Quit worrying. Fanny wrote. Her father's in Moscow, designing a railroad station. Her grandmother's ill and not expected to live very long. Fanny is considering entering a convent."

He didn't say as much to his mother, but a sudden memory of Fanny in bed didn't assimilate at all with images of her in a convent.

"Have you written back?"

"I'm thinking about writing. After all, she is Hank's mother. I don't want him to grow up and think I was unkind to her."

"Why did she leave?"

He grinned. "You've been champing at the bit to ask that question, haven't you?"

"I have. I thought you were happy." She reached out, wiggling her fingers, but Hal ignored her. She gave up trying to hold the baby. Instead, she played peek-a-boo with a flannel blanket. "You haven't answered my question, Hal."

"I thought Jack would have told you."

"Jack didn't tell me anything. What a strange young man. What exactly does he do?"

Hal had no idea how to answer her. Words just popped out of his mouth. "I don't know. Something with the President. Something secretive."

The train stopped for fuel and water near Downingtown. Hal stood, holding Hank against his shoulder. The baby's pale skin and golden down set against Hal's leathered face and dark hair made quite a contrast.

"Let's get some air," he said.

Once outside, he shrugged. "Don't blame Fanny, Mother. I wasn't a very good husband. When we get home, let's have one of those photographs taken of Hank. I'll send it to her. I know I'm biased, but isn't he the most beautiful child you've ever seen?"

"Do you want her back?" The sun glistened off Hal's crystal blue eyes and Hank's downy hair. Her grandson, so fair and smooth, her soldier son, so dark and weathered. Such a pretty and poignant picture. Her fingers itched to draw, and she thought of the sketchpad and pencils in her valise.

"I don't know, but I'd like Hank to get to know her." He put his free arm around Amelia. "It would be terrible to grow up without a mother."

CHAPTER 48

BOURBON AND TEACAKES

When he returned to the Shenandoah, Hal carried a bottle filled with Woodford Reserve bourbon and two glasses over to Daniel's tent when he knew Summer Rose wouldn't be there. They shared a drink and he told Daniel that the Zimmermans were taking care of the animals, that they had closed the house for the winter.

"Nip and Tuck will let Margie feed them. She spoils them." He reported on the status of their mutual holdings, then pulled out the photograph he'd had taken of Hank, and told Daniel he'd sent one similar to Fanny. "My mother's painting a portrait of Hank and me. It's pretty good."

Daniel and Hal spoke to each other about business or army matters. They asked about each other's sister and parents. But there was never any mention of the incident with Hal and Summer. Hal made certain that, even from a distance, he didn't make direct eye contact with her. One time, he found himself in the same room with her but immediately situated himself in a far corner, leaving a few minutes later. But he wasn't the only one having trouble adapting. Even Daniel, who longed to touch her, treated her as if he were her brother.

Daniel and Summer hardly had a chance to talk. She still slept on the cot in the warehouse. The sergeant, the general, most of the army noticed. No one commented. Chunks of the barriers between them fell, but the wall remained.

She told him she'd overheard him talking to his parents and knew about her grandparents. They talked about their deaths, how the bank had taken care of the funerals, how they'd tried to contact her, and how she could use the interest from their estate however she wanted. He didn't want her to know that the money would come to him, because women didn't own property. The minute they married, the money always went to their husbands. He'd forward the money to her, because her financial independence from him became important. He wanted her to want him for the same reasons he wanted her. He wanted her because he couldn't help himself. She was as much a part of him as were his bones and blood.

When they were together, he confused her. One minute she thought he wanted nothing to do with her, yet, at the same time, she felt the heat of him. His pale eyes smoldered, all but smoked. Without them as much as touching, desire swamped her. *All he needs to do is snap his fingers, and I will melt.* Then she shook her head and reminded herself about the gold piece. The devil in her told her to charge a lot more than two dollars.

When he talked about her grandparents' estate, she told Daniel, "I don't want to live anywhere but Camelann. I don't need money there."

He nodded. "I don't want to live anywhere else, either." He wanted to live in the valley with her and their child. He knew they'd need money eventually, but he didn't press the point.

Frustrated and a little frightened—frightened that it would never be right with her and Daniel—she marched directly to General Sheridan. He was sitting, hatless, at a folding table outside his headquarters, writing a letter and soaking in the weak afternoon sunlight. Rocks held his papers flat, keeping them from blowing about the camp.

Summer sat on a folding chair opposite him. The wind blew her short hair all about. She loved that it didn't tangle, even in all this wind. "We won't be longer than a week, Sir. We need to check out our property."

He pulled a chair beside her and signaled Sergeant Landon, who set about fixing them a tray with a tea service, cups and saucers, and a plate of cookies. The sergeant used his general's Spode.

"How much property do you have?" he asked. He stood and rearranged stacks of papers and rocks, and took the tray from Sergeant Landon. He poured her tea. "Sugar?"

She shook her head. "About eight thousand acres, Sir."

He moved his chair closer, and they talked together for over a half an hour. The soft autumn breeze wound round them. She described the lake and the valley, and its history with her family. Then she explained that Daniel and Hal had bought the original acres from her brother, then bought adjacent farms and leased them to veterans." Her eyes grew huge, and she whispered, "You know, a lot of soldiers didn't reenlist after their three years were up."

She took another cookie and he nodded, almost choking on his tea with surprise. He hadn't expected her to be informed.

She told him how she treasured the land, how she wanted to keep it a place where the eagles could come back to their nests year after year, a place where the beavers could find their lodges forever.

"You know, Sir, the Indians felled trees over the beaver lodges and used them as bridges across streams so as not to damage the beavers' homes." She made a sweeping motion with her hands. "I even want to keep the bears and the mountain lions, as long as they don't get too close to the house. It's truly God's country. You can't imagine, General, how beautiful it is. After the war, you must come for a visit."

She took a sip of tea. "Where do you get this tea? It's delicious. Did George make the cookies?"

Her presence, her voice, the way she grinned, all her questions, and the light sparkling in her eyes wove a web about him. How did she know about the dearth of reenlistments? The Indians? He noticed she still didn't have Daniel's ring on her finger. He knew better than to hope, but he could imagine. After all, he was a major general.

"Sergeant Landon's wife sends us the tea, and yes, George made the cookies. Try a tea cake. The ones with powdered sugar are my favorite."

—➤➤⏪⏪◄—

What little they saw of the Shenandoah Valley was deserted. Because of the mild weather, some green showed through the scorched earth, but the ground was still predominantly blackened grass. Those farmhouses still standing were vacant, the great barns were ashes, as were the mills. The miles of fence rows and the herds were gone. Even the field mice, gophers, groundhogs, and birds had deserted the now burned vistas. The vast richness inherent in the Shenandoah lay fallow.

They saw only one family, glassy-eyed with hunger. Even the children glared at them. Summer insisted they give them a ham, potatoes, flour, and coffee.

The first day they talked vaguely about the baby. Ray had told her she'd be all right on horseback as long as she took it easy. He advised her to dismount every few miles and walk a mile or so. "A blast in your backside didn't shake loose that baby. I think a nice ride won't hurt. Just don't push yourself too hard." He told Daniel much the same for different reasons.

As they walked in front of their horses, he asked, "Are you happy about the baby?"

"Very," she said.

He took her hand and her heart fluttered, then flew up to her throat. His hand, brown and strong, swallowed hers. The hardness, the warmth flooded right up her arm. Memories tripped over each other. She remembered his forearms on their wedding night. How strong, how gentle, how they'd held her.

"I remember the first time I held your hand. Do you?" he asked.

She nodded, feeling suddenly shy. "Right after I killed the snake."

"You know, I always suspected something wasn't quite right about Kip." His eyes danced. "I even asked Hal if Kip could be a girl's name."

"You're making that up. You had no idea Kip was a girl."

They walked in silence for a while, still holding hands. "I suspected. I certainly like Kip as a girl."

"You do, do you? Maybe we should name the baby Kip. What do you think?"

He shook his head. "Only you could ever be Kip. I've given a little thought to the names. If it's a boy, I'd like to name him Micah Angus. Is that okay with you? I have great admiration for your father, even though I never met him. He's one of my heroes."

He looked at her again, his eyes soft. "If it's a girl, you'll probably want to name her after your mother. I like Lillian. I'd like to call her Lillian Rose, after you and your mother. I wish I'd known her."

"Does that mean we'll have to name the next babies Flora and Louis?"

"Good lord. I didn't think about that." He smiled and squeezed her hand. "We'll worry about that later."

He kept holding her hand and warmth flowed all the way to her chest. *At least he didn't run away when I mentioned more babies.* Hope mingled with the soup of emotions sloshing inside her, and she reached in her pocket, fingering the gold piece.

That first night, they made a fire and fixed their bedrolls under the stars near a shallow pool in a rocky stream. The night was exceptionally clear, and they watched the flames lick toward the stars. The heat fell on their faces and Summer half-wondered if they might be the last two people on earth. He'd skewered pieces of steaks, onions and peppers on his sword, and now sat on a rock by the fire, roasting their dinner.

"The best use for it I've seen so far," he said, then gestured toward their pack of food. "I know the army has an abundance of beef. George gave us bread, apple tarts, and a quart of cider."

As they settled down for the night, the awkwardness seemed palpable. Daniel kept his back to her while she bathed and changed by the pool, and she did the same for him. Once settled near the fire, he tentatively ran a finger along the line of her jaw. The fire created soft shadows on the contours of his face. His voice came out low and shy.

"I'm so sorry I hurt you that night."

She pressed a finger to his lips and studied the fire for a long moment. The words came out awkwardly. "You … you hurt me, but I was partly at fault. What must you have thought?" She brought her eyes around and focused on him. "Daniel, I deserved your anger. I'm sorry, too. You're my life." One side of her mouth pulled up. "I could no more stop loving you than I could pluck a star from the sky."

Her head rested on his arm. She sighed sadly. "There's one more thing we need to talk about."

"What?"

"The baby. I don't know what happened that night. I was drunk. I'm so ashamed."

He pressed a finger to her lips. "Shush. The baby's my child. I hope someday I can forget how he was conceived."

He touched the tip of her nose. "It doesn't matter, Rosie, who fathered the child. More than likely we'll never know. The baby's mine because he's yours, and you and I are the same."

He slipped the rawhide from around his neck and held up the ring. "Remember, we're married. The moment Ray told me about the baby, I decided I wanted both you and the child, even if, by some wild chance, he is Hal's. What's important is that we're together. Will you forgive me for hurting you, for the anger, for the wasted days of being apart? Will you wear my ring again?"

Tears gathered in her eyes. "Oh, Daniel, I forgave you a long time ago." She took the ring in the palm of her hand, then closed her fingers over it. "I thought I'd lost it," she whispered. "I thought I'd lost you. Can you forgive me? I don't know what happened with Hal. I know I didn't want him. I have no memory of anything."

He kissed her salty eyes. "I told you it doesn't matter. You're here, alive, carrying my child." His big hand covered her abdomen. "I never quit loving you. What happened, happened. I know you were frightened, grief stricken. I'm sure Hal had more in mind, but he's sorry, too. I haven't yet figured out how to reconcile with him, but I love you, Rosie. I've been going crazy not touching you." His voice broke and grew softer. "Ray told me I could." His hand rested on her waist. "What we have is worth keeping. So many men I knew are dead. We're alive, sweetheart. You're a part of me as much as my hand is a part of me. I want you."

He opened his arms, and she burrowed into them. As he ran his hands through her short hair and kissed her face and neck, he told her, "I didn't feel I had the right. Not after what

I did." He rolled against her, holding her face between his big hands. "I'm so ashamed of what happened and so, so sorry." He moved his hands down the sides of her body. "I've about gone crazy keeping my hands off you. I love your short hair, and the baby ..." He showered kisses all over her face, her neck. His big hands shook, but he chuckled. "I was so dumb." He held up her sock. "I even saw your purple-toed sock and didn't realize it was you. You cut your hair." He hugged her tightly. "Oh, Rosie. I was dead inside without you. I never want to feel like that again. I'm so sorry I hurt you."

She brushed the tears out of her eyes. "Hush now." She pressed her lips against his neck. His skin smelled good enough to lick. His shirt came off and her hands stroked the skin of his shoulders, his chest.

"You are my heart," she said, wiggling out of her nightgown. "I never stopped loving you." Her voice grew husky. "Though I'm still a little miffed about that two dollar gold piece."

He lowered his head. "That was just meanness. Dirty meanness. I'm so sorry."

He buried his face against her breasts and didn't see the imp in her eyes. "Daniel, meanness or not, I'm worth much more than two dollars."

He growled and sucked in a deep breath, then rolled over on his back, holding her close to him. His eyes swept across the night sky. "Oh, sweetheart, how right you are. If every star were a two dollar gold piece, I'd trade them all for right now with you." He kissed her hard and long and held her so tight she could barely breathe. His voice came out raspy and low. "I don't ever want to live without you again."

CHAPTER 49

ACROSS THE STONE BRIDGE

She danced through Maryland and Pennsylvania, grinning constantly at her ring, which she'd assumed had been lost on the battlefield when she was wounded. Having it back on her finger thrilled her; having Daniel back in her arms completed her.

They spent another night under the stars. The following afternoon they came to the stone bridge her brothers and father had built. Both basked in the happiness of being together and coming home. No evidence of war showed in their part of Pennsylvania. Peace permeated deep inside them, very much like the purple haze of Indian Summer that veiled the valley.

From a distance, they saw a note nailed to the boarded up door. Daniel took it out of the envelope and unfolded the paper. When he read the words, all warmth left him. He handed it to Summer Rose.

JUST WANTED YOU TO KNOW
THERE IS NO PLACE FOR YOU TO GO.
THERE IS NOWHERE YOU CAN HIDE.
I KNOW ALL THE PLACES YOU ABIDE.

SWEET, LOVELY SUMMER ROSE
DO NOT ALLOW THOSE HAUNTING EYES TO CLOSE.
WHAT I HAVE IN MIND FOR THEE
IS FAR WORSE THAN WHAT YOU DID TO ME.

– H.

She went to rip it to shreds, but Daniel stopped her and pocketed the note. "Remember, I'm the son of a lawyer. Evidence."

They took down the boards that had been nailed over the door. Chaos and ruin greeted them. The piano had been axed, the mattresses, the quilts her mother had made, all were shredded. The chair and couch cushions smelled of urine. The books were ripped and thrown on the floor; some had been burned in the fireplace. Flour had been dumped all over the house. Dishes and glasses lay in shiny shards. Even her mother's china, stored in an odd little chest, hadn't escaped detection. Every piece had been deliberately destroyed. Becca must have canned quarts and quarts of tomatoes, for the jars were splattered all over the kitchen. They found three different sets of tracks around the house.

Daniel took her hand and led her to the bench by the lake. "We'll hire someone to clean it. Your heart will break a thousand times if we do it. Let's check the barn."

No damage had been done to Hal and Fanny's house or to the barn, but something still didn't feel right. They both sensed that Hobbs and his gang had been in the barn. In her greenhouse, Daniel and Summer found the glass destroyed and another verse nailed to the wall. Summer Rose felt her heart tear as she read.

> CHECKED EVERY CRANNY, EVERY NOOK
> TWO DOGS WE FOUND, TWO DOGS WE TOOK.
> SMART AND FIERCE, WE'LL TEACH 'EM RIGHT
> TO TEAR AND BITE AND REALLY FIGHT.
>
> SWEET, LOVELY SUMMER ROSE
> I WANT YOUR EYES, YOUR LIPS, YOUR NOSE.
> I WANT THE PIECES OF YOUR GORGEOUS FACE
>   SCRAPED OFF THE BONE.
> I WANT YOU NAKED AND ALONE.
>
> — H

Summer gasped through sobs. She leaned her forehead against one of the support posts and pounded the wood with her fists. "I'm going to kill him, Daniel. If he hurts my dogs, I'll kill him. I don't care who his father is. They can hang me. I do not care. I'll kill that son of a bitch." She looked up at him, her faced streaked with tears. "How did he find our valley?"

He took her hands and pulled her into his arms. "Maybe he followed Hal when he came here." He ran his fingers through her short hair and pressed her cheek to his chest. "I'm so sorry."

They rode first to Morgan's Corner where Daniel composed three telegrams: one to General Sheridan, concisely giving him an idea of what had happened and requesting Boy Criel be sent to their valley. Boy Criel, part Iroquois, part French-Canadian, was the best tracker in the Army of the Shenandoah. The next telegram went to Hal, asking him to give Boy Criel directions and search the army camps for the dogs. If Hobbs used them for sport, the most money would be made around the Yankee camps. The last telegram was to Jack McAllister. They received three responses within an hour. Boy Criel and Jack would leave immediately: Jack from Washington, Boy Criel from Harper's Ferry. Jack asked that they not clean up the house until after he arrived. Hal would scour the camps.

They stopped at Ezra and Margie's farm and told them. No one had seen a thing. They had been to the lake two days previously and no note had been nailed to the door at that time. Margie promised to clean the house with her older boys, and Ezra said he'd repair the greenhouse, but they said they would wait for Jack. Everyone was sick about the dogs and thrilled about the baby. Margie packed them a basket of food, and Ezra returned with them, taking their horses back to his farm.

"I'll send one of the boys with them first thing," he promised.

They packed firewood, Margie's basket, bedding, and the tent into the canoe and headed for the island.

The owls still hooted and flapped their soft wings. The moon inched over the mountains, tossing a silken sheet of silver across the water. The rocks and pines still whispered.

But nothing seemed the same. Was that bastard on the mountain spying on them with a rifle scope? Was he waiting for first light so he could pick them off like ducks in a row? Their wonderful, secluded valley had been violated.

On the side of the island facing the meadow, Daniel built a small fire. They made coffee and halfheartedly picked at the chicken Margie had sent. They sat amid the rocks and made sure their silhouettes didn't show. Later, when the fire died to embers, they swam and bathed on the side of the island that faced away from the mountains. Being clean was the best part of the day. .Later still, they lay in each others' arms. Neither of them slept very much.

Jack arrived before ten o'clock the next morning. He touched the destroyed piano and shook his head with disgust. "I remember hauling this monster from Lancaster, and your mother playing it, teaching you." He walked through the house, touching, remembering. He picked up the pieces of a small porcelain dog. "We brought this from Scotland. It came from my mother's family."

Boy Criel arrived around eleven. Boy, white-haired, skin like supple, well-cured doeskin, was tall for an Indian, and very lean. He claimed to have scouted for President Zachary Taylor. Boy showed them how poorly the nails that tacked the notes up had been nailed.

"He's using his right hand, and he's left-handed. The handwriting on the notes isn't good either."

Boy showed them where the intruders had tied their horses in the barn. Outside, he pointed out how one man's right foot turned in, another wore two inch heels. "The third man is probably big. His footprints are deep." He found the remains of several cigarettes. "English brand. Expensive. The sulters don't sell these. They were purchased in Baltimore or Washington."

He pointed out the droppings and tracks of their three horses and followed them upstream from the bridge to where they had crossed the stream, headed for the Gettysburg Road. A little south of where the lane met the road, he found more droppings. He knelt beside the dung and dissected it with a stick.

"This is clean. No grass, nothing except hay, winter oats, and a few pecan shells. I can track their horseshit all the way to Virginia."

Jack shook his head and said to Daniel. "You were wise to send for him."

Boy said he wanted to continue tracking while the trail was fresh. They agreed to keep in touch by telegraph.

Margie and Ezra, along with the four older boys, arrived with a picnic lunch. Everyone pitched in to clean the house. It was a huge undertaking. They heaped the living room furniture and mattresses into a pile and burned everything they could. The parts of the destroyed piano that couldn't be burned were lifted into Ezra's wagon to be taken to the dump. They scrubbed the remaining furniture, spread the rugs out in the sunlight. The boys took every pot, every towel outside, then swept and mopped the entire house.

Margie put a final coat of lemon oil on the floors and shook her head. "Come February I'll think of those smashed tomatoes and cry. Becca showed me how to can. That girl sure is a cook."

CHAPTER 50

ASHES

Jack nailed the last board over the door and the three of them rode to Morgan's Corner, where Jack sent a telegram. When they arrived at the railhead, a private locomotive and car waited for them. It whisked them and their horses through the night to General Sheridan's headquarters.

"How do we rate our own private train, Jack?" asked Summer.

He chuckled. The car was a simple, empty boxcar with horse stalls at one end and cushioned wooden benches at the other. It certainly wasn't luxurious, like some of the private cars of the affluent. Daniel surveyed the interior, then pulled up a bag of oats and set in front of her seat.

He patted the makeshift footstool. "Put your feet up."

Jack didn't like how tired she looked, either. He took off his jacket and tucked it around her shoulders. "I have friends in high places. A cabinet member's daughter has been threatened. Kate Chase received a poem last week. We believe the blood sports, the rapes, the threats are all related. Did I tell you Pearl Mason was released?"

They both whipped their heads around. "What?"

"The Darlings dropped the charges."

"They *what?*"

He shrugged. "Someone paid off someone. Mrs. Mason was out of prison and long gone before we knew anything about it."

Summer leaned forward. She put her feet back on the floor, her elbows on her knees, and her head in her hands. "What's going on? That horrible woman *sold* their daughter to Hal."

"The President's reaction was about the same as yours."

Daniel asked, "Who was the judge?"

"Judge Turner."

"Ephraim Turner?"

Jack nodded.

"He has a good record. What has he to say?"

Jack's dark eyes were hooded. "He shot himself before we could ask."

Daniel and Summer stared at him.

"The Darlings?" Summer finally asked.

Jack shook his head. "I think threats on the girl's life may have been made. Neither parent will say a word, except that he requested transfer to the Indian Territories, which the President approved."

Daniel arched an eyebrow.

"He and Sam Grant both said to let them go." He dusted dirt off his boot. "I've found both Lincoln and Grant to be honorable men. Hard, but honorable men."

The train pulled into Harper's Ferry and Jack stood. "Let's find ourselves some dog thieves." He pointed to his sister. "You, however, will get off your feet. Otherwise I'll ask General Sheridan to confine you to quarters."

While Summer Rose rested in Daniel's tent, night searches were made. Jack set up a central desk in one corner of Daniel's headquarters so he could watch all communications. Jack was good at that. He stayed near her, keeping a close watch on her. At the same time she didn't feel left out. Word came from Daniel that Devin's command had found the remains of what appeared to be dog pits near Staunton. Boy Criel reported finding more of the expensive cigarette butts at Rockfish Gap.

General Sheridan demanded a powwow with Jack, Daniel, Hal, and Summer Rose. For the first time, Hal and Summer Rose stood near enough to see the whites of each others' eyes. When they entered Sheridan's headquarters and saw the red glint in the general's black eyes, all thoughts of their own problems evaporated. In the flickering lantern light, Sheridan sat behind his field desk, his back West Point-straight, his face set in stone. The men who served under him knew that face. That was the face which rallied his troops and pushed men *uphill* to take Missionary Ridge.

When they were all settled, he said, "I'm in the middle of a goddamn war. I have 60,000 men under my command. Sam Grant is counting on me. We almost have Lee boxed in a corner. What the hell is going on?" He pointed to Jack. "Major McAllister. Start."

Jack summarized the blood sports, old and new, the numerous rapes and murders, the gutted girl, Liza, the attack on Summer after the Christmas Ball in Washington, how she'd slashed Hobbs, suspicion that he was a spy, and how he'd fled to Virginia. He told of Pearl Mason's high class brothel, and the rescue of Liza by Hal and Daniel. He relayed what he'd uncovered regarding Mrs. Mason's operation, the money involved, the notebooks. He explained Summer and Ray's involvement, Mrs. Mason's release, then moved on to Judge Turner's suicide, missing evidence, Sergeant Darling's request for transfer, and the threatening poem received by Kate Chase, the daughter of Lincoln's Secretary of the Treasury. Jack finished by handing the general his orders, signed by the President. He nodded to Daniel, who reached in his shirt pocket and gave General Sheridan the two poems they'd found in their valley.

Little Phil spent a few minutes studying Jack's orders and the poems, then looked up, his eyes pausing momentarily to her hand and Daniel's ring. He leaned back, his hands laced across his buttons. "I'm up to my eyeballs in this whether I want to be or not, aren't I?" One corner of his mouth curled up. "I knew you were trouble the minute I laid eyes on you. You slashed him with a Bowie knife that you just *happened* to have beneath your goddamn ball gown?"

Summer lowered her eyes. The silence was loud and long.

"Jesus Christ, General Sheridan, would you expect anything less?" blurted Hal, effectively breaking the ice with the general, Summer Rose, Daniel, and himself.

The general shook his head, a little smile threatened his stern demeanor.   Everyone laughed. His eyes sited to Summer Rose. "Next time slice the bastard's throat."

He cleared his own throat then turned to Hal and Daniel. "Have you considered offering a reward for the dogs? Post it in the local towns. Someone will squeal. Men who deal in these sports would sell their mothers for the right price."

The next day posters were printed and sent out by courier to all the towns up and down the valley. They offered a $200 reward for the recovery of Nip and Tuck. Just about every rebel in Virginia and the entire Army of the Shenandoah now knew some version of the Lieutenant Lady's dog story. The reward was huge and just about every Yank, rebel, and civilian wanted it.

Just before dawn of the following day, a rider galloped by Daniel's headquarters, and a package hit the dirt at the entrance with a thud. Daniel awoke with a jerk, and his wife stirred, but he patted her hand. "Relax. It's just a mail packet."

But he knew it wasn't a mail packet. When she'd fallen back to sleep, he pulled on his pants and boots. Jack, who had bunked across the road, knelt beside the burlap bag and pointed to the blood. Daniel heard a noise behind him, but didn't turn. "Go back to bed, Rosie. You don't want to see this."

Sergeant Landon and Boy Criel arrived just as the sun was coming up. Daniel took Summer by the arm and led her toward the guard post by the river. She still wore her nightgown with his army jacket over her shoulders. He questioned the guard and watched the men in the distance as they examined the hoof prints, the bag, and the murdered dogs. He held her close.

"I'm going back, Daniel. I'm not a child."

She sat in the dirt and dust of the road beside the dogs' mangled bodies and pulled them onto her lap. Her hands stroked their bloody paws and muzzles. Their nails and teeth had been pulled. As she ran her hands over the burn marks, a half-sob, a half-cry escaped. Daniel sat in the dirt beside her. A huge sob knifed through her, and she buried her face in the fur by their necks.

"How could anyone do such things? What kind of people are they?"

He sat beside her until Sergeant Landon knelt on her other side. "I'll take them, Summer. Let me have them. I know just the place for them."

All afternoon she lay on Daniel's cot, her body coiled into a ball. Later that day Sergeant Landon took her up to the hillside to Maryland Heights where they had first met, on the ledge where she'd waited for General Sheridan. He'd buried Nip and Tuck under a scrawny pine tree and marked their grave with a large oval stone. The mighty Potomac and Shenandoah Rivers roared below them.

"I've always loved dogs," he told her. "So much easier than people."

CHAPTER 51

TRUEST FORM OF FLATTERY

They sat for a long time, not talking. From down below they heard the bugler call evening mess.

"You'll miss your dinner, Sergeant."

He nodded toward the large cloud of dust making its way up the hillside. "I was waiting for him."

General Sheridan came into view, riding Winchester. She stood as he neared and walked out to greet him. Rienzi, now Winchester, nuzzled her shoulder while Sergeant Landon held the reins of all the horses.

The general jumped down. "I wanted to tell you in private how very sorry I am. If I hadn't made that suggestion about the reward … Well, I feel terrible." He took her hand. "Your husband and Hal are both sick about it, too."

She placed her other hand on his. "They're probably better off dead." Her breath caught, and she started to cry again. "You know what was done to them." She sniffed back her tears and tried to smile, noticing that even his eyes looked wet. "You have been so kind in so many ways, General."

Somehow neither of them found it strange that while they had to stay composed, keep a stiff upper lip for the half-million men who had given their lives in the war, they could still cry for a couple of slaughtered mongrel dogs.

He pressed her hand in the crook of his arm, and they walked together to the oval stone. His presence calmed her. The general removed his hat and she stopped her tears, dabbed her eyes with her handkerchief. Rabbit bravely snorted at Winchester; a skein of geese honked across the sky.

They stood for a few minutes until he broke the silence. "I questioned some rebel prisoners. I vaguely remember that bastard, Hobbs. He was in my company at West Point my first year, then he dropped out or was kicked out. Even then he was a misfit." He squeezed her hand. "I'm concerned for your safety, Summer. His verses made my skin crawl.

"We're staying here for a while, until the spring perhaps. I'm putting your husband in command of headquarters. Whether he likes it or not, he won't be going on patrol. Sergeant Landon knows of a house for rent in town where I want you to stay. I believe you know Colonel Stone's wife. Several wives are coming for the winter. We'll put round the clock guards on you. Have you a pistol?"

She shook her head.

"Ever use one?"

"I fired one a few times."

"We'll get you a good one. Not one of those little pea shooters. Sergeant Landon can set you up for some target practice." One side of his mouth curled. "We'll get the bastard even though Boy Criel said he's long gone." He petted her hand. "The President asked about you." He smiled at her reaction. "So I'd better take good care of you."

He walked with her to where Winchester waited then motioned Sergeant Landon to bring Rabbit forward. "Now for the real reason I'm up here." He removed his hat again. "We can change all those plans. All you have to do is leave that big lout of a husband of yours and marry me." His dark eyes shimmered. "I could arrange to have him—"

She arched her eyebrows and made a mock face of horror. "You know how hard I worked to get him back, and you want me to leave him now?" Her face smoothed into a smile. "He found me first, Sir, or else I'd be honored to be your wife. I have a feeling that once this war is over, General, you'll find the perfect girl." She stepped back, but her hand lingered on his sleeve. All laughter left her face. "And she will be a most fortunate woman."

She leaned forward and kissed his cheek. He picked up her hand, the hand with Daniel's ring on it, and kissed it. For a long moment he didn't say anything. Then he bent and laced his hands into a step and helped her mount Rabbit. With surprising grace, he pulled himself onto Winchester.

"I'm going to be particular. I know exactly the kind of woman I want." He nodded to his sergeant. "Lead us slowly down this mountain, and tomorrow I want you to make sure our girl has a Smith and Wesson."

CHAPTER 52

LEWIS AND CLARK

Just before Christmas, Daniel moved his office into the brick headquarters in Harper's Ferry. Late that Thursday afternoon, Hal ducked into the new office, his great coat dripping with moisture from the storm outside. Sleet peppered the windows. Hal stood in the dim afternoon light and studied the room. "Nice. At least you have solid walls."

Daniel knew Hal's headquarters were still a large tent.

Hal sniffed and swiped his arm across his face, trying to dry it, but only smearing more moisture. "One of my troopers needs to get rid of a couple of puppies. They're good looking dogs. Would it be too soon to give them to your wife?"

Daniel noticed how Hal always now referred to Summer Rose as 'your wife'. They still avoided speaking about the incident, though the knowledge of what had happened would always be there, like a bastard child.

Daniel slowly put his feet on the floor. "Where are they?"

"Right behind my headquarters."

He stood and reached for his greatcoat. "Let's take a look."

The wind picked up, rippling the canvas between blasts of ice pellets. The puppies, both males, had identical markings, but in reverse. One was tan with back markings, the other black with tan markings. They didn't resemble the mother.

The soldier who owned the mother looked about sixteen. He shrugged when they asked about the father. "Sergeant Nolan told me I had to get rid of them by tomorrow. If I don't, he will." He shuffled some straw with the toe of his boot.

Daniel knelt and picked up the puppies. Short-haired and healthy, they were a handful to hold. Their paws were big and their faces square. Both had black eyes and wet noses. He handed the black one to Hal. Neither puppy seemed shy. Little pink tongues lapped at their fingers. Hal pulled a bill from his pocket and gave it to the boy, who beamed.

Daniel grinned. They both knew how difficult parting with cold cash was for Hal. "I'll split the cost with you."

Hal shook his head.

They mounted their horses, both automatically sheltering the little dogs under their capes. The sleet increased, starting to harden into snow and cover the ground. They turned uphill and into the wind, toward Daniel and Summer's house on Washington Street, where they met General Sheridan coming from the armory. They saluted and Sheridan nodded toward the puppy sticking its head out from Daniel's cape.

"For Summer Rose?"

Daniel nodded. General Sheridan saw the other puppy; he shyly smiled at his colonels. "I would like very much to see this, if you don't mind."

Daniel led them to the rear of the house via an alley, their chins tucked down as they fought the roaring wind. A groom took their horses, and they entered the house through the warm kitchen. Daniel introduced them to Ida, the Negro woman making biscuits at the kitchen table, and she nodded her approval when they wiped their boots on the mat by the door and hung their dripping hats on the hooks. She beamed at General Sheridan and made no comment about the puppies.

"How is Winchester, Sir?" She moved her head toward the barn. "Is he …?"

General Sheridan shook his head. "The weather's too nasty for Winchester. He's snug in his stable."

Ida nodded. "That's good, Sir. You can't be too careful of our hero."

Daniel led them through a narrow hallway to the living room. Summer sat by the fire with her feet up on an ottoman. Dressed in a soft raspberry-colored wool jumper and a white blouse with Garibaldi sleeves, she looked the picture of health. Her shining sable hair had grown a little, so she could tuck it around her ears. Holding a half-knitted, tiny yellow sweater, she stood quickly when she saw who her guests were.

"How …" Her eye caught the tiny nose poking out from her husband's cape and she squeaked, dropping the little sweater and crumbling to the floor. The skirt of her jumper billowed around her like the petals of a peony and she held out her hands, her fingers wiggling. All three men grinned from ear to ear, watching her cuddle the tan puppy to her chest, beaming as the puppy licked her face and neck. Hal knelt beside her, showing her the other black nose as it poked out of his cape. She hooted again, and he put the second puppy in her arms.

Daniel took the men's coats and hung them in the hallway, then poured each a glass of bourbon. Daniel and Hal sat on a wooden bench by the fire while General Sheridan joined her on the floor and played with the puppies. Hard sleet splattered against the glass windows, and the fire cast a golden glow like a spell over the general, the girl, and the puppies.

Daniel's heart rose in his throat and caught there. He stuck out his hand and Hal took it, knocking down a chunk of the wall of hard feelings between them. They had been friends since before they could walk, and Daniel couldn't blame any man for wanting Summer Rose. But while his Rosie was, without any doubt, the most gorgeous girl any of them had ever seen, she was also so much more.

He knew Hal would never touch her again, not like he had that night, and he knew she'd never again be so innocent. The hardest thing for Daniel was forgiving himself. He should have focused on her fears, her innocence, rather than his miserable jealousy. He should have spoken to Hal earlier about his inappropriate actions, let Hal know he wouldn't tolerate such behavior. He was aware of the ease with which General Sheridan joked with his wife. It hadn't gone unnoticed that the general glanced at her secretly, admiring her, perhaps more than he should.

Daniel lowered himself to the floor and picked up the tan puppy. "What are you going to name them?"

General Sheridan picked up the black mongrel. "When your tenacious and shameless wife was convincing me to let her play soldier in order to worm her way back into your affection, Daniel, she told me that the two of you were, and I quote,"—he raised his voice to a falsetto—"'General Sheridan, Sir, we're like bacon and eggs, bread and butter, salt and pepper, even Lewis and Clark.'"

Summer blushed to the shade of her jumper. General Sheridan's grin spread across his face, and he held up the black puppy. "May I suggest that this one reminds me of Meriwether Lewis? See those big black eyes? Did you know that sixty years ago Meriwether Lewis and William Clark's expedition started here at Harper's Ferry?"

The tan puppy squirmed out of Daniel's hands and wiggled toward Hal who lifted the second puppy. "My father, when he was a boy, met General Clark. He spoke at length about his fine appearance and said he had a lot of teeth. I think the tan one looks just like William Clark."

Summer laughed. "You're teasing me." The tan puppy squirmed out of Hal's hand and made its way across the lush wool of her skirt. "Are you making this up?"

Little Phil shook his head. "Meriwether Lewis did come here. And I distinctly remember you saying, 'bacon and eggs, bread and butter, salt and pepper, even Lewis and Clark.'"

She hugged Clark, who nibbled her nose. "I vaguely remember saying Lewis and Clark. I guess I *was* tenacious, wasn't I?" She grinned at her husband and mouthed, thank you, then smiled at Hal.

Ida stuck her head in from the kitchen. "Mrs. Charteris, I set two more places for dinner and made an apple pie for dessert." She motioned to Hal. "Colonel St. Clair, there's a nice wooden crate in the cellar. Would you bring it up to the kitchen for the puppies? Daniel, go with him and bring up a couple of bottles of wine. General, Sir, I warmed some water. You may wash your hands in the kitchen."

As the general followed Ida to the kitchen, she turned and handed General Sheridan a small apple. "For Winchester, Sir. Do you think possibly you could arrange it so I could meet him?"

CHAPTER 53

THE END AT LAST

They spent the winter in Harper's Ferry waiting for the roads to dry out and the ice to crack on the upper Potomac. By Christmas, Summer Rose's waistline had thickened, and the baby occasionally gave a soft flutter. At night Daniel laid his head against her abdomen and waited for the baby to bump his cheek.

Summer giggled. "That's my stomach gurgling, not the baby."

The puppies slept in the crate beside their bed. Daniel ran them outside a couple of times during the night then came back to their bed, shivering, with his report. "Clark peed. I almost lost Lewis. His black coat fades into the night."

She wrapped her warm body around her husband. "Come here. The baby is a little furnace."

They ate Christmas dinner in one of the warehouses with all the soldiers and danced at a military ball in the same warehouse less than a week later. Harvey, Amelia, Emily, and Abbey with Hank all came for a visit and stayed at a hotel near the parade grounds. Becca and Ned came to help take care of everyone and stayed at Daniel and Summer Rose's quarters.

Hal spent as much time as possible with his son. They sat for another photograph, and Hal enclosed it in a letter to Fanny. For the next few days, Hal could be seen walking and riding around the post, the baby tucked in his arms.

Amelia and Harvey gave Daniel and Summer a fluffy Swiss comforter, which they put to immediate use. Frostbite had become the hospital's biggest affliction; however, Ray had his hands full that winter with more than frostbite. Grace was expecting their first child. Her sister had won the hundred dollar gold piece from their father for producing the first grandchild. Grace made such a big fuss over losing the gold piece that Summer considered suggesting an easy way to earn gold pieces. She confessed her wicked thoughts to Daniel, expecting him to admonish her, but instead, he told her she should go ahead and tell Grace.

"It might shut her up," he said.

Becca laced Summer Rose's stays tight and adjusted the black velvet ball gown so it fit her expanding figure. "No one would ever guess you have a baby in there. You look sinfully gorgeous."

Daniel thought so, too. They walked through the post, he in his dress uniform, she with her black, hooded cape billowing about her. They couldn't help but remember the last ball they had attended.

"I wonder where Hobbs is?"

Summer Rose had a knife strapped to her leg and Smith and Wesson in her pocket. Two guards trailed behind them. "I hope he's under six feet of dirt."

Daniel filled her entire dance card, but she danced twice with General Sheridan and once each with the gallant George Custer and handsome Myles Keogh, the Irish Soldier of Fortune. The charming young Lieutenant Colonels, Jake Hunt and Ed Kincaid, danced several times with Emily and Abbey. Both couples seemed quite interested in their partners.

Neither Harper's Ferry nor Winchester offered many diversions; however, over the next few nights, the young officers took the ladies ice skating, as well as to a play. They spent some time every day in Harper's Ferry, escorting the girls around the village. The girls didn't complain at all. Harper's Ferry didn't offer the shops Philadelphia did; however, Philadelphia lacked handsome colonels to escort them. The puppies were a huge draw, and the four of them stopped to take Lewis and Clark for walks at least twice a day. Every afternoon the couples ended up in Summer Rose's kitchen, making hot chocolate or fudge and often playing cards. Summer Rose enjoyed getting to know Daniel's sister.

When everyone left in mid-January, the village settled into silence. Summer took long afternoon naps and Daniel did an impromptu tap dance when the baby bumped against his cheek. That night, Lewis and Clark slept through the night.

In early February, word came through accurate channels that Lincoln and Seward had met with a delegation from the Confederacy. They'd met with John Campbell, who had been a High Court Justice before the war, Alexander Stephens, a nine-term congressman, and Robert Hunter, a former senator. President Lincoln suggested a meeting "with a view of securing peace to the people of our one common country."

They met with Lincoln and Seward aboard the river steamer *River Queen,* which was anchored at Hampton Roads.

On the surface it appeared that little came from the conference, but Little Phil, who came to dinner at Daniel and Summer Rose's home about once a week, explained at one of the dinners just how important the meeting had been. The officers and the sprinkling of wives about the table listened carefully.

"Mr. Lincoln let them know he considered them traitors who had committed treason. He told them they had forfeited any rights, and essentially were proper subjects for the hangman. In other words, he made clear, 'We are not going to dance, gentlemen. We still demand what we have demanded all along: restoration of the national authority throughout *all* the states, no backsliding on the slavery issue, and unconditional surrender and disbandment of Lee's Army. If Lee falls, the rest will collapse.'"

Phil Sheridan slammed his fist on the table. "Over half a million men have given their lives in this conflict. I, for one, am very pleased with our President and very proud of Sam Grant. They're not going to allow those men's deaths to be in vain."

Lewis and Clark grew into their giant paws, and around Valentine's Day, Summer began serious training. Wrapped in her winter cape of Union blue, lined with black cotton like the cavalrymen's capes, she took them, along with her ever-present bodyguards, everywhere she went. The baby grew rapidly and Summer was forced to clutch her cape about her.

Twice a week she walked to target practice with Daniel and General Sheridan. The officers who ran the range had a little building where they doled out ammunition and kept a potbellied stove. She commanded the dogs, which were still big puppies, to sit just inside the door. They waited in the warm hut while she practiced with the Smith and Wesson, then the Spencer. Her bodyguards stayed with the dogs. Captain John Cray, who ran the range, took an avuncular fancy to her. Often he had a new gun or scope, and he'd ask her to try it out. Occasionally she'd show off with her knife or use a new pistol. Just about every practice session she drew a crowd, and invariably someone would ask her, what's the trick?

She'd point to her eyes. "No tricks involved. My eagle eyes are just very good. That, and a few thousand hours of practice."

On the 20th, Daniel asked General Sheridan if he'd walk Summer Rose back to headquarters. "General Custer called a meeting with all his staff," Daniel said. "I need to be there."

"It would be a pleasure." As Daniel rode off, Sheridan offered his arm. Summer took it and signaled to Lewis and Clark, who walked obediently just ahead of them. The bodyguards walked behind.

"I've wanted to talk with you alone." He placed his other hand over hers. "The big offensive will start soon. Before March 1st, I plan to take Merritt's, Devin's, and Custer's divisions and join Grant below City Point. We'll clean out the valley on our way and destroy Confederate stores. Hal is coming. I'd like Daniel to have a shot at the finale, too. He's given four hard years. I'm sure he'd like to be there at the end, and I'd like to give both our boys stars." He glanced at her growing belly. "I'd like Lieutenant Ross to be there; however, I can't risk taking you, Mrs. Charteris."

She nodded, smelling conspiracy between her husband and the general. Her heart caught in her throat; every muscle seemed to freeze at the memory of sending him to war. Daniel, of course, wanted to go. He was a soldier. There was something about soldiers: the loyalty, the camaraderie between and among the men that rode and fought together. In war they were brothers, a bond stronger than family, in some senses stronger than marriage. She smiled, summoning every bit of feminine mystic she could muster. *Women have their loyalties, too. I'll wave goodbye again, smiling while my heart breaks.*

She petted his arm. "The baby isn't due until the end of April. I believe our child would like his daddy to be a general."

"I insist you stay here. There's a local doctor." He gestured to Evers and Saxon. "I still want bodyguards assigned to you. Be kind to these men, Mrs. Charteris. You'll be a general's wife soon, but I insist you listen to these men."

On the 27th of February, General Phil Sheridan rode out of Winchester with 10,000 cavalrymen. They thundered through the Shenandoah to Staunton and Rockfish Gap where they came against Jubal Early's entrenched troops and quickly disposed of them, capturing more than half of the 6500. The rebels were outnumbered, outgunned, ill-clad, ill-shod, and famished. If the truth be known, many of them knew the end was near. The knowledge made it easier for the Yankees to catch them. They had fought long and hard, and now they simply wanted a decent meal. Sheridan's troops took eleven guns, seventeen battle flags, and 200 wagons loaded with supplies.

Ordinary major generals would have rested on their laurels. Sheridan, never ordinary, pushed his horsemen over the Blue Ridge Mountains in a drenching rain and entered Charlottesville late the next day. There he waited for his pontoons and ammunition to come through the mud and over the mountain. His troopers, in the meantime, destroyed bridges, factories, depots, and all railroads in the direction of Lynchburg. When the pontoons arrived, the James was too swollen to cross, so they proceeded eastward and destroyed the James River Canal, the conduit for supplies to Richmond. This last act cut supplies to the high officials and their families in Richmond, sending panic through the officers of the Confederate government.

Sheridan was relentless. His army destroyed railroads, bridges, rolling stock, warehouses, and over 200 miles of railroad as the Confederacy wobbled. Toward the end of March, he swept around Lee's army and joined Grant below City Point below Petersburg.

In Daniel's letter to Summer, he told her,

The men have learned to sleep in the saddle. I want a hot bath and your warm body next to me beneath our comforter more than you can imagine. I have been damp to the bone since the night we left the post

On March 30th, Grant halted all operations, stating, "The rain has made forward movement impossible."

Sheridan, on hearing Grant's orders, rode seven miles through a downpour, racing through water as high as Winchester's knees. Upon reaching headquarters, he paced like a leashed cougar.

"I can drive them where we want them with ease. Give me infantry and I'll roll up their flank. I'm ready to go out tomorrow and start smashing things!"

He finally made enough noise that Grant saw him. One thing Grant did better than any other general, either Union or Confederate, was recognize and use the momentum of his subordinates. Sheridan's enthusiasm somehow moved Grant, for he finally said, "We will go on."

They did go on, for five more days. Sheridan's flankers and scouting parties of cavalry brought in scores of prisoners from the nearby woods on either side of his columns.

"The rebs were lost from the main body of their army. They were hungry and tired, and if there was a Confederacy to sustain, they couldn't find it in the woods," said a member of Sheridan's staff.

The end, so long in approaching, came swiftly. Richmond and Petersburg collapsed and emptied. The day Richmond fell, Grant woke Washington with a 900 gun salute and Lee's army moved west. On April 7th, Grant stayed at the Prince Edward Hotel in Farmville, where Lee had stayed the night before. The men sensed an end to the war, and they gave General Grant an impromptu pass and review that evening.

Later that night Grant wrote to General Lee.

The results of the last week must convince you of the hopelessness of further resistance on the part of the Army of Northern Virginia. I feel that it is so, and regard it as my duty to shift from myself any further responsibility of any further effusion of blood, by asking of you the surrender of that portion of the Confederate States army known as the Army of Northern Virginia.

Half a mile west of the village of Appomattox Court House, Sheridan, the bantam worth his weight in gold, proved his mettle again. Men under the command of Generals Merritt, Devin, Custer, and Crook, as well as Brigadiers Charteris and St. Clair, were placed in an enormous semi-circle in front of Lee's Army. The men had only a few hours sleep, the generals had none, but by the time daylight came, they were ready.

The proud II Corps of Lee's Army of Northern Virginia seemed to bite through the middle of the horseshoe-shaped Union line; however, Sheridan's long line of cavalry withdrew, allowing a gap to open in the middle. The joyous Confederates moved over the crest of the hill, where they were met by the Federal Infantry, 28,000 strong. They couldn't move forward, backward, or to either side.

By eight o'clock in the morning, Lee said, "There's nothing left but to go and see General Grant, and I'd rather die a thousand deaths."

From somewhere white flags emerged and crossed the skirmish lines several times, carrying notes back and forth. Tensions on both sides stood on an edge as sharp as a well tempered sword. Emotions swirled with relief, elation, and heartbreaking disappointment. Sheridan and Winchester rode into the thick of it, looking unshakably confident, as if he'd done this a hundred times. He understood the fine line between resolution and strength, as well as between vainglory and courage.

CHAPTER 54

WILD GEESE

D aniel and Hal stood with their men outside the McLean
residence in the town of Appomattox Court House as
the high brass of both sides gathered in front of the steep
stairs. Lee, immaculate in sword and solid gold spurs, came
first on Traveler, his favorite mount. With him was Colonel
Marshall, Lee's longtime aide, who rode a good-looking dark
mare. Behind General Lee and Colonel Marshall waited a
small herd of Union generals, including Sheridan, who accompanied a dusty General Grant into the redbrick house.

Around three o'clock, Lee stepped out onto the porch.
The men could tell by the way Lee, Grant, and the other
generals held themselves that Lee had surrendered the
Army of Northern Virginia. The war was essentially over. In
the distance a few cheers echoed but soon quelled as, like
a soft wind, word flew down the line that cheers would be
inappropriate.

Daniel heard only the stomping and snorting of the
horses. Someone led Traveler to Lee, who straightened a

forelock on his faithful warrior's forehead and mounted. Grant removed his hat, a motion repeated by every man, Confederate or Union, within sight.

That night, General Sheridan sent Daniel to City Point where he and Colonel Ray Stone saw to the transfer of wounded to the trains, and started north.

Early the next morning in Harper's Ferry, Summer with her bodyguards and Lewis and Clark, waited at the small depot for the early train from Washington. The Potomac roared by, high from recent rains, and April couldn't make up her mind. Sunshine dazzled with diamond brilliance, yet frost still clung to the grass. Despite the vestiges of winter, robins dug between the icy blades to search for worms.

After Daniel and Hal left with Sheridan's columns of horsemen, Amelia, still besotted with her grandson, remembered she had promised to be with Summer Rose during her confinement. Unable to leave Hank, she sent Becca, who traveled along with Summer's brother, quite by accident, on the train from Washington to Harper's Ferry. While the two women hugged and cried, Jack knelt and played with the dogs. Summer Rose's two bodyguards saw to the scant luggage.

After the women had mopped their tears, Jack McAllister, now Colonel Jack McAllister, kissed his sister and hugged her as best he could, then backed away from the substantial bulk of her belly. There was no pretending it wasn't there.

"I'm excited to finally have another relative. It's up to you, dear sister, to multiply and produce many McAllister descendents. I'll just observe." His face lost all hint of humor. "Are you sure it's just one baby? You are …very large. Enormous, actually."

She giggled. "He must just be a big boy. No girl, not even me, could be as cantankerous as this child."

He held her at arm's length, looking reassured. "A telegram arrived this morning from General Charteris. They're transferring the wounded from the hospital ship to the trains today and tomorrow. Daniel should be here, at the latest, the day after tomorrow."

Thrilled with the news, Summer hugged everyone, even her bodyguards, though it was difficult to get at them from around her belly. The dogs barked and jumped, but Jack reached out and brought her to a stop. "You're frightening me. You'll tip over!"

Laughing, she linked arms with Jack and Becca and walked to the carriage. Her bodyguards helped her up the little step while Lewis and Clark ran circles around everyone.

As they settled in the carriage, she asked, "What's it like in Washington? It must be crazy. Even here with the garrison almost empty the fireworks haven't ceased."

Becca nodded. "It's been wild. They had a 500 gun salute yesterday, fireworks all the time. It's been a party. I think half the city is drunk. Every once in a while someone throws his hat up and leaps into the air, and the entire street will start dancing. Amelia is beside herself with joy because Hal is on his way home to see Hank." Becca shook his head. "I've never seen a man as crazy about his son as General Hal is."

"We see the other side, too," said Jack. "Washington has always been a southern city. Her citizens have politely nursed their sentiments for four years, tolerating the Yankees. Now they realize the Yankees are here to stay. The anger and the fear are thick. They've lost, and they fear the enormous changes they know are coming."

In an effort to sound less gloomy, Jack reached over and grabbed her hand. "Are you feeling well?"

She blew out a long breath. "I'm miserable." She giggled and shook her head. "No, I'm not. Now that I know Daniel will be here soon, I'm ecstatic." She studied her bulging coat. "But this child has already let me know he's in charge. I sleep in a chair sitting up. He's an acrobat, and I waddle like a fat sow. He's a little tyrant. Right now, he's letting me know he's starved."

Less than a week later, Summer Rose began labor. Ray tried to shoo Daniel and Jack out of the house. Jack dutifully took a walk to Jefferson's Rock then settled in at the hotel bar down the street. Daniel refused to leave. He sat on the bed beside her, at first making jokes and telling stories to divert her, then shuddering along with every contraction. At one point she asked him to leave, then screamed for him to return before he got to the door.

Finally, at nine o'clock on the evening of Good Friday, she delivered a healthy boy.

Four minutes later, she delivered another fine, healthy boy.

The twins were a huge surprise, but everyone in the house fell madly in love with them. The first boy, the larger of the two, had a lion's mane of pale curls, while the second had a mop of dark hair just like his mother.

No one had warned Summer about the emotions that would consume her when she first held her sons. She loved her family, her parents, her brothers. She loved Daniel with every piece of her heart, and she'd expected to love her children. But she didn't know she could love so passionately, so tenaciously. Their tiny hands, their miniature toes, their adorable ears and sweet lips, the tiny wrinkles at their wrists … she couldn't look at them enough.

"Do all babies have such velvety skin?" she asked Ray, her voice soft with awe.

She hugged each child and felt their strong heartbeats matching her own rhythm. They sighed and snuggled against her as if they knew they were home. They sighed, too, when they squeezed up against each other. In those moments her boys stole her heart.

Two days later, a somber Jack presented them with a telegram he'd received, as well as the newspapers. The news was the worst they could have imagined. President Lincoln had been assassinated.

Jack hadn't told them right away, wanting to give them a night and half a day of absolute joy with their new sons before dampening their moods, but the news had hit him as if his own father had died again. As they devoured the papers, disbelief became sadness and depression settled over the house, as it did over the entire country. Summer Rose, who had met the President only that one time, asked her husband, who had met with Lincoln, listened to his wonderful stories, grown to love him, if he'd mind giving each of their boys

Abraham as a middle name. He didn't mind. In fact, the act brought comfort. Both boys were named after her father, becoming Micah Abraham Charteris and Angus Abraham Charteris.

Jack dubbed the oldest baby Mac, because of his initials, and the younger Gus, because Angus was too formal for a baby. Now, with the war ended and no marauders tearing up the tracks, the train ride between Washington and the garrison took only a few hours, so he spent his weekends in Harper's Ferry.

One Sunday morning in early May, Jack found himself alone near the cradles, situated in a dim corner of the dining room. He pulled a straight-backed chair between them and studied his nephews, slightly frightened by their smallness. Mac lay content on his back, wiggling his legs and gurgling, but Gus fussed. Jack tried making faces and rubbing his finger against the boy's cheek, but he still whimpered. Finally, convincing himself he was brave enough to pick up a baby, he lifted his nephew. Gus curled into his arm and quieted immediately.

"You know, Gus, you come from some mighty fine stock. Your blood runs thick with heroes and patriots." He turned to Mac, who was studying his toes with great interest. "Not many boys have a true American hero for a mother, and a daddy who is a general. If you want some plain bread pudding, remember your Uncle Jack. I'll teach you how to throw a knife, hold a rifle, and ride a horse. And I have a lot of stories to tell. When you're old enough, I'll tell you how your mother killed a bear."

Jack kissed the baby's forehead and the bridge of his nose then turned and studied Mac's nose. "I think you both have the McAllister nose." He turned sideways and showed the boys his profile, featuring the proud hawk hook of a beak. "Be proud of it, fellows. It's a good Scots nose." He studied the boys' eyes. Mac's were pale green like his father's. In fact, there wasn't much about Mac that wasn't a miniature of Daniel. Gus' eyes matched the unusual blue-green of his mother. "I must return to Washington, but remember, boys, your Uncle Jack will be around. I'm a bit of a stuffed shirt, but I do care. You and I'll do all the fun stuff."

With newfound courage, he manipulated Gus into the cradle so he lay on his stomach. Gus squawked at being put back in bed, so Jack rubbed the tiny back. The hem of his little shirt slid up, and Jack peered down at a birthmark he hadn't noticed before.

"By damn, Gus, you have a flying goose on your ass. Huh. I guess that's a good thing. At least there's no chance they'll mix you up with your brother."

Daniel had seen the wild goose, too. Right after the babies were born, Ida and Becca shooed the men and babies to the guest room which they had set up as a nursery. When Ray unwrapped the first boy, he joked how the screaming, red-faced, baby with the wild mane of pale hair looked just like Daniel.

Ray had laughed. "Has your temper, too."

Immense relief flooded Daniel. Tears hovered.

Daniel had prepared himself in his mind, ready for the baby to be the spitting image of Hal, but when Ray unwrapped the second baby and Daniel spotted the goose, his knees gave out. All six foot two inches of him thumped to the floor. As his head cleared from the smelling salts, Ray chuckled and helped him sit up.

"Now I know what having a rug pulled out from beneath me feels like," mumbled Daniel.

"Easy, big guy. Sit there with your knees up and your head down. Let me take care of your boys. You'd be surprised how many new fathers faint."

Thoughts whirled, too fast to grab hold of. Fear threatened to consume him, but it was fear for Summer Rose, not him. If she learned they were Hal's babies, she'd be crushed. Daniel shook his head. "Ray, I've made a horrible mess."

"Give me a minute. Can't be that bad," said Ray, as he tapped the dark-haired baby's back and listened to his lungs.

Daniel, still on the floor with his head between his knees, mumbled. "Christ, Ray, you don't know the half of it."

All of it, all that had happened last fall, spewed out, loosed by the reality of Hal's birthmark. He told him how Summer Rose had been drunk after hearing he'd been hanged.

"I found them naked in my bed, and I saw red." As he told the story, the words came out faster and faster. "I don't give a damn if the babies are Hal's or mine. You can't imagine how angry I am at myself for everything that happened. Until that night, I always prided myself on being an honorable man. But good lord, Ray, I went crazy. I raped my wife. I hurt her. I didn't even have the excuse of being drunk. What I'm afraid of now is that this will devastate her. She doesn't think anything happened with Hal, but she can't remember."

His hands shook, and he sucked in another chestful of air. "I don't want her hurt any more than she's already been hurt. I swore I'd never lie to her, and now I can barely keep the lies I've already told her straight. What am I going to do?"

Ray let out a long, slow whistle, then busied himself with swaddling the dark-haired twin and rechecking the fair one.

"God Almighty, Danny," he said, shaking his head. "I'm surprised she didn't shoot the two of you. If I'd known, I'd have helped her. I can't imagine what Grace might do to me if I did anything like what—" He placed the dark-haired boy in the cradle and scowled at Daniel. "You always were a hothead. When are you going to learn to control that temper?"

His head still bent, Daniel lifted one weak hand. "Believe me, my temper is gone."

Ray took a deep breath and wrapped up the fair-haired baby, laying him at the other end of the cradle. "They're healthy, beautiful baby boys. And they're big for twins. You're lucky."

Daniel pulled himself up and sat on the edge of the bed. Ray moved the cradle and put the babies between them, then sat on a chair facing Daniel, looking thoughtful. He used his foot to rock the cradle.

"I believe something rare happened here, Daniel. Very rare. I'd like to write it up for a medical journal, but I won't, because I consider you a friend and because I respect your wife."

He let out a loud breath. "In my opinion, the blond twin is yours. He looks just like you, has your big bone structure.

The dark one has to be Hal's. There's no denying that goose." He shook his head and let loose a chuckle. "Only Hal would have a wild goose on his ass."

Serious again, Ray continued. "It's not unheard of for fraternal twins to be fathered by different men. In the animal kingdom it's common with mammals bearing multiple offspring. In humans it's rare, but it's been documented since about 1810." He sighed. "My advice is to tell no one. Few people know it can happen, and who would bother putting two and two together? Who else knows about Hal's birthmark?"

Daniel, stunned, shook his head. "Me, Amelia, Harvey, Fanny, maybe a doctor, and half the whores in Washington ..."

Ray grinned. "I wouldn't worry too much about the whores. The army's breaking up, the whores will dissipate, too. You need to keep Summer Rose from seeing Hal's ass, and Hal from seeing the baby's bottom. Summer wouldn't remember the goose from ... would she?"

"She has no idea what happened with Hal. I'm sure she doesn't remember the damn goose."

Ray chuckled again. "God punishes in mysterious ways, Danny. You deserve a lot worse." His face softened. "You must feel like hell."

He stood up and walked to the dresser, where he began to pack his bag. "I may be able to help you. You need a good nurse, one who isn't a gossip. I know a German girl who may be perfect. It would help her, too. She's only twelve, maybe thirteen, and has no one. Lost her parents. She's painfully shy, hardly talks at all. She's living with Irene Wood."

Ray expelled a big breath. "She's a pretty little thing and I'm afraid she'll end up where the other pretty little girls end up. She's wonderful with children. Her name is Mercy Hamil. I'll speak to Irene." He narrowed his eyes and gave Daniel a half-smile. "I do this for your lovely wife. You, my friend, should be horsewhipped."

CHAPTER 55

MERCY

In late April, Amelia wrote:

Dear Summer Rose,

I hope this letter finds you safe and healthy. Rumors whisper President Johnson and General Grant have scheduled The Grand Review for the last week of May. Every one of our gallant soldiers, including Danny and Hal, will be honored by our President, the Senators, the Congressmen, by all America. Plan to stay at the 18th Street House.

My fingers itch to hold Micah and Angus. I am so happy Hal and Danny's sons will grow up together. Hal arrived last Monday. He steals Hank from me all the time. If I weren't so thrilled to have my son home, I'd send him somewhere so I could have Hank to myself.

Tell Becca that I cannot find a thing without her, and Harvey is complaining about desserts. We will have a houseful that week. Ray and Grace shall be here, as will Danny's parents and Nan Charlotte. Tell Danny I know how he loves the Rose Room, the one that you stayed in the last time you were here in Washington. I'll save it for him.

By all means, bring the boys' nurse. Grace wrote me that Mercy is a marvel. I think Grace is a little peeved at Ray for not keeping her as their son's nurse. I miss you.

Love, Amelia

Summer found Daniel in his study and showed him the letter. "Can you imagine Grace wanting Mercy?"

"Yes, I can. Mercy's a godsend."

Mercy had fit into their household as snug as four fingers and a thumb fit in a mitten. Quiet, neat little Mercy, with her golden curls and honey-colored eyes, managed the boys beautifully. Neither parent knew what they would do without her.

"Thank Amelia for saving the Rose Room for us. You haven't stayed there in May. The roses climb all about the upstairs porch. The scent is beautiful. The light—"

Summer dropped a quick kiss on his mouth. "I forgot how much you love roses."

"I haven't." He pulled her onto his lap and kissed her long and hard. "I love you, Rosie Charteris. Love you, love you, love you."

General Sheridan invited them to ride on his train. "We have dozens of trains taking us. I'll reserve seats on my train for your party."

Becca laced Summer Rose into her stays and helped her into a new traveling suit of navy blue with a crisp white blouse and yellow silk scarf. The jacket wasn't an exact replica of a cavalry officer's jacket, but it was close enough.

Becca tutted. "It's sinful how good you look after just having twins. The soldiers will love you in this jacket." She helped her with the hat, which imitated a soldier's forager cap. "Even Daniel will like this hat."

Summer Rose made a face in the mirror. "Don't count on it. He dislikes hats on me."

The train brimmed with military brass, handsome horseflesh, and a well-stocked bar. It chugged out of the station before ten in the morning and both champagne and spirits flowed as it cleared Harper's Ferry. A few women sat here and there, or partied along with the men, but mostly the train carried officers out to have a good time. Piano music and singing came from the car behind them. Few men kept their seats, but sloshed their drinks as they roamed the train. The war was over, they had stories to tell, and, for most of them, the most exciting four years of their lives were about to end. The next few days promised a hiatus before civilian responsibilities returned.

Summer and Daniel sat with a fussy Gus on a pillow between them. Mercy and Becca sat in front of them, with Mac asleep also on another pillow. Summer picked up Gus and patted his back; she regretted accepting General Sheridan's invitation. How, in all this noise, would she ever keep two babies asleep?

Daniel winked at her and took Gus. Her heart did a flutter as it always did. She loved how Daniel took part in the babies' care. Not many men would touch a baby, but he loved helping with their bath. Sometimes he even dressed them. She smiled, feeling fortunate. Because of Daniel and Mercy, she was healthy and strong.

Daniel interrupted her thoughts. "I'll walk him about and show him off. It might be quieter further along on the train. Maybe he'll fall asleep."

He moved toward the rear and she waved him a kiss then leaned over the seat. Becca rested with her head against the glass while Mercy sat with one hand balancing *A Tale of Two Cities*, the other on Mac's back.

The rhythm of the train hypnotized her. So did General Rosecrans who stood in the aisle alongside her, telling an unbelievably long, boring joke about two rebels in a Presbyterian church with a parrot. Her head drooped and she drifted into a half sleep, allowing the muscles in her shoulders to relax. She awoke with a jerk when something dropped onto her lap.

It was a note. The stationery was Daniel's, but the script wasn't. She knew the handwriting. Her heart stopped then raced. Frantic, her eyes darted back and forth in search of who might have delivered the note, but found no one. She tore open the envelope.

SWEET, LOVELY CHILD, SO FRESH, SO FRAIL, AND FAIR,
I SEE YOUR FUTURE: DARK, BLEAK, CHOKED WITH DESPAIR.
GOOD THING NEITHER DADDY NOR MOMMY YET KNOW
HOW YOUR FACE WILL BE SLASHED BY THEIR WICKED FOE.

SWEET, LOVELY, SUMMER ROSE, DON'T SOUND THE ALARM;
LAST CAR, LAST HORSE, THEY HAVE NOT YET COME TO HARM.
COME ALONE, COME FAST, YOUR FACE FOR THEIR LIVES,
DON'T TARRY, DON'T TALK. I HAVE SEVERAL SHARP KNIVES.

— H.

She sat for a long minute, trying to think straight. Her heart pounded, and hot blood surged through her veins and arteries so fast her body numbed. She forced a couple of deep breaths, tried to slow her heart. She'd lost her head when she'd thought Daniel was dead. She did not intend to repeat that behavior. She searched the car, but saw nothing untoward. Nothing except every soldier appeared flush with alcohol. Even Ray, the most serious of officers, looked bright-eyed and pink. She needed a clear head.

She stood, bent over, and whispered to Mercy. "Stay with Mac. I'll be right back."

At mid-car, she stopped Sergeant Boyle, one of her favorite young soldiers. He smelled of beer but seemed relatively sober. "Sergeant, be so kind as to sit in my seat behind Mercy." She forced a smile. "Watch over her and the baby."

He nodded, trying not to act put-upon, but she knew he'd obey because she was a general's wife. She moved toward the rear of the car and was surprised when she spotted Sergeant Landon. He'd broken his foot at the Battle of Five Forks, and just this week had started walking with a cane. When they'd worked together in the warehouse, he'd told her his wife made him sign the pledge. *Thank you, dear, dear Mrs. Landon. Thank you.* Her guards sat behind him, pouting. Sergeant Landon probably wouldn't allow them near the beer, which explained their sour faces. Sergeant Landon stood as she neared, and she bent forward and touched his right arm, slipping him the note with her right.

As he opened it, she whispered. "None of these men can help. They're beyond drunk."

He glanced at the note; she watched fear gather in his face, like a pebble creating expanding circles in a pond. He'd seen the other notes and knew what had been done to Nip and Tuck. She motioned with her head for him to come along with her.

She bent and whispered to the guards. "Follow us."

Once inside one of the compartments in the third car, she drew the blinds. She ripped off her hat, sending pins plunking against the cushions. She stepped out of her skirt and petticoats, and tossed them across the back of the seat. The boys' jaws dropped and she turned her back to them, speaking over her shoulder.

"I'm sure you've seen pantaloons before, gentlemen. My husband is being held hostage. They have our baby. They want me." She glanced back. "Private Saxon, I need your pants."

He hesitated.

"Now, please!"

In her mind she saw again her dogs in the burlap bag, remembered what had been done to them. Panic roared through her, freezing her hands, soaking the fabric beneath her armpits. This man will show no mercy to either Daniel or Gus. She forced the pictures away and slowed her breathing, steadied her heart. She lifted her chin and her eyes, then turned her back to Sergeant Landon, who knew exactly what to do. He reached beneath her little jacket and unlaced her corset. Ignoring them all, she shimmied out of it and slung the contraption over the back of the seat. Sergeant Landon motioned for Private Saxon to remove his pants, and when he had them off, the sergeant set about shortening the suspenders.

They made no pretense of not watching as she removed the knife strapped to her leg, nor as she pulled the trousers over her long pantaloons or bloused both ruffled drawers and trousers over the top of her boots. Sergeant Landon helped her adjust the suspenders.

"Summer," he said, "Let me find Captain Case. He'll be sober."

She ignored him, stuck the knife in its sheath in her right boot and pulled the revolver from the pocket of her skirt.

She checked the chambers and slipped the gun into the back of her pants, then transferred spare bullets from her skirt pocket to that of her trousers.

"The note said, 'Come alone'. I can't risk doing otherwise. You know what he can do. For the love of God. He has Gus and Daniel."

She pointed to Sergeant Landon. "I'll follow you to the next to the last car. I'd like you and Private Evers to walk through to the end and reconnoiter. I noticed, when we pulled out of Harper's Ferry, that there's no caboose on this train. I want you to unlock all the windows and open them so that there's a lot of noise inside that car. Use your rank, Sergeant. Make a loud comment about General Custer complaining about the smell. That's something he would do. You'll have to go into each stall and make sure no one is hiding beneath a horse. Be careful. We have to assume he's not alone. When you get to the back, step out onto the platform and when you return make sure the door is unlocked. Do it nonchalantly."

She swallowed and took a deep breath, praying for strength. "They have Daniel back there someplace. God only knows what Hobbs might do to Gus or him. He's insane. You know he wants to maim me, even kill us all."

She focused on Sergeant Landon. "Once you're back at the front of the car, stay here and cover me with your carbine." Her teeth set. "I'm going over the top of the car and in the back door. The hinges on that little compartment swing out so it'll hide me. Also, keep everyone out of the last car. Do any of you have a knife?"

Private Evers handed her a switch blade, and Sergeant Landon gave her the stiletto from his boot. It went in her left boot and the switch blade in her pocket.

She smiled sweetly at them all. "I'm going to slice out his gizzard." Her smile hardened until it looked as if she might use her teeth to do the deed. "I'll dig out his heart."

Private Saxon glanced down, looking as if he might throw up.

"I'm sorry, Private Saxon, but sometimes you just have to pretend. Tell anyone that looks cross-eyed at you that you ripped your pants and someone is mending them. Or tell them you lost them at cards."

CHAPTER 56

JUST PRETEND

She took the hat that had come with her suit, ripped off the veil and slammed it on her head. Sergeant Landon shook his head and removed it, replacing it with Private Evers' cap. He removed her pearl earrings and stuck them in his trouser pocket. "I'll keep these safe for you."

Private Evers paled and for a moment Summer Rose feared he might really throw up. "Mrs. Charteris, don't go," he pleaded. "I'll go."

She squeezed his arm. "Thanks, Henry. But nobody on this train is better with a knife than I am." She reached to the back of her pants and brought the Smith and Wesson around so she could check it again. "And not many can outshoot me, either. Right, Sergeant?"

He swallowed hard and nodded. "She's good. Damn good."

Following her directions, they walked through the remaining cars of soldiers. No one paid them any attention, and not one person seemed to notice that Private Saxon didn't have on any pants. George Custer stood on a seat, the top of his blond curls brushing the ceiling as he led the singing of *John Brown's Body*. They made their way through another car, then two containing horses, and stopped when they came to the last car.

She and Private Saxon stood at attention while Sergeant Landon and Evers moved into the last horse car. She'd already guessed where Hobbs had probably stowed Daniel and Gus. At the ends of each horse car stood a closet-sized room for pitchforks, feed, shovels and tools. Some had a small window. Often she'd seen the grooms sitting there on buckets or crates, even sleeping on a mound of straw. Now she stole glances through the set of windows in the connecting doors as the soldiers moved up the aisle. Sergeant Landon limped along the outside wall and opened windows while Evers went in each stall. She heard the men's voices, but couldn't make out what was said. They seemed to take forever.

When Sergeant Landon returned, he whispered, "The door to that little room on the left is closed, but I heard thumps." His big arms came around and hugged her, fitting her face against his rough cheek. "I wish I could go for you." He checked her over. "Tuck your cap in your belt. The wind will take it otherwise."

She climbed the brakeman's ladder and hoisted herself to the roof. From there she could see the blur of gravel, wooden ties, and rails. She crouched for a moment, getting her balance, acclimating to the wind. The vast Potomac River Basin spread before her, an enormous boa of brown water, frothing and curling through the brilliant green of forests. A silent thank you came to her lips as she thought of her brothers. They'd been the ones who had taught her to climb and swing from tree to tree, to inch along a branch like a tight rope walker. Pewter-colored sky stretched for miles, and the wind, smelling of spring and soft against her skin, plastered her clothing against her body. The endless bowl of the sky, the earth, the river surrounded her, became part of her.

Iron rungs, maybe a foot wide, marched down the center of the roof, leading to the end of the train. She supposed they'd been placed there to hold onto, and she did just that as she half-crawled, half-walked toward the end of the car. The train clacked over a trestle, bridging a small stream, and she saw the Potomac now narrowed, boiling with spring rains, rolling muddy and powerful beside her. A red-tailed hawk startled her as it shot like an arrow toward the river, intent on its prey.

She pressed her ear against the roof, listening hard. She could hear the horses and her heart leapt at the sound of her baby's hungry whimpers. Her breasts ached in response. The great train blew its mournful whistle, wailing through the countryside like some prehistoric beast.

At the end of the car, a ladder was bolted into the side. She lowered herself a quarter of the way down, squashing her body tight to the ladder just to the left of the small window, which was closed and almost opaque with filth. She dared a quick glimpse down and inside, fighting the constant tug as the wind whipped against her. Her clothing flapped like battle flags and her hair flew wild. *Thank God, it's short.*

A man in a tan felt hat, who she assumed must be a cohort of Hobbs, pressed his back to the window. He couldn't see her from her perch on the ladder. However, from her odd angle and even through the filth on the window, she could see the glint of the dagger he held to Daniel's throat. She made out Daniel's face and she knew he saw her, because he quickly diverted his eyes. He held Gus tightly against his shoulder, and his big hand gently tapped the baby's back. She noticed he was only using two fingers. *Is he telling me there are two of them?* She thought so. He lowered his eyelids and peeked at her through his lashes, so she turned and showed him the gun in her belt.

Gus began to wail; he was hungry. Fear for his safety made her mouth dry, and she scurried up the rungs to the roof, scrambling to the end of the car. With ease, she descended the other ladder, the one at the end of the train, and gained access to the rear platform. For a long moment she rested, taking a respite from the wind and catching her breath. Her heart slowed, readying for the fight.

Right away she noticed Sergeant Landon had wedged open the rear door with a flat stone. As a secondary precaution, he'd jammed a wad of paper into the lock's catch. She stood with her body plastered against the back wall of the car, plotting her course and orchestrating every move she planned to make. In her head, she ran through exactly when she'd withdraw the stiletto, where she'd place her foot, her hand, how she'd swing her body, her other foot, her other hand. In her mind, she tested what could go wrong with each move then adjusted and refined her plan. She knew Hobbs was watching the front of the train, and he'd expect her to have a knife.

Well, I'll give the bastard a knife. The stiletto will be first. She hefted it in her right hand, liking its weight then she checked the Bowie, her old friend, making sure it was still in her boot. The gun, in those close quarters, would either be backup or it would be for Daniel. She ran through the scenario two more times, imprinting it in her mind. She peeked through the outside door and caught sight of the back of Hobbs' head as he checked up the aisle toward the front of the train. *He's expecting me to come like a lamb.* She smiled.

"This lamb," she said under her breath, "has knives, teeth, and a Smith and Wesson."

The door to the room swung out and blocked the view of her approach. Hobbs' head disappeared as he stepped into the car. She slipped inside and pressed her back against the door to the room.

Daniel was so right. Anyone going into battle who says he's not afraid is an idiot. She wiped her palms on the sides of her trousers. She knew Daniel. He'd die for his son. *Well, so will I, dammit.*

Before anyone knew she was there, she'd caught Tan Hat with her stiletto, thrusting up and under his ribs, into his heart with all her strength. She twisted and plunged with her whole weight behind the knife, rocking it back and forth. Blood gushed, shot up like a flooding spring and blinded her. Kicking off from the wall, she pulled out the stiletto, letting the man slide as if boneless to the floor.

She felt a quick pressure against her back as Daniel slipped the gun from her waistband. She turned swiftly, letting momentum throw her out the door into Hobbs who just now stepped back into the room. She roared into him, spinning him with her into the boxcar, wanting him as far from her baby as possible. They spun in an awkward, lethal dance, and when Hobbs' back was to Daniel, a shot fired. The smoke choked her and Gus screamed, sounding terrified. Hobbs' hold loosened and he shoved her toward the front of the car, where she slammed into the wooden wall of one of the stalls. She grabbed at the wall, stunned from the impact. The horses along the length of the car screamed and pulled at their tethers, threatening to break loose. The entire boxcar tilted with their movements.

Hobbs staggered away from her, laughing. "I'll hack off your nose, bitch." He lurched toward the rear door, but Daniel had shot him in his hip and he stood unsteadily, clutching the door frame.

Still dazed, Summer Rose let the stiletto slide to the floor then rose to one knee. "You won't have that chance, you bastard!"

In one smooth move, she gripped the Bowie with her right hand and sent the knife home. The Bowie spun fast, hard, and true, catching his throat. The razor edge sliced the cartilage at his windpipe, giving a telltale crunch. Blood bubbled in a slow, small leak from his wound and he fell forward, lunging and spinning onto her. His face was frozen, his claws stretched like those of a beast. A spurt of blood blossomed into a geyser, spraying in front of him. With her left sleeve she cleared some of the blood from her eyes and the baby screeched louder.

Hobbs's eyes popped wide, and he twisted to claw at her throat. Her knife still stuck from his windpipe. She dropped to her back, arched her spine, and levered her legs against him, reeling him away from her. Another shot fired, then another. She thought at first the bullets missed then Hobbs fell like a great bloody side of beef on top of her. Daniel stood on the other side, the baby tight against his shoulder, the Smith and Wesson smoking in his hand.

Henry Evers pulled Hobbs off her while Wally Saxon set about calming the horses. Sergeant Landon stepped over her, helped her sit up, then bent and checked Hobbs. "This one's dead. How about the other, General?

Daniel pushed toward her through white smoke which filled the end of the car. "They're both dead."

He knelt on one knee beside her, Gus cradled against his waist. He stuck the gun in his belt, and from somewhere he produced a handkerchief. With his free hand he wiped the blood off her face, then pulled her under his leg and kissed the top of her head.

"I was afraid to fire," he whispered into her hair, choking on the words. "Afraid I'd hit you."

"I'm a bloody mess."

Daniel smiled and sobbed at the same time. He crumbled, cross-legged onto the straw beside her and laughed, tears rolling down his soot-darkened cheeks. "You're the best looking bloody mess I've ever seen." He rubbed a finger across Gus' cheek, his voice soft and low, rich with love. "My brave son wants his mama. Don't you?" He kissed the baby's forehead and held him out to Summer Rose. "He was so good. I think he has your courage."

He glanced up at Saxon. "Where are your pants?" His gaze slid to his wife. "You took his pants?"

She nodded and smiled. Wally Saxon took off his shirt and tossed it across her bloody chest, grinning from ear to ear. "Lousy cards, Mrs. Charteris."

Summer took Gus and breathed in his sweet, sweet baby smell. "Thank you." She kissed the top of her howling son's head. "Gentlemen, I'm going to crawl over into that corner and nurse my baby. Don't pay any attention to me."

CHAPTER 57

NO MORE LIES

Cleaning up took more time and more effort than the entire harrowing event. The amazing thing was that through it all, the party went on around them. The band got louder, the singing more boisterous. Even through three cars of horses they could still hear them singing *Garry Owen*. Summer Rose curled up facing a corner, and gave Gus access to his lunch.

Sergeant Landon directed Privates Evers and Saxon to throw the bodies off the side of the moving train. "Send the scum back to Maryland."

Midway across a trestle Hobbs and his cohort dropped into a tributary of the Potomac. The soldiers then scooped the bloody straw out the back door and off the platform, and one of her guards laid her cleaned Bowie knife beside her. Daniel and Sergeant Landon calmed and treated the horses to oats as Gus contentedly nursed, and the train chugged to Washington.

With his back against one of the stalls, Daniel slid to the floor. "Thank you," he whispered to no one in particular, maybe to God. "I'm truly amazed any of us are alive. Thank you."

He turned to Summer Rose and mouthed, "I love you."

Gus drooped, asleep, and she buttoned up her bloody blouse. She slipped her arms into Private Saxon's shirt, which covered most of the blood. "I love you ten times more," she whispered.

He smiled, feeling restored. "Not in a million years."

Sergeant Landon approached and offered his hand to Summer. "You've got to quit scaring me half to death. Thank heavens you're all right." He pulled her to her feet then turned to Evers and Saxon. "Do either of you have another uniform?"

Daniel pulled himself again to his feet as Evers nodded. "I know where to get one."

"Find it, give it to Saxon, then find Mrs. Charteris' luggage. It's probably in the first car. Then the two of you find two big buckets of hot water—George is in the kitchen car—some soap and towels. Bring them to the compartment where she changed earlier. If anyone gives you an inch of trouble, tell them Sergeant Major Landon ordered you. Also, everyone, listen up. None of this happened. We weren't attacked. We didn't kill anyone or throw any bodies off the train. Everyone understand?"

They nodded. Sergeant Landon glanced at Daniel and Summer Rose and tilted his head toward the front of the train. "Follow me," he said, lifting his cane as if it were a sword. "I know how to clear these aisles."

Within half an hour, Summer had her valise and hot water. Sergeant Landon returned her earrings and reported

Mac was still asleep. She bathed and changed Gus, then handed him to Daniel.

"Hold him for a minute," she said as she ran a washcloth over her hair. "This short hair has its advantages. Can you imagine the mess the blood would have made if I still had long hair?"

The train rocked and lurched; Gus wiggled free of the blanket. The wild goose and the memory of his lie jolted Daniel. He swallowed hard. "I hope we never need to know."

He rewrapped the baby and gently wedged him on the seat with a pillow. Without being asked, he took the stays from her hand and laced them up. She smiled as he helped her into her clean blouse, the one trimmed with daisies. While he stripped to the waist and washed himself, she tucked her blouse into the soft, gauzy skirt. He dried his hands and face and automatically fastened the hooks at her waist, then smoothed his hands over her hips. She leaned back against his naked chest.

His touch, combined with the smell of the soap and his skin, made her aware of every male inch of him. Desire seared through her. She wanted him fiercely and became very aware he wanted her, too.

Gus chose that exact moment to bunch up his tiny fists, turn a frightful purplish-red, and wail.

With practiced expertise she swooped up the baby and nestled his flailing body between them. The blanket fell away and Daniel stared down at the conspicuous wild goose, dark against the virgin white of his son's bottom. He wilted onto the seat, folding Summer and Gus onto his lap. Words spilled out of him, making him feel sick with guilt and relief.

"He's Hal's son. The goose … Hal has the same goose on his backside. I've known all along. I've tried to keep it from you, but … it doesn't seem to matter if he's mine or Hal's. I love him so much. Mac is—"

She pressed a finger to his lips. "Shush! I know. I've known all along. Fanny told me ages ago about the goose on Hal's bum." She sighed. "You know girls tell secrets to each other." Her expression grew serious. "I was so afraid you wouldn't love Gus like you love Mac." She smiled and pressed a kiss on his forehead. "I knew Mac was your son right away."

"How on earth—"

"The goats." She wiggled deeper into Daniel's lap and cuddled Gus on his chest. "Those randy old billys could care less who they poke, and it shows up in their kids. Tomcats do the same thing." She leaned her head on his shoulder. "I suspected you might know. You made such a fuss about hiding the goose." She bent forward and kissed Gus' forehead. "But Daniel, Hal must never know, nor Amelia. We'll just have to be prudes about nakedness. I couldn't bear for them to know." Her voice softened. "He's our son."

She paused for a second, dropping her eyes. "So this means I must have slept with Hal. I truly don't remember. Can you really forgive me?"

He snorted then stood, depositing her on the opposite seat. She stared up at him, wide-eyed as he diapered and dressed Gus, then bundled him into a blanket. He nodded to Summer. "Close your eyes, put your feet up, look distraught."

"But—"

"Just do it." Shirtless, Daniel slid open the door to their compartment and called for Privates Evers and Saxon. "Do you know who Mercy, the boys' nursemaid is?" he asked.

Private Evers nodded.

"Good." He handed the baby to the soldier. "Mrs. Charteris needs to rest. I'm sure you can understand how exhausted she is. Mercy's in the first car. Ask her to take care of Gus for a while. If she needs help, stay with her." He glanced at Private Saxon. "Please make sure we aren't disturbed."

He slid the door shut, hooked the latch, and picked up Summer. He twirled her around, holding her tightly against him then fell back onto the seat. His dexterous hands disposed of hooks and buttons and burrowed beneath clouds of crinolines. "I have a question for you, Mrs. Charteris. If Fanny told you about Hal's goose, what exactly did you tell her about me?"

She reached up and snapped closed the blind and rolled her eyes then giggled. "I told her you didn't need a goose."

CHAPTER 58

GRAND REVIEW

O n the evening prior to the Grand Review, Daniel's father came round to the back door of the 18th Street
house. There Louie found Summer Rose and Daniel sitting
on the back porch steps, watching the songbirds at the feeder.
Daniel stood and shook his hand.

"Your mother has a bad cold, Danny. She didn't feel up to
the trip. Abbey stayed in Philadelphia, too. I took a room at
Willard's. Too much hubbub around here."

Mercy and Becca came around to the porch with the
babies in the buggy. Daniel introduced Mercy to his father,
and Louie peered into the carriage. "What handsome boys,
Summer dear. I'm pleased to see the Charteris name carried
on. Thank you." His voice cracked as he kissed her cheek.

Summer Rose swallowed hard.

Louie cleared his throat. "You heard, didn't you? That
Sheridan left for the border?"

When he realized they hadn't, he explained that General Sheridan wouldn't be riding down Pennsylvania Avenue at the head of his seven mile long column of horse soldiers.

"Grant had a hell of a time convincing him he was needed on the border of Texas and Mexico to keep down defiance by the French in Mexico. Maximilian was pro-Confederate during the war. Now he needs to get out of Mexico. His ilk on our borders isn't good. We need someone tenacious and single-minded like Sheridan to convince them to leave."

He frowned, and Summer thought his eyes flitted strangely.

"I'm surprised he didn't take you, Daniel," he said. "Sheridan, of course, argued for all he was worth, trying to delay his departure until after the Grand Review, but Grant convinced Sheridan to speed to the border. He'll be in New Orleans sometime tomorrow."

After he left, Summer asked, "Did he seem odd to you?"

Daniel chuckled and gave a halfhearted shrug. "My father always acts squirrelly."

Summer Rose managed to go to the first day of the Grand Review. Although the parade meant to celebrate the end of the war, the music, even the cheering brought her sadness. It didn't help that she sat with an empty lap. Mercy held Gus, and Becca held Mac. Hank stood on Amelia's lap, waving a tiny flag. It amazed her how the babies had so quickly become family.

Meade's infantry marched down Pennsylvania Avenue, twelve abreast, in close order drill. The weather was perfect, and the Union's grand army sparkled with pride as division after division passed the stands in front of the Executive Mansion. Despite the excitement of the day, it was impossible not to notice how so many divisions were a shell of their former strength. Summer Rose's eyes, as well as most of the other spectators, blurred. The ranks were filled with men in their prime who looked no different from the marching soldiers, except a shade paler. These were the ghost soldiers, memories of men, like her father and brothers, men who had given their full and true measure for the great republic. Line after line, company after company, thousands upon ten thousands who had died, joined and marched beside the men who would carry on.

She stopped her tears when the cavalry came into view. She held up Mac's arm and waved it. Seven long miles of horsemen, a great many of whom she knew. She pointed out Daniel and Hal, and waved to Sergeant Landon, who somehow managed a horse with his ankle still splinted. Flamboyant George Custer was instantly recognizable, with his foot-long blond curls and flashy showmanship. His horse spooked—no doubt startled by a spur—and cavorted wildly in front of the viewing stands, putting on a show. Handsome Myles Keogh, then Tom Devin, Wes Merritt, Bill Rosecrans, Jim Wilson, many of Sheridan's generals trotted by. Memories rode with them: General Sheridan's bowling game, dancing with the generals in the warehouse at Harper's Ferry; singing around the campfires.

She caught the eyes of Ed Kincaid and Jake Hunt. She waved. Ed winked at her. He'd stopped by the house after Louie had left, and told Daniel he planned to ask Abbey to marry him. "I'll ask your father, but I wanted your blessing, too." Her eyes misted again at the thought of all the men who didn't return, men like her father and brothers, who would never have a chance to marry or hold their own child.

They didn't attend the second day of the Grand Review. While General William Sherman's great army and ragtag followers marched down Pennsylvania Avenue, Summer Rose and Daniel sat outside on the upstairs porch. Mac and Gus lay sound asleep in their bassinets just inside the door. Summer had sent Mercy with Becca and Amelia to the grandstands. Daniel and she needed time alone.

Huge magnolias and roses, all in full leaf, kept the porch shaded and cool, and dimmed the greenish light. The long, sheer curtains at the French doors billowed and fanned perfume from the white climbing roses. Summer and Daniel sat next to each other on a long swing. She leaned against him, her legs curled beneath her dress of white batiste. Daniel, in uniform, but jacketless, seemed a million miles away, his big hand slowly made its way up and down her back. They could hear drums and cannon, even horses, but they also heard bees feasting on nectar from the roses.

They had begged off attending the review, using Mac's fussiness as an excuse. Both babies were fine; their parents were not. Late last evening, Daniel, out for a walk amidst all the celebrating, had been shocked almost speechless by what he'd seen.

Even though he'd related the whole encounter the night before, Summer asked again, "You saw her with your father?"

She ran her hands across the straining muscles of his upper arm and felt a knot tightening in her stomach, erasing the tranquility of Amelia's porch.

His voice came out parched and bitter. "Oh, yes. And the whore knew I saw her. The carriage stopped a block from Willard's. When the door opened and Mary's father stepped down. I couldn't miss her. A streetlight shone right into the cab. She leaned against him, her hands clamped on his arm like she owned him. She wore that damned ruby bracelet, too."

"Did you father see you?"

"No. He and Hugh were talking. Arguing, actually."

"Maybe there's an—"

"Hell, sweetheart, what possible explanation could there be?" He pulled her tight against him and growled and kissed the back of her neck, then unbuttoned the top button of her dress. His arms tightened around her pulling her onto his lap, and he pushed his head against the back of the swing.

"I don't give a damn who he's sleeping with. I just want to know if he's involved with the children.

"I knew children were abused, but I'd never really thought about it. Seeing the house with all the contraptions, the straps, the lotions, it brought home what child prostitution is. They use boys, too. Can you imagine someone abusing our boys?" He shuddered and clenched his fists. "I'd tear them apart."

Summer Rose's heart ached for him, but she didn't have any magic words.

Finally, she said, "He certainly has demonstrated that he likes grown-up women. I'm sure he's not part of such evil."

He didn't seem to hear her. His eyes darkened. "Abbey? I've racked my brain, but I've never seen anything odd with Abbey? Nothing. If he touched her, I don't know what I'd do. Thank heavens for Ed. I'll be glad to get her out of that house."

When he turned to Summer, his face was creased with tension, his eyes dark and smudged. "I can't speak to anyone. Maybe Jack. Where is he?"

The tension left her body. She sighed. "On Saturday, when we go to Philadelphia, he'll be traveling with us. I thought he could come with us to my grandparents' house. I know they weren't his family, but he might like some of the furniture before we auction the rest."

They had planned to make a fast trip to Philadelphia to go through her grandparents' home, and see if they could use any of the furnishings to replace the things Hobbs' gang had destroyed. They had already arranged with Louie and Harvey's firm, as well as Mr. Crenshaw of Girard Bank, to sell the house and auction the furnishings.

"You could talk to him on the train," she said. "Jack would be a good choice. Why don't you see if we could go visit your family later that day? You don't really think he was involved with the children, do you?"

Daniel shrugged. "Did he know about the children? And do nothing."

They heard the crowd roar, then several cannon firing. The long white curtains danced and billowed like sails on the high seas above 18th Street. His hands moved through her hair, and she smiled, pulling his face into where her neck and shoulder met.

"I sort of like your hair short," he murmured, changing the subject.. "How much time before a child awakens? I want some time where I just don't think."

She shrugged and leaned into him.

He sat her up and kissed the back of her neck, then eased her down to the cushion. "Can you smell the roses?"

That evening after dinner, Amelia and Hal surprised them. "Next week," Hal said, "Mother and I are sailing from New York for Southampton. I've been writing to Fanny and we plan to meet in London."

Daniel hesitated. "Does that mean you and Fanny ..."

Hal shrugged. "Danny, I have no reason to believe she'll have me." He chuckled. "I'm not sure of much of anything right now. But I want Hank to know his mother. I won't live abroad, and Hank is going to live where I live, but I want him, at the very least, to know her. If it entails an ocean voyage every year or so, I'll do it. I don't know if she'd be content to come back here." His voice cracked a little. "God, I was such a bastard. I don't blame her at all for leaving me."

He shrugged again. "I wouldn't mind spending the winters in town, but I want to live in the valley most of the year. You're going to have to put up with me, with or without Fanny." His eyes slid from Daniel to Summer, then back to Daniel. "I want my son to grow up in the valley, grow up with your sons. We'll see. Perhaps his mother will come back so we can raise him together."

Amelia was holding Hank and frowning. "Mark my words, Hal. She'll come back with you. How could she resist this darling boy? I've been writing to her father. They're meeting us in London. I believe Fanny's father would like to see her settled. Her grandmother passed away a few weeks ago."

She cleared her throat. "Regardless, when I return, Harvey and I want to buy some land near the lake and build a house, a summer house for us. I have to be near Hank." She kissed her grandson's forehead. "I guess you'll have to put up with me, too."

Daniel stooped and kissed her cheek. "Amelia, I can't think of anyone I'd like to put up with more than you." He straightened and rested his big hand on Hal's shoulder.

PART FIVE

CAMELANN

CHAPTER 59

PIECES OF THE PAST

On the morning train to Philadelphia, they arranged to have two compartments, one for Daniel and Summer, and Jack, and one for Mercy and the boys.

Daniel was pale while he spoke. "I have trouble even talking about it. Regardless of what he has done, he is my father. Thoughts of repercussions make me ill. My mother, my sister …"

Jack nodded. "I'll be discreet. Perhaps I'll find that he's just enamored. He won't be the first middle-age man to be infatuated with a hooker. If that is the case, I'll warn him to back away from her. I'll keep you out of it."

"If it's the worst scenario?"

Jack shrugged. "We can't charge her. We'll just have to watch. One step out of line, and I'd have to arrest either of them."

"Would you let me know before that becomes necessary?"

Jack nodded again. "I'll do what I can, Daniel. Thank you for this information. It gives us another avenue to investigate.

A judge. Now your father. We'll look under every rock, every business deal. I have to tell you, much is done to cover up this kind of evil. Powerful men and women tend to protect the wrongdoers rather than the children. It's the children who should be protected, but that's not how it works. We're still hunting for the money."

He changed the subject. "I heard your mother is ill. I hope she's better."

"She sent a note yesterday. Apparently she's improved. We plan to stay at the house tonight. Remember Colonel Ed Kincaid? He proposed to my sister. There's a small celebration of their engagement, a dinner. Plan to come with us and stay at the house. I've already made arrangements. It might prove helpful."

Mr. Crenshaw met them at Fitzmartin Manor, and they spent several hours there. Summer walked through the gardens with Pat McCall, the gardener. She remembered him from when she had visited her grandparents as a child. The excess of early spring had passed, but the shadow of the earlier garden still showed. Mercy sat on a blanket near the lily pond, in the dappled shadow of a sycamore, and played with the babies.

"Thank you for coming today," Summer Rose said to Pat McCall. "I want to preserve some of the things he loved: his roses, the tulips, the lovely irises, and especially the lilies. My love of gardening probably came from him."

Pat nodded. "I'll put together a couple of crates of bulbs and tubers. He loved that climber rose back by the garden shed. I'll send shoots of all the roses, and I also have envelopes of seeds. I'll include those, as well."

She smiled brightly, "Mr. McCall, why don't you come along with all your packets? I'd love it. We have close to 8000 acres, now. Plenty of room."

He surprised her. "I'm tempted. I may show up on your doorstep some morning. I have nothing to keep me here." Mr. Crenshaw had told her he'd lost two sons in the war and his wife had died.

"We'd love that."

Once they were inside the house, she, Daniel, and Jack moved from room to room. A lifetime of debris and sadness permeated every corner like dust. Their lives seemed so futile. They were dead, dead forever. Like a dandelion blowing in the wind, she was the single seed, the one left, the one to pass some of the good forward. Her grandfather had left enough money that, if she and Daniel were careful, they could fund generations and keep their valley pristine for years. They would pass on Micah's strong pride in America, both grandfathers' work ethic, their love of the land, and their tenacity.

Now, as she walked through the rooms, she admired the good taste beneath the dust. She tagged the piano—she'd teach all her children to play—several pieces of furniture, and all the books in the library. She collected a large set of flow-blue china, to replace what Hobbs' gang had smashed.

When she took kitchen dishes and a copper kettle, Daniel lifted a blond eyebrow. "Why? We have lots of our own."

She arched one dark eyebrow. "Daniel, the twins won't be our only children. Be forewarned. I want a flock of children.

And they'll grow up and have children." She closed her eyes. A dreamy expression spread over her face. "Envision long tables down by the lake, covered by fluttering white tablecloths, filled with friends, family, and children. You and Hal can build an empire. I'm going to build a family."

Mr. Crenshaw smiled. "We'll have it all packed up and shipped. The auction is scheduled for the third week in June. Do you plan to come?"

She shook her head. "I'm sure I'll regret not taking more, but no, we won't attend. The war is over. We have a lot to do."

She knew that the Grand Army of the Potomac was scheduled to dissolve by mid-June, since it was costing a million dollars a day to maintain. The vast multitudes of veterans were eager to melt back into society.

She hoped to plant her garden soon. Margie had written that the boys had plowed and raked the ground, and Margie had planted a big patch of onions and potatoes just for Summer Rose. At Harper's Ferry, Summer Rose had started hundreds of vegetable plants, and now imagined the expression on Daniel's face when he saw what she planned to haul to the valley.

From Fitzmartin Manor the six of them piled into a large carriage, and as they neared Daniel's childhood home, Summer turned to Jack and Mercy. "I haven't seen the house but I've heard it's magnificent."

Daniel shook his head. His mother's grandiose ways embarrassed him. She laughed at his expression. "Honest. It has a greenhouse. Can you imagine, Mercy? Daniel tells me they grow lemon and orange trees in a glass room that has chairs and tables and palm trees. The kitchen is big enough to feed the garrison at Harper's Ferry. At night they light a mile of gaslights."

The carriage turned, heading into the long lane of gaslights and elm trees. Daniel's mother came out to greet them.

Flora held out her hands, beaming, and wanting to hold one of her grandsons. "I'm all over my cold," she said, assuring them. To Summer Rose she added, "I imagine you'd love a bath and a nap. Come, Mercy. I have bassinets in the children's old nursery. May I hold Micah?"

She smiled at Jack. "Colonel McAllister, so good to see you. I've put you around the corner from your sister. I know how seldom you see each other."

As the three of them walked up the grand staircase, Daniel leaned in close and whispered. "Was that my mother?"

Chapter 60

RUNNING THE GAUNTLET

While Summer napped and Flora's household saw to the twins and Mercy and Jack, Daniel walked in the gardens, thinking of Hugh McGill, Mary's father, and his father, all together in the carriage with Mrs. Mason the other night. He shuddered slightly. *God, I hope they both wanted her for fun and games, not business.* As unpleasant as the picture of his father in bed with Pearl Mason was, the thought of his involvement in the business end of prostitution sent bile into his throat.

He rounded a rhododendron and came upon Ed and Abbey on a bench, tangled in each other's arms by the fish pond. Daniel decided they appeared very much as if they needed to be interrupted. He chucked a small rock over their bench and it plunked noisily into the pond.

Ed turned and, when he saw who it was, hollered good-naturedly, "Go away."

Abbey stood and ran to Daniel. Her cheeks were flushed, her blouse askew, and her mass of blonde curls mussed. She looked more beautiful than he'd ever seen her. She jumped in his arms and hugged him. "I'm so glad you could come. Are the babies here? Summer Rose?"

"Mother's with them in our old nursery. Please let Summer Rose sleep. She's exhausted."

"Oh, I can't wait to hold them!" Abbey blew a kiss to her fiancé and ran toward the house.

Daniel hollered. "Tuck in your blouse!"

She stopped short, straightened her clothes, then waved and ran off again.

Ed stood and Daniel shook hands with him. "So you made the big step?"

Ed was several inches shorter than Daniel but well-built. Dark haired, clean-shaven, with bright whiskey-colored eyes, he was a good looking man. "Yes. And I've never been happier, General Charteris."

"I think you can call me Daniel. Hell, the war is over. We'll be brothers-in-law soon. Have you set a date?"

Ed nodded. "Next Tuesday, in the chapel at West Point. Just your mother and my dad are attending. He doesn't live far from West Point. You're welcome, but it's quite a trip right now with everyone mustering out. We'll understand if you can't attend. I'm to report to Ft. Laramie on the 15th, and I want Abbey to come with me."

"Good luck." Daniel cleared his throat. "Will there be other wives where you're posted?"

Ed's voice softened. "A few. Mary and Emmett Hathaway are also headed there. I'll take good care of her, Daniel. I promise. I love her."

"I know. I'm just being protective."

They walked back to the house, talking about who was going where. Jake Hunt had requested duty in Washington. "He's still courting Emily St. Clair."

Daniel told him of his own plans to study and set up a law practice in Camelann. He shrugged. "I've had enough fighting. Summer Rose's valley is God's country. I'm going to leave the Indians and the Mexicans to you younger men."

As they neared the house, Jack McAllister came down the long backstairs. Despite his freshly shaved face, spit-shined boots, and knife-edge creases to his trousers, Jack shifted from foot-to-foot, skittish as colt. He looked as if he needed a stiff drink.

Ed and Jack spoke for a few minutes then Ed begged off. "I want to find Abbey. Think I'll be able to drag her away from those twins?"

As Ed walked away, Jack asked, "Do you have time for a smoke?"

Daniel nodded. Jack held out a silver case and offered a cheroot to Daniel. They took a minute to light their smokes then walked along the path by the long row of English Hawthorne trees. Pale pink petals floated on the soft air. Fine gravel crunched beneath their boots.

"Your mother sent me a gossipy, carrot-topped housemaid to help me unpack. Do you know who she is?"

Daniel nodded and grinned. "Ah. Mimi. Did she seduce you?"

Jack blushed, but shook his head. "I settled for a scrubbed back, though I'm hardly a priest. It was amazing, though. She spewed gossip with me barely asking a question. Her accent ... what *is* that?"

Daniel shook his head. "Just Philadelphia. Nerve-jarring, isn't it?" He peered sideways at Jack. "What did Mimi tell you?"

They continued back along the path, followed by the smoke from their cheroots. "She was a fount of information. You won't want to hear much of it."

Daniel's head jerked around. Dread, as harsh as acid, flushed into his veins.

"There's no way I can soften this." Jack let out a long breath. "It appears your mother is greatly relieved that Abbey will be married and that the wedding is next week."

He saw Daniel's stricken face and held up one hand. "No, no. Nothing untoward with Abbey and Ed." Jack took a drag from his smoke. "Your mother is just relieved because she can now avoid being humiliated at a big wedding."

He blew a long stream of smoke and gazed into the sky. "Your mother wasn't sick this past week, Daniel. Louie filed for a divorce. Everyone in town, or at least their servants, knows your father is seeing another woman, and he plans to marry her once the divorce is finalized. Mimi told me even his best friend, Hugh McGill, is upset with him. He went to Washington to try to talk sense into him. Harvey, also, is barely speaking to your father.

"Your father's involvement isn't new, Daniel. Mimi didn't mention her name, but she knows the woman has a reputation. According to Mimi, 'He's been seeing the ho' for a couple of years. He was probably seeing her when we arrested her. At first, your mother didn't want the divorce, but now she does. She hired an attorney, Roger McIlwraith, who I know personally. He's excellent. To quote Mimi, who quotes your mother, 'I will squeeze out every dime he's ever made or hopes to make.'

"According to Mimi, your father agreed to everything she requested. As you know, getting a divorce is next to impossible, but money has crossed many palms. All the hullabaloo hasn't escaped your sister. Even Mimi, who appears to have a newt-sized heart, feels sorry your sister. Louie isn't attending Abbey's wedding. He won't even be here tonight. 'That poor girl has cried and cried,' she told me." He shook his head. "Ed's the one who suggested to your mother that they speed up the wedding. He used the excuse of being sent to the Dakotas." Jack took another drag of his cheroot. "The Indian Territories appear to be more desirable than her staying in Philly."

Jack walked a few feet away and studied the back of the big house. "I don't know what to tell you to do, Daniel. We have no grounds on which to arrest Mrs. Mason. We have no papers on her. Any paperwork was lost or destroyed with Judge Turner's suicide. Apparently he made sure of that before he pulled the trigger. We only have Hal's word against hers."

"What about mine? Summer Rose? The soldiers?"

"Were you involved with the commercial transaction? She'll claim she was just caring for the child." He let out a bitter laugh. "Pearl claimed the house was a school." He shook his head. "You know those notebooks I collected? According to her, those notebooks were records of tuition payments. The house burned completely so we have no physical evidence, and Liza is out west."

Daniel ground out the butt with the heel of his boot. "Do you have any idea who really owned that house? Was my father connected with buying or selling that child? Any child? In any way?"

"We've found no connection."

Neither spoke for a good five minutes. Finally, Jack said, "Want some advice?"

"God knows I need it. Tell me not to drag him out to the pond and drown him. On the other hand, where's that whore? I have no qualms about putting a bullet through her head. Why in hell didn't we do that?"

"I know. And if I knew where she was, I'd help you." Jack ground out his smoke as well. "I doubt if your father was involved with the child, but you may as well try and change the tide as change his mind about Mrs. Mason. He's giving up his political ambitions, his practice, and his family."

He swung around and faced Daniel. "Go to Abbey and Ed's wedding. Step in for your father. And I suggest you plant a seed in your mother's ear. Tell her to go to England with Amelia. Nan Charlotte, too. Get them out of the country. Make that suggestion tonight." Jack laughed without any mirth. "Think of it as punishment for Hal. All those women on a ship for ten days will drive him mad. Then take Summer Rose home. She needs to spend quiet days with her sons and start her garden."

He led Daniel toward the greenhouse. They peered through the glass where Summer sat on a rattan couch beneath a large, leafy tree, holding Gus. Mac lay beside them on a sofa cushion. She'd braced one leg to keep him from rolling, allowing one slim ankle to peek from her petticoats. Her dark and silky hair had grown enough so she could sweep it back into a curled chignon. Her skin glowed with health.

"Now isn't that a gorgeous sight?"

Daniel nodded, speechless. Tears threatened. Since the train, tears snuck up on him often. *I almost lost them.*

She wore a pale blue-green dress of silk with wide vertical ribbons of the same colored crocheted lace between every panel of her skirt. Bands of the exquisite lace softened the hem and the low neckline, letting him admire the cleavage of her breasts, the downy petals of her petticoats.

"Danny, forget all about the things you can't do anything about. Those problems aren't going away. If you ask me, I think you should take your wife home and start another baby. You're good at that." He flushed. "Sorry. That didn't exactly roll off my tongue right. You know what I mean. Your twins have to be the most beautiful babies I've ever seen. I'm just their half uncle, but I'm so proud of them I could bust."

He cleared his throat. "Study the law. Buy more land." He elbowed Daniel. "I wasn't joking. Life's short."

Daniel let out a long sigh and opened the door to the greenhouse. Summer Rose turned to him and smiled. Beside her, Mac kicked his feet and Gus grinned, wiggling all over. Daniel's heart thumped and he smiled back. Mac held out his arms and Daniel's eyes filled up, which he blinked back. *I am a general who bawls like a woman.*

Jack sniffed the air, rich with the scent of oranges. "And ask your mother for an orange tree. Tell her how oranges during the winter would benefit her grandsons. I'll help haul it from the depot. Ask for a lemon tree, too."

CHAPTER 61

CHARM

Louie Charteris left without saying goodbye to his family. He left his affairs in good order, with Harvey St. Clair administering his interests. He left no notes. No one in the family ever saw him again.

Despite all this, Abbey and Ed's wedding was well attended. In addition to Flora and Nan Charlotte, Amelia and Harvey brought Emily, Hal, and Hank, along with his nurse, Miss Pitt, a tiny, prune of a woman. Summer Rose and Daniel also attended, with Mercy tending to both Gus and Mac. Except for the babies and their nurses, everyone drank champagne on the train to New York and West Point. They stayed the night in an elegant guesthouse which overlooked the Hudson and met Jake Hunt and Ed's father at the chapel the next morning. Several weddings took place that day; however, Abbey and Ed were the only couple who had two generals crossing swords for them.

Only one unsettling incident occurred. In the carriage, on the way to the inn for the wedding luncheon, Hal positioned himself next to Mercy and made quite a fuss over her. Daniel, sitting opposite him, grew angrier by the second as Hal used his glib charm on the sweet girl. He envisioned Hal seducing her. Not only did he worry about Mercy's virtue, but also that damn goose on Gus' bottom telling secrets he didn't want told.

At the inn, he pulled Hal to the opposite side of the carriage, away from any eyes. He slammed him against the door and held him still, his big hand splayed on Hal's chest. He kept his voice low, but each word hissed crisp and clear between his teeth.

"I consider Mercy under my protection. I'm warning you up front, Hal, if you even look at her cross-eyed you'll be lucky if I stop at gelding you."

Hal sputtered. "Danny, I'd never—"

"I've heard that before. Jesus Christ, Hal, keep your hands off her. I should have spoken to you upfront when you first sniffed around Summer. Consider yourself warned."

"I was just having some fun."

Daniel's voice didn't increase even a decibel. "I repeat. She lives under my roof. I consider her my daughter. You touch her and …" He released Hal, and straightened his own jacket. "Today is my sister's wedding day. The war is over. We're alive. You're my oldest and best friend." He swiped the hair off his forehead. "I've lost too many friends, Hal. I don't want to lose you, too. But if you touch her, you may as well be dead."

He spun on his heel and walked into the inn, leaving Hal in stunned silence.

After a splendid lunch along with champagne toasts, the bridal couple left for a two day honeymoon in Saratoga. Serious goodbyes were said all around. Amelia, Emily, Flora, and Nan Charlotte along with Hal, Hank, and Miss Pitt departed by rail for New York, then sailed on the *Adrianna* for England. Harvey accompanied them to New York. Everyone else painfully noticed that Jake Hunt did not. Emily, all blotchy-faced, left without saying goodbye to him.

Daniel personally mustered out all his men. To give Summer plenty of time to plant her garden, he sent Wally Saxon and Henry Evers, now retired veterans, home with her. They took two covered wagons full of hundreds of seedlings as well as the runners and plants from her grandfather's estate. Rabbit and Matilda clomped along behind them while Lewis and Clark loped in large circles around them. Wally and Henry helped her plant all the seedlings. Daniel came home in time to help them haul the enormous lemon and orange trees from the railhead. Ezra raised the roof of the greenhouse to accommodate them. The young veterans liked the valley so much they leased adjoining farms.

"We've got girls back home. After we marry, we can find work here, can't we? At least until the next harvest?"

"You can always help out around here or at the Feed and Seed Store in town."

In November, Summer Rose and Daniel celebrated the first Thanksgiving. The Zimmermans visited early in the afternoon, and Jack, the Evers, and the Saxons stayed for dinner. Jack, now with Allan Pinkerton Investigators, left in the late afternoon for Chicago where an important case involving smuggling loomed. Irene Wood had taken Mercy to Gettysburg for the new official American holiday, so they had the twins to themselves. Everyone else left at twilight.

After their visit to England and subsequent tour of the continent, Daniel's mother and grandmother traveled to St. Andrews and stayed with Nan Charlotte's Cousin Elsie in Scotland. Daniel knew they feared coming home to face the inevitable gossip. Amelia and Emily returned to Philadelphia in September. Rumors still rippled about Emily's breakup with Captain Jake Hunt. No one had a clue as to why. Hal, Fanny, Hank and Miss Pitt were aboard ship somewhere in the North Atlantic. Daniel expected them home the following week. Hal wrote that he was ready to practice law and that he with Fanny and Hank would live in Philadelphia during the winter. By spring though, they planned to finish the house and live in the valley during the nice weather. Everyone planned to celebrate Christmas at Amelia and Harvey's house in Philadelphia.

The day after Thanksgiving, Daniel received a letter postmarked from Chicago. When he opened it, a newspaper clipping from the *Chicago Tribune* fell out.

Louis Woodward Charteris
Louis Woodward Charteris, 54, ended his life this morning at 6:45 o'clock in the living room of his home. He had fired a 20-22 calibre pistol into the right side of his head. His body was found by his wife who immediately sent for a doctor. He

is survived by his wife, Pearl Mason Charteris, and an infant daughter, Louisa Lenore, a son and daughter from a former marriage, Daniel Charteris and Abigail Charteris Kincaid. His mother, Charlotte Charteris, is traveling in Europe. No foul play is suspected.

During the past year, Mr. Charteris had been an attorney with Hatch, Angst, Mercer, and Hoyt. He formerly lived and practiced law in Philadelphia with Charteris and St. Clair. He belonged to Trinity Presbyterian Church in Oak Park, Illinois.

Mr. Charteris, son of William Wallace Charteris and Charlotte Woodward, was born in Philadelphia on February 17, 1811 and spent most of his life in Pennsylvania. He attended and graduated from the University of Pennsylvania in 1833. Services will be held in Mr. Charteris' home in Oak Park at two o'clock on Friday. The Reverend D.L. Dawson will officiate. Interment will be made at Peace Valley Cemetery in Oak Park, Illinois.

The attached note simply said:

> Dear General Charteris,
>
> Your father and I were married in Indianapolis this past August. I wanted you to know that during the short time we were together, he was very happy. He delighted in your half-sister, Louisa Lenore Charteris, who was born in October. Shortly after Louisa's birth, Louie learned he had terminal cancer which precipitated his suicide. I thought him very brave.

I send my condolences to you, General Charteris. Your father was very proud of your accomplishments, and Louie's most fervent wish was to make amends. I also send my congratulations on the birth of your twin sons. I hope someday your sons and my daughter will be friends.

My Kindest Regards,
Pearl Mason Charteris
Oak Park, Illinois

Daniel eased down onto the porch steps, afraid he might faint for the second time in his life. Summer Rose picked up the note and the clipping and read them, then sat beside him and placed her hand on his knee. He covered her hand with his.

A thousand memories, some good, some not so good, flashed through his mind. Daniel thought he'd mourned his father when he'd left last spring, but all of it came rolling back in crushing waves of memories.

A mix of emotions: sadness, helplessness, anger, regret, guilt, and mostly relief came over him. His mother, grandmother, and sister could come home, and he could stop worrying about his father's involvement in things untoward. Little chance existed that he would ever know absolutely whether or not his father knew about Pearl's dealings with the children. Still an unending emptiness remained.

Jack, of all people, helped him the most in accepting his father's desertion, helped him keep his own sanity. "Your time here, Danny, is too valuable to waste being angry at someone who happgened to be your father."

Daniel took a deep breath. He'd survived the war; the woman he loved sat beside him; his sons napped inside their home. Could I be luckier, he asked himself? To Summer he said, "Jack and I talked about times like this."

"Jack?"

He nodded and picked up her hand, rubbing it between his palms. His pale eyes stared out toward the lake for a long time. The view, the smell, the cool air touching his cheek, the squawk of the ducks, this place, Camelann, never failed to bring him peace. Among the cascade of memories, he recalled the first time he'd seen Camelann. His mind moved on to Summer Rose healing his leg, and those magic days when he'd first loved her, when his love for her was a grain of sand compared to the mountain of love today. His throat ached with emotion.

He glanced sideways at her, his eyes crinkling. Still seated on the top step, he leaned back on one elbow and his one hand reached beneath her hair. She folded into the crook of his arm. "My father's gone. I have a new sister, and now a relationship with a woman I abhor. No chance I'll ever acknowledge her child as my sister or the boys' aunt." He cringed at the thought. "It's one of those times where I can't do a damn thing about anything." He lifted her hand and his lips brushed the inside of her wrist. "The war taught me, above all else, to simply live in the moment."

"Easier in thought than practice."

"I know. Hal wants to work together. Would that bother you?"

She ran her hand down his forearm and slipped it into his. "I have no problem with Hal, and I love Fanny. Have you two forgiven each other?"

He let out a chortle. "Has the South forgiven the North yet? We're not quite that bad. I have forgiven him. Myself?" He shrugged. "I'm working on it."

"You'd make a good team."

"I know. Hal has the brains. I, on the other hand, always had the charm."

She rolled her eyes. "Oh, yes."

"Hal, in his letters, tells me we need clients. Financial opportunities, he says, are mushrooming all over the place. He mentioned Andrew Carnegie, who plans to make steel in Pittsburgh. And a fellow he knows named Rogers in Venango County in western Pennsylvania. His father was a whaler, and now he's drilling that rock oil from the ground. He made $ 30,000 last year. As soon as Hal is home, he thinks we should make a trip out there."

His fingers undid a button, and she smiled at him, lifting one eyebrow. "Ah! Is this the trick to staying in the moment?"

He undid another button. "Yes, but more importantly is choosing just the right moment. The boys are asleep, Mercy's visiting Irene, you are here. I'm here." He undid another button. "And choosing just the right someone is the most important."

"You make it sound easy."

"As long as I have you, it will be."

ACKNOWLEDGEMENTS

First, I must thank Sergeant Luther Calvin Furst, Co. D. 10th Pa Reg. Inf., my great-grandfather who fought in the American Civil War with the Army of the Potomac. He kept a detailed diary of his experience from 1861 to 1864. The original diary in his handwriting is in the Army War College Library in Carlisle, Pennsylvania. Next, I must thank his son, Pop, my grandfather, John Kieffer Furst, for sparking my interest in Civil War history.

Once I caught the history bug, the world of books bloomed and further whetted my appetite for American Civil War knowledge. Somewhere in the vicinity of 16,000 books on the American Civil War have been published. Often when researching a point, I'd find conflicting information. Since *Summer Rose* is a work of fiction, I usually went with the better story. Serious historians may notice that in one incident I manipulated the timing of events during the Shenandoah Campaign to work better with the story. And although, at times, I felt as if I read all 16.000 books, I depended on the writings of a few experts. James McPherson, Bruce Cannon, U. S. Grant, and Shelby Foote were invaluable sources of historical material. I read stacks of autobiographies, biographies, and first person accounts of soldiers and generals. *Harpers Weekly* newspaper provided stories and details of the war as it happened. The wonderful story of General Sheridan's bowling game came directly from *Harpers Weekly* as did the Winslow Homer drawing in the locket on the cover. Reading these articles and stories reminded me that when they were written, no one knew the outcome of the war.

I send thanks to my family and friends who supported and encouraged me. Sue Giordano, my daughter, and Pat Hartman, my daughter-in-law provided immeasurable help by reviewing early drafts. In addition to my children, I send huge amounts of thanks to my sister Joyce Gaw for her encouragement. She and her friends in Columbia, Maryland became my first fan club. My cousin Linda Pearson provided invaluable assistance and accompanied me to battlefields and points of interest. She and Nancy Dugan, a dear friend, who died before Summer Rose could be published, gave good common sense advice regarding fashion. Genevieve Graham of Writing Wildly Editorial Services and author of *Under the Same Sky,* professionally edited *Summer Rose.* I highly recommend her services as an editor. Her support as a friend has been invaluable.

Many kudos go to Bradley Wind and Cheryl Wilder Krass. Brad created the beautiful cover and the map. In addition to his talent, he possesses amazing patience. Cheryl, my publisher, kept me sane. She took care of all the details, and Elizabeth Wilder, her mother and a dear friend and fellow author, gave invaluable insight into a writer's world.

Anna McGarry, also known as Anna Rossi, my lovely British friend and author of *Black Damask*, gave much needed support when *Summer Rose* was little more than an idea. To many others who supported me, I send heartfelt thanks.

As a footnote to history, Elvis Presley used the melody of *Aura Lea*, Summer and Daniel's wedding song, for *Love Me Tender*.

Made in the USA
Lexington, KY
09 August 2013

This book is presented to

_____

on

_____

Published 2008 by Concordia Publishing House
3558 S. Jefferson Avenue, St. Louis, MO 63118-3968
1-800-325-3040 • www.cph.org

Illustrations © 2008 by Concordia Publishing House
Verses 1 and 2, written by unknown; Verse 3 written by
John Thomas McFarland (1851-1913)

Manufactured in Heshan China/047365/407928

5 6 7 8 9 10   17 16 15 14 13 12

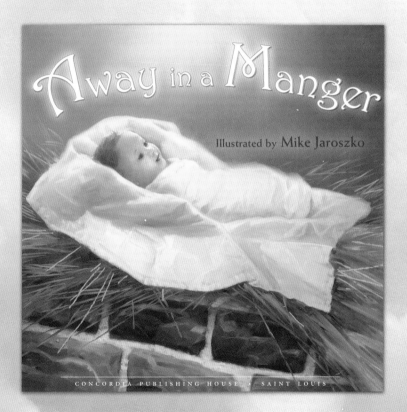

Away in a Manger

Illustrated by Mike Jaroszko

CONCORDIA PUBLISHING HOUSE · SAINT LOUIS

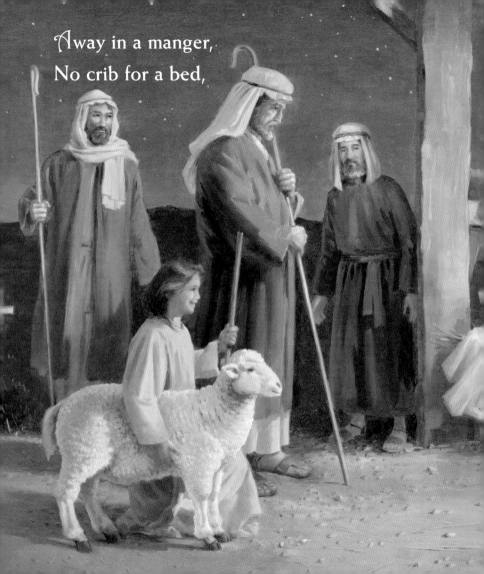

Away in a manger,
No crib for a bed,

The little Lord Jesus
Laid down His sweet head.

The stars in the sky
Looked down where He lay,

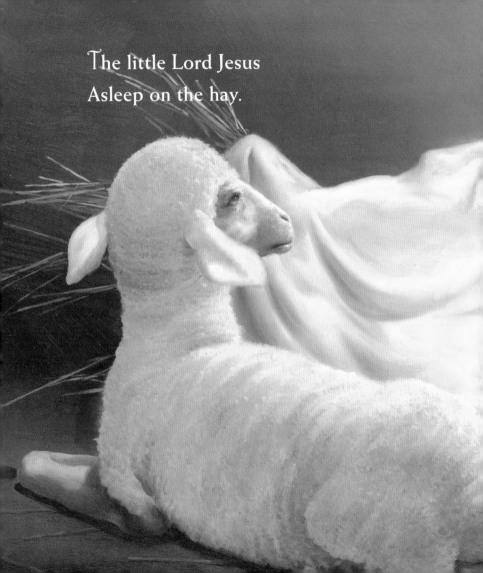

The little Lord Jesus
Asleep on the hay.

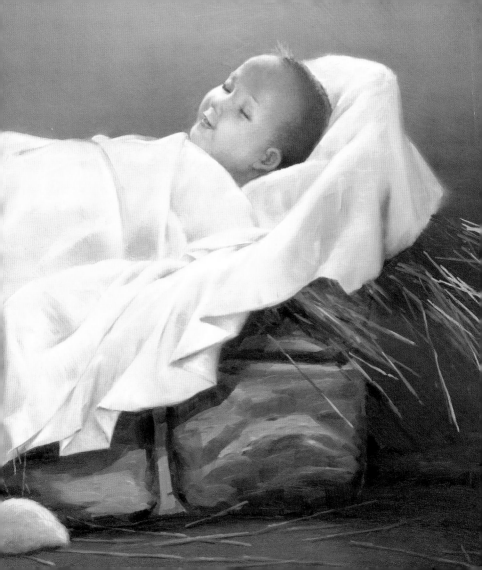

The cattle are lowing,
The baby awakes,

But little Lord Jesus,
No crying He makes.

I love Thee, Lord Jesus!
Look down from the sky,

And stay by my cradle
Till morning is nigh.

Be near me, Lord Jesus;
I ask Thee to stay

Close by me forever
And love me, I pray.

Bless all the dear children
In Thy tender care,

And take us to heaven
To live with Thee there.

Away in a Manger

1 A - way   in a   man - ger, no crib for   a   bed,
2 The cat - tle are   low - ing, the ba - by a - wakes,
3 Be near me, Lord Je - sus; I   ask Thee to   stay

The lit - tle Lord Je - sus laid down His sweet head.
But lit - tle Lord Je - sus, no   cry - ing He makes.
Close by   me for - ev - er and love me, I   pray.

The stars in the sky____ looked down where He lay,
I   love Thee, Lord Je - sus! Look down from the sky,
Bless all the dear chil - dren in Thy ten - der care,

The lit - tle Lord Je - sus a - sleep on   the hay.
And stay by   my   cra - dle till morn - ing is nigh.
And take us   to   heav - en to live with Thee there.

Text: *Little Children's Book*, Philadelphia, 1885, sts. 1–2;
Vineyard Songs, Louisville, 1892, st. 3, alt.
Tune: AWAY IN A MANGER, James R. Murray, 1841–1905